D1398903

1

2

GAIUS IS DEAD

A MURDER MYSTERY OF ANCIENT ROME

BY: ALARIC LONGWARD

GAIUS IS DEAD © 2018 Alaric Longward

REVIEWS

Thank you for getting this story. If you enjoyed it, I would be grateful if you could leave a review. You need not write an elaborate one, just one line and a rating is enough. Readers who do not enjoy the story, will write such reviews, and a bad rating will make it hard for any author to sell the story, and to write new ones. Your help is truly needed, and well appreciated. This author reads them all and is very grateful for your help.

NEWSLETTER

Do sign up for our newsletter at: www.alariclongward.com. You will find our blog, latest news, competitions, and lists of our stories in these pages.

FREE BOOKS

We are often offering free e-books for our readers. These are not short stories, but full, often gigantic tales. In many cases, you might get Book 2 free, by signing up to our newsletter. Please check out our author pages in the various retailers, or in our homepage to find out what is available.

OUR OTHER STORIES

If you enjoyed this story, be sure to check our other historical and fantasy tales. We have many related series that often tie together and are related. We have Medieval stories, several Roman Era tales, story set in the Napoleonic Era, historical mysteries, and many Norse Mythology related fantasy series. None of them are suitable for children, and will serve people who enjoy a surprising plot, fierce battles, and practical heroes and heroines. You can find list of these in our various retail author pages, and our home- or Facebook pages.

TABLE OF CONTENTS

GLOSSARY

Alecto – the Fury dealing with crimes against moral

Alexander – the captain of Limyra

Amyntas – Kyrillos's son

Andromache – Kyrillos's wife

Antius – centurion with a reputation for cruelty

Apollon – the actor

Ariane – slave of Vipsania

Bernike – Meliton's wife

Cassius – scribe of Gaius

Corinne – Meliton's daughter

Dareios – the cook

Decimus – centurion of the Praetorian guards

Drakon – a historian in Limyra

Eudoxia – daughter of Laodamia

Eurydike – the owner of the theatre

Gaius – Gaius Caesar, the heir apparent of Rome

Hiratius – the food taster

Kyrillos – the second councilman of Limyra

Laodamia – Pericles's wife

Larissa – slave of Vipsania

Lysirate – daughter of Laodamia

Megaera – the Fury dealing with crimes of love

Meliton – the third member of the Limyran council

Pericles – the first councilman of Limyra

Ptolemy – Alexander the Great's general of old

Tisiphone – the Fury dealing with crimes of murder

PROLOGUE

I walked the dark, slippery corridor for the noise of the river, and for the pale light. It was an eerie noise, like a gurgling, strangling man fighting for breath, on his last steps in life. I went forward, ever towards it, against all my instincts. I held my gladius, and my chainmail was heavy and cold around me, but neither offered me no comfort. The past days had given me no reason to believe in steel, when dealing with the killers of so many of my men. I walked forward, holding my hand on the wall to my left, and tried to hear something besides the gurgling noise. Only echoes could be heard, mostly my own steps. I passed under roots hanging from a ceiling, and imagined moist, dead fingers touching my face as I pushed past them. I walked through them and arrived in an old cave.

It was lit by many small fires, and by dozens of oil-lamps.

The way in had begun in a tomb, and the road ended in another. There was an ancient, old as time block of stone, carved with figure that had lost their features long before. A river, an off-shoot of Limyrus was gushing to the side, its waters eerily silent, dark, dangerous as a beast, as they rushed far down to the roots of the mountain, and the world far under. The sound of gurgling death came from far below, where the chilly water surged beneath the stone.

The sight was eerie, but not as eerie as the room itself.

There were holes on the walls, moist, and dark, deep black, and large as doorways.

Skulls lined the walls.

There were hundreds.

They were the victims of a generation of murderers, a generation of killers who had come there with their trophies, denying their victims afterlife, mocking them with the very gates of Hades. They were the seeds of the killers.

"Obol for the ferryman," I whispered. None of these had had a mouth where the coin could be placed.

No obol for their mouths.

They were all dead, most long dead, and I felt, I swore it, the ancient dead lining the room, staring at me, staring down to where the river should have carried their souls for Hades, and they wept.

There too, would be people I had known.

On one wall, there were heads of many of my men. They stared ahead in frozen horror, and I saw rats, and something else had gnawed on their ears, on their noses, and some had lost eyeballs, leaving behind a garish, pale-red hole filled with meat. It was a line of dead, out to greet me. And they were not alone at all.

She was there, gagged, by the river's edge, tied on a stake.

Before her, there was a bottle.

I stepped closer and felt malignant eyes on me. They might have stared at me from the depths of the hole, where the river plummeted below. They might have stared at me from a dozen cracks in the walls. They were filled with anger, full of hate, righteous rage. They hated me.

I heard a voice. One, more. I heard something shifting in the dark caves, and then, I saw a dog-faced mask, and the horns.

I prepared for a desperate fight, I, Decimus, the Pretorian, the warrior for Augustus, one of his best men. Not days before, I had arrived in Limyra with my men. We were there to punish a criminal, to bring home Romans, to pick up Gaius.

Now, I was facing a bloody fight on the gates of Hades, many of my men lost.

How did it happen?

Listen.

BOOK 1: THE SNAKE AND THE CRANE

CHAPTER 1

The storm-clouds were racing over the beautiful Lycian countryside. They were swarming over the morning sky like a herd of wild horses thundering across the plains of vast Scythia. The fine sight offered no comfort to the men we had picked up in Rhodes. Our party had been at sea only for twelve days since leaving Rome, and the poor bastard traders and locals we had picked up in Rhodes had been on the deck for two days only, and it still seemed they were having a by far worse trip. They had not been prepared, and the sea didn't agree with them. While we were camped on the deck of the Nefarious, the trireme of *Classis Misenensis*, under a make-shift tent, the fools had no tent or even a hat, and we didn't share ours. They had likely thought this would be a merchant ship where they might camp below the deck, but it wasn't, and they couldn't. That the captain had taken on civilians was a rare thing. He had profited greatly for it, and it was none of my business.

The traders were young men and likely regretted ever trying to establish a connection in Lycia. An older one in a stained tunic was the only one amongst them who seemed at ease. He was carrying scrolls, and occasionally, bent down to relieve his boredom by reading some.

The ship went up and down as an unfavorable wave

struck us. Oars stuck air and crashed at each other, and my men, and even young Segolia, whooped.

The ship righted itself.

I heard feet thrumming the wet deck.

"Try not to die, man!" yelled Antius, the other centurion, when a thin merchant rushed for the vale. He was followed by three others, all holding their mouths with their palms. The captain couldn't abide vomit on the deck, and they feared him more than the possibility of falling to the sea.

"I've got silver on him!" another complained. "I made that bet when they boarded, remember? He dies first!"

"I do, I do," Antius called back. "But I bet on the fat one, so let this one live a while!"

The fat one slid on the deck to throw up, right next to the thin one. "Die, Greek! Drop over for my silver's sake!" yelled Antius.

I smiled.

Soldiers were a crude lot, and nothing gave them more pleasure than seeing fools baking under the rays of Helios, and few things relieved boredom more than making imaginative bets on the lives of those who showed such weaknesses.

Every man, save for Antius, I had seen weeping with fear and suffering terribly from wounds. Every one of them had fought in wars and served Augustus.

Let them jest on the expense of the others.

I leaned on the creaking mast. I squinted at the

14

clouds and lifted the rim of my floppy hat. I decided the rain we had enjoyed that morning, just after we had left the latest cove, would not return. It had been scorching hot for most of the trip, though you could barely notice it while out in the sea. It had been an idle excursion, save for some visits in a few major ports, where Antius had gotten into trouble. The sea had been calm through most of it, and Neptune probably had regrets for the fact, for just on the last day of our trip, the sea had suddenly turned choppy.

"Who is doing that?" yelled a rower below. "Which one of you dog-humped bastards can't keep their food?"

I chuckled. The sight of now four men, all arse up, leaning over the sides of the ship and vomiting their guts out was humorous enough. It was, until you remembered how many ships had sunk on these waters. We had had a meager dinner the last night, cold goat and rotten cabbage, and now that was being distributed to Neptune. The men were also making life hard for the rowers, who would be spattered, their oars smeared and fouled momentarily. Many lives hinged on insignificant things.

A life could be ended by simple 'yea,' or 'nay.'

Hercules, the hulking optio, was shaking his head as he joined me on my scrutiny of the men and the rugged coast. His night dark face gleamed with a film of sweat as he looked over the mountains far away.

"Donor," the man said. "Donor is welcoming us."

I smiled. The African had adopted my northern gods alongside his, and I nodded gratefully. We had been together for long years, and I returned his respect.

"Oh?" I asked and tilted my head. "Is he now? Did you see him riding his chariot?"

He grinned. "He might be too far, sir."

He was right, though. There was no more rain for us, but the thunderous boom could be heard echoing from the mountains to the north, and I saw a stabbing flash over the green, hilly land. Then, again, a jagged line joined two white-topped mountains of which only the tips could be seen, half-hidden in the clouds. "Donor," he said again. "He is killing your giants."

"Taranis," said one of our men. He didn't say it to us, but he was simply in awe of the thunder and the lighting.

"Zeus!" called out another, laughing.

There were men of Rome, but all had unusual backgrounds. All had once been in the legions, and then, Praetorians, the best, of the best.

"They see it as a good sign," Hercules rumbled.

I nodded. The men were serious, no longer watching the slowly recovering merchants, who were pulling back from the sides of the ship, panting and exhausted.

"Lazy mission, this," Hercules said. "Gods, I am already ready to go back home. It looks no more serious a land than one purged of men."

I grunted. "Look around you."

He did.

"Look at the men," I said. "Our men."

He did and nodded. "You are expecting trouble? Truly?"

I nodded. I was.

The contubernium I had chosen were all tough as nails. They were veterans, not suitable for parades and drunken guard duty in the Palatine, but men who expected trouble and delivered solutions. They were a silent lot of fellow Praetorians who would not flinch when trouble found them, and I had handpicked them from men I had worked with before. All spoke Greek and Latin. Many spoke Germanic dialects, Gaulish, and all had killed for Rome a dozen times, and not always in a battle.

I, Decimus, believed in all the men, trusted them, and knew there would be trouble indeed. "We are here on serious business. We'll deal with the murders, and Gaius. We know little about Lycia, Limyra, or these coasts. Aye, I expect trouble."

He grinned. "You always do, and granted, it has saved our arses a few times. I know what you have prepared here as well. I've seen them."

I shrugged. "Antius knows best what must be done to apprehend the killer. I am here to assist him in that, and so are you. While we do this, I shall speak to Gaius and see what the boy is up to."

"He is no longer a boy," the man rumbled. "I am not sure why you Romans insist on calling a full-grown man a boy. Cursus Honorum aside, at his age, he should have a dozen boys and girls running around his house."

I nodded. "That is part of the trouble. Gaius and Vipsania are not making heirs. He must come home. It is high time for them to settle in Rome."

He laughed. "Ah, she griped to Augustus for so many months, and now, she must come home. Gaius didn't complain."

I smiled. "She is not the only one who has complained. Ennius, the scribe has been sending alarming reports of the coin Gaius lost, all of it. And there is someone else there, someone who is keeping an eye on things."

"Spy," he said.

I didn't confirm it. "He is happy, Gaius is, I think. Far from duties, far from trouble, he simply ignores Rome, and Augustus."

Hercules went serious. "There are Romans getting killed in Limyra and he said nothing."

I agreed. "Pericles, the first man in Limyra sent word. He told Augustus about these deaths. And that there is a witness."

"Sounds like a bloody mess."

"Centurion Antius," he said, "will deal with the murderer of Kleitos the Golden, and the killer of the three merchants, and we shall help." We both grinned. "We must be careful. We are allies, Lycia and Rome, and they are a free city under Roman protection, but they are also old and proud nation."

He grinned. "Gods help us if they find our methods

18

unsavory."

"We keep them secret," I said. "As well as we can."

Gods.

When there was none talking about them, I believed in none of them.

When people spoke about gods, I nodded. I didn't want to antagonize my men. So, I watched the thunder and nodded my head with them. My mother had been a Germani, my father, a Roman centurion, we had lived outside the camp, and when he had retired, we, too, had become Romans, eventually. Then, I chose my profession. I knew little else than soldiering. The rest was history. My beliefs had been those of my mother, and my skill in arms and the capability for Roman treachery those of my father's. I lost my mother's pious beliefs in gods soon under the standards, but I developed my Roman skills. Now, at thirty, I was a Praetorian and a centurion, and it had nothing to do with gods.

Only me.

"They speak Greek?" Hercules asked. "Not some obscure Lycian dialect?"

"They speak both. Many speak Latin. Can you see it?" I asked Hercules, and spat, as one of the traders rolled on his back like a beached turtle not too far. His face was smeared in vomit. "They'll never leave land, if they make it to the port," I murmured.

Hercules grinned. "If? If they make it?"

"We'll all make it," I said. "Do you see it?" I asked.

"The city?"

He squinted. "I see a river and a…wait. Is that it? That shitty hamlet? That's Limyra?"

I shook my head. He was looking at Phoneica, the harbor of Limyra. The sprawling harbor area on the mouth of the river Limyra was easy to spot. The piers were full of traders, and a colorful stream of people were moving back and forth the few streets, past the warehouses and taverns on the quayside.

"Look over the green hills and the fields," I murmured. "Up the river, or down, as you like."

He shook his head. "I see the crops and the baked hillsides, the cypress forests, the many mountains, and the river. That's all."

"The mountain, you blind idiot," I murmured. "Look at the one next to the river. Few miles off."

He squinted. "The river goes past the mountain, and part of it seems…a new smaller river comes from the mountain and curls around to join the big one?"

We heard footsteps. We turned to look at the Celt woman we had brought along. She was a medicus, worked for Rome and the Guard, and we all thought she was far too beautiful to be anything but a distraction.

I also knew her.

I had asked for her father, with whom we had worked many times before.

As it happened, she was the only one available. Her father was too old to travel.

She had endured the trip, and she was tough enough to suffer the heat, and the crude conditions. She also had a foul temper that morning.

"Springs, you piss-smelling oaf," said Segolia to Hercules. The daughter to the medicus of our Pretorian Cohort had moved out from under the tent, where she had been tending to a slowly healing wound on the chest of Antius. He had picked a fight when we had beached in Herculaneum. Incredibly, he had found another in Mons Crippius, in Crete. The man had a knack for getting into trouble.

He had also a way of staring at Segolia, which I didn't like.

Segolia was not a Roman citizen but a Gaul. Outwardly, to a casual onlooker, she seemed either a whore we had picked up, or a slave.

She should not be that to our fellow praetorian.

Hercules grinned at the short, strong brunette with a pert nose and thick braid of a hair hanging over her shoulder. Her ankle length tunic was smudged but did nothing to hide her shapes.

"Springs, lady Segolia?" he murmured. "How would you see them?"

"Springs are under the ground, oaf," she insulted him. "Limyra River makes the plains fertile. They flood, oaf. They flood a great deal. The ground beneath the city is filled with water, and there are springs, where the river's waters that has been sucked below, and much of it comes up again. You don't see the city? The spring-

21

born bit of side-river is right in the middle of the city."

He shrugged. "There's a something on the mountain behind? It is Mount Tocak?"

She nodded. "Yes. That's the one. The last mountain in a string of them." We had gone it all over before, and during our trip, but Hercules liked to ask again, and again, until he was sure he knew everything. "The Pericles's Heart, the citadel on the spur of the mountain, is visible enough. It is stadia up the hillside. High walls and with two hundred local troops stationed there. They are armed and armored, much like Romans these days."

"Not trained like us, though. Gaius's men are bound to be staying there," I murmured. "Unless he suffers them in his house."

Hercules, a thick as horse Greek, was shaking his head. "Acropolis is for the locals, not Romans. They won't let a century of Roman legionnaires in their citadel."

I shrugged. "We'll see. They might use it to for a herd of goats. They are not a very disciplined troop."

Segolia nodded. "Lycians have good soldiers. Father said they will be much better than you will think. He also said you will belittle the enemy for the benefit of your men."

I gave her an annoyed grimace.

She was far too witty, her father knew me far too well, and she had grown up fast. "Fine," I said. "They are not bad soldiers. We should be happy Gaius didn't mistake some savage hill men for Lycians when he arrived. Then, the century would be quartered in a necropolis."

"Oh, I see the walls!" Hercules said, as we raced on top of a large wave.

We could all see the city now. We dipped and glided in the choppy waves, and then, I caught a glimpse of it again. Segolia had a great eyesight, but the rest of us soon saw it as well as she did. I could see the tombs and the greenery of a large necropolis on the slopes of the city. No, there were many such necropolises around the northern side of the city, and even over the river. There were walls of decent height, and great agora near the mountains. Hundreds and hundreds of buildings ran in a chaotic mess across the plain under the mountain, and over the river, I wasn't sure, but I thought I saw a temple and a white-stoned theatre with statues, even from so far away, just behind the Agora.

Our medicus was murmuring, "They worship the Ptolemy blood-line, and especially Alexander, and the gods as well," Segolia said. "Not the proper, Celt gods, but the Greek ones."

"Oh, not proper?" Hercules murmured. "Mother would switch your rear, girl. Zeus is not to be mocked. No god is."

"A rare bastard." I laughed. "A rare one. Zeus, not Segolia."

"Not like Cerunnos, none of them," Segolia said.

Hercules looked ready to defend Zeus but sighed

instead. "I only agree this service to the Ptolemy is odd. Men should not be worshipped. Alexander, perhaps, but not the other ones. Never the others."

"We shall love all their ways," I said. "They are not Greek, nor are they of the east. They are odd in many ways, they say."

Segolia nodded. "Lycian League is practically gone, Alexander and the Persians are dead, there are few pirates left, and they are a federation of free cities. It means, of course, they are soon Roman, and some will detest it. I hear there have been trouble against Rome here before. You are wise to be cautious."

She had been busy listening in on rumors in Rhodes. She did annoy me.

I also couldn't stop looking at her.

"Which one of you commands?" she asked. "Antius thinks he does."

"I command my men, he tells me what to do when it comes to this murderer," I told her, with a cold smile. "But, of course, in the end I decide what my men do. There are limits to his influence. He is bothering you?"

She frowned.

"If he is, I can—"

"I can deal with it. We are there soon." She was right about the latter point. We were closing to the end of a small peninsula, and I watched the rugged coastlines with curiosity. I had seen the northern sea, and the plains beyond the lofty mountains ranges of Taurus. Alexander had marched through this land. Great

Alexander. Hercules was right. There was a man worth celebrating. It had seen conquerors and wars and Greek tragedies before Rome ever existed. The land was eternal, old as time, and I could see why Gaius came here, to rest. He had been planning to return to Rome through Lycia, but perhaps not through Limyra.

"Myra," said Antius as he appeared near us. He inched closer to Segolia, who had just checked his wound, and she stepped away, closer to me. Antius, undaunted, his thin face sporting a grin, spoke on. "Gaius should have gone to Myra. They seem much livelier. Must more civilized."

"Antius," I said softly. "We won't be doing any fooling around here. No wine, no women, especially. Myra's a nest of ribald jokes and whores. Keep your cock in your loincloth."

Antius snorted and looked at the two dagger wounds on his skin. He shook his head, as he traced one wound from his forearm to his palm, and another from his shoulder to his chest. "Herculaneum, Mons Crippius. That's what I will call them scars. They join the others, eh? We are lucky they didn't catch me in Tairano and Gythion."

I snorted. "You are lucky. I lost a bet in Tairano."

Antius spat, risking the wrath of the captain who had a religious respect for the sanctity of the deck.

I chuckled. "Come, let us see if we can find out when we will disgorge."

I moved to the bow with Segolia, and Hercules

25

standing before Antius.

"You don't have to guard me," she said, as she looked behind. "You know that."

"I do not," I told her. "But he doesn't need any encouragements either."

"He is what he is," she said. "Swathed in madness, shit dangerous. But I can guard my own honor." She put a hand on a hilt of a hidden pugio. She knew how to use it, if I knew her father.

"Fine," I told her. "Just don't stab him before we get things done. He is here for a purpose"

"If he puts his hand on my thigh again," she snarled, "you will need to take over. Remember what you are, Decimus. You and Father were friends, but you were his superior. You are no brother to me. Not anymore"

Brother.

That's what she called me.

That's what I was, in a way. We went back a long way. All the way to legion camps, where her father had been a medicus. I had seen her grow. I had been like a brother to her those years, but now?

She was to serve Rome with the Guard?

It seemed impossible. For me.

I shook away my thoughts and tried to find the trierarch. I spotted the captain looking at the coast in the aft of the ship. He was standing next to the old Lycian and speaking softly to him.

We walked the slippery, watery deck, and I nodded at him. We had been no bother, had helped well in the ship, helped guard the ship with the mariners and the rowers when we anchored for the nights, and the captain liked us fine. The man knew the waters and had been leading galleys in the Lycian waters for ages. He looked old as bark and turned to watch us. He winked at Segolia, as he had all the past days, like a father to a daughter, and the Celt showed supreme patience as she muttered silent curses.

"You should not be walking about," he told her. "Women don't have the balance for the deck, especially in a weather like this. It is the hips, and the tits, and it's not your fault."

"I've not fallen *once*," Segolia said, for the hundredth of time. "Tits and hips don't have a thing to do with it."

"You will," he said. "They all do."

"Fish-Bait," I told him. He insisted on being called that. He also claimed it was lucky, and that's why he wouldn't be a bait to fish, ever.

"Giant," he answered, and looked up at me. True, I was tall as a horse, as was Hercules. He insisted we ate more than five men. It was true. He nodded to the coast. "Soon there. His highness will get his mail. It is as it should be. The mortals risk their necks, so the high can learn the gossip. Mail for Gaius."

I grunted and clapped a hand over the large leather pouch I was carrying. "And perhaps more."

He looked up at me. "More than mail. You will not give him crabs?"

I liked his humor. He was like one of his rowers, only

27

worse. "Only if he insists. One cannot refuse such as he."

He nodded, grinning toothlessly. "I had a man with crabs last time around here. His cock was swarming with them. His hair and arse-hair were full of eggs." He winked at Segolia. "She should check your hair and arse," he laughed, "but she would just fall over on the deck."

She turned away and walked off. I shrugged. "You have a talent for annoying her."

"You are a lucky man," he said happily. "She possesses more patience than any woman I've seen. Most would have made life uncomfortable for me by now." He sighed. "I should have married."

"She has no interest in me, and I am no good for her," I told him.

"She stares at you centurion. All the time. When you sleep."

I looked at him with suspicion and thought he might be lying. He ignored me and gave a quick look at the harbor. "Well, it seems they will take us in right away. The pier is free, the one I've been to before. It is good luck to get to dock on the same pier. Never had any issues in these waters when I was in that pier. I am that good, of course," he murmured unhappily. "Though, of course, if Fortuna takes you for her toy, you are going to sink anyway. I will be humble." He seemed to be addressing Fortuna. He looked at me. "Tell her you like her, centurion. Someone will, otherwise. They get married young."

I nodded and looked back at my men. And at her.

They were now all sitting under our make-shift tent on the deck, all mumbling prayers, and packing. Segolia was watching, and ready. She was observing the city and memorizing all she could. And then, she looked my way, and I felt happy.

We had spent a week and a half on the deck of the miserable galley, Nefarious, and had had excellent weather, a speedy passage from Italy, along the Greek coasts, Crete, past Rhodes, and it still had been miserable. Segolia's closeness had been a torture.

Her father would kill me for looking at her.

"No, I'm not as lucky as you think," I mumbled.

"Eh?"

I waved to the land. "It will be a relief to step to the land."

"It's a large one," Fish-Bait muttered, leaning on an oar. "Fairly so. It is no Alexandria, or Rome, but it is large in these waters, Limyra. Very rich. It doesn't look like it, but it is. There are some ten noble houses that own most of it, and they like their modest ways. Many loves the place." He leaned closer, trying to avoid the old man who was sitting close. "But I hate it. I do hate it."

"You do?" I asked him. "Why?"

I kept watching Segolia. Her green eyes were fixated on the city and the port. And then, again, at me.

I didn't hear what the captain said. "Sorry, sir?" I

said.

He crinkled his nose. "You bastard. Weak shit, you are. Tell her. I said; I do. I do hate it. Just look at it." I turned to look at it again. We were much closer, and the celeusta below growled an order, and the flutist played a note, and the galley turned and aimed its bow for the piers, not too far now. There men were rushing about, preparing. On the beaches, where the round rocks were slowly turning into sand, goats were moving in mottled herds, jumping from one rock to the other, avoiding splashes of waves. The blue, green, and white beauty of the sea was complemented by the mighty mountains, the hills full of cypress forests, the valleys and green orchards, swathes of arid and dry land for the summer's heat. All this was split by a mighty, pale-blue river. It didn't look something one might hate. It was a Greek city, with what was clearly an agora, and a gigantic theatre, and oikoi, the Greek houses which were not really that different from an average domus in Rome, filled the land beyond the wall and over the river. Green mixed pleasantly with whites and grays, and red roofs complemented the oranges, and I could enjoy it, I decided.

"I don't see it."

Fish-Bait smiled. "Oh, you don't? I tell you now. There is a curse on the land."

"A curse?" I laughed. "Truly? A *real curse*? A curse of the gods? They have pissed on the land."

The old man laughed gutturally. We turned to watch

him. He had sun burns on his face and his ears were red. I took my hat and gave it to him.

He looked surprised and took the hat with a bow. "Thank you."

"I have a thick skin," I said. "You should not let sun burn your skin so."

He nodded at the captain. "I know, but I lost mine. He is right, though. Can't you see it? Your woman can sense it," he said. "She's looking at the land like she knows what is wrong with it. The captain here is right. He can see it too. It is like visiting a beautiful house, only to see everyone were sad, but nobody tells you why."

"She's not my woman," I snarled. "Can you tell me why the city is sad?"

"Just look," he said. "Don't look at the buildings, the people, the mountains or the walls. Forget the wealth, and the ships. Do what the lady does. She is looking at a land, but she sees its past."

I tried. I watched the land, the wind touching the trees gently.

It looked beautiful still.

And perhaps, with the storm clouds racing across the sky, the sun seemed paler, and the great graves on the sides of the mountain...everywhere across the landscape...seemed to be...waiting.

Yea. It was the set of necropolises that seemed to wait...for new people.

Rome had them as well. Here, they seemed ominous, rather than sad.

Looking back. Looking at the history.

"Deaths," said Fish-Bait. "You sense old deaths."

The man nodded. "Deaths by tens of thousands. The land it too old. Far too old. My mother told me about it. When a land grows far too old, ghosts escape Hades. They do. Spirits claim people There are few places like this in the world. One is near Acheron River. People go there…even Odysseus did, to speak with the lost ones. One is here, in the heart of the mountain. There the dead come out to look at the living. Perhaps they never get to leave. It is an unhappy land. Rich, affluent, the people still hold onto some old ways, but sadly. For some, their hair is long, our old names are used, the odd customs, and some of those customs are harsh. They still sacrifice lambs to seek the dead ones inside the mountain."

I nodded. It was not odd to me to hold on to your old ways. And still, Greece was different, as was the east. It wasn't Italy, nor was it Gaul. I loved the former, and I understood the latter, but these lands were abodes of old grudges, homes to old feuds, and angry, bloody gods. They were the land of the old ways.

And still, it was just a land. I pushed away the fear, and the doubt.

"You see?" the old man asked.

"I see it." I didn't. He saw through the lie.

He smiled and nodded. "Be very careful, centurion, with whatever you are doing here," he said. "I smell death. There have been deaths here. Murders. There are very many murders in Limyra. Some were Roman

32

murders."

I shrugged. "I know. We are here to investigate them. Amongst other things."

He shook his head. "What other things? An actor was killed here. A famous Roman actor. The great Kleitos the Golden. Few other Romans, a trio of merchants in one house, and one servant," he said. "You will solve the deaths? Will you? Ah, of course. You must protect Gaius, Lady Vipsania, and to bring him home. The ruler of Rome, the young hero must be taken home." He smiled sadly. "Ah, you will have to wade through the three families, their malice, their greed, their lies to get him home. He will have to go, but he will be much changed by Limyra."

I gave him a suspicious glance. "What do you know? And who are you?"

"I?" he asked, surprised. "I am a poet. I am a historian. Drakon, they call me. I'm of the oldest of families, friend, and know the city well. My ancestors spoke the local language and still know it." He stretched his back and smiled as the captain was frowning at the approach. Drakon squinted up to me. "It is but a city with two votes in the League and still as ambitious as those who have three. I hear Pericles sent word to Rome about these dead Romans?"

I nodded. "He did. Others have told me other things about the happenings in the city."

He snorted. "The Great Caesar made our alliance quite wordy. We are to acknowledge the pre-eminence and power of Rome in all aspects of our lives. We may keep our laws, and ways, unless we wish to declare wars or break alliances. And if you find this killer, and he is a Lycian, is it not so he should be condemned and judged by Lycians?"

I nodded. "That is the law."

"And if Roman," he said. "In Rome?"

I nodded. "That, too, is the law."

"And they have not been able to find the killer," he said. "It is a tragedy. Still, you are here to find it, since they cannot, or will not."

I gave him a quick look. "Him."

"It."

I ignored him, until I couldn't. I sighed and asked him the question. "It?"

He slapped his knee happily. "Indeed! It! There is a ghost that is killing people here. A ghost! A head hunting ghost. Atropos cuts the strings, but this one? It is no kind spirit. It punishes them for evil. Do you want to hear?"

"A champion for evil." I laughed softly. "You mean some kind of spirit, who hunts the wicked?"

"The Furies!" he said happily. "You know? Alecto, Tisiphone, Megaera."

"One punishes the murderers," I said. "Another, those who betray their spouses. One, I think, is very concerned about the crimes against morals. Dog-headed things, the lot, no?"

He was nodding. "I do love a man who knows his

tales. Aye. Tisiphone, the murderous one. Megaera, the jealous one, and Alecto, punisher for the moral crimes. Aye, dog-headed beasts." He winked. "And you think you will find them. They have been killing here for ages, punishing those guilty of these crimes."

I shook my head. "Which one killed the four Romans?"

He scratched his neck. "Depends on their crimes. They were an actor and three merchants?"

I nodded. I smelled the dead things of the sea as we came close to the pier. His words made me nervous. Nefarious turned slowly, oars beating the water gently, and we slid closer under the expert guidance of Fish-Bait's pilot.

I turned and looked at the mountain, the great fortress, and the walls of the city. My eyes went up to the tombs.

"Kleitos, they say," the man was saying, "was prideful, greedy. He came here to entertain your Gaius as requested by the great Augustus, and while his skills in the theatre were many, he despised the local actors. In the end, he had them replaced. Alecto would not like that."

I snorted. "Sounds like I should look at the local actors," I said.

"The merchants were all working with Pericles," he said. "Pericles has the very best wine and vast fields with herds of horses and wheat. Perhaps the Romans were trying to cheat? Perhaps they bribed Pericles and hurt other traders, merchants, and locals? Deals with Rome are precious. Indeed, such as Gaius can shake the entire land apart, without him knowing it."

"Perhaps they should have killed Pericles instead," I said. "If he takes such advantage of it."

"Perhaps so," the man said. "I know not their crimes."

"And what crime did this servant of the third merchant commit?" I wondered. "Murder, adultery, and perhaps thievery? Nay, old man. We shall investigate."

He squinted at me. "And if it is a Lycian?"

"Then, we shall have to administer Lycian justice on him."

He nodded. "Him. Eh? You know this murderer?"

I said nothing to that, but instead nodded at him. "I wish you well, old man."

"I am Drakon, the Historian," he said. "Find my house near the Temple of Apollo, on the western edge. I will offer you a dinner. Be careful of the city. It has old bones, wet beneath, built on swamp, and older cities. Keep your eyes open. And call on me, truly. I can tell you about the Furies, and about the old families. Or, about the present families. I know all the rumors. Be careful with the Pericles family. They have slithered through holes in the ground before to escape trouble. Like the snakes they so love!"

I smiled gratefully at the old, lonely man, determined not to have any more discussion with him. "Thank you.

I will be very busy in the city."

He looked uncertain and nodded. "You will. Hope it goes well."

I cursed, walked off, and nodded at Fish-Bait, who was totally preoccupied with the approach.

I got to the bow of the ship and dodged under our makeshift tent.

Antius was there, busy. "Get ready, boys," he was saying. "Hurry up now."

"Centurion," Hercules muttered, right next to me, and I turned to look at him. "The harbor is near. What shall we do?"

Antius gave him an incredulous look, but I appreciated Hercules and he a proper chain of command. They were my men.

"Finish packing, make sure we have everything, and get ready," I said. "We shall get out and make our discreet way to Gaius, and we'll meet this Pericles in his house. Keep quiet and try to walk with the bastard traders. Make it seem like you work with them, at least until we get out of the harbor. No need to tell everyone Rome sent men to discover who is killing our people, especially if the locals are touchy about their future and place in this world of Rome. Low profile, and we do well."

Antius was nodding, his eyes on Segolia.

Hercules frowned. "Yes, sir. Easy and invisible. We'll fit right in."

They chuckled, because there were no other men our

size, and he was dark.

I grinned at him. "We'll stick out like a turd in trousers. But keep the swords hidden and close. We'll do our best."

He nodded. "Hidden and close," he said with a smile that made him look like a gorgon.

"Yes," I told him. "Nobody calls me or Antius 'sir.' Any more questions?"

He nodded. One of the men perked up. "This killer. He used poison, eh? The actor was poisoned?"

I nodded.

The men asked a lot of questions that had been answered previously, they always did, but none were fools and were simply making sure they knew everything, and nothing had changed. You could sense their demeanor shifting. No longer would they make bets or careless jokes, and no longer would the men be relaxed. They were now going to prowl around what could be enemy land, and they were ready for most anything.

Poison had killed a Roman actor.

A famous one, a man Gaius had been a great fan of and a friend to Augustus, had died three weeks past. The man's name had been Kleitos, and he had come to Limyra to entertain Gaius, and now, he was dead. No matter what laws were observed or how, what our alliances said, Rome was there to administer justice.

Our orders had been given.

After, we were there to find out why Gaius wasn't

coming home.

That was the mission. That was what had been agreed on. And few other things.

"We won't have any trouble," Hercules said, as we watched many people moving on the pier. "We'll speak Greek and look like mules."

"That is how we do it," I said, and turned to Antius. "You will speak with Pericles today?"

He grunted assent. "Why, we all know this."

"Go it over one more time," I said. "Act. For me, dear."

He cursed and nodded. "Fine. Pericles claims he has a witness to the murder. We shall meet him in the house of Gaius."

"Good." I nodded.

"We are going to talk about the murders. We will hunt down the killer," he said.

"Good. Go on."

The men were chuckling.

Praetorians all, ours was a unit Augustus trusted even better than he did his Germani Guards. I had solved a problem that had risked the entire Gaul, and then smaller ones for Augustus himself for years, and while I was there to hunt a killer, I was there also to fetch Gaius home.

I was there on the request of Augustus. He knew I was a hunter.

A hunter was needed.

A man who could get things done was what

Augustus had asked for.

Hercules grunted. "Do you think he will accept his fate?"

I shrugged. I knew he meant Gaius. "It matters little. Now, I want to hear Antius go this over."

Hercules spoke on. "And if his centurion, this Marius, disagrees? They might be very loyal to him," he ventured.

"They will be," I said. "But they also know Gaius is no soldier. Rebelling with Gaius would lead to a swift end. Do not worry. He will be on a ship out of here in a week."

The scrolls from his wife, Vipsania, had been urgent and alarming. The scribe, Ennius, had sent lists of expenses, and they had quickly grown to a degree where Gaius was spending fortunes on food, feasts, horses, poems, and entertainment. He had no coin. Augustus had not sent him more coin.

And still, he kept living in Limyra.

Still, he kept spending coin he didn't have.

The man had always been fastidious in Rome. He had been like the Romans of old, careful, and calm. He had always been faithful, and honorable, and polite to women.

Now?

Not so much. He was broke, by all accounts, and paying for his upkeep by attracting roman traders to deal with his chosen friends. Vipsania hated him. Our spy said the houses were upset.

Gaius had…changed.

So, a hunter of men, beasts, and truths had been sent. Antius and I, we had such reputations.

The murderer was one thing. We had the full support of Lycia to capture him. We knew nothing of Gaius, though. I, the man called Decimus, but whom they also called Celcus the Tall, had been known to catch everything.

If Gaius refused to go to Rome, we would take him by force.

That's what Augustus had told us to do.

The galley lurched in the waves near the pier, making the flute-player below lose his rhythm. Men were yelling complaints, or curses. The oars clattered together unkindly. Fish-Bait rushed past, yelling in Greek, and he wasn't happy. "A trireme of Rome should look better docking to a foreign port! What are you trying to do? You are trying to make me look like I never left the farm? Are you fondling each other below? Eh?" he yelled. "Pay attention!"

I turned to Antius. "So. Go on. Tell me the details."

"So," the man said softly as he dodged past Segolia, touching her shoulder needlessly. "Here is the thing. We know who did it."

I forced myself to calm down. Segolia was cursing and shaking her head. Antius's eyes twinkled as he saw my struggle. "We," I said harshly, "know that, and more. How will we apprehend him?"

He smiled. "We will be helped by the Lycians in the

city. Alexander, a captain of the local soldiers, is a relative to Pericles, who leads the city. There are three families. That of Kyrillos, the second richest in the city, and that of Meliton, who is related to great city of Myra through his wife, Bernike. Pericles and the three decide everything in Limyra, and Pericles sits on the Council of Lycia. Kyrillos is opposed to Pericles. Meliton is allied to Pericles. Or has been."

"I didn't ask about the politics of the city," I said. "I asked what we shall be doing *today*."

He gave me an unkind look and gnashed his teeth together. "I know we dislike each other. But I am here to command this part of the mission. It will be finished primarily. We don't want the killer to escape. You need not question me. I know what—"

"Get on with it, Antius, because you are right; we dislike each other," I told him harshly. "Tell me the details. More of them."

He pushed hair out of his eyes with deliberate slowness, as if collecting himself. He nodded and spoke on. "There was a witness to one of the deaths. Lucius, a servant to the three merchants, saw a man leaving a house where the three had been staying. This was one week before Kleitos was killed in a house not far."

"There was a servant who died."

He nodded. "The three merchants and a servant died, yes. All were found naked and without their heads the next morning in their beds, save for the servant who only lost fingers and face, in an alley behind the house."

I shook my head. "These three and the servant were murdered a month ago. The witness came forth only after Kleitos died a week later."

He shrugged. "The man had been in shock. He came forth with what he had seen a day after the death of Kleitos."

I smiled. "I bet he was well rewarded."

Antius grunted. "I don't care if he was. He is hiding in the house of Pericles now. He is called Lucius."

"A Roman."

"A bastard of some sort. A drunk in the city, but a local. Pericles is holding him safe."

"And what did he see?" I asked.

Antius smiled darkly. "Son of Kyrillos. A man called Amyntas. Young, harsh boy of one of the richest men in the city. He came out of the house of the traders, and he carried a wet sack. This Lucius said Amyntas was bloodied to his armpits."

I stared at him, and then shrugged. "So. Why did Amyntas kill them?"

"Why?" he asked. "Pericles is a friend to Gaius. He leads the city. He is growing wealthier on Roman favor. Due to Gaius, Roman business is shifting from what was a balanced one into Pericles's lap. The others are suffering. So, they killed the three Romans who came to treat with Pericles. A warning? Perhaps they claim gods punished them for the injustices? The man has been talking against Rome. He hopes to supplant Pericles as the lead in Limyra. He took a step too far."

I nodded. "He hasn't been captured, but why?"

"Kyrillos has a lot of men and clients," he said. "It is for us to capture him, and then, we shall condemn him together with his son. It has been planned."

I smiled. He had taken his orders from Augustus himself. I had simply wanted to make sure he knew what was to take place that very day.

He winked. "It can get a bit hairy. No mistakes allowed. We shall move this very night. No need to worry about me."

I shrugged at Antius. I wasn't too concerned with the hunt for the killer. Augustus wanted the man found, but Gaius was our main concern.

"You are not afraid, are you?" he asked with some mockery.

I gave him a small, cruel smile. "Where are you from, Antius?"

He blinked. "I'm of Thracian blood," he said. "Father's rich, so he was given a citizenship. But I also had a brother, so I am not rich. They appreciated my skills in the legions, though."

I placed a hand on his shoulder and looked down at him. "I remember now. You killed a Gaul queen, after capturing her son. Spared us a war. Well done." I smiled at his face. "See, Hercules there, and I, we killed a Gaul king. A real king. A king with tens of thousands of warriors. He and I, we have hunted for the jewels of Augustus in Scythia, and come back with them, tales,

44

and scars. I've seen the rivers of the Germani, when we set out to slay a centurion who stole an eagle, and we came back then as well, though the centurion did not. I have travelled in Egypt and escaped their gods, and I have seen the king of Parthia weep in his palace. No, Antius, I am not afraid. I suggest you stop thinking about challenging me every fucking moment, that you stop harassing my friend Segolia, and if you do not?" I shrugged. "I show you how we get rid of Roman officers. Not all who become heroes in Rome come back to it."

I pushed him back and stared at him. Segolia moved off, and was packing a blanket away from us.

He was swallowing, face white with rage. "Segolia. It is about her."

"It might be," I said. "She knows very little about this, and our business. She is here to heal, and to help. She is not your plaything, and we will avoid upsetting her."

"A friend you call her, but you want more," he suggested.

I stared at him like I would at a corpse I had just made, and he flinched, for I had a bad reputation and told no lies. I was cruel when I had to be, and it would be easy for such as he to disappear.

He nodded. "I shall not touch her. I know better. But perhaps, a woman so pure and innocent as she is, so young, might not want you after she learns what the praetorians like us do abroad."

"I have warned you now," I said. "Be careful. More details, Antius. What is the word like in the city? They dislike us?"

He cleared his throat. "People cheer the deaths, and some fear what may follow. They think it is one of the Furies, punishing the foreigners for greed. You know what that means? Furies."

"Yes," I said. "I just spoke of them with the old man."

"The city thinks we are being condemned by their gods," he said. "This is what they whisper in the city. Marius, the centurion, sent word and information. So, we must show it is nonsense, and one of their own is making a fool of them all. No mistakes must be allowed."

"How did he die?" I asked. "What poison was used?"

"Hemlock, this Marius thinks," he said. "The killer waits until the victim falls victim to the paralyzing effects—"

Hercules frowned. "But hemlock doesn't affect everyone in a comparable manner. I saw once—"

"In any case, the victims make no noise," he told me. "And they died...later. Heads were sawn off. The servant? That was different. That centurion's report said they removed fingers and skin from face. It was done in a hurry, but they were outside. Perhaps the man escaped, and Amyntas had to chase him."

"Like a wild animal," I muttered. "Like a sated animal, hunting for sport, not for food. Still had to take something."

"Ah, yes," Antius said, his cruel, small eyes on Segolia who was moving past.

He seemed to recall my words and tore his eyes off her.

"The heads found?" I asked darkly.

"No."

"Indeed? Where do they take them? Do they feed them to the dogs?" I wondered.

"Not found," he said. "And there is one more thing. The horn," he said. "There is a horn. And I don't mean a drinking one."

"Horn?" I asked, confused and he smiled wickedly.

He nodded towards Limyra. "The killer likes to announce the kill to the hills. They blow a horn. One time, they say, he or she blows it only once per victim. Always after the kills."

"How dramatic," I said.

"Hope Kleitos got applauded," Antius grumbled. "Must have been his last drama, that night."

"We are there," I said. "Good man. You still remember why we are here, and most of the details. I hope you remember the rest I just told you, as well."

He shook his head at me, and turned away, seething with anger.

We watched the galley make its way to the harbor that had a long quay protecting more than dozen ships. I turned to see our men sitting down, ready, and packed. No furca for these men, and no military gear.

Speculatores, scouts, and infiltrators, looking more like ruffians, they would try to pass as merchants and mercenaries to avoid trouble. A Praetorian uniform was not easy to miss. I pulled my well-travelled cloak around my shoulders to hide chainmail.

"Discreetly, boys," I said. "We shall visit the governor, and I will present our orders. Then, we will find a tavern near the agora and get to the work."

The galley lurched past the quay, and Segolia cursed as she grasped me.

"By the balls of Bel," Segolia said. "That's not too good."

We turned to watch the approach, and I understand, she had not cursed the rough approach.

Indeed, on the pier stood a large, colorful group of men and women in togae and local, rich garb, and dozen legionnaires, another dozen local soldiers.

"Shit," I said. I turned to my men and looked at them. "The act starts *now*. Follow my lead, and that of centurion Antius, and optio Hercules. Consider them all enemies, but act like friends. Keep your eyes open. And mouths shut. We don't want anyone knowing too much about our business."

CHAPTER 2

We stood on the deck, confused. The ship's oars were pulled inside, and slowly, the ship made port. Lines were secured, people were looking on, a sea of faces.

"Stand still," Antius snarled to the men. "Maybe they are here for someone else."

"It is not of any use," I said tiredly. "Vipsania is out there. They are here for us."

Indeed, the small blonde girl stood to the back, her servants holding shades over her head. She was wearing a pale red palla over bone-white stola.

Hercules chortled. "You could hide under my tunic. We could hide behind the mast?"

"Shut up," I said. "She has seen us. And they brought everyone."

She was gesturing at us and speaking to a tall, handsome man with gray hair, who was wearing a rich, silver lined himaton with a silvery peronei, a brooch. The man nodded at Vipsania and turned to look at us. A group of guards and women stepped forward after him. Then, the man waved.

"That would be Pericles, no doubt," Antius said. "Shit. This is...not secret. He will kiss and hug and dance around us like a whore looking for a rich cock."

"We just go and get this over with," I said wearily. "It will make us look like cowards."

"Out, then," he said. "This will be an act I shall hate."

I led us. Hercules and Segolia followed. I stepped out

of the Nefarious, following the traders, who looked confused by the reception. The old man had followed them just before us and pushed them past the group of people not so far. Slowly and discovering the reception was not for them, they walked past the group of people, looking at them with some fear.

There were a dozen legionnaires and guards, and the reason was clear.

The highest-ranking people in the city were there.

I watched the local soldiers with bronze helmets and horsehair hanging to their shoulders. They had round shields with a black helmet painted in the middle of it. Their spears were long, and swords slightly curved. All sported long hair and few had trimmed spears. They looked at us with the captain, a man in a steel cuirass, and there was a golden sword's hilt under his palm. The man was handsome as a god of love, but his face had no emotion. He looked at us relentlessly, as if expecting the lot of us to either die or burst wings out of our backs.

A thin, harried looking man in a toga looked confused and disappointed. Clearly, he expected someone with all the trappings of rank to come forth before us.

Instead, it was just us.

They eyed our salty, sweat-stained gear, our filthy cloaks, the bearded faces under hats, and looking over our shoulders again, the man, Pericles no doubt, slumped. The thin man, with stained fingers, a scribe in a toga, scuttled over to the man and started to whisper to him.

We walked towards the group, and I avoided Vipsania's eyes and watched the people before me.

Anyone but her.

Antius tried to step past me, but I lifted my hand, and my men stood on either side of me, their hands near sword hilts, all well-hidden. All of them wore chain under their gear, and none showed it.

I waited, and Antius cursed softly under his breath.

Two girls, one a short, incredibly pretty one with curly dark hair and the other one, a taller blonde with a quirky smile, eyed us past Pericles. What had to be their mother, a beautiful, tall woman, pulled them back, and stayed closer to the tiny one, while ignoring the tall one.

On one side of Pericles stood another family. There, a man with gray hair and tunic, in a wide, simple hat, and his wife, a short and gaunt woman, stared at us anxiously. A crane was sown on his tunic.

Kyrillos, perhaps. Yes. The crane.

Next to that one, a pudgy, thick-necked man with a wife hidden by a hood, and a daughter, strong-imbed beauty with long, very long, hair and pale eyes. Her mother was a very delicate, older lady, but also very beautiful.

Meliton's family.

The woman's cloak bore an elaborate tortoise paint.

Yes, Meliton. Bernike, his wife from great Myra.

Pericles and his wife, the tall woman, listened to the scribe in a toga, and I took time to study the people.

Snake was their symbol, embroidered in all their clothing, one way or the other.

All, save for Kyrillos and his wife, wore fine, ankle-length chitons, strapped around their arms, and silver and golden fibulae held their undergarments in place on their shoulders. The cloth was mostly silken. The soldiers were draped in peplos, the square cloak fastened on both shoulders.

The nobles looked as rich as any Roman senators.

I waited, and then, Pericles stepped forward with the scribe. His stern face broke into a nervous smile as he spread his hands towards us. "You are…"

Antius grunted. "We are. You Pericles?"

He looked shocked for a moment and then gave us a small bow, one which I answered, but not Antius. "You are from Rome, no?" he went on. "I am sorry, I must make sure. It is possible men die on the journey. And I know such journeys can make a god look like a beggar."

There was an ice-cold reception of his words.

He sighed and stepped forward. "This is the…" He squinted at the galley. "The name of the galley?"

I shook my head. "Nefarious. Aye, it is the right ship. No man died on the journey. Things went well, and yes, we have had little opportunity to wash." I waved my hands around the scruffy team. "This is what you get. I am sorry."

He nodded. "Pericles. Yes, I am Pericles. This scribe, a freedman, is Cassius. Gaius is not here, so he is in charge."

The thin man bowed. "I am here to welcome you on his behalf."

Segolia was muttering, "I doubt Gaius knows we are here."

Antius grunted. "Thank you. Wait. Gaius had another scribe. Ennius?"

Pericles shook his head. "Alas, Ennius left. It is something we should discuss later. Cassius here was the second scribe, but now, the first. He deals with the affairs in the house, for both lady Vipsania, and Gaius himself. He is most efficient. They rely on him for everything."

"Indeed, but we have things we need to discuss, sir," he said.

"There are many things we would all like to discuss," said the gruff man in tunic. "But apparently, Rome only sends soldiers." Kyrillos was not happy.

Pericles scratched his head. "This is Kyrillos, one of the three who rule Limyra. He would have words with you, even when he had not been invited here to welcome you."

"One of the three, and the only one with sense," said his wife. "We would—"

"Aristomache," Kyrillos said darkly. "Wait. We have a grudge we would like to discuss, but if it is soldiers only—"

Antius waved his hand around us. "Soldiers with a mandate from Augustus himself, dear Kyrillos. We shall speak soon."

Kyrillos opened his mouth, looked at Pericles, and shook his head. "I demand we speak now."

There was a silence.

Pericles looked red of face, and his wife had the sort of a statue-like look which suggested she was doing her very best not to shout at the man.

The thick, wide man stepped forward.

Meliton, ally of Pericles.

Though, that was no longer so.

"Reluctantly, I must agree. I am Meliton, the third ruler of the city. My wife, Bernike, and daughter Corinne." They bowed, though the pale eyes were looking at me and Hercules with interest, the sort that did not suit any decently reared girl. "While our esteemed friend Pericles here stands for Limyra, we all decide on its matters. Rome has, previously, dealt with local tyrants, and we fear—"

"Silence," said the soldier in a cuirass. "This is no time for such talk."

Alexander.

Kyrillos sneered. "The captain, a nephew to Pericles, speaks thus. See, Roman. Your Gaius is making a tyrant of our friend."

Antius looked puzzled and uncertain. He licked his lips until Cassius, the scribe, bowed. "May I help? This evening, Pericles is hosting a party in the house of Gaius. Perhaps the Roman ear might be well rested and more willing to hear all sides in the local disputes?"

Antius nodded gratefully, Kyrillos spat and stormed

off with Aristomache in tow.

His son, the killer. That man wasn't there.

Meliton took a long breath and bowed to us. "So be it. It must be settled. We must speak."

What must be settled?

Bernike clutched his arm and cast a worried look at the departing Kyrillos. "Perhaps then, we can settle this affair with Corinne."

Corinne looked down.

"Your names?" asked the wife of Pericles. "We have no time for sordid tales of love. Your husband, Bernike, chose to break Alexander and Corinne up, and to give her to Amyntas. It is no fault of ours."

Bernike stared at her with hate. "It is your fault. You are making us beggars with the roman support. With the support of Gaius!"

Pericles lifted his hand first. "Alas, let us deal with unpleasant misunderstandings later. This is Laodamia, my clever wife."

She bowed her head. Her eyes never left us.

"My girls, Lysirate. The tall one."

She smiled. Laodamia looked enraged.

"Eudoxia, the smaller darling of mine," he murmured.

Eudoxia looked down, her eyes closed demurely. She was like the most delicate of flowers.

We nodded, and Antius bowed, his eyes gleaming dangerously at the sight of the young women.

The man nodded at Alexander. "And our captain,

who is indeed related to us."

Alexander didn't bow or nod.

Pericles twitched nervously. "This is…welcome. This is…not expected. I mean you didn't expect us? You have not dressed in your armor, and—"

I nodded, feeling wobbly on my feet. The long days in the sea had left us all shaken. I spoke. "No. It was not expected. We expected something entirely different, to be honest, sir. We didn't expect to be met on the pier, since we were supposed to come unannounced. Hence, our shock. Who told you of our arrival?"

Pericles looked dazed. Cassius, sweating with some fear, stepped forward. His arm was tattooed with a blue sun and a moon.

"Sir, Laodamia was told of your visit. A ship arrived a few days ago with some communications from Rome."

"To whom? You?" Antius asked him.

"They were informal letters," he said. "Very informal. Nothing was sent to me but to—"

Alexander stepped forward. "Nonetheless, a visit by Roman soldiers is unusual. Praetorian," he said with mild surprise. "The letter spoke of praetorians. You look like alley rats. Would one not wear something more suitable to his position when he meets the leader of an allied city?"

Antius smiled. "An allied city? It sounds very fancy. Yours is a free city, a status granted to you by Augustus, or was it Julius Caesar? I cannot remember. We are not disrespectful, but we are here on Roman business, and one must wonder who knew about our trip, which was supposed to be clandestine. I have our orders, of course, if something needs to be proven."

Alexander snapped his head forth. "Indeed. Your status must be proven."

They looked mortified. Antius looked like he was choking on a chicken's bone.

Laodamia stepped forward. "Now, this is unfortunate and wrong, Alexander. They are tired, husband, and are understandably upset, and we need no such acts here in the heat of the sun. They had not been expecting to be met at all, considering the nature of their business here," his wife said dryly.

Pericles straightened his back and let out a long breath. He lifted a finger at her, showing he was under control. He smiled. "Welcome, nonetheless. Do you have more gear?"

I shrugged and waved my hands around the men. "We travel light, sir. Nothing too much on us."

Then, from the back of the people, a sea of color was moving, and I saw two slaves, one red-headed and the other blonde, walking to us with Vipsania.

Cassius gave me a nervous smile. "The letters, sir, were for her. She told us—"

"I know," I said groggily.

She was followed by legionnaires. One was a centurion with a wide chin and wild eyes under his helmet. My eyes went to their shields and gear. Their bronze and steel helmets were flashing, and chainmail gleamed, as the soldiers pushed forward. Alexander and his men gave them an evil eye as they stepped away. The legionnaires were the guard whom had followed Gaius for home but were now stranded in Limyra. From Legio XI Ferrata, veteran legion of both glorious victories and saddest losses, they were all bronzed in skin and scarred as old dogs.

The centurion pulled off his helmet.

That would be a man called Marius.

The Centurion examined me steadily. He moved aside, and then, I saw the woman in a red Roman stola.

I groaned slightly. I had known her in one way, or other, most of my military life.

Vipsania, the fair, beautiful wife of Gaius, stepped forward from under the shade held by her beautiful slaves, holding a hand over her mouth. "You arrived! Finally!" She hesitated and smiled. "I have seen you! In Rome! In Gaul too! Celcus!"

"That is I," I said carefully, my eyes on her. "Decimus. But some…Celcus is fine. We have seen each other often."

Antius didn't look happy about that. It immediately lessened his power.

"You are so tall!" she said breathlessly.

"I have not shrunk," I said dryly.

She giggled. "Ariane! Larissa! Celcus! The Tall one."

They nodded. Ariane, the blonde, smiled gently, but she looked like she was slightly ill. She moved gingerly.

Larissa, the red-headed one, her eyes were on the ship, and there was a haunted, longing look on them.

"I am," I agreed. "Tall, lady. This has now been established."

Hercules snorted softly.

Vipsania.

She was slight and beautiful, energetic, and oddly, somewhat rattled, as if she was slightly drunk. She waved her hand around her with some pride. "I have no idea how they learnt of you, friends. I simply do not. Never mind the lot!"

The 'lot' looked mortified.

She went on. "I have so awaited you. Or any official. But I am happy it was you." She suddenly looked nervous. "Did Augustus send someone with authority?"

I smiled. "As has been said here, we have authority from him to do several things. We have plenty of authority, lady. And I happen to carry his letters and gifts."

I put a hand on a large bag on Segolia's side.

She gave the beautiful Celt a quizzical look, and then, she let out a long breath. "Your slave must take diligent care of the bag. So. We are going back to Rome now?" Her eyes went back to the sack on her side, and she begged and guessed there would be an order to just that effect.

"Vipsania, please," Pericles chortled. "You are in such a hurry to leave Limyra! It is almost hurtful. Do you dislike our home?"

She shook her head and smiled at him. The women in the two remaining Greek families adopted stony faces and looked like they were trying to be very still, as if a slithering snake had surprised them. Vipsania, irrational and angry that she was, gathered her manners and dignity. "Pericles! It is not so. Not at all. Things are much simpler here, and life easy. Who would not love that? For a time, at least. For me, that time has passed. I need the bustle of Rome again." She smiled gently, like a master manipulator might. "I am merely homesick. Not sick of your home. Every guest must leave at some point."

They all nodded at that, save for Pericles, who was bowing to her as he stepped forward. Pericles put a hand over hers. "I understand well enough. No need to worry. I was simply teasing you. Now, as for our guests." He said the last word with some strain and worry. "The good…?"

"Decimus, the centurion," I told him, and nodded at Antius. "Antius."

The man had a terrible memory.

"The Centurion Decimus is here, but they must also rest, and I hear they have other quests to perform, no? The city needs to find unity."

Meliton nodded. "The city is fine. It is the rulership that needs to change…its ways."

The silence was heavy. He meant Pericles should go.

I noticed Laodamia was holding one of her hands,

and it was shaking nervously. She was fair and proud otherwise. "We should not discuss such matters here, now. Shall we go back to Limyra?"

Pericles smiled wryly. "Laodamia. My wife. She is truly the brain and heart of our outfit. We all know there are families who yearn for my position, but are neither rich or intelligent enough to aspire for it without trying to smear me into shit. Shall we go?"

Meliton's eyes flashed.

I stepped closer and looked at Marius and Alexander and the two girls until they stepped back. She stood there, smiling.

I offered her my hand, and she walked off, holding hers over it.

The soldiers surrounded us, Alexander led us off, and Pericles and his family and Antius walked just behind us. Vipsania was giving me longing glances, and I tried my best to ignore the small, beautiful, but clearly unhappy woman. Her slaves walked around us, and Segolia kept looking back at me, and I knew she was rolling her eyes.

Meliton and his family and servants walked far behind, and when I looked at his face, he was fuming.

"We will start today," I heard Antius saying. "We will meet with Gaius," he told Pericles, "and Decimus oversees that part. You have this man Lucius?"

Laodamia spoke. "We have him. These deaths have simply crushed us. We are happy to help Augustus, and ourselves while we do."

"It must be done within law," said Pericles darkly. "There has been trouble with Roman soldiers so visible in the city. People gossip, they are unhappy. There were the three traders, all men who wanted to set up a profitable business with me. They were all men I sponsored and helped."

"The witness will be heard," Antius said. "Right now, if you please. Rome will find the underlying cause of things, and we are grateful you have protected this man."

He nodded. "Yes. I am more than happy to help. Lately, things have been changing here in Limyra, and not for the better. We need Rome, and still, there are men who would put their personal interests before the nation's. They see me, a fine ally to Rome, and they know how to apply pressure to those who know Lycia must change. We have changed before. From Lycian into Greek, and now, we must..." He shrugged.

I smiled at Vipsania and spoke softly. "Is leading Limyra such an honor that the other families, all wealthy, no doubt, try to topple him by speaking against Rome?"

She shook her head. "People risk much for freedom and for power. You know this. The others have been hammered by Gaius's favor to Pericles. All the romans and locals try to trade with Pericles. Look. I would speak with you."

I nodded and listened to Pericles speaking. "I lead Limyra. There have been many men called Pericles in this land ever since my family settled here, ages ago. One fought the Persians; would you believe it? In many ways, I lead many smaller cities as well, for business ties them to us." He smiled sadly. "There are many old families in the land. One is that of Kyrillos, the cursed dog, and the other the brooding dog behind us, who has formerly been neutral in my and Kyrillos's feud, but he has lately helped him. He even broke the betrothal between Alexander and Corinne off, just to promise her to the brute...Amyntas." He was hissing curses and spoke again. "We all trade in fruit, wine, and dabble in slaves and shipping, and since I have been doing well in business of late, so they have stepped up their game. This Amyntas's crime is a desperate act to discredit me. The bastard came here, acting like—"

"We shall speak with this Lucius," Antius said with a cruel, knowing smile. "Now, as I asked."

I heard Laodamia speaking to Pericles.

Soon, Pericles was speaking to Antius. "Listen," Pericles said, and leaned close to Antius. "When Kleitos the Golden died, I have started to lose business to those men again. We must hurry."

"Was Kleitos guarded?" Antius asked.

"Marius, your centurion had guards, but still, he was killed," the man said. "There were guards in the house of the traders as well. On both doors. They keep saying it is this ancient murderer in Limyra that had a hand in it."

"Have any locals been murdered like this?" Antius

asked.

Pericles shrugged. "Not that I know of it. Not in ages, long years. They simply reinvented this ghost, this myth of the Furies, and are discrediting me, and Rome."

Antius nodded. "As said, we shall deal with it. Carefully. Where is Marius's cohort staying?"

"Next door to Gaius," the man said. "He has bought his house and rented the one next to it."

Rented? Gaius had no coin.

I nodded. "Sounds suspicious," I whispered to Vipsania. "Ghosts and grudges."

"It is very much so," she said. "Terribly suspicious. But I want to leave the lot here and go home."

I shrugged. "It is no less suspicious in Rome, as you well know. We shall discuss that with Gaius. And, if you like, you can tell me how he is doing."

"When we get to the wagons," she said impatiently. "I dislike being under the Greek eyes. Gods, but Cassius gets things done. The wagons are excellent."

"Indeed?" I asked and glanced at Antius.

"Where do we meet Lucius?" he was asking, a bit loud.

Pericles suppressed a quick look of panic. "Please, not so loudly. The Romans were killed and Kleitos as well, under guard. Lucius might be murdered as well. We are not having any guards, just family. My slaves are his only companions. We will swing by a house where we hold him, and you may speak to him at once. Then, Gaius later."

Antius nodded and looked up at the Acropolis in the faraway city. "Why is Gaius not in the safely of the fortress? Gaius should be kept alive more than any."

"He won't go," said Pericles with shame. "He is not really interested in his safety, the fool. It is hot as in a volcanic disaster up there, and he likes his comfort. He lived in my house for a while, while he recovered, but now, he has his own."

"Still," Antius said softly. "He should be up there."

Laodamia bowed. "We suggested it. He trusts us well. We cared for him, sir, when he came to Limyra. And when he was better, he bought a house near the Agora and is very reluctant to let go of it. It is a modest thing for a man like him. But it is very well guarded. We told you the legionnaires were settled in a building next to it. It even has a wall. Our men guard out, and his men inside. Alexander's men know their business and so do the legionnaires."

Antius snorted. "And still, Kleitos the Golden was killed, no matter how many legionnaires had been guarding his house."

"Kleitos was a stupid, lecherous bastard," Laodamia said scathingly. "I wouldn't wonder if he invited the murderer in. He had had a feast that night, see? We are doing well enough. Gaius is impossible with security. He dislikes all of it, of course. He hates the attention and the guards. He is a gentle soul, the poor man. Plagued with duty and wounds, like a hero of ancient times. He would do anything for a life out in the countryside."

Lysirate spoke. "I must wonder; did he truly lead armies? He seems like no solider to me. No adventure in his soul!"

"This is why," Laodamia said darkly, "why Eudoxia is the family favorite, Lysirate. She knows better."

Lysirate's face went taut, and Antius gave her wry smile. Pericles spoke apologetically. "Forgive me. My daughter is a wild soul. She'd rather write tales, than behave like a lady of Limyra. Gaius is of no trouble. He and I share a passion for poetry, and both agree none equal Greek ones in this form of art. He prefers the city to make it easy for his clients to visit him every morning. Vipsania too, I imagine, has a respectable number of people who call on her each morning."

"Too many," Vipsania whispered.

I muttered, "He does prefer Greek ones, does he? And life out in the countryside?"

"My husband, Celcus, is threatening to stay here," Vipsania whispered. "He has threatened me with many things."

I let that sink in.

It was no surprise.

Antius nodded as we walked the haphazard, hot, colorful streets where people stopped to stare at us. "Well. I suppose we can get on with it. Actually, I want to see the house where Kleitos died. Bring Lucius there, Pericles."

"It will be so," he agreed. "Of course."

Laodamia spoke. "And," she asked. "If the son of

66

Kyrillos killed them, we will condemn Kyrillos?"

"It is your city," Antius said. "But we shall do our best. It will have to be discreet. I will need some things. For today, that is. You said you have a house full of Roman soldiers just next to that of Gaius."

He nodded. "We do. Anything to put this behind us."

I smiled and whispered to Vipsania. "To put your own trouble behind."

Vipsania smirked and said nothing.

Antius was speaking. "Of course, we shall question Amyntas. We shall. You and I."

"Thank you," he agreed. "We shall do that indeed. With the help of Zeus, the truth will be revealed, and all the crimes laid out to be seen by everyone."

Antius nodded up the street. "Zeus has not a thing to do with it. We will need guides. We shall stay with the legionnaires."

"No," I called out.

They stared at me.

"We will stay in a tavern, on our own," I said. "One will be provided to us. Near the agora."

Antius opened his mouth but noticed Hercules looking at him sternly, and then, he nodded. "Near agora. Inn."

Pericles nodded as well, though reluctantly. "Yes, and I can make arrangements. You will have two boys to guide you in our rather modest city. Both are clever servants of mine. There is also an inn not too far from his house, I mean that of Gaius, and the agora. I will send someone ahead to make arrangements."

He spoke to a man, who nodded, and rushed off.

Laodamia gave me a withering look. She was suspicious, and for a reason.

Pericles spoke on. "You shall like it, I am sure. It is mostly silent, and they serve excellent stew."

"Silence and stew," I said. "All a soldier requires."

He gave my bag a curious glance and took steps to walk with Vipsania and I. "Is he going home?"

I shrugged. "It is up to him."

He sighed and smiled. "Fine, centurion. First thing's first."

"Would you like him to go home?" I asked.

Laodamia smiled as she reached us and put a hand on Pericles's arm. "No, of course not. Naturally, these killings and the internal strife has created some unwanted tensions in our land, but we are what we are. Quarrelsome. We welcome him, but we also worry."

Larissa spoke gently. "My lady," she told Vipsania. "The sun, you must guard your skin. We should hurry. The shade can only guard you so much."

Pericles nodded. "Indeed. Wagons await. They are cushioned, my...centurion. Closed and with curtains like in Rome. But perhaps you would like to walk or ride?"

He looked briefly at my bedraggled state.

"The centurion will come with me," Vipsania said with a grin. "This one. The other one can walk or ride."

She pulled me along.

I nodded, feeling a brief stab of panic as she tugged me past the others. The legionnaires looked at me with simmering anger, and Marius was looking down, gnashing his teeth. She was probably a nightmare on any unit of bodyguards. Alexander was shaking his head as well, his dark eyes on Vipsania, then at Corinne far behind and then finally on the soldiers, especially on Hercules, who walked to stand by the wagon.

I had a hunch they were all praying Gaius would go home, and for him to take Vipsania with him.

All except the Pericles family, who had grown attached to the coin, and now fought the stain of Rome with roman soldiers.

At least, they had Alexander behind them as well.

Laodamia walked with me and kept a modest space between us. I realized I stank. Vipsania, for some reason, didn't seem to mind as she hooked a hand on my arm. I had to walk slightly stooped to keep her on her feet.

Cassius, the pudgy scribe, walked next to us and tried to say something, but Vipsania pushed us both forward. Laodamia stepped forward with us, her face a mask of calm.

I fell in step with her and Vipsania, who was speaking softly. "Cassius will deal with your schedules. Gaius is holding a party this night."

Laodamia and her girls who caught up shook their heads. "Gaius is hosting it, and my husband is paying for it," she said. "We shall all be there."

Vipsania looked ready to snap. Instead, she nodded. "Of course, Pericles is hosting it, or paying for it, but it is held in our house, and Gaius is the one inviting, and he sits in the middle. You must speak with him today."

Laodamia was speaking softly. "Before that, now, perhaps you should keep a low profile."

I snorted. "And therefore, you met us here in the harbor. To keep us from being noticed."

She smiled wryly. "We, as my husband said, expected someone from Rome, a man in a toga, and with power to decide on policy. Though, I suppose, there are many kinds of power, and it can be the more visible one. Be careful with Kyrillos."

"Why?"

"Because he is the sort of a man who lets his emotions control him." She shook her head. "It plays a part it. Gaius is oblivious to these things. He is far too gentle-hearted to ask about the deaths and what we are suffering for it, and what is going on with the council."

Vipsania frowned and muttered something.

I said nothing and walked on with Vipsania as she was sauntering along next to me, Ariana, her slave, holding a sunscreen over her fair head.

"Tell me, centurion," Laodamia went on, "since Gaius rarely speaks of Rome and Roman matters, is there truth to Kyrillos's fears and hatred for your nation?"

"I wouldn't be surprised," I answered. "I am sure

Rome would love this land."

She smiled at my honesty. "While Lycians are friends to Rome, ever since great Caesar signed a treaty with us, men do fear Rome has grander plans. Freedom is not freedom, if there is a possibility that a displeased Roman senator might call for our annexation over trade differences."

I nodded. "That happened. I heard of it. Last year, I think, but it was not a serious request."

She went on, unhappy. "It is politics, and things change, and perhaps Lycia would be better off with Rome. Some men still wear their hair long, many still speak ancient Lycian and Persian, but we are losing the old ways. We are increasingly like Rome, like Greece. Even our soldiers dress like yours now. There are those who hate it. Some of them clamor for the old days, for my husband's name-sake's heroics. Pericles, the first one, whose tomb is set before the Acropolis, is the lord of dissidents, not I." She sighed. "Silly, I know, to fight what must come, but there it is. They do fight it." She shook her head ruefully.

The woman is trying to sound friendly, submissive.

I felt very uncomfortable with her. I resisted the urge to agree with her on anything.

"Gaius and his soldiers have already made people uneasy. Sixty legionnaires and his officia, and the fact he bought a house, has put the tongues wagging. Pericles, as the lord, has the keys to his door, a way to access him, but that doesn't apply to the other people in the city, and many avoid him on purpose. The soldiers of Gaius are dangerous. And yet, I am starting to worry. Something is..." She looked deadly afraid. "The actor's death, it was the last straw. Men have been more vocal for and against Rome. It is a delicate matter, you see."

"I see."

And then she got to the meat of the matter. "Perhaps if you can tell Antius there that it is possible Meliton is part of this murderous act? He has lost as much as Kyrillos."

I nodded. "I see your worry. I see the opportunity you see in this. Perhaps the next two rulers of the city will be Roman-minded, and picked by you?"

"Perhaps," she agreed. "But these families, when they must fall, must fall totally. All of them. And some of them, the women, could be sent to Rome? Or at least, that would be the story."

Callous bitch.

I shrugged. "It would make sense. And still, if we find a murderer of Romans, the man will hang for weeks where everyone can see him. It should do to scare them all. But I shall talk to Antius about it." I gave her a long look. "I agree it is a dilemma for your family, lady. If these people survive, and Gaius goes home, you will have tough time holding onto power, since people responsible for the murders of Romans will have died, your people will be upset and angry at Rome, and hence to you, and Rome is no longer here to be profited from, or to guard you."

I pulled Vipsania off as Laodamia and Eudoxia frowned. I noticed Lysirate was grinning. I turned to Vipsania. "The inn where we will stay in? I assume it will be paid for?"

"Oh, you need not worry about payments," she said and whispered the rest. "It is all right. We send the bills to our host. We live off his generosity, after all since Augustus cut us off."

I nodded at Laodamia. "Thank you. Good."

Laodamia looked suspicious. "We are already hosting Gaius. I cannot pay—"

"You?" I asked. "You take care of the coin in your family?"

She shook her head and nodded. "Yes. My family is the rich one. My husband's was the noble one. I am not ashamed of it. But the expenses are huge already. We need..." She went quiet.

I smiled at the dismay on her face.

I spoke with an agreeable smile. "A good tavern will do well, and I suppose I can deal with the details on my own. I will pay for it." I told to her immediate relief. "Or, Augustus will. I shall let him know."

Laodamia shook her head and then nodded fast, as if catching herself in the dangerous act. "I shall, of course, cover the expenses of your stay. How long shall it be?"

"We won't eat much," I told him. "I don't expect us to stay more than a week."

Vipsania grasped my arm. "A week? Will we stay one more week? I don't have a week."

73

I looked at her curiously and clasped her hand as affectionately as a bear would a deer's neck. "A week, more, if the weather turns ugly." She sulked and walked ahead, likely cursing.

"Week?" she said. "More?"

"Depending on the weather, dear," I said. "You must pray to gods for kind winds."

She cursed.

"How did you find out we were going to arrive?" I asked her.

She smiled. "Your captain took a route that cut past Crete. Another ship, one bearing mail from my friends in Rome, came through Greece. It is much faster."

"You did invite Pericles—"

"I did no such thing," she said brusquely. "We met in the Agora, after he suggested it would make sense to go together. I simply told Gaius. I hopped to my wagon, when he refused to come."

"Hopped to your wagon, eh?"

"Yes," she said. "I told nobody."

I was nodding. Pericles, or perhaps rather Laodamia, has a spy in the house of Gaius, or Gaius had a confidant in the house of Pericles, one much closer to him than the others.

I turned to look at her servants. The red-headed girl flanked her, sturdy and powerful, and a tall blonde, both of whom looked at me with respect. I spotted some old scars on Ariane's back, the blonde flinching with each step. There was also blood, so there were newer wounds as well. The thin scribe took a small step forward as well.

"When can I see Gaius?" I asked him, before he could speak.

Cassius smiled nervously. "Centurion, if you have the time, I, too, would discuss several matters. The loss of Ennius, the head scribe. I must tell you that he has likely stolen—"

I nodded at him. "I shall need an audience with Gaius, as soon as possible. This very evening, if you please. Make sure Kyrillos and Meliton and their families are there, in this feast. The rest of such issues can wait."

He scratched his head. "Very well. I know where you are staying as well, so I shall send some finer gear for you for the feast. The tavern is but a few blocks away from the house of Gaius. It is rather a Roman-like house, as are many in that section of the city, near the agora. You will like it. Thank you for making him pay for it." He nodded towards Pericles. "It is resourceful to save coin."

"You mean Laodamia?" I asked him. "The smaller girl is precious to her, isn't she?"

"She is, Eudoxia," he agreed. His eyes went to my bag. "Sir, may I take them, and—"

I shrugged. "No, you many not," I said, clasping my bag. "It is not for you. It is from Augustus to Gaius. He needs to have the news today. From my hand, into his. In a very secluded setting."

75

He hesitated, just as Vipsania passed several taverns, and Laodamia and the guards crowded around us. Cassius took the chance to pull closer to me. He spoke breathlessly. "He has changed of late. He hates all official Roman business. He avoids letters, scrolls, and messengers. He has asked not to be bothered by such affairs. Let me—"

"He cannot avoid me," I told him. "Make sure he knows he cannot."

He bowed, looking distressed. "He will not like it. But I shall do my best. I would like to speak to you about the scribe. Ennius. It is—"

"I too, want to speak to you about him. Augustus does as well," I said. "It is surprising he is missing."

"It happened a month ago," he said. "Augustus?"

"Augustus wants to see all the expenses and wants an explanation for all of it."

He nodded and sighed. "He left. He left on the evening of the murders, and took all his scrolls with him, or burned them. Also, many precious things went missing. He is gone. I have been trying to see what he stole, and I think he has overpaid for many of Gaius's purchases here, and then pocketed the money, and ran. I must not be blamed for it. I would—"

"Later," I said.

I turned to Vipsania who was now tugging us through crowds of merchants and their customers, towards a pack of people and many horses at the end of a road. There, wagons, mounts, and litters awaited us.

She gave my men a wry glance. "Phoneica is a fine port, but the city is some four miles north, at the foot of the mountains. It would be two, but there is a small flood, and we must take a round-about way through some fields."

"We saw it from the sea," I said. "The city. It seems odd that in the summer, the hillsides are dry, and the plain and roads still filled with flowers and wheat."

She nodded, as she headed for the wagons. "Like a forgotten wife, that is. Dry on the outside, but still wet inside."

I squinted at her words, swallowed, and walked on. She was in an odd mood.

She was shaking her head and nodding at the mountain ahead. "That thing is dry as bone. Always is. The plains are heavy with wheat. I like the city, to a degree," she said tiredly. "I have Darius, my cook, and he constantly keeps me happy with his treats. The food is good." She sighed. "But is such an odd place. Those Greeks, they have Zeus and his brood watching over it all. They sacrifice to Alexander, which I find refreshing, but I do miss Rome's practical gods. I feel lost here without them. You will travel with me in the wagon, and I shall speak to you about our troubles. Worry not; they are not about the greed of Laodamia and Pericles, but about your mission to get Gaius home."

"Lady," I began, "I am here to bring mail and to investigate—"

"You are here to get Gaius home, so you will listen

to me first. Come," she said. "I need your company. These bone-dry soldiers and merchants bore me."

"I am a solider," I said.

She smiled. "But you are handsome, tall, and more than a soldier. I know you. Come."

I nodded with trepidation, and gave Segolia a small look, and handed her my mail. She cursed softly, grasped the bag, and held it close. Pericles wasn't far, with Laodamia following closely behind, but apparently, Vipsania had no need to wait for them, so we filed into a simple, closed wagon, which followed two cavalry men of Alexander and the captain himself. The legionnaires marched on both sides of us with Marius giving my men appraising, worried looks. Hercules was very close to our wagon, and the legionnaires were trying to be closer.

Ariane and Larissa walked outside the doors with Segolia.

The other people were getting ready to ride and march, and I looked up towards the ragged mountain by a gleaming river, and the city huddling behind the high walls. I felt uneasy, but shrugged off the odd…fear?

Aye, it had been fear.

Bone-dry, she had said.

I hopped in and sat across from Vipsania. She looked young, but I decided she also looked exhausted. Her rearing had hidden it, but now, it seemed she was like another person. Her eyes had rings under them, not something you might notice out in the light, but only inside. Worries raked her, it was clear, and I guessed the marriage to Gaius had not been a happy one. She sat still and smiled like a corpse as she moved her knees between mine. She took a long breath. "You served in the Legio XIX? I think you did, once. There were few other legions that were there, but…"

I wasn't surprised. I nodded. "It was one of the Capricorns. One of those that Octavianus raised. Yes, I was on the second, then first cohort, and I was a duplicarius."

"You had experience in hunting," she said. "You filled many pots with meat."

I nodded. "Your memory serves you very well. You were but eight."

She smiled and squeezed my hand briefly. It was icy cold and trembling. "More. Year or two more, Celcus. My father Drusus commanded you in his campaigns against the Chatti and the Sigambri. That's when I remember you were rewarded."

I smiled fondly at the memory, though I was acutely aware she was stripping me of all my defenses with flattery. "Corona aureus."

She shook her head. "You killed a great enemy"

"Enemy Thiuda, lady, a war-king," I said. "The man was trying to kill us, and I held the line and butchered him. Hercules was there as well."

"The African, I guess?" she asked. "I remember him as well. Chatti were ferocious enemies."

I shrugged. "They were, and are, I hear. There were many other tribes, lady," I said, at guard. "Many. They all turned out when your father went to war. Cherusci, Tencteri, Bructeri—"

"Quite so," she said, and smiled wistfully. "You know mother and the rest of us lived in Lugdunum and Moganticum much of that time. You lot would come and go, but you were so tall, I will always remember it, and always with that friend of yours. You were well liked by my father. Even a child could see it. The love of a general for his soldiers is a thing more sacred. As sacred as that of a soldier for his general. You loved him back."

"I know, lady," I said, uncomfortable and wary. "I loved him well."

"Oh, you did," she whispered. "Most men did, but some more than the others. You served him well. You respected each other and were loyal."

She looked away, and I saw a hint of a tear in her eye. Loyal.

Was Gaius having an affair? It would be a surprise. He was always known to shun the girls, and to respect them unlike most other men, who tried to bed every single one of them.

There was something bothering her, and that was as good a guess as any.

And yet, there would be a point to what she was doing, a purpose. She was trying to make me feel relaxed, charming me like she would coo at a drowsy kitten.

Nay, she was giving me a speech like a general to a heroic soldier, but the trouble was coming, and battle was about to begin. It was clear by the sudden jerk of her hand as she withdrew it from mine.

I spoke softly, eyeing her. "I often accompanied your great father on the winter breaks to Rome, and to you, his family, in Gaul. I was not a Centurion back then. I had other…skills."

"You were more than a hunter," she murmured. "Later. You were a speculatore," she said simply, and I was actually impressed. She saw it and nodded. "Scout. You rode the enemy lands, you found their secrets and guarded our lives. He gained his victories from the news you and yours gathered. I take your friend didn't take part in that?"

I smiled. His dark skin would have been odd in the camps of the Germani.

"Hercules had other duties," I agreed. "He killed our enemies and rescued me when I scouted."

"You guarded Father," she said gratefully. "Thank you."

"I didn't guard him well enough, lady," I answered stiffly, "when his horse fell, and he broke his leg."

She nodded, looking out of the small window at Ariane and the men beyond. "No man can change fate. Perhaps it was for the best. Gods saved lives."

"Lady?" I asked, shocked. "Gods saved lives by having a horse falling on his leg? The death was not a kind one, lady. He suffered terribly, for days."

"For the best, I said, yes," she whispered, as if someone might hear her. "Perhaps it had to happen, and it was for the best, indeed. He wanted to overthrow our Princeps, didn't he? Our Octavianus, our Augustus, the Princeps of Rome. That's what they all say, when they speak of my father. I was lucky Augustus allowed me to marry Gaius. It is only because Mother is a relative to him, and he saw a possibility for his blood to live on through us." She was frowning. "It was such a carefree day. It was the very best of days. The most beautiful day. I remember it well."

I nodded. "The day he announced it? Or the day you got married?"

I bit my tongue. It was foolish to assume she was truly friendly with her father's old soldier. She might just as well bite my head off.

She didn't.

She cocked her pretty head. "The day they announced it, Celcus. You assume one of the two was less than happy? Nay, do not blush. You are wise to do so. The day Augustus called me and joined our hands was a truly happy day." She smiled at my dismay. "It lasted until the marriage ceremony." She leaned forward. "Is it true? Did Drusus truly hope to overthrow him and restore the Republic?"

"The Republic?" I asked her innocently. "It never went away, did it? The Senate is still there. Rome is still a Republic."

"Oh, Celcus," she sighed. "Come now. It is I, Vipsania, who is of the blood and the family. I am one of the tools of Augustus, like you are, just prettier."

I said nothing. I shrugged. "I have no idea. I am not of the blood. I am a weapon for your family, but do not share in its secrets. Not the ones, at least, that truly matter."

And it mattered.

And I lied.

Drusus had hoped to overthrow the rule of Augustus. He had been for the old ways, always had been. The poor fool never made a secret about it.

She saw my face and read it like an augur of fame. "He would have tried to lead a rebellion, had he but taken Germania," she surmised. "He would have had war-hardened, loyal legions, and many others would have joined him, even some of our enemies. Oh, the Germani worshipped him, their mortal enemy. It would have condemned us all. All of Rome back in the civil war, with everything to win and lose. Ah, had he but done so, and won, I would not now have to weep my eyes out every night. I would be happy. If only even Gaius tried to rebel, and to summon his eastern legions, if he is so unhappy. If he only were a hero. He is not."

I shifted, considered leaving, but couldn't get out. Her knees were around mine. I turned to her and spoke very softly. "This discussion must end, lady. I told you; I am not party to your secrets. I must not know these things. I cannot—"

"No," she sighed and held her face for a moment. "You should not. But regretfully, you must. I remember you, Decimus Celcus. I have seen you with the Praetorians, tall as the Germani Guard, and often with our old Augustus himself, our patron whispering secrets to your ear. The brood of Pericles, the shit of Kyrillos, Meliton with his rancid high Myran wife and the ghost-eye daughter, let them all rot. I say let them rot with Limyra, with Lycia."

She was speaking harshly, and loudly.

I put a hand on her shoulder. "Lady, you must remember—"

She clasped the hand. "They say you are no official of Rome, these Greeks, no senator or fat confidant in a toga, but we know better. You are the man who solves issues for Augustus. You hunt killers, and you bury the secrets so deep, no enemy of Rome can ever find them. You carry his authority and deal with many terrible issues. And is not ours a terrible one?"

I nodded, and we lurched forward. The wagon and the roads were not very compatible. Few nations built roads like Rome did, and so we had to hold on as the great party left the harbor for the city. Her knees were still around mine, and we both grasped the sides of the wagon. The cushions helped but not much. When the last buildings could be glimpsed through the small window, I spoke to her. "It is a terrible one, indeed. These murders must be solved. It is no good for Rome, or Limyra, is it."

"Oh, the murders," she said with a bored voice. "It is a sad business indeed for the Lycians, and perhaps sadder still for Limyra when we leave. I told you; I care not for that part of your business. We must leave, no?"

"You must," I agreed. "Indeed, you must."

"In a week," she sighed. "Truly, I have been afraid for long months, but now, I do feel safer. You have the brains, and the muscle. You were wise to look like ruffians. Speculatores are the cream of the cream. Marius, his men? Just grunts."

"They have kept you safe and alive," I reminded her. "And they guard your husband as well."

She smiled. "By all means, solve the issues. Solve them all. Find murderers and blame the people whom Pericles fears. Do as her whore wife and bitch daughters would no doubt advise and spare the life of these men. Take them away and let none know better."

"She leads the family, no?" I asked her.

"She does, as she admitted," she said, swallowing. "She is a pushy bitch, and when we lived in their house, she basically kidnapped Gaius. Limyra, not large city at all, is suddenly filled with Roman business. Side, the city of Side, and Myra have suffered in trade because Gaius is giving Limyra special attention. There are some pirates, even, now that Gaius is the hub of attention in this city. His stay here is fraught with evil. I fear we are in danger, rather than at peace."

I bit my tongue. She had the looks and the smarts. She played a game of her own. They probably loved to

85

have Gaius in Limyra. They all, save for Kyrillos and the other families, benefitted from this stay.

She went on and slapped my knee. "So. Tell me. How is Rome?"

I squinted. "I thought you just now had mail from Rome?"

She nodded. "I have my correspondence but little else. Mother told me how you set out for Limyra, and I knew at once it would mean wonderful things for us. And while I know the gossip, I need to see lips moving and speaking of Rome, and I can then almost imagine what is taking place there. Every day, I see nothing but these cedar trees, the fucking mountains, the Greek dresses, and oiled faces, and it is literally making me sick. I read, but I want to hear. Tell me. Move your lips, Celcus."

She slapped my knee again. This time, her hand stayed on my knee.

I shrugged and ignored the hand. "Nothing much is different. Tiber floods the valleys every year, the boats are rowed on the River Tiber, and minor wars are won. Augustus is keeping peace, and they are heaping praise on him. Rome is eternal, the rich remain rich, the poor are dirt poor, and gossip, you know, as you say. I bet you even know Tiberius is back."

She blinked. "I read so much. Mother didn't tell me a lot. Uncle is back in Rome? His Rhodes exile is over?" she said, wonder in her voice. "They said he'd die in exile, but...no. I didn't think he would ever see Palatine again. Tell me; is he married?"

"No," I answered, smiling. She knew all about Tiberius. "He lives in the Palatine, indeed, but is no longer close to Augustus. The old man will never forgive him for leaving him when he was needed so badly in the east."

She wrung her fingers. "Who can blame him. Gaius had to go instead. Without Tiberius, we wouldn't be here. Augustus gave him more power than he ever did Agrippa. And Tiberius? He left for a permanent holiday."

I nodded. "He did. He didn't want to be Agrippa. He didn't want to fight Rome's wars, while Lucius and your Gaius were grown to power. He..." I began, suddenly passionate about the matter, and then went quiet. "He is out of power, he is. A citizen, and a peaceful one. Livia is worried for him, and Augustus still doesn't mention him. After Lollius and your husband speculated on taking his life, he has—"

"Gaius never did," she said, grasping my hands hard. "He never did. Ever. It was all Marcus Lollius."

I nodded, though I wasn't so sure. Marcus Lollius, the rector of Gaius, the teacher Augustus had trusted well, was dead. Riches had found their way to Marcus in the east, Parthian riches, and the man had guarded Gaius, the future Augustus of Rome, like his personal treasure, and Gaius had been blind. He was easy to lead, fast to trust. Marcus Lollius had made Gaius fearful of Tiberius, the great general, the son of Livia, who was the wife of Augustus. The quest of Augustus to have his own blood on the throne of Rome was well-known, and Lollius, after Tiberius's retreat to Rhodes, had found fertile ground in young Gaius, and he had done all he could to eliminate powerful men, so he might rule through Gaius.

Someone had told Gaius they might fetch Tiberius's head.

I wasn't sure how Gaius had answered. Gaius had not said, 'yes,' but he had not said, 'no,' either.

I held her hands, uncomfortable. "After Lollius threatened him, Tiberius has only wanted to go home. He knew there were men who would never trust he only wanted to retire, and his life was in danger. Livia, his mother meets him daily, and his few friends do as well. Gods know the Stone-Jaws was never one to make friends. But most importantly, he is back, a citizen, and, I suppose, happy."

She smiled. "You knew him well."

I nodded. "I served him after Drusus. He is not like...your father. Not at all. As I said, he is called the Stone-Jaws. But he is a great commander and a man with an unclouded vision."

"Of what?" she prompted, her eyes in a squint.

"Of life, I suppose," I said with a smile. "Few men dare defy Augustus and seek happiness, when they hold many of the powers Augustus himself does." I tried to take my hands off hers, but she held on, her fingernails digging in. I went on, nervous to the bone.

"Otherwise, there is nothing new. Augustus is getting over the death of your husband's brother. Slowly, he is. Poor Lucius."

"Poor Lucius," she echoed and breathed. "It changed everything. It changed Gaius. He had always been a bit sad, and bit timid, but Lucius's death in Gaul, the unexpected calamity? He had, despite the fact Augustus has placed the duty on his shoulders, always hoped Lucius would take the burden."

I nodded. "He told you this?"

She nodded. "The wound in Armenia, betrayal by people he trusted..." She sighed. "It was all too much for him. He came to this port, Phoneica, on his way home, saw the place, was greeted by Pericles, and then, he stayed. Here, he is like Tiberius was. On a holiday."

"It must end."

And so, she got to the point.

"He doesn't love me."

I looked away. "It is possible, Vipsania. Life isn't always fair."

"Fair," she snorted. "He married me. None forced him."

I wasn't sure that was true. Augustus made the decision.

She went on. "We do not have a child," she said sadly. "There is no boy, or even a girl to dote on."

I coughed softly. "No. There is no child."

She looked at me and read me like a book. "That's a problem."

I shrugged and tried to gather myself. "It is a problem."

"And they all blame me," she told me. "Even Gaius, who does not bed me."

I didn't deny it. "He is Gaius. He can blame anyone he wishes, and that will be the way of it."

She shook her head at my brutal honesty. "He is Gaius, and he is the sun of Rome, the future of the nation, and I, despite my bloodline, the glory of my family, I am woman and to be blamed," she said.

I nodded. "Yes. I suppose that is so. It is true. Augustus has spoken of it. He is very worried. I think he is desperate, even, though he doesn't show it. No," I said and decided to be honest. "He is worried. He expects a change."

"What sort of a change?" she asked with a nervous, small voice. "Because, dear Celcus, I am already hoping for one. I will have one. I shall have it. You will be surprised."

She smiled, and I wondered at what she might mean by that.

I spoke gently. "A major one," I told her. "He wants to see a grandchild."

She looked down. "Divorce?" She shook her head with despair. "Augustus will divorce us?"

"At least you must start trying, again," I said. "To be a pair."

Her eyes hardened. "A pair? Augustus commands us to be a pair? No, that won't change Gaius, since he already changed, as I said. He changed in the east, after his wound, and after he lost Lucius. And there is this. He cannot bed me."

I smiled nervously. "He cannot bed you?"

"He complains about his wound. When he tried the last time… I mean…he cannot make it…large?"

"Lady—" I began and tried to get away, but she pulled me back with ferocious force.

She placed her hand on my face and spoke desperately, like she would confess a crime and wanted none else to know. "It is not fair. Augustus will separate us. He will. He thinks it is I that is to be blamed, doesn't he? He thinks Gaius is bedding me day and night, on table and on bed, but he is not. Augustus is going to lure him back by promising him he can marry another."

I made a noncommittal voice. He had mentioned it.

She shook her head. "It was true. He wants to divorce us." She laughed bitterly. "Alas, he is not aware what Gaius is doing."

"It is for Gaius and for him to decide," I told her patiently, struggling to free myself. "It is as things are for many others as well."

"I am not barren," she hissed. "It is not my fault. I've followed him, nay, loved him. I am ready. He is not."

"I believe you," I answered, pushed her back, and put a hand on the door. "This is enough. I should not be here."

"I am not barren, and he is simply not interested in me," she told me, and blocked the door with a foot. "He is not flawed in that way, either. I am sure. He wants children. He and I used to speak about it. We got married in a terrible hurry back in Rome. You know, Augustus arranged it all and told me to make many boys for the family. He set it up, so Gaius, his grandson, and I, his sister's daughter, could make his dynasty powerful. There would be Lucius and Gaius, and through me, more boys to carry on the name far into the future. I knew it was all he ever wanted, this certainty his magnificent work won't be wasted. Love or devotion has nothing to do with marriages. Few marry for love, do they?"

I didn't like the look on her eyes. "No, lady. Then, you understand why he is looking at all the options. It is about Rome, and if Gaius is not...look. It is better for you as well, if you find a man who knows passion and love. You are worth it, no?"

Her eyes teared up. "Do you think so?"

"Yes," I said, and thought of the time I had ventured on a freshly iced river in a Gaulish winter, chased by the enemy. That ice had been perilous.

This felt exactly like that.

She went on, tears falling from her eyes. I tried to turn away, but she reached out, pulled me close, and held my rough cheek on hers. "He left for east. His tasks in Syria, his travels and that small war in Arabia, and the Parthian threat to Armenia's new king; he had to settle it all. He was busy. Very busy. I dealt with...everything else. I am too tired to deal with everything on my own."

I sighed. "He needs to get busy again. And you need to stop worrying. You will both find love again, if not with each other."

She looked slightly hurt and then went on. "Yes. It is so. But it is only I who needs to find love. He has love. He has had a lover, at least. Ariane has been trying to find out who it is, but you know, they have all been paraded before him. Bernike holds his hand, and the ugly Andromache sings to him. Corinne, she has been hunting with him, and Lysirate, she has tried to make him tell of his adventures in Armenia. While holding his hand. Eudoxia, she is always with Laodamia, and Laodamia meets with him daily. He has a lover. Someone of substance."

I glanced out of the window where Ariane was walking on, in pain.

"Lady—"

"Shh. Stay there." She held on to me, her cheek on mine, her perfumed neck close, and the blonde hair billowing around my shoulders and on my face.

She put her lips on my cheek and then leaned back, looking at me with longing.

I, the man, felt desire. I felt protective of her.

"Stay for a moment," she said sadly.

I rubbed my face and watched the countryside. A shadow moved past the doorway, and dust billowed in. I coughed and shook my head. Outside, there were riders, and we were surging to a lesser used road for north, a trail at best. The wagon was jumping up and down. I saw my men around us, and Hercules speaking to one of Pericles's daughters, who was astride a horse, her skin gleaming with oil and sweat. Lysirate. They rode together like best of friends. Segolia was not far from them.

Behind us, I caught a glimpse of a marching troop of soldiers, ours and Lycian, and the wagons of Pericles.

I turned back to Vipsania. "Lady. I have I tried to help your family for ages. I have and will. But I cannot control Gaius, and you must let them decide what needs to be done. I am sorry for your sorrow, of course. You must accept your fate. In the end, it will all end well."

She clenched her fists. "I? I let others decide my fate?"

I said nothing. She had always been a hard to control as a child. Germanicus was the same, and while Claudius was an utter idiot, and a cripple to boot, I sensed he, too, had a drop of Drusus's wild blood.

"Yes."

She took a long breath. "No. I shall not wait. Didn't I learn strategy from my father, and his legates? Antonia, Mother, is a clever one. I shall not be controlled, and I'll never be a leaf and let the currents take me along for a ride. Never."

"Why am I here, in this wagon?" I asked her. "I have listened to secrets that can condemn a man, and I will not hear more of them. I—"

The wagon hit a rock, and she bounced up and

down, and I caught her, before she could strike her head on the ceiling. She smiled thankfully and kept my hands on her waist.

Shit.

She smiled. "I will tell you what I must do, and what you must do to help me. Gaius rests. He spends his time in his study. I hate that study. The house is a haven of peace. Large, almost Roman, far bigger than most in Rome, the gardens blossom, every room has a mosaic floor, and waters flow, and music is played by the very best local musicians. The feasts are slow, and people are kind, and he has nothing to worry about but his wound and recovery."

"The wound," I said simply. "Such wounds often sap the energy…"

"He has plenty of energy to waste," she said acidly. "He spends it in poetry, in search of old tales, walking the paths of the mountains, by fishing in the river. He lets Cassius, and Laodamia deal with everything. He is…he wasn't wounded in the balls, was he? This place is sapping Gaius. He is…too happy here. He is forgetting his promises, his oaths to his father, like Tiberius did. He is no longer Roman."

"In a week, I shall take you away," I said resolutely. "There will be two more galleys, and a ship."

She was nodding. "I don't have a week. But if it is so, and we must accept it. There is more. I have things I must do. You do as well. If I go home," she said sadly. "If I go home like this, Augustus will divorce us."

I shook my head. "What? You will not go home like this?" I said, wondering what she meant. "Perhaps Augustus will give Gaius a fiery speech and make demands. Gaius must change. He won't simply throw you out. Gaius will wither like a sand tower before tide. He'll be in your bed, cock ready in no time."

She didn't buy it.

I bit my tongue, and she laughed. "Oh, I missed soldier's speech. I occasionally catch Marius, the centurion, speaking thus to his men, and it makes me smile."

Her eyes twinkled.

I would have rather faced a Gaul with a gigantic sword, right then.

"Alas, you don't know everything. Augustus warned me." She sighed. "He sent me a warning first time in Armenia. Then, one again, three weeks ago. Gaius has slept—"

"I cannot, must not know—"

"Has slept with me three times this past year. Last time, was two weeks ago. He couldn't finish. I am not sure he could even really get started; it was truly that pitiful. I must be with a child, Celcus, to go back home. Then, I cannot be divorced. And if something happens, and I am a widow, then at least I can stay in the family, and carry the great name of Augustus."

She leaned back and wiped tears off her eyes, gathering herself. I sat back as well. "I am sorry, I said."

"Did you know, that he has told me he, Gaius that is,

will divorce me," she said. "The insult. I cannot bear it. He told me he will divorce me this very night. He said he will write it up."

We sat there, and I watched out of the window.

Was it true? It could be.

Men were marching there, the scribes very near, and my men were riding. Segolia kept a close eye on the roadside where wheat was swaying gently in the wind. Not too far, I saw the walls rising high, and a city growing behind them like an anthill. It was one of the oldest city in Lycia, with a proud history, and I could see why Gaius had settled there to rest.

And still, I wondered if Fish-Bait and that old man had indeed been right.

It felt cold, sad, as if the time had stopped. A city of dying people, of forgotten myths. A city of crying people. Vipsania was crying bitterly.

Hades. A killer from Hades haunted the land, one from the past.

I'd love to meet one then, or the Gaul I had just thought of, or even the enraged Augustus, rather than sit there with her.

I smiled and then shook my head at her.

"I have no power over that, or child-making," I said simply, purposefully misunderstanding her on the latter point. "None. I cannot tell Gaius to bed anyone. I cannot instruct him how to make his cock hard. It would be awkward, and I won't touch it. He would have my head if I so much as suggested it. And I cannot stop him from—"

She giggled.

I went on. "He would likely have my cock before my head. He might be gentle as summer rain, but no man must be told how to bed a woman, or even if they should. I can pray for you, pray to Vesta, but—"

She shook her head. "No. You can help me."

I frowned and cursed. I had read her right. "How could I possibly do so?" I tried one more time.

She smiled, the exhaustion in her being becoming more evident. "First, you will force him home. You will tell him he must not divorce me this night. That he must wait until Rome. It is a matter Augustus has to be part of."

"I can do this," I told her. "But—"

"You can. Second, you will listen carefully. I will explain why, before I tell you what that particular thing I require is. Listen. I was a child when I saw you serving Rome with my father. I was a child, when I, and our little Germanicus, sneaked around our villa in Moganticum. Remember it? It was just to the west of the castra, fortified and guarded and secluded. I loved it. Claudius was just born, the poor, crippled bastard. I was a child, when we heard Father screaming at you in his study."

"What?" I asked her, my blood running ice cold. "You heard him screaming at me?"

She nodded. "I have been trying out the waters for a while, Celcus. I have been telling Augustus Gaius is not well. I wrote to Augustus many times that Gaius is strange, that he plans to stay far longer, but he ignored my complaints and told me to do better. This last time, when I heard Augustus is making his move here, I think the gods heard me. Oh, I prayed to be rid of this city. Another ship came here, carrying messages from my friends, and then, I saw your name in the letters and thanked the lares and the goddesses, and they rewarded me. Of all his men, he sent you. I have been thinking, you see. I have had a plan, and now, I have more than one. First, as I said, you will boot him to Rome. And second?"

I nearly swallowed and, instead, kept looking deep into her eyes.

Those eyes were half delirious with joy and hope.

I grasped the door. "This is enough. I must tell you that I have no idea—"

"You married," she said. "You married fifteen years ago, while you were in service."

The silence was uncanny. Even the sounds from outside seemed to fade. "Many men do," I managed.

She nodded. "Many men do, but few marry a Roman lady of almost the first class. She was a patrician, of one of the best houses in the land. It was, and would still be, I imagine, a disaster to know you seduced her in the camp and then pushed your cock inside her and gave her pleasure. Marriage? It adds to the flavor."

She was shivering, excited, and nervous.

So, that's it, then.

I stiffened and glared at her as I sat straight. "She is with her new husband. It was a madness, and we were young, and it is a part of history. It has been arranged."

She nodded. "It is a part of history my father arranged, and that new, or rather old, husband is raising your boy. Oh, he was fooled. She gave birth, and the boy was put before him, and he picked him up, raised him, and took him as his own. That family has been consuls for many times. Imagine, Decimus, what would happen if anyone so much as suggested the boy was not his in public? If someone were to gossip of such a travesty, and people in Rome would start whispering from Aventine to the cattle market? It would ruin her, it would ruin your boy, and things would be very awkward, unless I, too, have a boy of my own."

She put a hand on my knee, and I knew she wasn't entirely sane.

"See? Do you understand what I am saying? I will outsmart both Augustus, and I will outsmart Gaius, and gods sent you here. I could do this with someone else, but with you, I can be sure there is silence after the fact. I hold nothing over any other man. A child will give Augustus a reason to keep us married. I shall not be shamed. All I need is seed."

I cursed under my breath. "I see. I understand."

"A week, centurion, is enough. We start tomorrow. You tell him to hold the divorce."

I laughed bitterly. "It is enough? And what if it isn't? I am not even entertaining such notions, my lady, that I might agree to this, but what do I know —"

"I know," she whispered. "Women do. I was upset when you said we shall not leave for a week. Perhaps that, too, is a plan of the gods. Perhaps it will not be so hard to spend the week here, after all. It is your duty to calm me, isn't it?"

It wasn't. I was simply to fetch her.

She eyed me. "Do you have a woman?" She looked out of the wagon. "She is one? Your slave."

I shook my head. "No. She is a medicus. Not a slave. I know her father. I do like her. But she is not our kind."

"Crude?"

"No, she is crude, and swears like a sailor," I said. "But she is…innocent."

"A female medicus," she murmured and looked at me. "Never heard of one. But she likes you, and you like her. I like her innocence. Think of her, when you do it."

I rubbed my face. "It is complicated. It is not usual…she is a friend," I said. "No more. I won't think of her."

She winked. "But you desire her? You have had her?"

I didn't shake my head.

I wanted to, but I didn't want to give her the satisfaction of talking about my desires.

It wasn't a door I wanted to open for her.

Instead, I tried to sound arrogant. "Whatever happened to little Vipsania, the tiny wisp of girl we all loved so well?"

Her eyes flashed. "Why, Celcus, she grew up. And can you not see it?"

She leaned back and placed a leg over my hip. Her clothing slipped, and I saw a leg, and a flash of the hair curling between her legs. She was trembling under my gaze.

I pushed away the thought of her beauty.

My eyes rebelled.

I tried harder, turned mine to her eyes, and managed to keep myself intact. Her foot stayed.

"Let me see," she told me with a whisper. "Let me see what I have bought."

I blinked. "Let you see? Bought?"

"You saw what you will have," she whispered. "Let me enjoy what I shall have. Sight and a touch."

Her foot slipped between my legs and slid along my inner things. She was so fast, I could hardly blink before the foot slide under my ass—quite forcefully—and her toes sunk into my ball sack.

I grasped her leg.

She shook her head and held the foot there. I hesitated, and she shrugged my hand off.

She moved the toes and wrestled my thighs open with her other leg, and I cursed her as she slid her foot over my loincloth, and cock.

I was mortified.

I had faced all sort of enemies in my short life, but this one was far too surprising and well equipped to deal with a man who had been spending weeks on a galley. I had no allies, certainly not my cock, which was suddenly not at rest. She ran the length of her foot under the fabric.

I nearly fell out of the wagon, the touch of her bare foot on my hardened manhood far too much.

She slipped her leg off, nearly snapping my ball off. She moved very fast.

She jumped to her knees between my legs, and her hands were sliding up my thighs while her face was blushed, her lips moist. She placed a hand over my manhood, and I tried to grasp the hand. She giggled and pushed her hand under the loincloth and over my balls.

"No!" I said. "This is not—"

"Lady!" someone called outside.

She closed her eyes. She leaned on my leg and pulled it out. She sighed and bent down to kiss the tip, very gently, and then fully, and finally let go, far too slowly, her eyes full of fire, and climbed up and sat back. I adjusted my tunic and my loincloth and tried to figure out something to say.

She looked up, took a deep breath, and spoke out of the window. "Yes?"

Ariane was there. "The city. We are here."

"I know we are," she said softly. "Be gone."

Alexander took her place, looking inside and watching us for a moment. "They will be going to the Agora, lady, and perhaps it would make sense you are not there."

She rolled her eyes. "Fine. Take us to the Agora,

where the centurion will jump out. I shall go home, as I must."

He turned his eyes on me.

"Centurion," he said. "We are stopping by the house of Kleitos. The victim's house first. The houses of all the victims, where they stayed, are very close to each other."

I nodded and didn't move. He rode off, unhappy.

Vipsania sat back and stared at me. I leaned forward. "That must never happen again. It will not."

She smiled and shook her head. "But you didn't fight too hard. It cannot be hidden, the fact. You desire me. And perhaps you know a desperate woman will have her vengeance, if nothing else."

"I desire release after a voyage," I said brutally. "My cock is not my ally when it comes to keeping my honor and upholding decency. You must never do that again. To do so, would condemn you, and me both. No revenge is worth it."

"And your son," she whispered. "He is worth it."

I shut my mouth.

She nodded, satisfied, a winner in her mind. "Gaius is never like that. Never. I have never seen one so hard. The way you reacted. The way I did...I could just..."

I looked outside. "You did. I'm the one who should scream."

"Is it always like that?" she asked.

"What?" I asked, and watched the walls suddenly looming above us. "No, of course not. Especially if I am drunk."

"He is never hard," she said sadly. "So large. Gaius never is. I never thought it could do that...you were hard for me. Are. It is his fault, isn't it?"

I nodded.

It was.

She was ferocious as a vixen, but she was also very desirable. And still, while I was no saint, she was the wife of Gaius Caesar, and I was playing with my life. "It is not you, certainly. Few men would deny you your wishes."

"But it must be you, to protect my future. Thank you. So, you shall serve me, from now on," she told me, suddenly happy, and relaxed.

I wanted to slap her. I was a damned fool, and felt I needed Segolia to tell me so. "It is as you say. Unless it stops me from my duty."

"The duty to make a son for Augustus is above other duties," she informed me. "Now, we must be careful."

I nearly chuckled.

Careful?

I held my face and looked out of the wagon's window.

We sat in silence, as she eyed me, and I watched as the people thronged on the road, and we passed into the city. We traversed a less wealthy part of the city, filled with surprisingly corroded homes, old warehouses, a mix of Roman, with simple doorway on a many storied houses, Greek, with sun-dried mud bricks and open courtyards with modest fountains, shuttered windows on many stories. There were old Lycian paintings on many walls and very life-like statues of heroes, gods, families.

The city was not like Rome.

Like most Greek cities, it was a jumble of streets, a true chaotic cauldron filled with people, buildings, and temples, and the streets ran in every direction. It would be a nightmare for any conqueror to take it, even if they get through the walls. There were beggars on the stony streets, peddlers, criminals, and street urchins surrounded the wagons and the riders.

Soon, we went up to the better part of city, and I gazed at the pillared, stone hewn catacombs that stretched on the slopes and at the Acropolis above. The glimpses of the busy Agora, the theater, and the mazes of alleys filled me with unease, and then, suddenly, we stopped. I gave Vipsania a quick look, and she smiled softly.

"I expect you to do your duties, centurion," she said virtuously. "All of them, no matter how bad you might feel about them."

"I will endure and conquer," I told her, and I hopped out.

Bitch. And still, had I fought hard enough? Had I pushed that foot off, and had I not seen her coming for me?

I had enjoyed it. She is beautiful, and I am a man.

I cursed myself and looked around. Vipsania's

wagon moved off, Marius and his legionnaires surrounding it, as well as some of the local soldiers.

We, on the other hand, stayed, and so did some of Alexander's soldiers. It was very hot, scorching, and even the rich section of the city looked dusty.

Alexander rode up to us, eyeing the people around him, and pointed at a Greek house with a wide gate. "That's where Kleitos stayed. We shall see Lucius inside."

I squinted. "While we wait, where did the traders die?"

He nodded at the house next to us.

I looked at the place. Between it, and the house of dead Kleitos, was an alley. On it, a servant's exit. It was a clean, straight alley, dark, even during the day. Nothing was blocking it. I took a step that way, and I looked at the building.

"Where," I asked, "were the bodies found?"

Alexander shrugged. "Inside, in the lower rooms. They each had their own. Nothing special about them. Save for the lack of heads. Look, this Kleitos was the friend of Augustus, and Gaius. The traders do not matter—"

"Nobody else in the house?" I asked.

"Servants, in the upstairs," he told me with an unpleasant scowl. "Some say they left that night without leave. If there were any inside?" He spat. "None moved a muscle. The traders were killed, one by one, and none heard a thing."

107

"And the servant," I asked. "The one that was killed. How many servants were there? Slaves?"

Alexander hesitated. "Right down there in the alley. Not far from the servant's door. He had escaped, we think. We have no idea how many people they employed. They come, they go, and none track them. One was killed. Nobody is sure who it was. Most of the servants never came back."

"So, it could have been anyone. Who claimed it was a servant?"

He glowered. "Pericles wrote up the report. You romans were here to investigate. That Marius, and the scribe, and others. They brought Pericles all the information that was needed to write a report to Augustus."

"This servant. He wasn't poisoned?"

He shook his head. "Stabbed in the throat, and his face had been mutilated. All of it, the skin, taken off. His fingers were missing. Looks like he ran to the killer, and the killer had time to enjoy a new fantasy."

"Oh," I said. "And the heads off the others?"

He nodded. "This Lucius—"

"Saw him, this Amyntas, leaving here," I said. "The heads have not been found? No? Shall we go to the house of Kleitos?"

He nodded and pointed that way. I walked over, and my men followed me. Painted with pale blues and faded red, the main doorway stood open. Two forlorn looking fish were painted on each side of it.

"You must ask Marius," Alexander said as he walked behind. "Ask his men why they didn't guard the alley. He says they did, but obviously, it is not true. They failed to protect the merchants. And Kleitos. Here too, someone came in from the servant's doorway. Your guards are rotten."

"I will ask," I said. "Antius will."

"Also, do not come to agora alone," he said. "Lately, past week, Kyrillos has been here spewing hate against Gaius, and Pericles, and of course, Rome. Some clients of Meliton as well. They are desperate, for people who serve them are starving. They can be quite compelling, but also dangerous. Keep out of here, if you can. My men keep the peace, but anything might happen."

I nodded. The situation had deteriorated.

I saw Pericles and Laodamia arriving, and they were looking at Antius, who had travelled with them. Antius jumped from a horse and flicked the reins to a man. I noticed Eudoxia sitting in the wagons, but not Lysirate. She had been riding with Hercules, I remembered.

There were only the brood of Pericles, Alexander, and us there. The two girls of Pericles stayed next to the wagons, staring at us intently. Lysirate, the tall one, and Eudoxia, the small one, watched, as their parents and soldiers walked for us. I noticed Laodamia speaking to Pericles, and then Pericles nodded, and walked off to the edge of the agora, where a building of some sort was coming up. It was dusty, windy so I couldn't see much of it.

Alexander stood by the door as he looked at Antius. Antius grinned at me, his eyes on Segolia, and we waited as they entered. Hercules looked at me, and he led our men after Antius.

We both wanted to strangle the centurion.

I gave Segolia a quick look and took the bag from her. "Thank you."

She nodded, her eyes flashing. "Was your journey a pleasant one?" she asked me. "The lady was so pleased to see you."

I nodded. "She thought a world of you," I said. "She thought you might be my pretty slave."

"She did?" she asked, upset. "That would be unpleasant."

"It would," I said. "I have never had one."

"What did she want?" she asked.

I shook my head. "I have known her since she was a child. I served her father."

She nodded slowly, her eyes full of amusement. "She looks all grown up now. I heard her laughing, and I heard her weeping, and I have never seen a woman do determined to do something stupid. Did you have an affair with her in Palatine? I would like to know, because I will make myself scarce if you did. Touch her, and we shall all hang."

I adjusted the bag. "I didn't touch her. Shall you look inside? This Lucius will be there."

"I'll just have a look," she told me. "That girl is dangerous. All women are, but she is more than the others."

She is right. She was dangerous. She seemed truly dangerous.

I should have hopped out immediately when she touched me.

I was a dog.

We looked inside the doorway. There were soldiers working on oil lamps, and the sun was lighting up the garden in the middle. Rows of open doors stood on each side, and corridors as well. It looked abandoned, save for some cats, who stared at their new friends with curiosity.

Segolia was hovering around me. "No, seriously," she said. "What did she want?"

I turned to look around and saw the agora beyond her. It was busy as a battlefield. Vendors of all kinds littered the stalls, by the dozens. Temples loomed over it, where lawyers, like in Rome, were speaking to their prospective clients. There were also witnesses for sale, men who would do anything for coin. On one corner, the dust had settled, and I saw Pericles before a building, speaking to a man with a scroll open on a table. A mighty, new structure was being built. It was new, and I read words on its side. "Augustus," I whispered. "A temple to Augustus?"

Segolia grunted assent. "Roman temple, in Lycia. For Augustus. It looks very expensive. They must be doing well, the Pericles family. Perhaps the council is making the city pay for it."

I nodded and watched her. "Why do you wish to know? About Vipsania?"

She seemed to gag, and then she brushed dust off her tunic. She seemed to make up her mind about something. "Because you have been looking at me for years, and I have liked it, and I would know what sort of a man you are," she said, and blushed as she walked past. "Father warned me of you. I am just curious."

I blinked. She was beautiful, smart, desirable, and hinted that she had liked my longing looks? And suddenly, I was afraid.

So, without thinking, I hung my guilt on her neck.

I'd scare her off.

"She tried to rape me. She grabbed my cock and wanted a child."

I walked in and left her taking deep breaths.

She stumbled after me and kicked over a bronze vase. I couldn't help but grin when everyone turned to look at her.

The courtyard was dusty, filled with debris, and remains of an old celebration, with dead flowers on the bottom of the dry Roman-style impluvium. It was a forlorn sight.

Antius turned to Alexander. "Where was he found?"

Alexander lifted his finger. "The yellow door to the right. That's where. Not a pretty sight back then. Flies, shit, piss, and vomit. All the ingredients of a bad death. The head was gone. Poison, decapitation. Like in the other cases. Then, the horn again."

Antius nodded and walked that way. I stepped after him to the doorway and pushed it open for us.

Antius cursed. "Shit."

"That too," I said.

A pungent stench came to my nose, and I walked in and looked around the room where Kleitos the Golden had died. The actor had been a devoted friend of Augustus and Gaius both, but now, he was simply a pool of blood in the corner of a rotten, stinking room.

Segolia came in and kneeled next to me as she eyed the room. Antius looked around and walked out.

I stayed and so did Segolia. I looked at her. "Well?"

"Bad death, but a silent one," she said. "The poison was potent. Hemlock, perhaps, but a huge dose. The head was taken. The bodies are not kept?"

"I doubt it," I said. "I do doubt it. Burned or buried away. Antius will know."

"Will he?" she said, more than asked. "This Amyntas has a history for such violence?"

"They say he does," I told her. "That he is a soldier, and a troublemaker, and is the future of Lycia in his own mind. Ruthless."

"You have none," she said.

"Eh?"

"No. Future," she spelled out for me. "A child?"

I rubbed my face. "Yes, a child," I said, as I examined the room. "She wants a child."

"Truly?" Segolia asked. "A child? She is missing a child. Any child will do?"

113

"She wants," I snarled, "my child, Segolia, to pass as that of Gaius, so she wouldn't be booted from the family. Gaius has no interest in her."

She chuckled and rubbed her neck as she flicked her eyes over the blood. "Oh, you and Gaius look so much alike. The child will certainly pass as yours. Why are you considering it?"

"I am not!"

"You are," she hissed. "Do you think I am stupid? Father warned me. You have a weakness for women." She shook her head. "Though that is a common issue with your kind. She needs a willing cock to make it all happen, and the little wench is holding something over you? Will you tell me?"

"An old story," I said. "A very old one."

"My father," she said as she got up, "would tell you to step away from her. You know this, right? They will find out. They always will. The child would look as ugly as you. Imagine if it was tall as a giant? Imagine, idiot, you serve in Capitolium at the time they hold the child up to Juppiter, and someone notices... They will—"

"I know."

"And if things go sour for her, and she doesn't feel like taking her secrets to the grave? You will follow her. Do you see? Of course, you see, right?" She traced the scratch marks on the floor where the actor had dragged himself to where an old pool of blood had dried. "And you just sat there and smiled. Did you tell her it is dangerous while she was grasping your..."

114

I rubbed my face. "I did tell her it is dangerous."

"Gods, if she had insisted you hump her there and then," she whispered. Then, she looked at me.

I looked down.

She tossed a stone at me. "You what? You humped her there?" she asked with such a furious voice, I actually flinched. "You told her it is a bad idea, but still let her do it? Why didn't you…you…" She took a long breath.

"You tell your father you tried to talk sense into me," I said. "No, I stopped her."

It was a lie, but at least technically, I had not touched her.

Hercules leaned on the doorway. "They are bringing Lucius in now. He looks like shit." He gave us a pondering look. "What? Did he do something?"

"Yes," she said. "And perhaps not. I don't know when he is lying."

"You will," Hercules said with a wink. "He is a speculatore. We all lie and act all the time. Everything you see, is a lie. We all act while on the job."

"If we are lucky, you might lie your way out of it," she said, and walked past us. "Tell her you are used to cows. Come."

I walked after her and endured Hercules's smug smiles. I found Alexander in the atrium, speaking with Laodamia and her daughters, and Antius was looking at his nails as if they held profitable secrets.

Two soldiers walked in.

With them was a man.

He was tall and looked strong, but also terrified. His hands were gnarled and scarred, and he had a nervous tick on his eye. "This is Lucius," said Hercules. "The man who saw the slayings."

Alexander scoffed. "He didn't see them. He saw the killer. Servant of one of the dead merchants."

Antius eyed the man. "Ah, yes. He wasn't in the house. Lucius? Do you speak Latin?"

"I do, sir," he answered. "I do, indeed. I serve many people. I was not born here, but in Side."

Alexander lifted his head. "Of course, you were."

"I...know nothing of this place or the killing here, only of the house and the murders next door," he said, gathering confidence.

"Tell us about the night you saw the murderer," Antius said.

Lucius bowed. He was so nervous, he might have shat himself. "The house was actually entirely empty, save for the three merchants. I was the only servant."

"And, where were you?" I asked him.

"We were attending a feast," he said. "The traders were not aware of it. There was a birthday for one of the girls in the house, and we went to the river to toast her."

Hercules grunted. "You didn't get lucky?"

He grinned. "Alas, no. I came home. I walked the alley for the entrance."

"Did the guard greet you?" I asked. "There is only one servant entrance to that house?"

"Only one, and there was no guard," he said. "That's why I was worried. I was afraid they had noticed our absence. You see, one can climb down and jump out from the windows of the higher floor, from the servant's quarters where none can see you, but you cannot easily get back up." He looked down. "I was worried. I hid behind the corner."

Antius smiled and walked back and forth. "And?"

"I saw him," he whispered. "I did. The door opened. There was a man. It was a shadowy figure, and a large one. He wore a cloak, gray and blue, which I saw when he turned to look back in. He left the place by the same door I had tried to enter. I knew the man. He is called Amyntas, and he is son of Kyrillos. The man had clearly bought off a guard and had entered in secret. He had probably paid off the same guard to poison the men before he went in. His face, I cannot forget it. It was ferocious, bloody, and he carried a sack. Filled with heads, no doubt. Oh, he had a horn on his belt."

Alexander was caressing his sword, and Antius looked bored.

I grunted. "What of the servant who had been mutilated? He died in the alley."

He looked uncertain. "I fled and saw nothing. I am not sure which servant it would have been, but clearly, the killer was still in the house when the servant came back. Or a slave. There were many people living in the house, serving them." He shivered. "I heard the horn. Three times it rang, and I was terrified. I dared not go in. I ran to lord Pericles."

I nodded.

Laodamia stepped forward and gave the man a coin. "We have been protecting him and wondering how to deal with it."

Antius shrugged. "Well, we have a witness. A credible one, if I ever saw one."

Hercules snorted, and I smiled.

I scratched my neck. "Amyntas? A strong man?"

Lucius nodded. "Strong. Odd. Strange as shit. He is one evil bastard. He beats his slaves with a cane, and people say he does other things to them. Uncouth things. They say he ate man flesh in war, years back. He is always alone."

Laodamia nodded. "The slave speaks the truth. Our laws and yours are draconian."

"It seems so," Antius said. "His boy shall have to be questioned."

She nodded. "His father will be at the feast today."

"And his boy?" I asked her.

"He will not be there," she said. "He stays at home and hates such affairs."

Antius nodded. "We go. I shall find Marius, and then, we will prepare a room, where the law shall be put into effect. This will be easy. Listen," he said, and we did, though I already knew. The ritual that was about to be played out was a brutal one.

He bowed his head at Laodamia, and we turned to go.

Outside, Lucius was taken away, and Laodamia and Pericles stopped to discuss before the doors. Our men, and Antius turned to watch a play. In Rome, such street plays were common, and even women acted, or played tricks in them. An older woman, white of hair, and with beautiful, smooth face was singing. A few young men, and women in death masks, were writing around torches, dodging them, vaulting over them. The two women were in loincloths, their breasts bared, the white masks eerie. The two or three men, danced around them, nearly naked. One had old scars in his arms, but was young, and very muscular man. He was fast, moved smoothly, his arms tied, and he slipped the bonds as deftly as a snake.

People were cheering.

Our men were as well, though I was sure they were looking at the women, who were now bowing.

Pericles was smiling gently.

Laodamia, however, looked on with fury, and suspicion.

Then, they left, and Cassius appeared, and our guides as well, and we marched for our inn.

CHAPTER 3

I was buying fruit, and men were joining me. We had walked a short way up a winding, chaotic street and pressed through throngs of people. When we got to a busy street, where many buildings clearly served as taverns and eateries, my belly rumbled. We all yearned for something fresh, and I felt I could eat a horse. I pressed to a stall, found meat buried in flies, opted for fruit, and handed Segolia a pear.

Then, I looked at a pair of young boys, our guides, who were staring at us, at the fruit, and were both fidgeting.

"Lucius is a shaky one," she observed.

"He is our witness," I told her. "And based on his testimony, we shall question Kyrillos's son. And Kyrillos."

She gave me a long look and tugged at her braid. She shook her head. "Too bad for this Amyntas. He is risking everyone in his family and other families besides his. Sins of sons are heavy. But it is just."

I said nothing. Her father served Rome for the sins of her brother.

As for justice, she believed in it.

"Do you want to tell me about this Vipsania business?" she asked. "I was asked to join the troop to make sure you survive, and Gaius as well. It is odd. There are doctors here."

I shrugged. "I was going to tell you about that. Might

as well. Vipsania is afraid. Gaius is odd. You might be needed."

She thrummed her fingers on the pear. "You will force him, if he refuses?"

"We will," I said. "And it might get ugly, if he has a loyal set of guards..."

"He is my mission," she stated. "If he is hurt."

"He is your mission, should he get hurt," I said. "And perhaps, if we need to make him compliant."

She patted her bags. "You want me to drug him."

"If he is not compliant," I said simply.

She smiled softly. "Oh."

I turned. "Enough. We must get to work." I looked at the two boys. One was tall and gangly. The other one short and curly-haired.

Antius was speaking with the scribe Cassius, who bowed and hovered around us.

Antius walked to me, and our men gathered around us. Eight pair of eyes were on Antius, but all kept giving me glances. Antius lifted an eyebrow my way. "Well?"

"It seems straightforward," I said. "Justice will be had."

He nodded and looked at Segolia. "This very night. I have my business, and you have yours, and we all know our part?"

I shrugged. "It will be no big deal. Hercules knows his part."

Hercules looked grim but nodded.

"Bloody business, but I know," he murmured. "This

121

Marius has been told?"

Antius shook his hair, and dust billowed around him. "In a bit, he will know all we can share." He gave the two boys a quick look. "Which one will show Decimus here the house of Gaius?"

The short one raised his hand. "I will, sir," he said in heavy Latin.

I nodded and winked the tall one closer. "And you are to show my men and Antius where to go?"

The boys blinked and the latter one spoke uncertainly. "I can do that," he said, with very broken Latin.

I nodded. "Good."

Antius eyed the tavern. "Looks good enough. You are right. Better than a barrack."

I shook my head. "A wonderful place, but we won't stay there."

Antius blinked. "What?"

"I said," I snarled, "that we won't stay there." I lifted my head. "You, Cassius?"

"Sir?"

"Step back for a moment."

He frowned and did. I turned to the two guides. "Boys?" Both stepped forward. "You work for Pericles?" I asked them. "Or for his wife?"

Both shook their heads. "Mainly for the lady," the tall one said.

"Does she...they pay you well?" I asked them, and silver gleamed between my fingers.

They shook their heads. The short one whispered, "The family feeds us. Often, at least. And gives us clothes. Says we get paid one day, if we prove our worth. We are no slaves, but distant relatives."

I smiled. "Bastards?"

They looked down.

"Bastards of the family," I said. "Worry not, bastards. I guessed that might be the case. Pericles?"

They shook their heads. "His brother," said the tall one mournfully. "The father of Alexander."

I clapped a hand on his shoulder. "No slave collars for you lot, but shame delivers the same effect, eh? So, I will make you a deal. You look properly smart. You want to move up in life? You won't with Pericles. You want a life without the stain of being a bastard? Possibilities?"

They looked at me with shock and then nodded.

I smiled like a cheating merchant. "You are going to do well." I flashed three silver coins before their eyes. They were denarii, rich, fat, new. Then three more. They stammered. "What will you do?"

They flinched, and both licked their lips. They were smart enough to understand the question. "We shall obey him, but you over him?" the small one added.

The tall one smiled. "We work for you."

"Exactly," I said. "The latter one more than the former one." I flashed the coins to my pouch, which was jingling with coin. Their fingers clenched involuntarily. Then, I flipped one coin to each, and I was sure they would cry. I snapped my fingers, and they lifted their eyes. "We shall do just that. We shall work together. You shall work for me and the Praetorian Guard itself. When we are done, you will leave with us for Rome. You do what I tell you to do, and you get paid very well," I told him. "Hercules!"

The man nodded, mouth full of fruit. "Sir?"

"This is your boy," I told him and pushed the tall one forward. "Do not eat him."

"No, sir," he said, and the small one shivered. "I'll not nibble or take a bite. I promise, sir. Not like it was last time around. I'll be good."

The men laughed, and the boys didn't.

"He is just jesting," I told the boy. "Worry not. He is known to eat like the rest of us do."

"No, sir, I do not worry," he said. "He looks sated."

Hercules roared and slapped his back and threw him a fruit.

"You'll be called Tall and Short," I said. "You know which is which. It will be easier. You will be very busy." I eyed the tavern. "What is it called? It is this one?"

Tall stepped close. "Pericles asked his men to do the reservations. This is the tavern. It's called Apollo's Flute and hosts musicians most every night, and the wine is good and cheap. Upstairs is for you, I think. You must share rooms."

"We won't have time for music or sharing of rooms," I said, suddenly tired and in a terrible mood, "and I would rather sleep when I can, instead of being tortured by some fool who play their flute until they are too deep in their cups for it to be enjoyable. But I shall deal with that. Cassius!" I yelled.

The scribe scuttled forward, dodging a goat. "Sir?"

I pulled him next to me and placed a strong arm around his shoulders. "The tavern suffices. Make sure we meet Gaius this night."

He flinched. "I will try. I am in in charge of his daily routine, ever since the head scribe disappeared."

"He did, did he?" I asked. "Why? Stealing, you said?"

"He was stealing, of course," he said coldly. "The bastard was stealing from Gaius. Purchases at three times the price, and I spotted it. I asked him about it. Then, he left. Pericles has been kind enough to help, what with the funds that are no longer arriving from Rome." He looked at me with disapproval.

"That is right. The money ran out, and still you stay," I said. "Very odd. Perhaps Kyrillos and the other one has cause to be upset. Gaius is favoring one family and making them rich."

"Pericles appreciates the business he brings here," Cassius said neutrally. "For me, it has been trying time, and I apologize for failing to control the unfortunate affairs that have taken place here. The theft and the...rest."

I snorted. "Control. Do you think you should control Gaius Caesar, do you?"

He stammered. "No, sir. Of course not. But there are

things that would have best been dealt with in a better manner. I lack the strength and wisdom, I am afraid. I do not think I should control the great lord, but—"

"Well," I snarled. "You should have. You should do your best, at least. I hope, for your sakes, that we will meet with him today," I said. "I have to see him this very day, after we have… spoken with Amyntas."

"Gaius will see you this evening," he said with some hesitation. "I have not asked yet, but I will tell him. It will be after your…well. He has some business with me, as usual, in the evening, after the party. He likes to eat in his study after such feasts, since he doesn't like to bother his food taster Hiratius in such a crowded setting. Finds it tedious and awkward. Hiratius is not well liked here. Vipsania rather has her slaves taste her food. Doesn't want to see Hiratius at all. Doesn't trust him. The man, did you know, never tastes the fish. He is shit terrible in his job. Everyone knows this." He sighed. "This evening then. That time is when I usually brief him and take his orders for the next day. I can cut it off quickly and persuade him you should see him."

"His business goes first, of course," I said. "But mine must come after."

He looked bothered. "It does. It will."

"Has he been writing a lot?" I asked.

"Poetry. He is working on something else as well," he said. "He says it is important."

"He is divorcing?"

He stammered. "This is only a rumor. I know not."

126

I nodded and peered deep into his blue eyes. "Our meeting. It will have to be a personal meeting, where there are no prying ears," I told him. "I'll not share the words of Augustus in the presence of curious Lycians, thieving merchants, and other ears. It is not compliment I am brining, but a stern warning."

"Thank Apollo." The man was trembling. "Home is calling."

I placed a hand on his shoulder. "We shall have words tomorrow about the theft of coin by this scribe Ennius. Today, my words will have to be delivered in privacy. Also," I said, pushing away the thought of Vipsania, "I must not be bothered by his wife. Not by anyone. That includes the lady."

He nodded, looking down. "Not even by her. I understand. I fully do. She has been having terrible time with Gaius. She is pushing poor people around her to spy on him, and after yesterday…well. She is desperate. I worry about her. Her mood goes from hopeful to darkness."

I gave him a curious look and found Antius walking past us. "Are we going, Decimus?"

I nodded, and Cassius smiled gently. "Good, though," I said. "His wound? Wait." I pushed off a street urchin that had been sneaking around me, a red-nosed imp, who was pulling at my belt, and then grasped him, my pouch, and a bit of his hair as well, and booted him gently down the street. I watched him stand there, sullen, and pulled bronze coin from my pouch and tossed it to him. He grasped it from air, looked shocked, grinned, and ran for his life, for others of his kind soon followed him.

I snorted. "Yes. His wound?"

"Healed." He nodded. "Fully so. It is not more than a scar on his chest." He hesitated.

"Speak."

"Some say it was never more than a scratch," he said, blushing. "It seems it was little more than—"

I nodded and moved off. "I expect you to send me presentable clothing for the evening. For me, and for her. Send the bill to Pericles."

"Oh, Pericles won't like that," he said, shaking his head. "He is very stingy with his coin."

"She will pay for it," I told him. "Laodamia. So, she will," I said, and he bowed, and moved off.

I considered his back.

"Decimus?" Antius snarled. "Why did you say we won't stay here? We will. You listen to me. I—"

I pushed past him and went inside the tavern.

"Decimus!" he called after me.

The establishment was clean, well furnished with heavy tables and counters, and beautiful, exotic, painted jars. Oil lams sputtered, creating an eerie luminance from the corners, and a nervous, bearded man was standing ready to receive us. Some other guests, with rooms on the first floor, were looking at me. A flute was being played near the back of the tavern.

The tavern keeper nodded upstairs, but I walked to

him.

"I trust everyone knows who we are?" I asked. "The rumors have spread?"

"None will bother you," he confirmed, his voice a silky whisper. "They know, of course, where you come from. I was paid well, though I had to empty some rooms. It was unexpected. Praetorian Guard has the first pick, of course."

I rubbed my face. "Mars's balls."

"Indeed, sir," he said with pity. "It is a shame people gossip so much. They say you seek the killer of the Romans."

I sighed. "We seek many things. How many rooms?"

"Five," he said, his eyes going over my men, the two boys, and Segolia. "One for you and her, and the rest for your officers and men. The red-door one is for you. It is the best one. Has a large bed."

I ignored Antius's hissing complaints.

I nodded. "She is not with me." I gave Antius a quick glance. "But she stays with me."

Segolia cursed softly.

"And you will not pay?" he ventured. "Pericles will?"

I nodded outside. "The great man. Pericles. He pays for all of this. The scribe, Cassius, will be sent a bill, and he will charge Pericles, and that's all there is to it."

"Cassius. This scribe of Gaius Caesar? I know him. And Pericles chose this?" He laughed. "The man's not known for his generosity."

"He agreed to it," I sniffed. "But you might get paid even more, if you can accommodate some unusual requests."

He squinted. "Indeed. I can arrange most anything. If it is not to be found in Limyra, then in Phoneica, surely. We will be able to provide. I can help out, if you but explain in detail."

I chuckled and clasped a hand on his shoulder. "Rarely seen a better man than you, friend."

He smiled. "I can understand the value of coin."

I leaned close. "Here is the thing. If someone asks about us or seeks to know who we are and what we are doing here, you will have them followed. If you do so, Augustus himself will pay you well."

"Augustus?" he asked. "Surely you are making an over statement?"

I shook my head. I flashed a golden coin under his nose.

He frowned. "How well will he pay, and for what? I must live here, see? I'd prefer to know a bit more."

"Very well," I said with asperity. "And discreetly. You will be paid well. You have servants?"

He nodded. "I know a boy or two."

"One tried to pick my pocket just now," I said.

He grinned. "Sorry. He is bored. They know how to get things done. As discreetly as they get paid, of course."

I leaned even closer to him. "Your inn is fine. One of the best I have seen."

He leaned closer as well. Our noses nearly touched. "But?"

I shrugged. "It is not what I chose. I'd like for you to seek another accommodation for us. A rat hole."

He lifted his eyebrow. "You would like to sleep in a rat hole?"

I nodded. "We need something like that. A place few would willingly go near. We'll eat here, we will, but will have access to your rear doors. In short, we shall sleep elsewhere, while apparently staying in here."

He scratched his face. "That will mean you cannot stay upstairs. You need to be down here."

"We need the entire inn," I said. "All of it." His face twitched. "And I will get doubly paid for it?"

"Triply," I said maliciously. "Pericles will pay for the inn. I shall pay you for the rest. Though you must wait a bit for the payment. It takes time to travel back and forth from Palatine."

His eyes brightened, and he nodded. "To Rome, and back, eh? Indeed. I will see to it. I will make sure it all goes well. I know a place, close to here, in a rotten street caked with dust, mud, cats, and vermin. A large room it is, to be honest, but dry. It is empty. Will be, at least, shortly."

I nodded. "In the meantime, I shall enjoy some rest here, and I'll wash my face." I said with thanks, and gave him the aureus, a heavy one. I had a pouch full of them, worth a fortune. "Make sure the rat hole is something people would avoid."

His eyes went round as plates, nodded, and I walked up the stairs. The others followed us.

Antius was trying to catch up. "We are not—"

"We don't sleep where the enemy knows we are. It might be a city, but we act like it is a forest filled with enemies," I said. "You deal with what you know, Antius. I shall deal with what I know. Now, freshen up, centurion. We have work to do."

"You are pushing me too far, friend," he said with an angry hiss. "I will snap at some point."

"I'll push you over, if you are not careful," I told him. "And then I'll snap you." We came to the upstairs, and there, Hercules with two men sat in the shadows, swords out. I turned to him. "Follow the boy and do what we have agreed on."

Hercules nodded with a serious look on his face. "Aye. I know how."

"I am sorry it is distasteful, but it is for Rome. You have your coin?" I asked.

He nodded. "I do. We shall go as soon as Antius is ready."

"Do so," I said, and went to a room with a red door.

There, Segolia was washing herself, her skin gleaming with water. She was hunched over a bowl and poured water over her face with her palm, and her neck was dripping with it. The door closed behind me, and I knew Hercules had made sure we would be alone. We would be properly attired soon, with Cassius delivering us clothing.

She gave me a quick look.

I rubbed my face. "Fine. She was daughter of a senator," I said as I leaned on a door. "Long years past. Before I knew your father."

"And?" she asked. "You had an affair?"

I shook my head. "And we were married, but she carried a child, and that boy is now raised by a senator," I told her.

She turned her eyes to me. "You married her? I had no idea a Praetorian centurion might have such a romantic, sweet soul."

"You know little about me, Segolia," I said. "But, yes. I had a soul. I lost it somewhere in Germania."

She smiled. "Do you still think of your first wife?"

"We never divorced, not really," I told her, unable to look away.

"So, you are," she said sourly. "I doubt you lost the soul in Germania, then. That's why you never fall in love. You are already in it."

"At least I do not lie," I answered. "At least to you. And how would you know I never fall in love?"

She turned to face me. "My father told me. You like women, but only their bodies."

"And you asked?" I wondered.

Her eyes hardened, and I walked past her and undressed. I pulled off the chainmail with great difficulty, fighting with the clasps on the shoulders, until I was on my loincloth. I went to the bowl of water and leaned over it.

She was right.

I thought of Servilia, still. I never stopped, really. Sometimes, when I entered a woman, nay, always, I thought of Servilia.

And now, Vipsania wanted a child?

"Here," she said, as she stepped next to me. She took a rag and wet it.

I closed my eyes.

She washed my face and shoulders. She moved to my arms and back. She spoke softly. "So. Gaius will be hard to convince. The people are very nervous. He must enjoy his stay here but dealing with him will be very risky. This will be much riskier than this Vipsania business."

"I know," I said.

"You have had many adventures, Celcus," she told me. "Many were dangerous."

I shivered as her hand moved up and down my belly. "Most were." I sighed and spoke. "Your father was a druid."

She shook her head. "Once."

"And sometimes, when he is in the mood, he senses things," I said. "He has a gift."

Silence.

"He has a gift of foresight," I said. "It has been useful. I don't believe in gods."

"Father told me."

"In a way, I do," I said. "But I don't think they care what we do, and so, they mean nothing. They have their own world, and we have ours. But I do believe in their power, and magic and what help one can gleam from them, when they are not watching. I wanted your father mainly for that power. I don't go to war without someone who knows how to read the signs."

She put the rag away and stood there, tugging at her braid. "I have it."

"You do."

"I do, and you know I do."

I faced her, and she looked down. "Well?" I asked.

She spoke with a soft voice. "Your plans are well-made. The murderers will be punished. Gaius will go home. You flash a golden coin, and people love you, and it all seems so very simple."

"It is not?"

She put a hand on my chest, and trembled as she touched me. I clasped the hand. "Look. I saw something. Father said you have had dangerous adventures. This will be doubly so."

"Indeed," I told her, close to her. "I know. What did you see?"

She sighed. "I saw it on the galley. I felt it. I walked the room of the dead one," she said. "I let the spirits speak to me. They did."

I stiffened. Her father had a gift, as far as any such gift still existed in Gaul after the purge of the druids.

I put a hand on her face, and she looked sad, and vulnerable. She leaned on the hand.

"It is dangerous to you?" I asked her. "What do they

look like, these spirits?"

She put her hands on my chest and looked at me. "The sprits…I don't see them. They speak. They deceive and lie, and they are not sane."

"You are in danger?"

She shrugged and leaned on my chest. "We all are."

"Tell me," I said. "Tell me what you saw."

She sighed. "I saw it in the galley. I felt it in the city, and in that room. Something terrible happened there. But something more terrible visited it after, and something walks the streets of the city. It was not human, nor was it a ghost. It was something older than men, and far more evil. I heard the spirits. They say people will die. Many people." She caressed my face and looked pale. "Perhaps you, or I. Or both. Perhaps neither. Nothing is certain. But what is certain is that there will be more deaths and something terrible is looking at us. This city is death itself, a playground for the dead, and those who never lived. I saw it. For Rome, and justice, we must go on, and save Gaius."

"I know. So are we."

She leaned on me, and hesitated, as she put her hands on my belly. Then she shook her head and opened my loincloth. It fell to the ground.

"Are you sure?" I asked her, as she leaned on my naked body, her eyes down on my erect manhood. She nodded, and let her fingers play along it, and then I picked her up, and carried her on a bed. There, we lay together, for a long while, enjoying each other.

Later, when she lay curled around me, and I held her as she slept, I felt regret.

I felt love for her, and fought it, for no speculatore should love. It was pointless, and it was a weakness, and she was now in a land of our enemies. Someone, anyone might use her to hurt me, and she was too young to know better.

I also felt like I had not felt for years. Not since Servilia had told me she loved me.

Love was simple. It was also rude. It was always born at the wrong time.

None must know. Not there, not in Limyra.

I thought of her words, and shivered, and buried my face in her hair. She woke up, kissed me, and turned around, and I, the fool, entered her, holding her hips, caressing her buttocks, and kissing her neck.

I heard a noise, and turned, and saw Short was there, carrying wealthy looking tunics, underwear, and shoes for us. "I—here."

He ran away fast to the right, and I stared at the doorway.

I was sure a shadow had moved the other way, to the left.

CHAPTER 4

The sun had nearly set when we were led to the riverside. There, the buildings were beautiful, the streets less busy, and the gardens blossomed. Short guided us, and we found the house Gaius had bought. Next to it was a brown, unassuming house where the legionnaires stayed. It was their barracks now. Men guarded it and watched us approaching the doors of Gaius, which were also guarded.

First, I walked around it.

I found, like it had been with the house of Kleitos and those poor traders, alleys and a river's bank filled with stones, flowers, and gardens. There were Lycian soldiers on all the corners.

There were Roman legionnaires on the servant's doorway to the alley, and the main one to the street.

I finally led us back to that one. "Short, you may wait here," I said.

The domus, for that's what it resembled, was a Roman house in many ways and still somewhat bastardized version between a Greek and a Roman one. Beautiful and tan, with red, intricate paintings on the outside walls, it was guarded by walls and Lycian soldiery, who walked the perimeter. It was a huge, sprawling estate on the edge of the River Limyros. Possibly built for a rich merchant, or an exiled royalty, it was still somewhat new, like most buildings near the bank of river. Around the main entrance, there were olive and cypress trees, with many sycamores as well, and a bountiful, colorful stretch of flowers you could see in the light of torches that were set on the walls and lit the entire area and street.

Inside, we heard a soft sound of flute and a drone of voices.

I smoothed my tunic.

Segolia smiled. "You look fine enough."

"Fine enough?" I wondered. "I am not convinced."

"You are begging for praise," she chided me. "Come."

She was right. I wore a rich red tunic, embroidered in silver, and a wide belt, where I had my pouch full of coin. I carried my mail bag, filled with missives. There was no sword, but Segolia was with me, wearing a long Greek chiton and had hidden the blade so expertly, I had no idea where it was. She looked splendid in a set of silver earrings and a necklace in the shape of a porpoise. Despite her fine looks, she seemed aloof. She smiled at me, when I spoke to her, but when I hazarded a glance her way, she was…looking at shadows.

Her sight had made her odd, fey.

Terrified. She controlled it well, but I knew.

We passed some local soldiers, all with odd bronze helmets with beaks and tassels and billowing horsehair, and they gave us a long, wondering look.

I met a legionnaire at the main gate.

The man's chainmail was immaculate, though his face held a long scar, and he had a many-times broken

139

nose. He gave me a long glance, and no words were needed, as he knew a fellow soldier from another.

"From Rome?" he asked. "You are the one? Celcus?"

"Aye," I answered. "Rowed in this morning. Salt in my mouth and bloody piss in the pot, but we made it alive."

"You are a Pretorian?" he asked with some spite, but not too much as he eyed me. Most praetorians had served in the legions, and my scars were visible on my arms.

"I am."

He tilted his head at Segolia. "And this is your slave?"

"No," I said. "She is a medicus."

He grinned at her. "Praetorians have their own medicus with them? One each, and pretty as a flower? Can I get a recommendation? I would love to join the guard."

Segolia gave him a small, cold smile.

He stiffened and looked at the main doors, where an optio was standing. "You served in Germania?" he asked me.

"Yes. I have seen the place," I said coldly. "I've served in Gaul, Germania, Greece, Illyria, and elsewhere before. Will you let me in?"

He grinned and saluted me, and he nodded me inside. "Go on in. You have not been in Egypt and Syria? Then, you've seen nothing, sir," he mocked me gently as we went past him. "Please, sir, get us out of

Limyra."

I nodded. "I was in Egypt as well."

"But not in Syria!" he called after me, and I grinned.

We joined a throng of people coming in and came to what was an atrium.

In Rome, they were relatively small affairs, but this one was large like a warehouse, and full of Lycian nobility, soldiers, slaves, and now, drunks. I looked around. The furniture were simple ones. The statues, the few that were there; simple. No gold, no silver adorned the walls, or the floor. It was wealthy enough looking place, but not…quite as rich as it should be.

People were happy. They were feasting, and in favor of their host. There was laughter, there were joyous calls, and in the middle of the side, laying on a sofa, was Gaius, flanked by men who wore their best. Men in toga and chitons were a colorful sea praying on Gaius's attention. There, too, were flute players and actors, all leaning over him to listen to his requests or banter.

But most of all, the women surrounded him.

There was nothing odd about it. Bernike, was listening intently on Gaius, and he touched her hand fondly. Eudoxia, the tiny, delicately beautiful girl sat behind him, nodding at his every word. Corinne, next to her, staring at the people around her, her eyes intently looking at Bernike.

"What do you think Bernike is talking to Gaius about?" Segolia wondered.

"She is a daughter of Myra's mightiest man," I said.

141

"She is a fine ally and has kept Meliton on the council for years. Now, Corinne is meant for brute Amyntas, and she is hoping to reverse the situation that forced Meliton into the camp of Kyrillos. She is doing it subtly, but I don't think Gaius even knows about the tensions around him."

"They must hate him for his stupidity," she said.

"Even Andromache, she stays close to him," I said.

Indeed, the wife of Kyrillos was staring at the people thronging around the great Gaius.

I watched the man carefully, so did Segolia.

I knew him but only barely.

He wore a chiton and not a toga. He was pale, and his hair had grown past what would be respectable in Rome, and he smiled lazily and arrogantly, like a drunken despot. He enjoyed the adulation, the bustle of people around him, the attention.

Wounds do that to a man.

Sometimes, a near-death wound can leave a man forever changed. It can also make one a drunk and a hedonistic bastard, bent on nothing but enjoyment.

And still, he was acting.

Under the façade of joy, I sensed he was unhappy, afraid, lost.

That was the Gaius I might have known.

Gaius had never been happy.

I had watched him as he grew up, all through his long years while he and his brother were being educated by Augustus and by his wife, Livia. He had never been loud, and while bravely taking part in all the expected duties, he had never smiled with a true passion, unlike his brother Lucius had, and never laughed as if he meant it. Emotion dies in Palatine, under the brutal supervision of Augustus, and for Gaius, it had been no different. His command had at first brought him some joy. Vipsania had been right. He had been dutiful and had become different.

He was on a holiday. And he was terrified it would end.

"Is he sick?" Segolia whispered, as she led me to the side, where we stood in silence for a moment.

"No."

"Drunk? He seems absent."

I shook my head. "He is acting. He is acting happy. He is like a child, playing at an adult, knowing he must pay the price for his actions. He is a bit drunk."

"He looks drunk," she said.

"Nervous," I said.

He was not too drunk.

I saw a fat, bald man, his food taster Hiratius, who stood behind him, and had apparently not been called to do more than taste the wine of Gaius. That was the man Vipsania hated, and no doubt only for the looks. The fat man was unhappy, for many fine dishes were being served to the guests, and he would not be called forward before Gaius ate later, and he would go hungry until the night. Fish, broiled and with expensive sauces, were carried past his eyes. He would likely visit the kitchens as soon as he could. I knew few fat food tasters who didn't spend much of their free time in the kitchen, and they were always friend to the cooks. Clearly, this was the case with Hiratius as well. Dareios, the cook Vipsania had spoken of, would give him anything he wanted. Indeed, many food tasters slept near the kitchen.

A servant offered him a plate filled with oysters. He shook his head, and turned back to speak to Corinne, who leaned closer.

Gaius truly didn't enjoy public eating.

He never had. If he ever got truly drunk, I had not seen him show it. He had not changed in that regard. I saw Corinne nodding towards us.

His eyes went to me. He looked away and touched the hem of his toga.

Bernike looked at us, surprised.

"He is scared of you," Segolia whispered. "And they now see you. Soon, they will swarm us. Maybe we should fight them off."

"He ought to be scared of me," I said darkly. "He knows we are here, and I am the one who will deliver his doom to him. I am the hand of Augustus, and he has been a naughty boy."

"Oh, shit. She's here," Segolia whispered.

I sighed. "Of course, she is."

I nodded as I saw Vipsania in the crowd, walking past guests, pushing past Corinne, and then she was hovering near her husband's sofa. Ariane and Larissa were with her. I struggled with the urgent need to run away and also to hide, but I stayed still instead.

"I'll guard your cock now," Segolia said. "Don't be afraid."

"Thank you."

Out of a door in atrium, Pericles appeared. He walked for Gaius, smiling, and holding his hands out. People were greeting the man, and nodding. He was followed by Laodamia, whose eyes took in everything. With her presence, Andromache, and Bernike stepped away, and so did Lysirate, and Corinne. Alexander was there as well, near Pericles, his armor gleaming, and dark, curly hair long on his shoulders. He was staring at Corinne, then Vipsania, giving both small bows. Next, his eyes were on mine, ice-cold and resentful. He waved a hand gently for me to come and greet Gaius.

Vipsania said something to her slaves, both of whom turned and walked away. We stood near the corridors that led to the garden, and to the kitchen beyond, and when Ariane was passing, I noticed there was blood on her tunic. I stopped her with an outstretched hand. "Are you well?" I asked.

She stopped and wiped the blond hair off her eyes. She gave a small nod.

"You have wounds," I stated. "Perhaps Segolia could have a look at them?"

She hesitated. "I must not. She asked me to hurry. I must go and tell the cook that she will dine in her room tonight. Alone. He must keep her dinner warm."

I looked behind us, and at a room that seemed unoccupied. I pulled her in there, despite her small protests, and eyed the room. Heavy desk was there, a fine mosaic with snakes and trees slithered across the floor, and a bed. I nodded at Segolia. "Close the door. Her dinner may wait."

Segolia stepped in. "Please, let me see."

"But—"

I turned to close the door, and saw Larissa, who was speaking gently to an older lady, her hair white, and curly, a thin older woman. I knew her from somewhere, and then I realized it had been her, who had been singing in the agora, when we watched the acrobats. She was apparently no commoner. Lysirate, and Corinne were around them, and the lady held Larissa's hand briefly, squeezing it, her face a kind smile. Larissa bowed, and left, and walked to the side of Vipsania. Cassius appeared, and was near, looking at people, and settled there, with the others. He turned to Larissa, spoke to her, she answered, and then went to fetch him wine.

Cassius's eyes were looking at each guest, seeking trouble, or ways to aid Gaius.

I turned to Ariane. She was sitting on the bed, her face stone-hard. She was bare from waist up, and she turned her face down at my scrutiny. I was not admiring her body. I was looking at her wounds. Her back had scars, most new ones, and some fresh. "You must be a very poor slave," I wondered, "for Vipsania to punish you like this."

"I hear no complaints for my work," she said with a small voice. "Only for my failures. The house is clean. Larissa and I, we clean and swipe the floors every day. We must make sure the furniture is in place. It is unheard of, but we do. Pericles wants things to be just perfect here, all the time. He doesn't even own the house, but we work to make this a pristine paradise. We serve, and carry, and listen to her woes. Alas, that Larissa is such a hard, sad girl, and the mistress thinks I might be better suited to be her spy."

The words were not meek, but bitter. They bordered on insolent.

She shook her head in silent apology and covered her breasts in shame. "She is worried. I understand that."

"And you," Segolia said, applying some sort of salve to the wounds, "spy on whom?"

"Her husband," I said. "How do you spy on him?"

She opened her mouth, and then sighed. She twitched from pain, as Segolia worked, and spoke gently. "I usually take the food to him. She has asked me for weeks to try to seduce him. She thinks he has a lover. She doesn't mind if it is a slave. I pose no threat."

"And have you succeeded?" I asked. "Have you bedded Gaius. Has he opened up to you?"

She shook her head. "He once, in Syria, liked me, just a bit. Never much. I think he is with the girl, Eudoxia. I know not for sure. He has her around a lot, though she is also always with Laodamia, so it might be just a

147

coincidence. I have no news to give you. Nor to her. That is why she—"

Larissa opened the door, hissing softly. "What are you doing? What—"

She noticed us. She went silent, and still. "Yes?" I asked.

"She…has duties," Larissa said. "I am not trying to bother you, but…come. She wants us to be fast."

I stopped Larissa from leaving with my hand, as Ariane dressed up, painfully. "To be fast, slave? What for?"

Larissa straightened her tunic. "She expects her room to be ready. Soon. She cannot stand the crowd, especially when Laodamia is here."

I looked over her shoulder.

"Please, sir—" Larissa began.

I saw Vipsania. She was pointedly ignoring everyone. Her face was still as a marble bust, and even when Alexander tried to speak to her, she shook her head. Corinne, Lysirate, and even Bernike were now talking to the old, white haired woman, but Vipsania seemed to be focused on Laodamia's words. The woman was speaking to Gaius, Eudoxia hovering near. Then, Gaius smiled, and took Laodamia's hand to give it a kiss.

Vipsania's eyes were not on Laodamia.

They were on Gaius. She balled her fist.

I nodded. "It seems you must hurry. She is in not so very good mood, is she?"

"Laodamia," Larissa said.

"Or Gaius," I answered. "Make her food and let her prepare for the night."

Larissa looked bothered. "She asked me to tell you, sir, that she would like to see you in her rooms later, to discuss Augustus. After your meeting with Gaius, sir? May I tell her you will see her?"

I shrugged. "You may tell her I shall do my best."

She nodded, and Ariane dodged outside. Segolia sighed, and looked at the small jar of salve, and hid it in her bag. "Can you," I said, "mingle here for the rest of the evening?"

She looked at me with curiosity. "Why? I thought I was."

I scratched my neck, seeking words. "We shall speak with Kyrillos, and Meliton this night. It has all been arranged. I would appreciate it, if you stayed here, and gauged the mood of the people."

She looked curious.

"See, if you can find more about what you felt in Kleitos's house last night," I said. "If you can. Also, try to see where all the wealth in the house is. The reports of Ennius spoke of gold, and silver, and jewels, and statues Gaius used his war-chest on when he arrived."

"Of course," she said. "You go and catch the murdering curs and I will stay here. I…" she began, and then, instead, kissed me on the lips.

She slipped out.

I rubbed my face and shook my head. "Oh, shit."

149

"Oh, shit?" I heard a voice. I saw the taller of the two Pericles girls, leaning on the door. She cast Segolia an appraising eye. "A tryst, centurion?"

"No," I said brusquely. "Look. I have—"

"Nothing to say to a spoiled Lycian noble girl," she said. "Oh, I was just seeking adventure. Corinne's always more Eudoxia's friend, and I have nobody to play with."

I flinched at her tone, and her eyes. She had a crooked, bored smile.

I stepped forward. "You are the one who thinks Gaius is boring, no?"

"He is boring," she said frankly, looking at me as if I was an utter fool. "Eudoxia likes them boring, and mother as well, but then again, I am nothing like them. I like my men rough, and crude."

I smiled as she pushed into the room, closing the door almost entirely, looking around it like she would survey a barren cave. "Father treating you well?"

"He is, well enough," I said.

She smiled, as if she were grateful. "The inn pleases you? You do not get lost in the city?"

I shrugged. "The inn is fine. We have good rooms, Lysirate. We have guides. Your father's boys. They show us around. And it is not, after all, such a big city."

"Oh, it is not," she agreed. "Though it is old and has hollow bones."

I squinted at her, and she smiled at me gently. "Tell me, centurion. Father and mother wont. What is

150

happening here? I might be able to help you. I am quite bored. Are you seeking the killer?"

I nodded. "We are. You can talk to centurion Antius about it."

"I don't see centurion Antius here, nor the others," she said, winking. "What are they doing?"

"Same as I should be doing," I said. "Sleeping. It was a long trip. Tomorrow is a fine day to investigate murders."

"You have no idea who did it? I am fascinated by such crimes," she said. "A spurned lover, perhaps?"

"All four, five of them?" I asked. "Traders, all three, Kleitos, and the servant?"

"There were only four horn blows," she told me. "Those horn blows! They are fascinating. Imagine waking up in the middle of the night to such! Imagine it."

"I've woken up to Germani horns in the night," I said. "And we all shat ourselves."

She laughed brightly, and I found myself liking the girl.

"I wonder who that poor bastard was," she murmured. "The servant. Missing his fingers? Why would anyone take fingers, and face, hair, and all? The heads? It is an old thing here, but—"

"An old thing," I said dully.

"Aye, the Furies," she explained. "They hunt heads. Punishment, see, that lasts beyond death. But fingers?" She shook her head. "Oh, do not worry. Every city has its tales. I can tell you more of them later?"

I smiled. "You think I am a rough man. The sort you like."

"I think you are," she said, "though also, perhaps, dangerous."

"Why," I asked her, "does your mother dislike you? I do not, so I am wondering."

She looked sour and shook her head. "She is the sort of a woman," she said, and stepped close to me, and put her hand on my neck, "who believes spirit, and bravery, and a hunger for life do not belong to her slaves, servants, or family. She is, so to say, one who controls everything. She especially much hates girls who spin tales about her." She put her lips on my ear, and her breasts were hard on my chest. "Centurion. Might you take me to Rome with you? I need to escape the land. It could be very pleasant for both."

She was quite close, rather beguiling, and I was sure she was no virgin. I stepped back. "I shall consider it."

She grinned, and smiled, and squeezed my hands. "Fine! You know where to find me. Perhaps I shall ask your optio? He seemed a genuinely rough man, and also perhaps, not taken?"

I cursed her.

She shook her head in amusement. "No clues to what you are doing? You will not share? I shall remain bored?"

I smiled. "No, Lysirate. I cannot. As for Hercules, he would be your best choice."

She shook her head and opened the door. "So be it. Your loss. Look. There are people who are dying to meet you. I just wanted a quick word before them. I hope your Celt friend doesn't mind I tried to steal you for myself."

I followed her out and endured some looks from the guards. Some were envious looks, others less so. Alexander's look was especially chilling, before he turned back to Bernike. I decided to go and introduce myself to Gaius.

I stepped towards him, and then saw two legionnaires detaching themselves from pillars they had been leaning on, eyes on me.

The shit has told his guards not to let me close.

Gaius sensed the potential trouble and returned his gaze to me.

I bowed my head, he hesitated, and gave me a small smile. He lifted a finger.

Later.

And then, he turned away, back to Eudoxia, who leaned close to him, almost like a lover. I watched Gaius. He reached out to her hand, and Laodamia smiled, as Eudoxia took it. He pulled her to his side, and kissed the hand, in full sight of everyone.

He truly didn't want to be bothered by news from Rome, while flirting with the young beauty. Pericles gave me a helpless shrug and Laodamia smiled at the two.

I noticed Meliton, and Kyrillos.

Meliton was walking for me. Corinne, his daughter was looking on, her eyes full of hope, and Andromache joined Kyrillos in his approach.

I steeled myself. They all wanted peace, and return to what once was, before Gaius came there. They all thought I could bring about magic.

"Where is my sword?" I asked the air, but the air had no answer. Segolia was not there, but walking in the garden, where a pond, beautiful benches, and some guests were walking around a small stage. A tall guard stood on the doorway of an elaborate door.

Gaius's study.

She smiled at me though the corridor and stopped. She was beautiful. She was more. I gave her a speculative glance and turned to smile at Meliton.

He stopped before me.

He was a powerful man, his face thick-boned, his muscles suggesting he had done physical labor in his time. Now, he was heavy with fat and rich with a great frown on his face. He gave me the slightest of bows.

I nodded back.

He wasn't happy with that. "It is customary, Roman, to greet nobles of Lycia with more than a nod," he said. "Especially, if they sit in the Council."

"And is it not customary," I asked, "for people who are seeking favors, to show respect to those who might provide them?"

Both men looked shocked to the bone.

Andromache turned to them and shooed them back

a bit. They obeyed but with reluctance.

She gave me a small smile as she turned and collected herself before she spoke. "Favors we need, but we cannot beg for them. Please, won't you hear what we must say?"

"I will," I said. "I would like to speak later, though, where there are fewer eyes, and ears."

Meliton stepped forward and grasped a glass of wine from a servant. He tasted it and was gathering his thoughts. "Later is later, but now is better. See, roman, we are not without power. We know people, and are married into fine, influential women."

I bowed to Andromache, and she smiled gratefully.

"And still," Meliton rumbled, "we are afraid. We have people who rely on us. Our clients, their families. I still have many people, as does Kyrillos, who follow us. Kyrillos and I have hundreds of men who see our profits dwindling, and their families go hungry. I tell you this. We do not deserve what has happened to our family, and to our clients. Ever since Gaius came here, we have lost most of our business to Pericles. Rome and its allies, first find Pericles. We cannot sell much, we have not been able to buy any plots of land, nor build a thing to expand. Pericles does that all now. People sell to him, for through Pericles, they get to Rome. I must pay thrice what he does for my investments, and I end up with shit. Same with Kyrillos. My business is mostly ruined by now. My girl there, she was supposed to marry Alexander, did you know? I was forced to break their betrothal. What good is a marriage, if the family benefits nothing for it?"

I shrugged and eyed her, and she nodded at me. I turned to him. "You are marrying her to Amyntas. You two are making an alliance against Pericles. Or Laodamia? And you two? Are you natural allies?"

Kyrillos huffed. "He knows Pericles, doesn't he? Aye, against Laodamia. She is the one who is pulling all the strings. Pericles is a fine man, but he has no balls, unless they are those Gaius has between his legs."

Meliton croaked a warning, and Kyrillos went quiet. Then Meliton shook his head. "We are not natural allies. Kyrillos and I are natural enemies." Kyrillos nodded. "We hate each other. He is a plain, thieving liar. He calls me the same—"

"Both are right," Andromache said tiredly.

"Fine," Meliton said. "Both are right. We need to be together, see? Tied together like two drowning men. Gaius wouldn't so much as speak with us. Kyrillos and I wrote to Augustus about this."

I shrugged again. It annoyed him. "I know," I said. "Ennius wrote a letter about the costs of living here. Vipsania is complaining to Augustus. Yet another has told him about the trouble Gaius has caused. And you, as well. Augustus is up to his ears in Lycian trouble. What exactly do you want?" I asked him. "What can Augustus do? Gaius befriended Pericles. His clients follow him. The rest follows. Pericles leads the city but is it his fault Gaius attracts business to him. Hire a spy and find ways to cut him off."

Kyrillos grunted. "We do need a spy in the house. We will have one. But what we really need is to know if Rome is staying here. Rome, not Gaius. Is Gaius here to rule? If he is? No spy can save us. We are ruined."

I shrugged. "I don't know what Augustus thinks. He is not here to rule, but one day, he might come back. Perhaps you should set up shop elsewhere?"

"They say you are taking Gaius home," Meliton said tiredly. "That's what you are saying as well. He cannot return, if he doesn't leave. That would be fine with us. But will that end his influence here? Pericles is still his friend. Will he direct trade to Laodamia and Pericles, even from Rome?"

"I will take Gaius home," I told him. "As for his legacy in Limyra? I know not. I cannot tell Gaius what to do."

Kyrillos held his face, and Andromache, giving me an evil eye, pulled him away. Meliton looked after him, and I leaned to Meliton. "The future depends on many things, friend. It depends on your pride and your ability to make quick choices."

"My pride?" he asked. "It depends on my pride?"

"Yes."

He turned and watched someone over my back. "Do you hear this, Apollon? They warn me that to get justice, I might have to let go of my pride? Bah! May you all rot. We were getting richer than Pericles, on our own, with our own skills before Gaius came here. Now, they are ruining us. Laodamia be cursed for this."

I nodded at the side of the house. "Tell Kyrillos I shall come to him later this evening, and then I shall speak with you both," I told him. "I shall be there shortly. I agree we must give you something."

His eyes lit up, and he walked back to Kyrillos, and I looked over my shoulder and saw two people there.

A young, handsome man stood there, and grinned. His hair was golden, his skin bronzed, and he bowed before me. He wore a plainer tunic than most but seemed genuinely happy. "His pride, roman?" he asked. "Why would he need to be rid of his pride?"

I looked over his shoulder. There stood the older, white haired lady, smiling an infectious smile. She stepped forward and took my hand, tilting her head beguilingly. "He means, Apollon, my boy, that they must accept that some things will never return to be the same. It is a lesson we must all know, eh, son? I am Eurydike."

Apollon looked at Gaius, then at me, and gave me a reluctant nod. His good mood was half gone.

"Seems you are not a welcome guest in a hall full of them," Apollon said. "I noticed how Gaius made sure he would not have to speak to you."

"It wasn't subtle," I agreed as the old lady guided me to the side.

"Do not worry, Roman," she chortled. "The House of Joys will entertain you and chase your worries away. We are as much unwanted here as any. Just waiting to

158

speak to Pericles and Laodamia, we are. It might not happen. At least we are invited."

"House of Joys?" I asked.

"The Eagle's Joy," she said softly. "Eagle's Joy. That is the name of the theatre you see over the agora. I own it. It is a ramshackle mess, and needs repairs, but it was good enough for Kleitos the Golden, when he came here to entertain Gaius. We cannot stage plays now, though. We are not allowed, due to Kleitos dying. It was struggling, the theatre, before he died, but now it is closed until further notice. So, we are now acrobats, and sing in the agora until we are allowed to play." She kept smiling as she said it and looked at Pericles. "He is our lord, but also our family's patron. Lately, it has felt like he doesn't care for his clients at all."

I frowned at Apollon. His cheeks were oil-smeared, and so was his tunic. "Actors?"

"The best troop in Lycia!" he said. "We hope some promises will be kept soon, and are here, yet again, hoping to speak to the high and mighty. Bastard Gaius, I say."

Eurydike sighed. "He is still your friend, son." She winked at me. "Drama is our forte, and he writes the best, but sometimes, he acts like he is on the stage all the time. Have you seen any plays? In any theatre?"

I smiled. "Only before a battle. There people act like they will live forever and die in their shit. Nothing is more dramatic than a battle, lady."

"Ah, crude," Apollon chortled and handed me a mug

of wine. His eyes went to Gaius, and then, he shook his head. "Come to fetch him home? Ah, that is too bad."

"You said you are his friend?" I asked.

He nodded. "I have travelled."

I frowned, but Eurydike tugged my arm. "He was in Syria and acted for Gaius. He joined Gaius before Armenia, and Gaius appreciated a good actor. And, a good man."

"We were friends, indeed," he said darkly.

"And now?" I asked him.

"He came here with me, and met Laodamia, and now he has no more time for his old friends," he said, "but only for his new ones. And with this Kleitos business…we are penniless. They closed our livelihood. A friend would meet another, if they truly cared. I want the theatre to be opened. This mourning has gone on for long enough."

"At least they don't make you pay for it," I said. "In Rome, taxes would have to be paid still, open or close."

He grimaced. The man was rummaging around his bag and pulled forth a coin. It was a tarnished bronze one, a local coin.

"Here, we shall pay our taxes, immediately!" he chortled. "We are dirt poor, friend. I hear the Romans who enter the city shall leave it with all our coin."

He laughed, but his mother smiled nervously, and I took the coin. It held Apollo's face and on the other side, a face of some ancient king, or dignitary.

"That is Pericles's father," he said. "It is —"

"Who says Romans rob your people?" I asked.

"Why, everyone! Kyrillos and Meliton, especially. They have many men hanging around the Agora all day."

"Are you one of them?" I asked him. "Do you do more than acrobatics?"

He went quiet. Then, he shook his shoulders. "We are out of work. They can appreciate good theatrics in the Agora, see? More than acrobatics."

I nodded. "You are one of the people who rail against him. Gaius. Pericles."

Eurydike was watching carefully. Apollon spoke with some bravery. "You see many things. I am. We are all the actors. We have good reasons, the lot of us. It is easy to see we are being robbed. It is clear as rain."

"Rain's not all that clear," I told him. "It muddies the ponds, and people hide from rain. Smart people hide from it."

"It is, after you get wet," he insisted, and winked. "Then, you need not hide."

I smiled back at him. "That bad, eh? Your friend won't give you his ear, and if he did, and opened the theatre, you would forget all about Kyrillos and Meliton."

The man's face screwed in a stupid frown. "You are trying to insult me?"

"You do it on your own. Here." I flipped the coin back at him, but he let it fall.

The man was full of fire, and the pretty face couldn't

hide his faults. No wonder Gaius didn't meet this one. The scars on his hands were visible, as he pushed his hair back, trembling with anger. "I am not sure I won't punch you in the face."

"Try. I sense your kind and mine, will not be allies for long."

Eurydike calmed Apollon and put his hand on my arm. On it, a serpent ring gleamed with silver. Clients to Pericles, indeed, the Eagle's Joy was there to beg for a favor, but the boy did them no favors.

She shook her head. "We are allied, Roman, even if we argue. Hill men and other foes threatened Lycia from all over, and I think it will be time very soon when Roman legions will hold sway. But we are getting the hang of it already. We are ignored. It is simply sad. But it is better to be ruled by Rome than it was by the Persians, the Carians, or by Rhodes. Obol to you, then, and keep it well." She picked it up. "You might need it."

I smiled. "One obol. You want me to put it on my tongue?"

Apollon laughed loudly. People were turning to watch us. "You have a sense for drama, you do! Shall you come to Agora and act with us?"

"A lot of Romans have died here of late," I ventured. "And perhaps your visiting actor was not an unwelcome loss?"

They nodded and looked down. "You are seeking answer to his death?" Apollon asked. "He was killed by greed."

"Whose greed?" I asked him.

"Greed, in general. Greed kills men, even in real life. It is so," he said. "Greed killed the three Romans that one night. Greed killed Kleitos."

"How was Kleitos greedy?" I asked him.

Eurydike pushed Apollon. "Love, let us—"

"No." Apollon squared his shoulders. "Let me answer it. Wherever Gaius went, in Syria, in Arabia, in this city, greed followed him. I hate him not. It is not his fault, really. Such as he, invite trash into his wake. Such trash loves him, serves his needs, and makes him feel important." He laughed bitterly. "Corruption, evil, death. His glorious trip to the east brought that to every city he visited. Now, here? He came here and found new friends."

"Stop it," said Eurydike. "Please."

"Let him speak," I said, as I played with the obol. "You know much about him. Is it true Pericles was losing in business to Meliton and Kyrillos?"

Apollon scratched his neck. "Yes. I suppose so. Laodamia was upset about it."

"And your family are clients of Pericles and Laodamia," I stated. "And you were friends with Gaius. And you brought him here."

They were silent.

"I see Laodamia doesn't much like you," I said. "There a reason for it?"

They said nothing.

I looked at Gaius doting on Eudoxia. "Did Laodamia

163

send you to get Gaius here, where her daughter might seduce him?" I asked Apollon. "And if so, were you let down by both? Why does she dislike you? She dislikes many people. Lysirate, her daughter. The competition. And you. I saw her, in the agora. She hates you both."

Eurydike sighed. "There is a story you might like. But yes, we try to please her to appease her. It is impossible."

"What do you think about these murders?" I asked them. "I hear the city approves. If you, Apollon, are one of the rabble-rousers in the city, can you not also douse them?"

He blinked. "You think we could? That you could help us?"

"I might. Limyra is a deadly place. We need no more deaths here."

Eurydike looked nervous. "Indeed. There have been far too many murders in this city."

"But," Apollon said, "the people killed before, have been locals. Not visitors."

I gazed at him. "Locals."

"They Furies kill people who deserve it," he said. "I think Romans did this."

I shrugged. "No. We have our killer."

"Truly?" Apollon said with wonder in his voice. "You know who it was? I am sure it is no thing from Hades, but a creature of darkest soul, from Rome. I'd find him fast."

"Instead," I said, "I ask you to calm the people who

clamor against Rome. Do this, and let us find our killers, and deal with Gaius, and perhaps you will soon be rewarded. Will you not tell me what Laodamia asked you to do?"

Eurydike shook her head. "It is shameful."

"She asked you, in punishment for some past act, to send your talented son to convince Gaius to visit Limyra," I said. "They made friends, and he did. No? Laodamia has long planned to use Gaius to further her agenda. Rome has lost coin, and…Gaius. Go now, and I shall do my best for you."

Eurydike bowed her head and kissed my hand. "Thank you, my son. Thank you. I will, one day, tell you how we failed the family, years past. It is a story of a girl, and my failure to protect her."

Apollon smiled, his anger gone, and tugged at my arm. "Thank you indeed. I hope you forgive my harsh words."

I nodded, and they left.

My eyes were on Gaius, who was now walking around with Pericles, as the blonde servant, Ariane, was handing his food taster wine. Hiratius took it and tasted, and they walked around for a while. Then, when the man still lived, he served it to Gaius with a smile. Gaius took it. He drank frugally. He wasn't eating anything, still.

I saw Laodamia near them, with Eudoxia, and I decided I didn't like Laodamia much.

Vipsania was gone, and Larissa as well. I couldn't see

Cassius, but the other people were looking on, like hounds staring for a meal served only to the best few.

Gaius had caused quite a mess in the city.

I walked to a table filled with food and found bread, meat, and soon, I was playing with an olive and popped it into my mouth, savoring the arid taste. Then, I realized a man was standing next to me.

I turned and faced Alexander. He gave me a long look, and I gave his chainmail, sword, with a goat-headed, silver hilt, and powerful shoulders a casual glance.

"Celcus," he said coldly. "And you are ready?"

"Indeed, I am," I told him. "Decimus, to be truthful. Celcus is an insult from someone who doesn't know me. Tall and stupid, they called me when I joined up. It was unkind, though, later, few called me that if they were not my friends. The rest learnt better."

He turned without an apology and inclined his head towards Pericles. "He hopes to see you tomorrow morning at his pleasure, not too early, mind you, in his villa. I will fetch you from your place of residence. Then, you may discuss some private matters. After this night, it will be urgent you speak and deal together with what will follow."

"Antius will meet him," I told him. "I have my own business."

His eyes went to Gaius. "He wants you. Antius should be there as well."

I smiled. "Is he interested in what Gaius will tell me

this night? Is this why I must come as well?"

He said nothing to that.

"He knows I am carrying messages," I said. "He worries about his future in the city? Are we not dealing with that? At some point, he must make do without Gaius."

He ignored me again. "Pericles also wishes to point out that you will report to me for the next days while we deal with what must be very confusing to the city," he said stiffly. His face was stubborn, and mood challenging, but I wasn't one to back down.

"I'll see how that might work," I told him, and ate another olive. "You must seem to be in charge."

He tightened his jaws. "I am. He is."

I crudely spat the stone to my palm, and he flinched. "You lead your men and do what Pericles wants. I will take heed of what you say, as will Antius. But we also decide on our own what we shall do."

He chewed down an acid answer and spoke so softly, I barely heard him. "We will act soon."

The man was angry, petulant, and stubborn. The loss of Corinne must have left him so.

I watched Kyrillos and his family, and that of Meliton.

"Your men in place?" I asked. "All your men?

He nodded turned to go. "The garrison and my offices are up in the Acropolis," he said. "That's hundred and ninety men. You don't need them all down here, just a dozen. My men are all ready, and you will know when to act."

I nodded. "Antius planned it well." I looked around as he left and saw a sea of faces with Segolia's eyes on Kyrillos, who was speaking agitatedly to Meliton. Both gave me impatient looks.

I gave them a slight bow.

The servants were carrying platters of new dishes to the guests and seemed to know exactly whom were to be given most of them. There were two older men, both slaves, who appeared from a side corridor, and they handed the plates to two young girls, who served, and they were all so very busy. The music was drowning out most of the voice, the laugher much of the rest, but I did feel a breath of fresh air from the end of that corridor, and a clang of a kitchen as Dareios prepared food, still.

Apparently, the party would be going for a long while.

The atrium and the gardens beyond it were lined with studies, and the best painting I had ever seen, including those of Livia and some of the senators, lined the walls. One part of the wall, the artists had not yet finished. There, the wall-painting ended in a sea by a beach, and the ship that was to grace the surface of the stone was only partially sketched. The stairway began before the ways to the gardens and was rich and well-made, marble and wood. Up there, I could see a railing, and a guard watching down.

"An odd building," Segolia said, as she appeared. "They seem to be decorating. They are painting and building…" she stopped midsentence and stared at me.

I nodded and wondered at her. "They are, indeed. They are doing both."

She spoke softly. "I…you have been…something was close to you. Something…is watching you."

I stared at her, and then put a hand on her shoulder. She looked startled and spoke on. "No treasures here. The house is half empty, and if there is nothing in Vipsania's rooms, I don't know where Gaius's money went. They have guards on the kitchen doorway, a guard walking the perimeter, a guard or two upstairs, one in Gaius's garden study, and guard on the roof, one on the servant's door, one on the gate, and those buffoons walking around Gaius. Perhaps others. They are stretched. Only fifty to sixty of them in total." She gave me a curious glance. "Oh. Marius is outside. Men as well. This is part of the plan?"

"Good, yes," I told her. "Remember, you should stay here. There."

Gaius was getting up, and the room went quiet slowly. He swayed a bit on his feet, smiled inanely, and waved his hand around. "Good friends! The very best of friends! I feel almost like I have known you most of my life."

The twenty people around him cheered happily. They were minor merchants, local nobles, and their families. They were his and Pericles's clients, and Gaius was the Patron Supreme to the lot.

I shook my head. Segolia's words haunted me.

169

Something.

Gaius stepped forward and shifted his toga. "Pericles tells me great tales of your country every day. Every day, we hear and wonder at the heroes of old, the poets of the past, the land's long history. Truly, there is no other place I would rather be."

I thought he gave me a look, but I wasn't sure.

It didn't matter.

"We shall have many such feasts, my lords and ladies, and together, cement Roman and Lycian interests into a bond. I toast Pericles and his fine, wise wife for their hospitality, for their wisdom and generosity! I toast their beautiful daughter, who decorated any house like a goddess might."

Men and women cheered, eating, drinking. Eudoxia smiled. Lysirate didn't.

"I salute the rest of you, many of whom I have had precious little time to meet with. Alas, I have tried, but gods have conspired against us," he called out. "We shall remedy that soon." Gaius hesitated and looked unsure of himself. Then, he gathered his wits. He waved towards the garden. "Let us, friends, see a way to the gods. The good…" He stopped and looked at Pericles.

"Eurydike," he said.

"Eurydike!" Gaius said, and she stepped forward, "will sing for us today. The theatre is still closed, due to this unhappy issue over my friend Kleitos, but here, today, we may enjoy a moment of utter bliss you would not be able to hear in the theatre. In my house, women may act and sing, no matter what the gods say. Please, let us all move to the garden, where food and more drink will be served, and seats!"

It was then that someone began playing a flute in the gardens.

There, a woman with a trilling voice, aided by a pair of flutes, was singing a song of lament, and Eurydike and Apollon, both, were moving that way. The crowd cheered, and, delighted, Gaius joined them. The mass moved that way. Pericles went after him, gave me a nervous look, and Laodamia pushed him forward.

I spotted Hercules at the doorway to the kitchens, and he nodded. I saw Marius and Lycian soldiery there as well.

I smiled and walked for Kyrillos, who had just stepped out from the wall's shadow, and had taken steps forward to trail the group, uncertainly, still speaking with Meliton.

I walked forward and made a beeline for both.

Their eyes turned my way, and both stiffened visibly. Kyrillos opened his mouth to greet a servant, but they were all fleeing the atrium.

And the man sensed deceit.

He suddenly knew something was wrong.

He turned towards the door.

There, Alexander stood, staring at the man, a hand on his sword's hilt. With him were a pair of Lycian men. Behind them, two more men. Both were legionnaires, grimy and large.

Kyrillos stopped and turned, and his eyes spotted Marius and Hercules, and a few of my men spreading out from the servant's area. Meliton opened his throat.

"What is this, Roman?" he asked.

"Silence," I answered. He stood straight, his head high.

Kyrillos was not so graceful. Unable to control his fear, he was making involuntary starts. He stepped left and looked right, and then looked left and stepped right. He finally stopped and turned to look at me. The man's chine lifted up as I approached, trying to mimic the nobility of Meliton.

He stared at me and I at him.

Cassius, the scribe, peeked in, looking nervous. Some of the guests were turning on their seats, staring at us through the corridors. Soldiers, Lycian, stepped to stand between us and them. The families of the two men had not yet noticed a thing.

I stopped before the men. "Lords. Now, we may talk about your business and the Roman one."

"Not a music lover, Celcus?" Meliton asked me sarcastically. "You are uninterested in hearing Eurydike?"

"I have my own vices, but music is not one of them," I told him.

"Beautiful women are one, I think," Kyrillos murmured as he eyed Segolia briefly. "But not wine. You are here on duty, but not to hear our cases and grudges."

172

I shrugged. "I am here on duty. I am here to investigate murder."

Kyrillos looked scared. "The fool actor's?"

"Amongst others," I agreed. "There have been many, no?"

He shrugged. "Limyra has had plenty of murders. They are not usually people one misses."

I walked up to him. "I have heard this. However, Kleitos the Golden will be greatly missed by Augustus," I said. "Very well missed, Kyrillos."

He licked his lips, and his eyes rested on Laomedeia, who was looking back at him with a small smile. He sneered. "No. This is about her. This is about a personal vendetta. You are questioning me because she hates me. You told us to come here so we might talk about the issues we must face with Gaius giving one family all the power and advantages, but instead, you are here to frighten us to eat our soup, no matter how unappetizing, or hot. That's it, isn't it?"

Meliton opened his mouth, but closed it, a coerced look on his face.

"The bitch," Kyrillos spat. "They say she sleeps with your Gaius. Did you know this? She and her girl both. She fears us, because we are better traders than she is."

Laomedeia heard and still kept her cool, simply staring at the man with cold amusement. The song was raising in note, but more people were looking at us from the gardens behind two corridors and gossiping.

Laodamia? Possibly.

"They may say what they want, Kyrillos," I told him. "The fact is that we must find who butchered Kleitos. This we must—"

"You have a city full of suspects!" he yelled. "You have Gaius, who hated the man Kleitos for suggesting he should go home soon. You have Vipsania, whom Kleitos was harassing whenever he could! You even have Laomedeia, who hates the idea of losing Gaius's influence. Pericles, as well! You have the actors, who hated the shit!"

"And the city is full of angry people who hate Rome," I said stiffly, "because you have been railing against us."

"He was an arrogant Roman, and people who knew him, hated him!" Kyrillos yelled. "And I, nearly the only one who voice my concerns on Roman influence in our lands, get questioned by Romans?"

I shrugged. "Your own people shall question you."

He spread his arms. "Alexander is a relative of Pericles, no? No, this is—"

"We have a witness, Kyrillos," I said. "A man saw what happened to the three traders. Or, who carried their heads off."

There was a shocked silence.

Meliton realized what was happening was far more serious than he had thought. "Witness?" he asked. "You have been here all but few hours, and already you have found someone who saw this murder? Murders."

He was looking both furious and afraid.

Kyrillos slapped a hand across his chest. "You think I cut off heads? You think I murder people? Why?"

"You have constantly been telling everyone," I said steadily, "that Rome should leave Lycia. You have said, in several meetings by the Limyran council, that Rome is a pestilence. You have said that Pericles is too close to Rome and is trying to become a tyrant. You have written Augustus, but you failed to mention these acts. Naturally, sir, you are a person of interest in these murders, which target those people who work with Pericles. You hoped Rome would stop working with Pericles. You might have thought that Rome would blame him, your foe. You have, discreetly, suggested you would be a far fairer person to lead the city, a better man to deal with Rome, and you have followers too."

He fumed. "I have no reason to hide my ambitions. I also do think we must work with Rome, but not if it means we stop being Lycians. That he accepted Gaius to settle here? It is incredible. It is beyond understanding. It has changed everything. That Gaius keeps staying here, and spending our coin, is upsetting the entire nation. Guests are welcome, but they must go home soon! But you claim I am killing people? Do I look like a soldier? This is—"

"Be that as it may," I said, and stepped closer to him. He flinched and stepped away. "We are here to find a killer. We don't give a rat's ass if the killer is a seller of turnips, a rancid beggar, or a bastard son of some high house. The justice of Augustus must be carried, even to

175

Lycia. I'd carry it to Parthia, if I had to."

He stared at me.

Eurydike was holding a dramatic, rather appropriate note, and some other singer joined in, with an ominous note. There were appreciative gasps in the rooms beyond.

He pointed a finger at the doorway. "I, and Meliton, will leave now. Consider us warned. You can go home, or even to Parthia. They at least know how to welcome such as you."

They both turned to leave.

Alexander looked at them with mild boredom.

"You," Meliton hissed. "Again, you hurt my family. You will move. This is about Corinne? Amyntas is a better man for her, anyway. At least he thinks for himself. He has ambition."

Alexander sneered.

"Centurion," I told Marius. "Tell them what will happen."

Marius stepped next to me. "You are both leaving, but you are coming with us. We shall show you where to go."

Kyrillos took a step forward, tried to get past me, and bumped into me. I didn't budge and stopped him. "What is this?" Kyrillos hissed. "This is crude. This is beyond wrong. You cannot—"

"A man was seen leaving the house of those traders, when it was supposed to be empty," I said. "That man, lord, is your son, Amyntas. You shall accompany us."

"He what?" the man laughed. "That is not true!"

"Alexander? Have you...you are trying to take Corinne back! You—" Meliton began, but Kyrillos shook his head.

"It is hopeless," he hissed.

"It is true," I said, and nodded. Hercules stepped forward, so did the legionnaires, who pulled swords. "It is hopeless to resist. You will come with us."

"He wasn't in the city when the others were killed!" the man yelled.

A crowd was gathering around the atrium, filtering slowly from the garden.

"Husband?" asked Aristomache, wringing her hands, trying to get past the Lycian soldiers. Laodamia walked to deal with them.

"Will you come?" I asked. "He is waiting for you."

His face went ashen white, and his hands were shaking. "He is waiting for me?"

"Alexander's men fetched him from your house," I told him. "Mine helped. He is held. Your wife is here, as is yours, Meliton, and shall not go anywhere. Come. Let us deal with this nasty business. We must, after all."

He went limp, and Hercules grabbed him. Meliton raised his hand and pushed away one of the Lycians. Marius and his men flanked us, and we left after them. I cast Segolia a look, and she smiled uncertainly at me. We passed outside, and then to the street, hearing the song turn into terrible, screeching scream, as Aristomache screamed her pain to the winds, interrupting the singers. The Lycian guards were staring at us with uncertainty and doubt, but Alexander was there, looking on steadily, growling orders.

Meliton marched forth, and Kyrillos collected himself, and he was walking on his own. He kept glancing back at me anxiously.

I hardened my heart.

It was Rome, service to Rome, and a conquest for her glory, and Lycia be damned, I thought. Hercules kept pushing Kyrillos forward, and we had not far to go.

We came to the plain looking house, the one that housed the century of men, and found the door guarded by men, who opened it up fast.

Meliton turned to us. "Truly? He is in a Roman fort? What happened to our laws?"

"They will all be applied," I said. "In you go."

The two hesitated and looked like they were gazing to the jaws of a lion, as the doorway yawned. The legionnaires looked at me, and I nodded at Hercules.

He pushed both forward, and we entered.

The main floor was littered with gear and beds. Dozens of men were sitting on them, their armor near, weapons at hand, in their tunics. The rooms around them seemed to be empty. On the side, a set of stairs led up to the higher floors.

And some led down.

There was a yawning hole on the side of the great room, just next to the stairs leading up.

Kyrillos gasped.

Below, a man was weeping.

He took quick steps forward. Hercules stopped him. The man trembled so hard, his bones seemed like they would break. I walked past him, and we went down the stairs.

"Is he hurt?" Kyrillos gasped.

I looked up at him, then Meliton. "Yes. He is."

Below, a scene of horror opened before us.

Soldiers lined the room. Mine, Roman. There were Lycian ones. They were simply shadows, holding spears. A pan filled with burning charcoals, and various red-hot tools, was giving the light.

In the middle of the floor, a man had been chained by his wrists and ankles. He was naked, powerful, his skin gleaming with sweat. He was kneeling, his forehead on the dusty surface.

And bloody one.

The man's fingers were broken. The nails were gone. It was the same with his toes. I saw several wounds and burn marks in his tortured flesh. He was shaking with pain and exhaustion.

Antius, his upper body unclad, hands covered with wraps, so he could hold the hot instruments of pain, was kneeling next to the broken man.

He didn't look at me.

He seemed fully absorbed by his task. He was a known torturer, an artist, some said, in the art of inflicting pain and finding answers.

"Tell the men to come down," he said with an odd,

exhausted, almost cheerful voice.

I stepped aside as Kyrillos came down without me telling him to. He held to the wall and nearly fell in his haste. He saw his son and took a ragged breath, one of despair, and he, we all saw it, pissed himself. The man went to his knees, but Hercules pulled him upright.

Meliton came next, followed by Alexander, and now even Cassius, who looked surprisingly uncaring of what he saw. He was holding a tablet, a wax one, with a pen on the other hand, and his tattoos of suns seemed oddly fitting for a scribe of torture.

Antius sat down next to Amyntas, who looked up, trembling. His eyes went to his father, and I have never seen a man more beaten. "Father," he whispered, and spat blood. He was missing teeth, and his lips were split.

I looked at Alexander, who adopted his usual, steely face. This man was his competitor for Corinne, and he held his happiness in complete check.

The Lycian soldiers didn't. They all looked horrified and were whispering amongst each other. The ones already in the room, bearing witness, looked sick in their military pose, their faces pale.

The Greeks knew how to give a man a bad death.

But they rarely had seen a Roman one.

Hercules pushed both men to the side. I saw yet another man, descending to the bottom of the stairs.

It was Pericles. Laodamia was there as well. Someone was coming after.

Meliton stood to the side, holding his face, and Kyrillos looked like a lost dog.

Pericles gasped and gagged as he witnessed the terribly hurt man. Then, Laodamia pushed him, and he stepped closer.

"As the Lord of Limyra, as one of the speakers of Lycia, the Master of Law, I ask you, Amyntas, son of Kyrillos, do you confess your crimes?" he asked.

There was silence, save for the gasps of Amyntas, who was trying to shake his head, but couldn't, for he was in a terrible pain. His eyes went to a weapon held by one of my men.

It was a large ax.

Antius pulled out a knife and leaned closer to Amyntas. "So. We have had our chat. Do you have something to say? You would do well to repeat what you told us, not long before they came here."

I watched his eyes tear up. For hours, he had been tortured in the room. Rome knew no mercy when it came to the enemies of the wolf, and the man had received none. Lucius the witness was leaning on a dark part of the room, while guards stood on both sides of him.

Amyntas took a shuddering breath. "I haven't—"

"He said he did it," Antius snarled. "He did. Got shy now, did you? You said you did the very deed. Everyone here heard it. House of Kyrillos tried to destroy Pericles by killing its roman guests, but instead, they have destroyed themselves."

181

I watched Kyrillos. "Your son was involved in your treachery. Your little rebellion against Rome is finished."

Kyrillos gasped and seemed to convulse as he stepped forward half a step, shaking his head. "I have not rebelled. I have merely suggested—"

"You were braver not too long ago," I murmured. "Just now, in fact. You were saying Rome should go, and Pericles as well. Your son hid himself in the house of these traders, during the daylight. At night, he did his deed. He paid off a legionnaire and tried to escape. He blew the horn to celebrate and mark his success, and by taking the heads, tried to make it seem even your mythological creatures hate Rome and approve of its death. Alas, you were unlucky. He was seen by Lucius there." All eyes went to Lucius. "Alexander tells me your son was out of town on the days of murders of the traders, but he also tells me your son was visiting a city not far from here and could easily have come here. Did you tell Amyntas to do this, Kyrillos?"

"Please, sir," Amyntas. "He is not guilty of anything. He has not... I am a fool. It is truly not—"

"Silence," Antius whispered, and slapped him so hard, blood and sweat spattered the guards.

He lay on his side, shuddering with pain. Slowly, he lifted his head. "My father nor my mother knew anything of this. I accept full responsibility. Have another son, Father."

Kyrillos wailed softly.

Laodamia was whispering to Pericles, and Pericles shook his head and spoke. "We need more than his assurances. Surely, Kyrillos had an inkling of what his son was doing? Madness, madness, I say. Full madness to believe him in this. The pain has addled his judgement."

Meliton spoke softly. "But not when he confesses to a murder."

Antius nodded and scuttled to the other side of Amyntas, like an evil spider. Amyntas gasped with fear and guarded his face. He spoke. "Truth is important, Amyntas. Kyrillos is clearly guilty, if only of rousing up trouble that led to his son's rash, mad actions. But Rome can show clemency. He may live, in Rome, a captive, if someone steps forward and admits to it."

I pushed away the nausea and the horror and nodded. "Your father knew nothing? You did it on your own?"

"I did it for his reasons," he whispered. "For the future of our family. He would have disapproved. I went ahead anyway."

I nodded and looked at Meliton. The man's eyes widened, and then, he looked down. The silence was terrible.

"There is no proof, except by this torture," whispered Kyrillos. "This is a murder. No Lycian would approve of this travesty."

Pericles sneered at the man. "This is our justice. We have a murderer of Romans on our hands. We shall condemn him. What, do you think we do not torture those we suspect of crimes?"

"Not like this," Meliton whispered.

I snapped my fingers. Hercules stepped forth and spoke heavily. "We searched your house, Kyrillos, when we took your son. In his room, there is a curious artifact."

He tossed an ox-horn on the floor. It clattered across it and stopped before Kyrillos.

"There is also," said Hercules, "a sword. It was still stained in blood."

He showed it. It was long and heavy, local, and indeed, looked to hold traces of blood.

Kyrillos opened his mouth to protest; Amyntas looked away, spitting soft curses.

I turned to go. "Alas. We shall find everyone who was involved with this. Everyone. No clemency after this night."

Meliton raised his hand.

We turned to watch him. He spoke, with the pain of a broken honor behind the words. "Kyrillos mentioned this to me."

"What?" Kyrillos asked desperately. "You lie!"

"He did," Meliton said miserably. "He said that blood must flow for us to truly have momentum in our attempt to push Pericles out. He said it has been planned. He mentioned…Amyntas."

Cassius was writing furiously.

I watched Pericles, and Laodamia leaned to his ear.

He nodded and stepped forward. "It is a sad case, it is. Limyra's very best, its leaders, have put their personal gain before the needs of its people. It is far too much to bear. We must bear the shame." His eyes went to Kyrillos. "You are banished from the city. So is your wife and family. You will both go to Rome, and may Zeus give you peace after you understand what you did. Your fortune is forfeited to the state. You shall be held in your house until the Romans take you away." He looked at Meliton. "You shall no longer sit in the council. You may keep half your fortune, but never hold an office again, nor may you vote. You are closely watched. Your daughter will be given to Rome as a captive, so you always remember what you have been told."

Both stared at him with terrible rage.

He turned to Amyntas.

"Please—" Kyrillos begged. "No."

"Let them," Amyntas whispered. "It is time."

Antius looked at the man. "Say the words, Pericles. Speak them."

He rubbed his face and looked pale as a cloud.

He spoke, his voice cracking. "The Lycian state condemns you to death. Let the Romans do the deed for their revenge."

Antius nodded. "Centurion Marius?" Antius got up and stepped away.

"Centurion Antius?" the man said from the side.

"By the words of Pericles, and the honor of

185

Augustus, I order you to put this man to death," he said.

Marius walked to the man with the ax and grasped it. Then, he walked to the man.

Amyntas leaned forward, closing his eyes, shuddering with fear and pain.

Kyrillos surged forward, but Hercules had been ready for it. The man crashed to the dusty ground. "My son!" he wailed. "My sweet boy! This is madness. This is not right. I beg of you, son. I beg you spare him. Take me—"

Hercules pulled him back.

Antius stepped in front of him. "Marius."

Marius pulled back the ax and lifted it.

He hacked down. The blade sunk to the man's neck.

Amyntas wailed, a shriek so desperate, so filled with pain, it stabbed into your soul. He tried to get up, his head half severed, and instead, fell on his face, chains jingling. He spat and cried and howled, bit his lip, and Marius was struggling to find a place to hit him. Then, he and Antius pinned the man down, and Marius, grunting like a madman, hacked down heavily.

The head came free, blood spurting and flowing, and everyone in that room stared at the corpse with horror. It seemed incredible he had just been alive, so mangled and tortured the body looked. People stared in silence at the incredible sight, the body twitching its life away, and I stared at him regret.

Rome. It is no gentle father.

Thus, I hardened my heart, and stood up. I saw

186

Segolia.

She was standing on the stairs and looking down at us. Her eyes were filled with tears, and horror, and then, she turned away. She walked up.

My mind was whirling. I had told her to stay away...

I turned and saw Antius. His eyes were gleaming with pleasure. The bastard had invited her there.

"Rome has taken its revenge," Antius said evenly, smiling at me. "Those who killed Kleitos, and our traders are gone. Take his body, Kyrillos, and let you, Meliton, and others tell everyone what happened in Limyra. No man or woman shall escape justice, neither the laws of Lycia or those of Rome."

I walked past Meliton, who was on his knees holding his face. I got up, and there faced Segolia.

"That bastard," I whispered.

She shook her head. "He is, but he didn't do anything you didn't approve of. Justice? Torture to gain justice?"

I closed my eyes. "Nothing here changes what I am. I serve Rome. And I love—"

"No." She shook her head. "You do not. You must not. Perhaps the deaths I saw are warranted. I am a medicus, and a seer. I am not a murderer."

She left, and I followed her. Hercules followed me, and Marius stayed to deal with the issue of the body, and Cassius to record the names of those who had witnessed the death. Alexander was arranging for guards for Kyrillos.

I walked after Segolia, deep in my dark thoughts,

and felt the horror of it all clutching my heart.

I heard soft laughter, like wind with a wicked sense of humor, and turned. Shadows. There were only shadows, and wind touching the trees. I hesitated, and went to the house of Gaius, where I would have to deal with the great man himself.

CHAPTER 5

Laodamia was rushing after me, and I stopped to wait. Hercules rushed to guard Segolia, as I stood there, looking at the wife of Pericles.

Out of all the people that night, she was the happiest. She was very beautiful when she smiled, and it had been a great relief for her to be rid of her enemies. She walked to me and surprised me by giving me a crushing hug. She was shaking her head. "Centurion, oh centurion. I must thank you. This has greatly helped our cause."

I nodded.

She sighed, and leaned back, her hand on my cheek. "I am horrified by what Amyntas did—do not think I am not—but I am also relieved. If I can—please let me know how we can reward you."

Despite all her riches, and influence, she was also lonely.

I stepped back. "I serve Rome, and it shall reward me."

"But surely," she said, hurt, "we can do something. The cause—"

"The cause of getting rich?" I asked. "You created this whole problem by being a greedy shit, Laodamia. You did that. You lured Gaius here, and then used Gaius to put your enemies into a tight damned spot, and here we are. They reacted, and now, you remain."

She was nodding, the happiness and warmth gone.

"Gaius is going home, then?"

"He is," I said. "But I suppose you gained much from this misfortune and will remain a loyal ally. But be careful. Kyrillos might come home, one day."

She said nothing.

"Now, I must have words with Gaius," I told her. "Please leave me alone."

She kept walking after me. I looked behind and saw her eyes. Enormous, bottomless greed filled them. "Centurion. I know not what you know of Eurydike and I, and what Lysirate told you, or the lies Apollon spewed, I still warn you to keep an open mind. We have done nothing that Gaius doesn't agree with. You must keep your eyes clear. See the true evil lurking in these halls. It is not I."

I said nothing.

I walked the rest of the dark, garden-filled street, and saw the doorway to Gaius's, where Hercules had a hand on his sword-hilt. Street urchins, robbers, killers, and thieves stepped away at the sight as we hiked the short way, and we soon reached the doors. We walked past the guards and through the doorways to the atrium. Hercules followed us.

It was silent.

Who was left looked our way with worry.

Apparently, the feast had lost much of its spirit after we had left. I saw both Larissa and Ariane were collecting discarded garments and cups from the atrium, as well the other servants and slaves.

190

Laodamia went past us, to the garden, and approached Gaius. He and Vipsania listened carefully, and I saw Gaius looking down at his hands. Then, Laodamia turned to the other guests, some ten to fifteen of them, and began telling everyone a tale of what had taken place. Shocked eyes stared at her, and none more than Eurydike and Apollon's. The latter practically stormed out of the hall, past me, and only dodged Hercules, who didn't budge before the man's rage.

Eurydike followed, worried, deep in her thoughts. She stopped next to me. "A sad day."

I nodded. "A truly sad one."

She wept softly. "I must go and calm down Apollon. Do try to calm down your side of the quarrel." She was pulling and pushing at her ring. "Will you still speak on our behalf?"

"Aye, I shall," I said.

She sniffled, and tip-toed before me. She gave me a kiss on the cheek and left.

I tried to see Segolia, and spotted her sitting in the garden, deep in her thoughts.

I turned to see Cassius coming in. He looked tired and pale. He saw me and waved his hand around. "Nasty business, this. But thank Zeus, it is over."

"Not for me," I said. "Gaius? Then tomorrow, you and I have a chat about his bills."

He was clearing his throat as he tried to see to the gardens. "Yes. Gaius is going to his study now, as the guests are leaving, and we shall be meeting him," the

191

scribe said, pulling me along. "We shall wait for a bit. Then, I go in, and after, you shall too." He shook his head. "The business with Kyrillos. It was terrible. Very unfortunate. It makes one think Rome is bound to make trouble wherever it goes."

"Rome has made mistakes," I said, "but I correct them. Augustus wanted to see the score evened. Kleitos was close to his heart."

"It is even," he said, and hesitated a bit. "I must warn you. What you will hear from Gaius will not please you. It is most unfortunate business, that."

"He will hear Augustus's words and then he must make up his own mind," I said. "I have seen the bills he has raked here. I see he bought a house, and I see he, after running out of money, has attached himself to Pericles, who is making fortunes with his patronage. I will see all the bills tomorrow, Cassius."

"Yes," he said. "I heard you. There are no bills or scrolls left over from Ennius. I am happy to show what we spend, and what Pericles has paid since Ennius left. It is an unfortunate business, as I said. Come."

I walked after him for the garden and found a pond filled with yellow and red fish, and bright flowers were growing around it.

I stared at Segolia, not sure what to do.

Nothing, you fool, I thought.

I spotted Gaius near the door to his study, surrounded by the last of his local clients, a motley crew of men and women who were taking an advantage of the great man.

He raised his hand, tentatively, standing straight, his eyes moist. "Friends," he said with a sonorous voice. "As a guest in your city, you need not thank me. I, instead, am showering you with thanks and gratitude. I shall leave you now, and may the tomorrow be painless and without regrets. Alas, for the terrible discoveries this night."

The tremble in his voice betrayed him.

He knew it would not be so. It would be anything but. The city would be abuzz with rumors and anger.

Hercules appeared. I looked at Segolia, who was hugging her self. Her mood was odd.

Hercules, on the other hand, was chewing on a bit of dried meat and grapes he had stolen from the atrium. His dark eyes took in everything, especially the lanky legionnaire guard on the door of Gaius's study. His black skin gleamed with sweat, and I realized I was drenched as well.

He smiled at my scrutiny. "Torture. Nasty business. Antius is a damned maniac."

I nodded.

He shook his head. "Foolish to punish a man like that. You only have to give them poison," he mused, "and then, an antidote to cure it, if they cooperate. Then, head off. Antius is a crude bastard. And he should pay for what he did to you, and her."

"He will."

We watched as Cassius was speaking with Gaius

briefly. The man wasn't pleased.

"Augustus wanted Antius here," I said. "He knew what was needed and sent what he knew would hurt the enemy."

"Enemy," Hercules mused, munching on a seed painfully. "Shit. They are, are they not?"

"Enemy, Hercules," I told him. "Lycia is a free city that is seething with anger. They—"

I went silent, and Gaius turned to go. He smiled drowsily as he looked at the mostly drunken guests, who were moving out. Hiratius, the food taster, was walking past, on his way to the kitchens.

Gaius raised his hand one more time.

Many of the drunken guests roared their approvals and happily saluted Gaius back, who turned as if ashamed or shy, and walked for the doorway at the end of the gardens. The lanky soldier stood there, his chain gleaming, and the scribe came over. Cassius spoke hurriedly. "Wait. When I come out, you get to meet him. It has been agreed. Be fast. He is not in an agreeable mood, so this was a great victory."

I smiled. "It could be worse, I suppose."

The man hesitated, apparently also thinking about Kyrillos, and then dodged past people in the garden. He entered after Gaius, who had waited by the doorway. His eyes were on me.

Then, they disappeared inside.

I stood there, as the servants slowly herded the guests out. Many of those left the house as well.

Laodamia was moving away out as well. Guards were walking on top floors, and calls echoed from the outside and the roof, and then, Ariane carried a steaming plate of food past me and held an amphora of wine. The food taster, Hiratius, followed her, and together with the guard, they entered. Not too long after, they left. I could glimpse Gaius leaning over the scribe, who was sitting, shaking his head, and writing.

Gaius's eyes visited mine for a moment.

The guard came out and closed the door.

Hercules shook his head. "He is gathering resolve. I can feel it."

"He will try to defy Augustus," I said. "I know. Everyone here knows it."

"He is doing more," he whispered. "He has a lover, does he not? Eudoxia?"

"Laodamia might be the one as well," I told him. "Most everyone else wants him gone."

"It is a woman," Hercules said. "He seems confident he can stay. Someone wants him to stay." He shook his head. "I'd not defy my father and stay anywhere unless I loved someone enough."

"Who could be so important he wants to stay?" I mused.

"A young woman," Hercules suggested. "A clever one, a greedy one."

I shrugged. "Or someone who truly loves him. Someone who Gaius simply cannot live without."

"So, anyone?" he asked. "They all hover around him,

the girls. Lysirate less than the others, but perhaps she too, would fall into his bed, if he asked."

I rubbed my face. "Or, perhaps, there is nobody. Perhaps he just wants to forget Rome and hopes to become a gentle soul hidden in some valley nearby." I shook my head. "We wait. He must meet with us."

Cassius had been wrong. It was taking a very long time for them to finish their business.

Segolia, silent, waited. We as well.

Later, much later, in the middle of the night, the guards changed.

"My turn, Avila," said a squat, evil looking legionnaire who came to stand by the doorway and eyed me with an unkind look. "Who's this?"

"A butcher from Palatine," Avila said with a tired grin. "Have a good night, Marcus."

Marcus watched us. He smiled to Segolia, but his smile froze when she looked back at him. He cleared his throat. "You going to see him? Or are you just pissing in the garden?"

I didn't bother to answer.

"Let him sleep, centurion Butcher," he said distantly. "He needs his rest more than words."

Hercules chortled. I spoke softly, with a menacing tone. "Even those of Augustus?"

He flinched. "You carry the words of Augustus? In your bag?"

"He needs to hear what Augustus has got to say, that's what he needs," I told him. "Stop trying to pick a fight with me, or I'll tell Marius to send you to Syria."

He shrugged. "I listen to my centurion, and no other. No Syria for me, thank you. Seen it. And you are right, sir. I suppose our Gaius should listen to Augustus." He leaned forward and was whispering. "The man is crazy. We love him, of course. Women throw themselves at him, riches flow past him, but he? He just writes poetry." He made the word sound filthy.

I snorted and walked back and forth in the garden, and finally, the scribe opened the doorway. He was carrying a simple scroll, hesitated as he saw me, opened his mouth to croak out something, perhaps a warning, and instead, left the door open as he dodged past us. He headed upstairs for Vipsania's rooms.

I hesitated and walked past the guard, who turned to watch me, and glanced after me before he closed the door.

The room was huge.

It was dark as night at the edges. Only Gaius's desk was fully lit.

I heard a scratch at the end of the room. I stared that way but saw nothing. I turned to eye the furniture near the table.

There was a large sofa.

Nothing else. Besides the huge desk, and the sofa, there was nothing. I could see pillars of marble and red stone, and dark corners, an elaborate mosaic on the floor, snakes with deer and waterfall, and a large crack on the mosaic just before me.

There was an atmosphere of peace in the room. It looked like a cave fit to house a thrifty king.

I looked at the man himself.

Gaius was reading something, hovering over his meal, sitting down before his desk. I spotted figs, meats, vegetables, and fish on the plate, with no doubt bitter wine since he grimaced as he tasted it from a silver cup. Instead of looking back at me, he carried on reading, fully aware I was in the room.

"Lord?" I finally said.

He stiffened and turned to look at me. His face was very pale, his hair stiff, and he had rings under his eyes, as if he had just struggled mightily. "Centurion? That is right? You are a centurion?"

I raised my hands as if to make sure he knew I was none else.

He rubbed his face. "Thank you for helping my friend Pericles. It seems my stay here has flamed some old issues, and the deaths…Kleitos. Poor Kleitos. It is dealt with?"

"It is," I said. "Mostly."

"Mostly?"

"We have to see if someone takes the rebel's mantle in the coming days," I told him. "If they do?"

He nodded. "They will bleed." He laughed softly. "I am sorry if Vipsania surprised you. My wife…she is hoping you would give her some good news from Rome. Poor fool, she is. She is tedious and doesn't please me, bothers me constantly, and I find myself hating her. She thinks you are here to take us home." He gave me a quick look. "She somehow managed to bring the lot down to the harbor. Laodamia was frantic when she found out you are here."

I said nothing.

"Did you please her?" he said softly.

I flinched. "Lord?"

"Was she happy with what you told her? I know she asked you to share a ride with her."

"She has her answers, lord," I told him, relived.

Did he guess what else Vipsania was asking for?

He went on reading. If he did, he didn't care.

"I bring news from Rome," I said. "But also, gifts."

"Oh?" he laughed bitterly. "I take it my father does not send me coin, though."

"No coin," I said. "But there are gifts from him, if you will receive them." I opened the bag on my side. There, scrolls, and a wooden box.

He eyed the package, and the scrolls. "Thank you. For the gift. Though, I would prefer he sent me coin, so I would not have to rely on others. That has partly caused the issues here. How can I refuse helping those, who feed me?"

Silence.

He didn't move. Neither did I. He turned and stubbornly began reading a scroll.

I cursed and stepped forward. "Augustus insisted I give them to you in person. And discuss them."

"You may leave them on the chair," he said. "I am in

199

no mood to discuss Rome's business, when I am tired and have already made the effort to meet you. Besides," he said with a soft laugh, "it is clear the scrolls contain nothing more than the same order to return, but this time, my health cannot stave off the inevitable."

"He insisted," I said darkly, "that your health will not stop your return. He made sure you would know what he is saying, that he wants you to read them in my presence, and to provide me either with an answer, or one in writing before I leave your presence."

He turned again and frowned. He contemplated on being obstinate, and then, he saw in my eyes, that obstinate people were people I knew how to deal with. He still took time to acknowledge the fact he had little choice but to do this, and then, he picked up a pen, leaned back and nodded. I sighed and walked forward, and he took the bag from me.

"You are Decimus, eh?" he said. "The Tall? A Pretorian as tall as the Germani Guards?"

"Yes. I have guarded you often," I said.

He hefted it. "All for me?"

"We have others for other people," I said. "This is yours."

He chuckled. "I have just spent a better part of an hour with Cassius on Roman business, and now, more? All of this will keep me from my poetry. And from my will."

Will?

"All for you," I said. "Roman business never gets

smaller. Poetry will wait."

He gave me an unkind look. "Clearly, you do not know poetry. Aye, Roman business never shrinks. It only gets filthier, and there is more of it," he said. He looked at me with suspicion. "Your men? How many?"

"Enough," I said.

"And just eight men and a woman," he said, "spoiled the affairs of Kyrillos."

"There was a witness," I told him. "That witness identified Amyntas, son of Kyrillos."

"You came today, you met the witness immediately, and now, the family is dead and taken?" he asked softly, his eyes large with shock. "Today. Meliton shackled as well. I suppose your men are impressive."

"This very day, yes," I told him. "It could have waited, but your wife alerted the city to our arrival. We had to move fast."

He shook his head. "You did what, exactly?"

I sighed. "Nothing we would do to you. But, yes, Gaius, we know our business."

"What did you do to them?"

I nodded and hoped he could stomach it. "We tortured a man," I told him, brutally, simply, "and the man answered the question and admitted to his crimes. He sought to undermine Pericles, and you, and he hoped his father would be the new Pericles of Limyra. After that?" I shrugged. "They would likely have worked with Rome just as much as anyone."

He nodded. "How unlucky for them to have been

seen. I am also happy that, while effective, you can spare me from such unpleasantries."

"We have no orders to remove your toes," I said. "Men make mistakes. Some are forgiven."

He gave me a furious look. "Forgiven? Aye, even when there is nothing to forgive. Am I not a free man? Women have more rights than I do, and only dogs fewer still," he grunted. "I assume, by tomorrow, people will know Kyrillos made a move on Pericles, and that Rome simply investigated and found the truth? People will be mad. I think you are right. There will be blood."

I shrugged. "That is how it will go down. I have seen it often. You can crack open a skull, but a spine must also be snapped."

He sighed. "I do hate this. Skulls and spines. I hate all these intrigues and the weight that comes with Roman power."

"Rome fights like its enemies do," I said, and nodded at the bag. "It has been a long day. The guard outside —
"

"Marcus," he said. "He is a man more comfortable with night. He loves it here during the nighttime. He is in love with my wife's slaves, Ariane, and Larissa. Neither care for him. Yet, he keeps trying."

The man was trying to avoid the discussion so desperately, he was almost shaking.

"Marcus outside told me to let you sleep. Let us get this over with, lord, so we both may sleep," I said. "I have to be rested tomorrow."

He smiled softly. "May you sleep well after what you did today." He clapped the bag. "What's in there?"

I cursed in my mind. "Scrolls. There are many that are simple gossip."

"I do love gossip. I love it better than orders. It is nearly poetry, is it not?"

"Livia sent you a few filled with such," I said. "She has a good amount of gossip in her drawers."

"I never found Livia's gossip pleasing. Too purposeful. She causes damage with her gossip, more than you with your sword."

"Your friend, Lucius Paullus, sent you news of your house, and of your horses and dogs," I went on. "He is staying there occasionally."

"I will have my horses and dogs, for sure, one day," he muttered, opening the bag slowly. "I care nothing for the house."

"Young Germanicus sends you greetings, rather than to your wife," I told him. "He

"Germanicus will be happy," he murmured again, and opened the bag and looked inside. "He is very impatient and ambitious."

"There are few from Augustus."

He looked up. "I take it I don't have to read them, but I can hear them?"

I nodded. "He instructed me to give you all the news in person."

He gave me a quick look. "I remember you. Decimus, indeed. A guard. But more. His personal...man."

A dog. That's what the shit had been thinking about.

I nodded. "I remember you as well, as I said. His choice for the future of Rome."

He laughed bitterly. "Oh, so. That's it, then. You have a sting on your tongue. Come. Speak. Scrolls."

I nodded at the bag. "The gift. There is a package from you loving adopted father," I said. "He sends his warmest of greetings in writing and, in my speech, an ultimatum, but also a reminder of Rome."

He laughed and pulled out a parcel. "A taste, rather." He rattled the package, and a small smile flickered on his face. "Olives?"

"The same you always shared, lord," I said. "When you still loved him."

He pulled out one scroll and looked at it curiously. "Love, eh? Is Tiberius back in Rome yet?"

"He is, lord," I answered. "That one is from him, and he simply, I think, wishes you well. He is back and living comfortably. I told your wife this earlier this morning."

He nodded. "She tried to tell me. Oh, I feel sorry for her, almost as much as I hate her. She is so unhappy here. I know it. I hope we can fix that soon. Is Tiberius well?"

I shrugged. "As far as I know, he is. Rhodes was not overly hard on him. Seemed well rested and happy, in his quiet way."

"Happy," Gaius laughed. "Oh, he is happy. He is, and I am not."

I was silent for a moment until he waved his hand for me to go on. "He only wishes to obey Augustus and hopes for your success."

He smiled and nodded. "There was the business of Lollius, wasn't there? He thinks I wanted him dead? That I feared he would, one day, be my enemy and suggest he be killed?"

"No longer," I told him. "As I said, he wants to live in peace. He knows it was Marcus Lollius who offered to bring you his head, and you had nothing to do with that."

If that was true, it mattered little.

Gaius looked sick and nodded, while leaning on his hand. "This is exactly what I want to run from. This…need to scheme. To…think about my future, to fear everyone. Man is driven to evil, so often." He rubbed his eyes and smiled. "Good. I am sorry for the trouble between us, and I do prefer peace to war, like he does. We are two very peace-loving people, and well do we deserve it." He began to open the package, while placing the scrolls on top of the others, carefully. He took a hold of the box and played with the wrapping, ripped it open, and pulled out a box, which he smelled.

"Grandfather knows what I miss," he said sadly. "And perhaps he doesn't know me that well anymore, but he knows what I loved in Rome, if not him." He opened the box and stared at the dozens of olives. He took one, tossed it to me, and I caught it. I popped it into my mouth, and he took one, and ate it with a smile.

Then, he gave me a barely concealed look of disapproval. "So, my fool wife found out about you and told everyone. They all came?"

"All?" I said and shrugged. "No, not all. I don't know who these all are, even. Enough. Enough came."

"I have been expecting for you or one of yours," he said softly, playing with the package. "It has been coming, indeed. I learnt of you from my wife." He smiled. "I half contemplated on going to Side for a trip."

I smiled. "I can get to Side. I can ride, and I have the coin to find you even far in Mithradakert if I must."

"I know," he laughed softly. "So, tell me what I should do tomorrow when Amyntas's death hits the populace."

"You will act shocked," I said. "As per the deal made by Julius Caesar, and the Lycians, Rome may deal with Romans who get killed in Lycia. At least, we are allowed to be involved and to investigate. So. We are here to investigate, hunt, and kill this perpetrator, since the victim was a friend to Augustus. Let Pericles make sure everyone knows that he condemned the man. He will. Kyrillos is still alive, but I doubt he will make trouble. The death of Kleitos went too far."

He shook his head. "A hideous thing this. I do not know what Augustus saw in Kleitos. He was the Golden, but in here? Roman. Did he hope to drive me home by embarrassing me? Perhaps so? Sending such a bad actor here... They say he was badly disfigured?"

"As were the others," I agreed. "Had no heads."

"God Zeus," he whispered.

Zeus.

I spoke on, trying to make him focus. "It is done. The killer was beheaded. You will act shocked, but we must all be careful, Pericles and Alexander as well. We have experience in Gaul and Germania of hunting for men like this, and some of us have travelled in Greek lands, but few, here. This is a world between east and west."

He nodded, delighted. "Indeed! That is just so. A world between the two, and it holds, in my opinion, more of the good of both than the bad. No savagery of the east and deceit of the west. No pompousness and wars of the west. Even the gods are polite. I do like it here. They will be upset, but I shall be careful."

I nodded. "You like it? Enough to buy this house."

He shook his head. "My adopted father has houses all over the world. Why not I?" He gave me a baleful eye. "And now for the part I dread. Let me hear it."

I shifted on my feet. "We were to investigate the murders. We made an example of Amyntas for —"

"And that is what I consider one of the bad qualities of the west and east. Examples to keep power in your claws."

I kept going. "They will be your claws, Gaius. We are here to make sure you fall to no evil."

He snorted. "Truly? You have seen my guards? A century of men. And since Amyntas confessed, I am safe."

"A century of men," I said stiffly, "is a small force.

207

They are growing bored, fat, disgusted by their lost opportunities to grab loot, and they are, to be honest, stretched. Sixty men are a pittance, but they are now perhaps fifty, and many more will be sick. There are nearly two hundred men in the Lycian garrison alone. If a determined enemy would want to see what your lordship's scalp looks like inside out, they could do it, especially if the Lycians were in on it. Imagine if Amyntas had met you privately."

He looked unhappy with my words. "They say the four men were butchered like lambs. I heard the horn playing in the night."

"They say the men were butchered like lambs, indeed, if you don't intend to eat the lamb," I said brutally, and he shivered. "There is more. We have a job outside of catching killers and keeping your head on your shoulders."

He nodded. "You are here to show the Lycians that the Wolf has claws. You are here to make sure my useless century is going to do their job properly. And perhaps you are here to fetch me home? Finally?" he ventured, his eyes on mine. "Is that not what is in these scrolls and behind the olives he used to give us when he taught us our letters, Lucius and I?" He looked shocked for a moment and then down, his eyes filling with tears. He wiped them on his sleeve. "Poor Lucius."

"I am to take you home in a week's time," I told him. "You and your wife," I said. "That's what I am going it be doing, lord. More galleys and ships are on their merry way. They can fetch you from Side as well."

He chuckled and looked unhappy. "Indeed? Is that what you will be doing? And if I choose to extend my holiday?"

"Then," I said stiffly. "Augustus has make arrangements that your guards will bring you home. He does, after all, own the provinces where your legions are stationed, including the century in Limyra. You are well loved, Gaius, but your men won't rebel against Augustus, especially if you tell them you fight for the right to live peacefully in a cottage somewhere. They smell no money in peace. Also, you left your troops after Armenia. They have new commanders now. The legates love coin more than you and their future position in the Senate."

He shook his head, gnashing his teeth together.

I stepped forward. "We shall follow you wherever you go. We can. We have done it elsewhere. I once hunted a man to the depths of Gaul and found him. It is time, lord, for you to return Rome. I need your answer. In any case, no matter what it is, my men will guard your door and person from now on. We need not follow you anywhere."

Gaius turned to look at me with loathing, seething anger, and bitterness. I now had an enemy, a mighty one. "You have a scroll for my century?"

I nodded. "I will give it to Marius, if you refuse."

"I agree to discuss it with my former wife," he said neutrally. "I give you this promise. I shall not disappear, and I will give it consideration. In the meantime—"

"There is no discussion, lord," I said. "Former?"

He went on. "I trust Pericles will aid you while you wait? He is a good man. He deserves our help."

"I will speak with him and others again," I said. "But we need your answer right away. As to your former wife? What do you mean?"

He sat there and then placed the box on the desk and turned to me.

He scratched his hair and rubbed his face, gathering strength to open the scrolls from Augustus. "Very well. Here is my answer. I shall not obey. I shall not return to Rome. Give your scroll to Marius, man. I am sure he will obey it with pleasure."

I closed my eyes. "Very well, Gaius," I said. "We shall discuss the travel arrangements...later."

He slapped his knee. "I have my own weapons in this game. I have made my moves. I will stay here, soldiers or no soldiers. This is my home now. Go, for I have work to do. And finally, I shall finish my meal. I shall be drunk, I hope, but I feel good about our discussion. It was coming and has been had." He looked at me carefully. "I will now finish two scrolls. You are right. Poetry must wait this night." He pulled out two. He showed them to me. "This one," he said, and shook a thin one. "Is going to contain my divorce from Vipsania. I just had Cassius deliver her a notification, that I will divorce her this very night, and I also told her what I think about her. This one?" He smiled. "This is my will.

Call it my confession."

I was a thick bunder of scrolls.

"Lord?" I asked, tired.

"It spells out every single treachery, every lie, every secret of Rome I have encountered, or been party of. It also tells a tale of Gaius, and who he really is. I am in love, Decimus. I confess my love here, and if someone tries to remove me from this room, I assure you this scroll will not be found. It will travel, across the world. It will be duplicated, and Rome shall be shamed. It will rattle it to its core. Its allies will rage, the lies exposed shall tear the Senate apart. It will cause war, and destruction. It is my legacy, the price of having me in Rome. Consider well what you do, Decimus."

He got up and embraced me, and I embraced him, and he turned away to write his will. What little I glimpsed of it, the list of lies, made my hair stand out.

I turned and walked out, cast him a quick, worried look, and saw his hands reaching for drink.

I walked past the scowling guard, who shut the door, and then, I walked out. I found Segolia in the atrium. Her face was calm, but lifeless.

I watched her and Short and turned to look at Hercules. I spoke to him. "Guard the door, and the man. One of ours, from now on."

Hercules shook his head. "He said 'no.'"

I nodded. "He did much more than that."

He walked off to sit in the corner and proceeded to stare at Marcus, who returned the favor.

I watched Segolia. "Your sight?"

She shrugged. "Not changed. People will die. And I tell you this; the thing I sensed, this evil? It is now interested in you. You have made it curious."

"They will rebel tomorrow," I said, ignoring the dread her words caused.

She nodded. "Then, you just kill them."

"You, as well," I said. "You and Rome, us."

She looked away. "It is not that simple."

I sighed and watched Larissa in the servant's corridor. Ariane was carrying a tray up the stairs, but Larissa appeared and was speaking with Cassius, who nodded at her, and gave her a gentle pat on the cheek. Larissa sprung after Ariane and spoke gently. Then, she was carrying the tray up. Ariane walked down, and I saw her back was bloodied.

Again.

I nodded and turned to her. "You think I lied to you?"

She shook her head. "I know not. Father warned me. I wasn't prepared. I jumped and fell and found something I loved and then something beneath. You must not touch Antius. He never lied."

I instinctively touched her cheek, and she flinched and stepped away.

"Why?" I asked. "I would not hurt you."

"Would you," she said, "if I was an enemy of Rome?"

I shook my head. And I was honest. "I would not love you if you were an enemy of Rome. If you were, it would have a good reason, and perhaps, I would follow you. After Servilia…Segolia. I want you to know, what we do, has a good reason. Rome cannot survive if men follow laws, and morals."

She shook her head, turned to go, and I took a step forward. "Segolia!" Two of my men hesitated, and Short did as well, and I, shocked to my core, watched her go. I nodded, and they followed her.

I hesitated and looked upstairs. I turned and walked up, past guards, and saw Larissa coming out of a room.

Her eyes were huge as she stared at me. I stood before her. "I would speak with her."

She nodded, a dark scowl on her face. "She is still awake. But it is not right. You must not go there alone, and I cannot spare the time."

"Is it any more wrong than your affair with Cassius?" I asked.

She blushed, cursed, and pushed past me. "Cassius? He is what he is and serves whom he serves. He is not my lover. My lover is gone."

She went past me, and I went inside, past the guard, who gave me a curious, disapproving look.

There, I found a double room. The first one was filled with cabinets and chairs.

The second one had only a table, chair, and a large bed. No riches there either.

Vipsania gasped, as she saw me. She was hunched over her late dinner but choked as I came inside. She was teared up and shaking.

I leaned on the doorway. "Why do you beat your slave?"

She sobbed. "Because…I am angry. She failed me."

"And what," I asked her, "made Gaius divorce you?"

She held her face. She shivered. "He is in love. He is going to marry another." She showed me a scroll. "Here. He dictated it today. It is cold as if he were speaking to a stranger. He will divorce me this night. In the morning, when I wake up, I shall be shamed."

She looked angry, the sorrowful.

"Who is the lover?"

"I don't know," she said, shaking. "Laodamia? Eudoxia. Both?"

I shook my head. "I doubt it."

She wept. "Ariane couldn't seduce him. She had once, long ago, made him smile, but now? He doesn't want her, just someone else. It is painful. I need some happiness."

"Augustus will not approve of it," I told her. "He might divorce you, but not Gaius, no matter what the law is. And then, you thought you would be pregnant. That it would protect you."

She nodded.

I walked forward and kneeled next to her. I took her hand. "It makes no sense, Vipsania, to hang on to something that died. It makes no sense to try."

She held her face and wept bitterly. She was afraid, no, terrified. She pulled at me, and at my chain, and banged her fist at me, and I let her. Then, I lifted her and carried her to the bed.

"Do not go," she begged me, and I despaired.

I nodded.

There, I lay next to her, whispering to her ear. She needed encouragement, and she had nobody else to give them to her. She held me tight, she clutched me, she hugged me, and wept, and listened to me. She held on to me like a drowning person holds a piece of wood.

Then, she kissed me.

She was wet from tears, and wet for passion, and her lips sough mine out. She kissed me desperately, her tongue playing with my lips. She dug her hand into my manhood, desperately caressing, and pulling it out, and when she tried to pull me over her, I let her. I found her under me, wiggling, pulling at me, and then, I felt her warmth, and entered her. She shuddered with pleasure, gasping with surprise, and kissing me, she demanded more. I gave her the love she needed.

I did it for her.

And for Segolia. She felt betrayed. I had to betray her to justify it.

I felt like a dog, like a fool.

Despite that, I had Vipsania, many times, in many ways, and when I knew she was happy, I gave her what she graved. I came inside her, and she was given the seed she had asked for. She smiled, exhausted, holding on to me as I shuddered inside her, and only then, she let go of me, and curled besides me.

I stayed until she slept.

I got up, hesitated, arranged my gear, wiped myself clean and walked away.

With the tray.

I woke up Hercules, gave him orders, and found Tall below and followed him to the city.

Near to the inn, he took me another way.

"This way, sir," said the boy, and he led us to a back street of the inn, looked up and down it, and slipped to the left. Soon, he turned right, and we entered a way filled with trash, mud, and doors. A shadow moved, and I saw Antius.

He nodded at me as he watched us coming forward.

I stopped as the boy hesitated. Short joined him. "Tomorrow," I told him. "One must take a message to Nefarious, and one takes me to Pericles. Early morning. Before sun rise."

They nodded, and I sighed and flipped them a bronze coin each.

They caught them deftly and ran off.

Antius grunted as I came near. "You made your woman cry."

I turned and grasped his face and turned it to me. "You sure taught her about me, eh?"

He stared at me for a long while and held a hand on a hidden pugio's hilt. Then, he relaxed. "She is yours, and it is only fair," he agreed. "Just wanted to make it fair for her, eh? She has to know what she is bedding. We are doing well here, so let's not kill each other."

"Gaius is staying," I told him. "Your part is nearly

over. Stay low. And stay out of my way. In Rome, I shall kill you."

He flinched, and I let go of his face.

"They are all settled in?" I asked, as if I had not just promised him death. "The Lycians?"

He was massaging his face and nodded to the city. "Kyrillos went home with his wife. They have guards of Lycia. Meliton's family is home as well."

I nodded. "Good," I said. "We shall sleep and see what happens tomorrow. Guard duties set?"

The man nodded. "I have the first watch."

I went in and found a large room, and several cubicles where men were sharpening weapons and throwing dice.

I looked as Segolia, asleep already on her side, breathing gently. I rubbed my face and lay next to her and closed my eyes.

***

Late that night, or rather, or perhaps very early in the morning, deep and dreadful, a horn blared. The deep, sonorous sound echoed across the city and ended abruptly, leaving a hundred dogs barking.

BOOK 2: THE WOUND AND THE SCROLL

CHAPTER 6

"Gaius is dead," said the Centurion Marius stiffly, and Pericles was leaning on the door, Alexander staring at the corpse near him.

Gaius was indeed dead.

It was plain as a nose on a face.

"At least he was spared the mutilation," Alexander said softly, a white-knuckled hand holding his sword's pommel. He looked haggard. "He has his head."

Beyond him, in the atrium, the entire household sat in silence, guarded by legionnaires.

Antius pushed Pericles around. "You will get everyone in here. Everyone who was here last night for the feast. Meliton, Kyrillos, the nobles, and the merchants. Even their servants."

Pericles whispered. "Of course. I will get to it immediately."

Alexander rubbed his face with anger at the arrogance of the request. "I have already sent my men to the city to do this, and to keep peace."

I nodded as I walked in the room. It was cold and shadowy and stank of a bad death. Flies were buzzing around.

His head had not been taken, but he had died a terrible, humiliating death.

The centurion Marius was shaking his head. "This is…shit terrible. Poison again."

"Yes," I muttered, and squatted next to Gaius. "Is

Hiratius here? Where is the food taster? The cook, Darius?"

Alexander shrugged, his eyes flashing. "I will...we will make sure. We will check. He was missing from the house. The cook as well."

Marius grunted. "My guards saw them leaving during the night, in a hurry. There was no reason to hold them. They often went out."

A man came to Alexander and was whispering something. Alexander was whispering questions back and then turned to us. Everyone was looking at him, waiting for unwelcome news. "My guards. In Kyrillos's house. They have let him out. The man has gone crazy. He and his wife and the actor Apollon, a trouble maker, are in the..." He shook his head. "They are making trouble, indeed. They are in the Agora. Hundreds of people. Some of our guards joined them. Few, but..."

Antius was spitting and cursing and slammed his hand on the wall. "It was stupid to spare him. See? When you frighten your enemy, you must frighten them to the bone."

"Are they rebelling?" Marius asked. "Truly?"

"They are asking...demanding for Pericles to flee the city," Alexander said. "I would say, they are."

"Are they armed?" Marius asked. "The guards are, but the rabble?"

"They have some weapons, but mainly rocks and clubs," Alexander said. "They will get more people soon, and weapons, if the guards join them. I must go and control my men. We must be—"

"Decisive," I told him. "We must act. Make sure your men do not join this."

"I can deal with it," he said darkly. "They are my people, after all. Limyran people."

"Your men," Marius sneered. "They let the bastard go. More might be part of it."

"They say Apollon convinced them," Alexander answered. "He is famous in the city."

"Silence," I snarled, and my eyes travelled the room.

"Silence?" Alexander roared. "The murderer is my business. Mine! This is our city."

"Gaius was mine, and now, they are the same business, and you keep your mouth shut while I think."

He did, barely. Antius was also struggling.

I looked at the room. The sofa had moved. The food had been consumed, the wine was gone. The amphora was on its side.

Everything else was gone. Everything.

All the scrolls had been taken.

"Who touched his desk?" I asked. "Who did it?"

Nobody said a thing. Segolia walked past me to the desk, and Hercules flanked her. I kneeled next to Gaius.

The corpse of Gaius showed all the signs of death by poison. He was face down, pale-colored, his facial skin blotchy with red rashes. Vomit had poured out of the mouth and lay scattered all over the floor around his face and was spread all the way to the sofa, where he had apparently noticed things are wrong. He had clawed at his throat while he had crawled from the sofa to the spot he had died in before his desk.

"The pain," Alexander said softly. "He has been in so much pain."

I nodded. He had also shat himself, and the fluids—vomit, shit, and piss—were unfavorably spread on the floor in an unholy mess. It all stank terribly in the closed space. Around him, where he lay, there was also a lot of blood. Scratches showed on the floor, and I saw his nails were chipped.

I tried to see his face. He had probably bit his tongue through.

"The pain must have been so much," Pericles said softly, echoing Alexander with tears. "Terrible. Was it hemlock?"

I shook my head. "He had dragged himself. His legs had not worked. Aye, hemlock."

I walked to the couch and looked at it. There were stains on the sofa, a lot of them, and it looked like a well-used one. Then, I tracked the trail of vomit, shit, and scratches on the stone.

The centurion was nodding. "We must deal with the city, Decimus. We shall prepare him later and weep for our souls. We are all dead."

I stared at the blood. "Did he bite his tongue in half?" I wondered aloud.

"Oh, dear gods," Segolia whispered. "Augustus will be heartbroken."

"Oh, Zeus help me!" Pericles moaned, and held his

face. "We are all."

Marius spat. "No, Zeus is fucking us all in the arse, and laughing. His food taster. Where is the man?"

"Hiratius," I snarled. "Marius's men have locked this place down. We keep the house secure, and we must find that one, right away, as we also deal with the rebellion. How many men do we have?"

"Forty men, if we must hold this house, and our own," Marius said.

Alexander shrugged. "Hundred. I have some hundred. They will be near the Agora."

Marius cursed. "Hopefully, the shit-eaters have not joined the enemy."

I reached out to Gaius and moved the face, just a bit, and saw bloody scratches running down his throat, but no blood on the lips.

Pericles moaned again.

A legionnaire came to us, panting. "Here. In the kitchen, there was this. We turned it upside down."

He handed Marius a bag.

"It was hidden in a sack of flour," the man said, eyeing Gaius in shock. "And there was another." He handed the bewildered Marius another bag. I frowned. "This one was harder to find. It was inside a mattress. I think it belonged to Hiratius. He slept there, near the wine cellar."

Marius hefted two bags of what was obviously coins.

He poured both on the floor.

Gold and silver gleamed. They were heavy coins,

drachmae. The centurion picked up one of each. "Snake and crane."

Pericles shuddered. "What? My coins? Snake is mine and...crane. Kyrillos. Kyrillos used my coins. He is...that bastard. He must be killed. Tortured to death."

We gave the gentle Pericles a surprised look, and then stared at the coins.

"Did you pay to poison Gaius?" I asked Pericles. "Did you pay for Hiratius's soul?"

"No!" he yelled. "Of course not!"

"That's a lot of gold there, Pericles," I said softly. "A lot of it. Enough to pay for a dead king."

"Anyone can have my coin!" he yelled in fear. "I am a merchant, as well as a noble!" He had not forgotten how Amyntas had died. "Anyone!"

"Kyrillos," I said. "Apollon. All traitors. It seems, Pericles, that your Kyrillos stripped you of your Roman patronage after all."

"But—"

I silenced Pericles with a wave of hand. "Can this Hiratius leave the city?"

Alexander walked back and forth. "I have sent men all over the land. No ship or boat has left the harbor this morning, or night. All the fishermen have been contained. The roads are blocked. We have messengers riding like the wind to make sure Hiratius will not find refuge anywhere if he left the city. But I feel he is still in the city. Hiding. He will be hiding with Kyrillos, hoping their rebellion will succeed." He lifted his shoulders in a labored shrug.

"It seems we underestimated Kyrillos," I muttered. "Marius. How does the guard of Gaius take this? They want vengeance, no doubt."

Antius stepped forward. "Damned well they want that. I shall lead our men—"

"You be quiet, Antius," I said. "Marius?"

The centurion rubbed his head. "The century is in shock," he said. "They all expect to bleed the bastard."

"Many men will die for this," I said softly. "Arm my men. Shields and helmets. We have chain. Pila, if you have many. Lead your men to the street. We shall meet Alexander's men near the Agora. Find Short and Tall to guide us."

Marius nodded. He began yelling orders.

I got up and walked out. I turned to Segolia. "You must stay here."

"I am not here to be safe," she said coldly.

"You are here to help me," I told her. "No matter how unpleasant the duty. Trust me on this." Her eyes went to Antius.

The bastard would pay.

"Find out where the scrolls are," I told her. "It is important."

She nodded. I turned to Hercules. "Lock the door to this room if Segolia is not here. Do not let anyone enter, and make sure the guards keep everyone inside here." I saw Marcus the guard, looking dejected and alone in the corridor. "Marius!"

"Celcus?" the man said, turning.

"Marcus must stay here with the men who guard Vipsania and the house. And make sure that Avila is here as well."

"Why?"

"Because," I said, "both must survive this morning. Pericles, you shall go to war with us."

They pushed out Pericles, and we walked out to find gear.

Blood would spill.

CHAPTER 7

The Agora was full of people. The moneylenders, for a while, were quiet. The orators were listening to Apollon, their faces gleaming with oils, and the merchants were hawking their wares, but quietly, giving those who listened a refreshing drink or a fruit.

The whole area seemed to twitch with anger and heat.

There were two hundred people, mostly men, around Kyrillos, who was on his knees on a makeshift platform, and Apollon, who was speaking furiously.

I couldn't hear him them, but I would soon.

I cursed him to Hades. The hot-headed, pretty boy had created quite a trouble for us by freeing Kyrillos. He couldn't have afforded to pay for the murder, but he was guilty of much. He would be guilty of much more.

We marched forward with the century, their standard high, through a street, emptied of life, and dust billowed, shields clanked together, and chain jingled. The inexorable trump of hobnailed caligae promised brutal end to the small rebellion.

With me were Marius and forty legionnaires, and some hundred Lycians were waiting on the edge of Agora.

"I bet they are all cockless shits," Marius snarled. "Cockless. We'll do this alone."

I hefted my shield. "It will look bad. But it matters little now."

I held my sword, and Hercules and my men had pila, the javelins. Antius was coming last, silent and brooding. He and two others, Alexander with them, were escorting Pericles, who had a wide, floppy hat, and looked like he would have liked to be anywhere but there. There was no energy in the man, his body bereft of a soul.

I gazed at the men.

They all looked excited, happy, ferocious as a pack of damned dogs, and I felt sorry for the bastards we were about to meet. The century had missed battle, had been reduced to baby care duties in a land where there was little to do but to eat, drink, and stand guard. Now, they would show their mettle.

Gaius is dead, I thought.

Augustus will be looking for heads.

We'll give him some.

I watched Kyrillos. He was looking up to the sky, utterly crushed. His wife was there with him.

Apollon was the loud bastard amid them. The actor was holding a sword up to the air. And now, I could hear him. "Murderers! They are murderers, the lot! They came here, to our city, invited as a friend to one's house, and what happens? Not only do they favor those who lick their shitty arses, they try to make sure none can ever match them in riches and wealth! If one does? Woe to him! Look at Kyrillos! He sold wine to Rome, to Athens, and wine to Alexandria! He did better than Pericles! He had opinions! That's his crime!"

The crowd cheered wildly. They cheered themselves hoarse and stared at the powerful actor, someone they admired, and lamented Kyrillos's fate.

Apollon roared away. "A crime of having opinions, apparently, is a heavy one in Rome. This city, Limyra, to be part of Rome! That's what they want. Nay, say I! Nay! Let Gaius be gone! Let them all rot! And if they do not go? I say let them stay! Where, citizens? Where shall they stay?"

The crowd had apparently been taught the answer.

"Inside the mountain! In a tomb!" they called out hoarsely.

Marius growled like an animal. "I'll show you lot a tomb. I'll pull your guts out through your noses, you bastards."

His men mumbled assent.

On the edges of the group, many men were turning to see our approach. Apollon cared not, apparently.

"Tomb, tomb for the killers of Amyntas! The centurion who tortured him, he must be judged! The other one ripped apart!" he went on, frothing in mouth. "Liars both!"

"He is mine, if possible," Antius called out.

"No promises," Marius laughed. "Never killed one so pretty!"

Hercules grinned. "I'll get him ready for you, Celcus. I am lucky. He'll come for me."

"Make ready," Marius snarled, as we arrived in the Agora proper.

We spread out at the edge of the agora. We pushed to the stalls and the tents, trampled some, and stood in a line of three. The enemy watched us, and they were milling with confusion. Apollon kneeled next to Kyrillos and was speaking to some of his brutes softly. They spread out to push and bully the men to turn towards us. At least ten local soldiers were amongst them.

On the edges of the Agora, people were backing off in their thousands.

The two to three hundred in the middle didn't think about leaving.

We stared at them. I watched Alexander lead Pericles out and then look at his troop of a hundred local men. They stood near the northern edge of the agora, sullen and silent.

I grinned. "I doubt your boys want any part in this, Alexander. They look entirely cockless, as Marius predicted. Make sure it stays that way, so this will only be a small battle. It must not turn to a war, and you well know it."

He gave me an unkind eye and snarled an order to one of his men, a subordinate. The man rushed off to speak to the soldiers.

Antius walked to Pericles. He squinted up at the man. "You don't look like you are up to this task, Pericles. For your city, you must perform, little bird."

He closed his eyes. "Let the city burn."

I stared at him in surprise and then leaned closer. "If

the city burns, then your family will burn with it. For them, give it your best shot. For your girls, at least."

"And you think they will cave in?" he asked, with just a tiny bit of energy. "My sweet Eudoxia...my girls must survive, but I cannot..."

"Gaius is dead, Pericles," I said brutally. "Save your family, at least."

Pericles rode forward. I saw Apollon climbing to his feet, and he was pulling Kyrillos up with him. The man had torn his clothing, his skin, in his sorrow, in his terrible sorrow.

"Amyntas!" he called, and the crowd before him growled as they spread more to hold the middle of the Agora. "Are you bringing my boy, Pericles? Are you here to tell me how I am forfeited of my legacy, my blood, my city?"

The people roared their anger. Some stones were tossed, and they landed near us. The legionnaires were silent and deadly looking professionals. Pericles was shaking and gagging.

Antius spat. "Get your shit together, you useless bag of crap. Fix this, or I'll feed you to them piecemeal!"

Pericles was nodding and swallowing. He lifted his hand, but the crowd was laughing.

"Louder!" Antius sneered. "Your cries do not echo out of your mouth."

Alexander cursed and walked forward. He pulled a sword and took his helmet off. His long hair billowed in the wind, and he, his armor shining, looked like Mars himself. His voice echoed out of his mouth. "Citizens of Limyra!" he roared.

The crowd of hundreds shifted on their feet. They stared at him, and some spoke but not loudly. They were a milling mass in a rough halfmoon shape around us and in the middle of the agora but were contained for a moment.

Apollon scowled at Alexander. "A dog of Pericles, or not, Alexander, you and we have no reason to fight. Brother, stay your men from this, and let us deal justice. See, some of our soldiers joined us. You should too."

"Pericles," Alexander called out, "is the leader of the city! A member of Lycian rulership! He is the—" The crowed jeered him. "He is the lord of Limyra, who sees further than you do! You killed Gaius Caesar, Kyrillos. Apollon, no doubt, you are in on it as well. You attended the feast of Gaius and killed your host! There will be a price all Limyra must pay! All of us, even those who have done not a thing! Kyrillos! Your son paid for his crimes. Who is next? Tell your ragged bastards to go home!"

The silence was deafening.

They all stared at Alexander, hesitating.

"Who is next?" Alexander yelled. "Give yourself up, Apollon, and Kyrillos. The soldiers who betrayed me will be punished, no matter who their father is."

Kyrillos shook his head.

Apollon stepped forward. "Gaius is dead? The horn was for him?"

Alexander nodded. "Murdered!"

Apollon had doubts about his rebellion. You could see it in his shocked face. The fool had exploded into action, and now he realized he was in a boiling water.

Kyrillos closed his eyes and had no doubts.

From agony of despair, the man saw the crowds swaying with fear. He gave them new purpose.

"They took him!" he yelled. "They took my boy! And they ask us to fear Rome? Best die brave, people. I spit on Gaius and his ilk. I say, kill the Romans and make this a truly free city once more!"

"Yes!" yelled his wife, Aristomache, who had torn her face and hair. "They killed him like a dog. In his own shit, my poor boy, they tortured him. For a lie! For lies!" She was moaning and beating her chest next to Kyrillos. "The horn must be blown for all Romans!" she cried. "Death!"

The men, hundreds of them, snarled assent. "Death to the dogs! Death! Freedom for Limyra!"

"Death to them!" moaned Kyrillos. "For my son, and Limyra! Death to Pericles, the Roman loving dog! To the tomb with them! Obol for the brave, nothing for the others!"

The Lycian troop stepped back.

The thronging mass stepped forward, the more powerful, stronger ones propelling the others forward.

We stayed still.

Apollon jumped down with his sword and waded amidst his men. He turned to the toughest men in the

233

crowd, which was three hundred strong now, and pointed the sword at us. "Kill them! Kill the liars and show them Lycia stands as one."

A man hesitated, bearded and huge.

He stepped forward, holding a cudgel. Another, thin and with a very tanned face, stepped with him, picking up a rock.

The Lycians with us, stepped back, nervous. They pulled Pericles back, and Antius pointed a finger towards Gaius's house.

Alexander retreated to our troop as Pericles was taken away.

Marius shrugged. "Kill them, boys. Show them how Rome fills graves. Pila! Get ready!"

The legionnaires, all forty of them, lifted their javelins. The threatening flash of their shields, the gleam of our armor, the three ranks of sturdy legionnaires, killers the lot, should have made the enemy wither away.

"Kill them! For me, for Lycia!" hollered Kyrillos. "For Amyntas!"

The men roared and ran at us.

They moved in a chaotic wave, fastest and strongest first, others following, jostling each other, and came at us with vengeance. Rabble, young and wild, were all brave, many drunk, and all spoiling for a fight. No doubt with coin of Kyrillos in their hand, they were also genuinely enraged by the sight of our troops.

I lifted my shield. The praetorians stood around me

in the middle.

Marius growled an order. Arms pumped. The pila flashed in the air.

They sunk to the mass of men rushing for us in the middle.

The weapons ate lives, and nearly twenty men crashed down on their faces before us. They screamed, wept, and begged, and then, the mob rolled over them.

We lifted our shields and braced ourselves. I saw a man coming, just in front of me, aiming a cudgel for me. He was roaring, eyes wild. He swung the weapon but met my shield. The guard smashed to his face, the sword cut below it to his belly, and I pulled back. A man was on my side, and I cut to his neck and had no time to watch what happened to him as I saw a flash. An ax cut down at me. I threw my shield up, felt the jarring impact, and stabbed at the figure. The blade went in, and stayed in flesh, the man spitting blood on my face.

I stepped back and stabbed again.

The sword tore to his chest, and throat, and the man fell. I hazarded a glance around me, and saw a legionnaire down, bloodied and shivering, and two men laying over him, both crying with horrible wounds. Our men were bending, and tightening around the standard, and Hercules, smashing his shield on an angry woman, pulled me back.

We chanted and stabbed repeatedly, and suddenly, there was a great press of men all around us. Our shields were together, our blades were thrusting, and the smell of fear, that of piss and shit smearing the thighs of dying and dead, filled the air.

It was a Roman world, that battle line.

It was a Roman sport, a place where killers endured, and while the throng, massive and angry was pushing at us, panting and hacking at the men, it was inevitably a place where the enemy would die.

Unless they grew smart.

"Push around them!" I heard a man call. "Fast!"

One of the Lycian soldiers was maneuvering his men to the side. They were pressing forward to our right flank. I nodded at Hercules and found Antius just behind me, his eyes wild. "This way," I called to them, while men took my place in the middle, slamming shields at unarmored drunks, stabbing them down like cows.

I shifted through our men, and we came to the back of the troop. We hopped over corpses and wounded and ran to the very end of the line.

There, the Lycians soldiers were now facing us.

They hesitated. One of the legionnaires glanced at me, and he and his friends stepped next to me and Hercules. Antius was near.

"At them, at them," he was hissing.

We went at them.

I walked towards the mob. The Lycian soldiers, having anticipated a mighty military feat by getting behind us, found few madmen walking for them. I stared at the men before me from under my helmet's rim and smiled at them.

The trash, the mob, many of them wounded, afraid, parted before us.

The soldiers, seven, stayed.

"Kill them," hissed the leader, and his helmet gleaming, he charged.

He came too fast and left his friends behind.

His spear flashed, and Hercules took the blade with his shield.

I smashed the sword to the man's throat.

His chain turned red, and he died at the end of the blade. A man tossed a spear at me, and it tore to a back of a legionnaire, missing us.

I walked to him and sawed the blade on his thigh so deep, he fell and shivered in agony. Hercules stepped on him.

I went forward, and the rest came at me.

They descended on me with shields and swords. They slammed the guards on mine, the swords at me. One struck my helmet and left me dizzy. One grated on my chain but couldn't get through. I pressed back and spat at their faces.

Hercules stepped past me, toppled one like he would a small boy, hopped on the fallen man hard, and then over the man and went into enraged battle-frenzy. His sword cut at a soldier's neck. He blasted the hilt into another's face. I suddenly found myself free.

Marius called out behind us, "At the weak shits!"

Every eye had been following our battle.

As Hercules began killing, the throng had blinked and stepped back, and back.

The thirty legionnaires who were left attacked wildly.

Men vailed, fled, and died.

Hercules and I chased the soldiers. I kicked legs out from under one. I stabbed on his armpit and tore at the flesh and left him bleeding to death. Antius passed me and stabbed at one who was turning, and I took the man's throat. A man, then two, got past me, then behind me, but both died and fell. I staggered forward in the rush and found two men tearing at my shield. I braced and cursed and stabbed and pushed. A man fell, then another, and I stepped forward and stabbed down.

The mob was disintegrating.

They were falling and running away, and the merchants in the agora were hiding behind their stalls.

I didn't look around me. I heard someone screaming in Latin, a soldier in pain. I heard the storm of caligae around me, and the sound of blade opening flesh, scraping bone, the chants of our soldiers. Our men were now looting fast before moving after me. I walked forward, over corpses and wounded, and saw Kyrillos. He was still where we had seen him and was holding his wife, who was moaning with a wound on her temple.

He saw me coming and put her down.

Men were running past them, a stream of them, some wounded, and when I saw Kyrillos again, he was coming for me, and his wife was gone.

He seemed almost relieved.

He came forward and walked for me, the short sword trembling.

I nodded at him.

"Liars," he hissed. "Bastards. Murderers."

He roared, his eyes full of fear, and hacked down.

I bashed the shield into the blade, and him, the sword flashing. The blade split his chest; he made a croaking, horrified sound, and fell on his back heavily. I looked around and saw no sign of Apollon.

It was suddenly quiet.

The Lycians at the edge of the agora were still, and Alexander was there, talking to them.

Pericles was gone.

Men were rushing to the city, fleeing like hares. The legionnaires stopped wordlessly as Marius held his sword high. Some were looting still, and I let them. Marius was soon walking about, stabbing at corpses, and Alexander was soon approaching slowly, his face pale as he watched the carnage.

He stopped near me and eyed his soldiers. "I knew some of these men."

"You don't have the belly for it?" I asked him. "They came at us. They are piss-poor fighters, by the way."

"They were just fools," he lamented. "They will never forget this."

"They should, and they will," I told him. "Apollon?

"He ran for his theatre," Alexander said. "He was

pulling Andromache with him. Kyrillos…this changes things. No matter what was right and what was wrong, you must stay out of sight. We shall take to the streets and keep the peace, but many people will speak against you."

Antius spat. "You will keep the peace? Right."

I lifted my hand and infuriated Antius. "We shall guard lady Vipsania, and we will leave when we can. It seems our mission is finished, though with great loss. Alas for Gaius. May Juppiter guard us all from the wrath of Augustus. But first, we must finish this. I want Apollon."

"Let us go find him," said the Lycian. "The fool has gone too far."

Marius turned to me. I nodded at his dead and wounded. "Get them all back to the house of Gaius. We shall be there shortly. I doubt they dare to defy us now."

***

We found the theatre nestled on the slope of the mountain. Up above us were several tombs carved on the mountain's side, and above them, the Tomb of the original Pericles and the acropolis named after him. Hercules was wiping sweat of his face, and my other men, all of whom survived the butchery, were looking at the house right next to the theatre.

It was rather drab, almost ramshackle, and in need of repairs. The pillars on the outside were faded red, and while once glorious, it seemed birds now inhabited the upper floors. Eagle had been painted on one wall, and

240

you could not be sure of any of the other paintings.

The door was open, and inside, Apollon was wailing.

Eurydike was standing before the doors, looking at us and trembling. Her kind face was pale, and she was crying.

Alexander wiped sweat off his face. "We need him. You know this, Eurydike."

"You do?" she asked. "Amyntas. We need no other killings like that. If that is the plan, please, let him go. He was just upset. He has been under great deal of pressure. Can you believe me? His heart is broken for Gaius. They were, once, good friends. Please—"

Alexander shook his head.

She grimaced at him and went to her knees. "You are one of us. What have they promised you to make you fall this low? Where is your mercy? What did your uncle give you?"

"I serve the state, and not him," Alexander said. "And we need the peace-breaker."

Eurydike looked at us, and shuddered with fear, and revulsion. "Please," she whispered. "Do not kill him."

I was acutely aware I was bloodied, with my hair sticking up with the gore under my helmet. The rest were as well, their armor a grim reminder of what happens when you go against Rome.

"He shall live," I said. "We want Aristomache. And him. Both shall go to Rome. They will stay with the century. You have my word, Eurydike, that they shall survive me, if not Augustus."

241

Antius spat. "It is not for you to give. These dogs—"

I turned and slapped Antius. His helmet fell, and I kept my hand on a sword's hilt. "Shut the hell up."

He looked at me in shock and then stepped back. Hercules stood before him. I turned back to Eurydike. "You have my word."

She hesitated and then nodded. "Very well, then. I trust your word. But my son had better survive you, as you promised."

I shrugged. "His survival is in his hands."

She stepped towards us. "Look. Kyrillos. He betrayed us. He is trying to make it seem—"

"Kyrillos is dead," I said. "What do you mean?"

"Go and see," she said and wept.

Alexander and I walked forward and entered the rooms beyond. There, we found Aristomache also weeping, holding her face, and the wound. Apollon was standing to the side and stared at a corpse in his home.

Aristomache got up and trembled. "It was him. Apollon. Not my husband. I fled here, and when I came in, he was standing over the two."

Hiratius. Dead. On Hiratius's side, there was a horn. I looked up at Apollon. "You. Or Kyrillos as well."

He let out a deep breath and closed his eyes. "Him, if any! We didn't do this! I just wanted justice! I freed him, and he had obviously paid for this. That was Gaius's food taster. I know him, obviously. They tried to make me—"

"Take them to the house of Gaius," I said. "We shall

keep them there. Fetters on legs, and hands, and a locked room for both. His mother may see him."

She nodded at me, her old face tear-streaked, and mouthed 'thank you.'

And then, I saw Segolia. And I knew, something was terribly off.

Her face was a mask of worry, and she came to us. She gave Marius a nod, avoided Antius, and came to stand before me.

"Gaius," she whispered.

"What of Gaius?" I asked. "Did you find the missing scrolls? What happened to them?"

"You must come and see," she insisted. "It is more than about some scrolls. Someone was in there that night as he died."

CHAPTER 8

I kneeled next to Gaius and watched the body. I looked up at Segolia. She hesitated and pointed at him. "There was someone here," she said again.

"Why?" I asked and shook my head. "We just caught the killer. Kyrillos, though likely Apollon was on it. Hiratius's body was in his house, and he had silenced the man. There was another horn there as well."

Marius, Pericles, and Laodamia stood in the room looking at us, perplexed. Outside, in the house, a murmur of speech echoed as Apollon and Aristomache were brought forth, and a jingle of fetters. The screams of the wounded echoed from the house next to ours, and soldiers were moving about, nervous.

Alexander was looking at us as he brought the prisoners in, and I waited until he arrived in the study.

Segolia shook her head, annoyed. "Someone was in this room and watched him die."

"Did he scream out?" Pericles asked. "Surely, he would have screamed. She is right. I have been wondering about that. In the other cases, the killer watched them die, slowly go to Hades, incapable of crying out. Probably the man kept them quiet until they could no longer breathe. It must have been the case here as well."

"Segolia?" I asked.

"He bled," she said. "To death."

We watched the body.

"So much blood," said Pericles with soft horror.

"He shat his guts out," I said. "He might have bitten his tongue out while he thrashed, suffered, and died, and the blood here...something broke inside him."

"No," she said. "He bled to death."

"There's not enough blood for it," I insisted. "I've gutted men before, you know."

Segolia stepped forward. She came to the other side of Gaius and looked at me. "I'll move him a bit."

"Why?" Pericles asked. "You shouldn't. Let the servants wash him. Let them give him the coin here, in this room, but—"

She grunted as she examined the body. Then, she was pulling at the arm, which was rigid. Pericles's face was white with fear, and he winced as Segolia forced the arm to move, and then Gaius came off the floor, his chest and belly in sight.

"See," Segolia said as she looked at the bloody mess.

I reached closer.

The tunic was ripped, and there was a ghastly wound in his abdomen. Blue and red guts were oozing out of it, and blood and mucus still flowed to the floor. There was that wide crack on the stone, and it was filled with blood, and guts. Pericles gagged, stepped out, and ran out of the room. We heard him throwing up and weeping.

Segolia nodded. "I was seeking for evidence and moved him. I saw it. He bled out to the crack on the floor."

Alexander stared at the wound. "Poisoned and still stabbed?" he asked softly. "Who did it?"

I rubbed my face, thinking. "No. Wait. This is not possible."

Alexander was voicing my thoughts. "Did he do it himself? To escape the pain?"

"A wide dagger did it," Segolia said, eyeing the wound. "Pugio. Gladius. Something like you people use here in Limyra. It is no small knife." Her eyes travelled the room, and she got up. I pushed at the body of Gaius and groped under him desperately. After a search, we found nothing.

"I looked," Segolia said, her eyes serious as she stared into my eyes. "There is not a single weapon in this room. I searched the floor, the ceiling, the sofa, the desk. Nothing. Nothing on him either. The killer was in this room and left with the blade. And the scrolls."

"Who has entered this room this night?" I asked Marius.

The man twisted and stepped out, face pale. Then, in a moment, the guard, Marcus, looked in. He was the same brute of a man, with a scar on his chin, and his eyes rested on Gaius. There were tears in his eyes.

"Get in!" Marius roared. The man stiffened, and half pushed past Pericles to come inside and kept his head up. "Stand there and answer questions."

"Yes, sir," he murmured.

I pointed a finger at Gaius. "Who," I snarled, "have been in here this very night, or this morning? Speak, man."

"You, she," he said stiffly as he looked at Segolia. "The noble and this Pericles. Our centurion. That Lycian captain there. And none else, save for the ghosts."

Marius snarled. "That man has a stab wound."

He squinted. He looked uncertain. "Then, one of you must have given it to him. Sir. After he died."

"He bled to death," I snarled. "The wound was bleeding when he was alive."

Marcus was squinting and shrugged. "Nobody was in here, save for Gaius."

Alexander stood before him. "It was you then."

"How dare you, sir?" Marcus breathed. "How dare you."

Alexander dared. "Who found the body?"

The soldier shrugged and looked at Marius as if begging him to save him from the Lycian He spoke to me, past Alexander's shoulder. "His wife. Sort of. I did. She came here early and demanded to see him. Gaius never slept late, and Cassius had a dozen people asking to meet him. The local clients wanted to see their patron, and the morning reception was very late. She was up and about and worried. Cassius usually had lined up people who wanted to see her as well, minor clients who hoped she might influence Gaius, but not this morning. There were none for her. She was bored? She came here with a servant. Demanded I open the door for them. She claimed she wanted to tell Gaius he is a shivering little shit. I did, reluctantly open the door, for I thought it

247

might be amusing to hear her calling the great man shivering little shit." We stared at him, and he went on, shrugging. "Then she saw this. Then, she screamed. She passed out in the garden. Her servants stopped her from falling and got her up on her feet, and I sealed the door...until you arrived, that is."

I stared at him with fury. "And you told me to let him rest."

He said nothing.

"Did you sleep?" I asked him.

"Never! Death penalty, and loss of honor, sir! Not for me. Honor, and—"

"Did you fucking drink?" I snarled. "Were you drunk, soldier? Sodden to the bone? And perhaps fucking a woman? I know you fancy Vipsania's servants."

"Cup of wine, which we are allowed," he defended himself. "Two, perhaps. I don't fuck on duty, sir! Only in my thoughts. And neither girl cares for me. Not one bit. Larissa had an affair with the thief Ennius, and Ariane is...sad. Terrified. You have seen her. Would be no fun humping either one. I would, but it would not be worth losing my life for."

I walked to stare into his eyes. "None came in? None left? Not one person during the entire night?" I asked, and he shook his head. "Did the women go in? Ariane, Larissa? Did they have a sword?" I asked.

"Not unless the women had them up their arses," he retorted. "I didn't check, but I doubt it. No blades were

248

visible. And they didn't go in, did they? None of them. Not even Vipsania, who simply screamed right there on the doorway."

"Did you not hear anything?" I asked, stepped away while holding my face. "You stood here, like a stupid damned fucking mule, and you heard not a thing? It was a painful death."

He shuffled his feet. "I don't understand it. I heard nothing. I heard him laughing, of course, but that is it."

I blinked. "Laughing."

He looked uncertain. "Yes, sir. Laughing. I was here on night duty many a time this past month. He was always laughing, and very late. Perhaps those poems made him happy? He wrote many a night. Or, perhaps, he laughed in his sleep. Some people do that. Especially when they are hungry."

I looked at the desk. Only the remains of the meal were on it. "I don't suppose the door guards remember if they didn't see someone leaving?"

Marius sighed. "It was a feast. They were running in and out. Anyone might have stayed here. Most of the rooms are empty. I will ask, but no, I doubt it."

Segolia was still walking the dark edges of the room. She shook her head.

"There are no poems here," she said. "Nothing else. He died in company of someone. It is irrefutable fact there was someone in this room."

"He wrote the poems on scrolls," he said. "They were taken away each morning for safekeeping. Not this morning, obviously."

"Where?" I asked. "Who did that?"

"Hiratius," he said. "The man had no real duties, so he carried them off."

"By Juppiter's arse crack!" I roared. "He is dead!"

"I know not what to tell you!" Marcus answered. "Look, sir, I have no idea why he is dead. Well, yes, I see why, but—"

I stared at the wound. "Who stabbed him? He must have laughed with someone."

He shrugged. "I know not! He was happy, sir. He sounded happy. Perhaps he laughed because he was happy? He certainly was not dying unless he found a fondness for it."

"Perhaps he laughed," I said tiredly, "because he was not alone? He had a lover. The sofa's stained with his fluids."

He blinked. "His... no. I don't know. They all say he did. But if...well. One was inside?"

"None came in, none came out?" I asked him irascibly.

He shook his head. "I saw nobody. Ask Avila if someone came in earlier. I was here before him, that day, and saw it being cleaned, and it was empty then. Avila's an arse, so he might have left someone in and forgotten to order them out."

"No other doors to the room? Any side rooms to this one?"

"None, sir," he said, and turned to his centurion.

"Sir—"

"Silence," Marius snarled.

We were all silent and thinking. "There," Pericles said eventually, having recovered somewhat, "was someone in here. There were no screams for help. That someone stabbed him. Made sure he didn't make a sound. He—"

"Or she," Segolia said. "It might have been a woman. If he had a lover, he might have been here, reading poetry to the trollop, while they…"

Alexander was nodding, his eyes on the corpse. "It wasn't Hiratius, or the cook Dareios. Both left. I wonder where Dareios is."

"She, he," I said irascibly. "Gaius had someone here, and he knew the person."

"It is a her, then," the soldier said. "It is always so. Look, sir—"

"Silence, you bastard," Marius snarled. "Get out, and—"

"Let the mule speak," I said. "He will have to, anyway. Avila as well."

The man didn't like my tone. He had no reason to. He knew I was unhappy, and he saw the blood on my arms and face.

He began to speak. "I--

"The horn," Alexander interrupted Marcus. "I don't understand it."

"Why?" I asked him.

"Your boys said the horn was hidden in Amyntas's

room," he said. "If Apollon or Kyrillos did this, and got in here, or someone else for them, and murdered Gaius for his son and then Kyrillos tried to raise the people against you, then why hide the horn? He was trying to incite a rebellion. Why not proudly declare his accomplishment? He never mentioned it." He shook his head as he watched Gaius. "In fact, he looked surprised Gaius was dead. Apollon too."

Marcus stepped forward. "I can tell you this, sir, but I think I need not, for you look like you have been a proper soldier once." I glared at him, and he ignored my look. "Few men would die of poison without screaming for help. You would rush to the door and gag your life away where you are seen. Few men have the strength to kill themselves like this. Someone was here, and I know not what happened to that someone. I do not lie. As a soldier to a soldier, I swear on Mars, nobody came in or left. Sir, I think there is another explanation here. It might not sound feasible—"

"You think it was a ghost," I sneered. "This was the work of a Fury? That would be convenient, for you. I, too, could kill a man and then claim it were a god who struck him down before I could."

He nodded and glowered at me darkly. "It is possible Kleitos and the traders were killed by Amyntas, but this one seems like the work of something inhuman. See, no way out."

I rubbed my forehead. "Your rank?" I asked him.

"Duplicarius."

"Marcus the duplicarius," I said. "You will stay in this house until further notice. Is that clear?"

"My centurion—"

"Will obey," I said coldly, and Marius gave me an evil eye. "You are now in our troop. You are under arrest."

Marius bristled. "I will not see him—"

"You will," I told him. "Since Gaius cannot speak, Marcus must stay here."

"Your mutt was here too!" he roared. "Hercules. He can testify for me."

Antius and Hercules came forward. I turned to Hercules. "He guarded Vipsania, on my orders."

Marius nodded. "Let us not argue amongst ourselves. It is his study. We have a man here all the time. The man before him would have kept it sealed like Marcus did. Avila and Marcus were here yesterday, all day. Marcus, the night and up until late afternoon, since he hoped to attract the girls' attention, the fool, and Avila, from afternoon to evening. Neither will have let people come and go without a leave."

"That one is under arrest as well," I said. "Get him here. Into a room."

"They will not know a thing," Marius said, nervous. "They are all good soldiers and follow orders. They do not know a thing."

"They must know something," Segolia said. "They are under arrest, but for their own protection. They might know something, and someone might try to kill

253

them."

I gave her a small, grateful glance. She looked away, and I cursed silently. I had no time to think about our tragedy. Marius nodded, reluctantly. "I shall take them to our barrack instead. What next?"

Silence. We all stared at Gaius, as if hoping for him to tell us what had taken place.

He remained silent.

I walked to the desk and leaned on it. I looked at the remains of the meal and found most everything else gone from the desk. "This room is dark."

"The room is damned dark," Segolia said. "Someone might have hidden themselves here early last night."

I looked at the shadows. It was possible. "I was here. I didn't look. That killer might have been here."

Marius was nodding, and Alexander shook his head.

"Someone killed," Segolia said. "Someone left. All must be questioned."

"None entered," Marcus said stubbornly. "None left."

"Well," I said darkly, "we shall find out. Alexander, you shall keep a guard on the outer door and around the walls. I will set my men to guard the insides."

"What of lady Vipsania?" Marius asked, and looked annoyed as Pericles sobbed. "We must guard her now. She is the next highest target."

Pericles shook his head. "Are you saying Kyrillos didn't do these things? That there might be yet another person killing Romans?"

"All I am saying is we must find the person who was in this room," I said. "Kyrillos and Apollon clearly poisoned him, but who stabbed him? It wasn't Hiratius, and it wasn't Kyrillos or Apollon. There is someone else. Either they are connected or not."

Alexander stepped forward. "I will provide men to the doorways. And to walk the perimeter. But, after today…we need them outside on the streets as well."

"A question," I heard a woman say.

It was Vipsania. She was pale as she came forth.

"Lady?" I asked. She suppressed a smile. Not at me. At Gaius. She was happy to see him dead.

"You have the killer," she said. "Kyrillos. Apollon. Take him to Rome. Let Augustus kill him. Why worry about this?"

I shook my head at her. "Because the truth matters. It matters for all of us." I gave her a warning look and then turned Marius. "Gather everyone into the atrium, and let them drink, and rest. I shall speak with them shortly. Hercules, Marius, and Segolia. Antius. Stay here."

Alexander pushed away, face taut.

Marius looked at me. "What are you planning? There is no way to know who was here unless you can see the into the past."

"There are ways," I said. "But let us taunt the enemy into revealing itself. Tell me," I asked. "Do we have any prisoners from the battle?"

"A few?" he said. "I can find out." Segolia looked

255

down, trying to hide her fear.

I looked at Antius and Hercules and nodded inside the room. They filed in, and I closed the door.

We spoke for a long time, argued, and eventually, we came out, and I walked to the atrium.

There, a sea of sad, terrified faces greeted me.

***

Pericles stepped forward. "You have requested to have us here. What do you want to tell us? Did you find out who—"

"Who killed Gaius?" I asked. "Apollon. Kyrillos. They are guilty. At least Kyrillos is. It is clear. His coins, and his sorrow drove him to it. The food taster, greedy bastard, helped him. But as to who was there with him? Anyone of you is a possibility. You all had your reasons to hate him."

Eudoxia sobbed. Bernike shook her head. Pericles opened his arms to refute me. "Apollon. Surely he—"

"Perhaps not," I said. "Perhaps so. In any case, I have no idea how a person got in there, unless they paid our legionnaires. We will find out. Apollon, and Andromache, do pay attention."

The man was in the corner, in fetters, a hopeless look on his face. Eurydike was next to him. Andromache was next to him, in similar chains.

"There was someone else there," I said. "Why did he die? Two possibilities. Here is the first. One of you aided those two in the murder. He was first poisoned, and someone, somehow got into that room to make sure he

256

dies. The other one? One of you hated him so much, they were in there to kill him, regardless of Kyrillos, unaware Gaius had eaten poison. In any case, Gaius knew the person. He met the person there many a time. They laughed. Marcus was often on the doorway. He will know."

The lesser clients were shivering like leaves.

They were the drunkards and sycophants of Gaius, and I nodded at guards. "Take them to your barracks. We shall speak to them later. We look at the bigger fish now, as we rattle the nets."

We waited, as they were hauled out.

When they were gone, Laodamia spoke, having fumed. "He was a friend to the city," she said darkly. "Perhaps you should question Apollon as to who killed him. Andromache, also. I am sure they hired someone, and, like they bought off Hiratius and the cook Dareios, they bought off your guard. To be honest, I'd say your Marcus did it."

Alexander nodded. "I agree."

I looked at Apollon who leaned against the wall. "Certainly, he had a reason to hate Gaius. Kyrillos did as well. The death of Amyntas—"

Aristomache, her face smeared with tears, cursed us all. "Traitors. Betrayers and bastard dog-sons. Aye, my family, as that of Meliton, raised concerns for our well-being! Nothing more! We have killed no-one!"

I went on. "And you raised rabble to rail against Rome. You did. Do not deny it. After the death of

Amyntas, Apollon and Kyrillos tried to raise the city to rebellion. I agree they hired Hiratius, even, to bring low Gaius, the symbol of Roman power. They may act they didn't, but they would lie. The very son of Augustus! Dead? What better way to start a war."

Andromache vailed. "We did not!"

I laughed. "Oh, you did not? Kill Gaius! And let the world burn after." I shook my head at them. "You all had a reason to kill him. Wealth ruined your balance. Fear. Kyrillos, rich, even richer than Pericles before Gaius came, and rapidly gaining power in the city, was a threat. Meliton as well. Kyrillos did kill Gaius. But who would help him? And for what?"

"And Apollon?" asked the man himself miserably. "What of him? Surely I am guilty as well."

Eurydike was crouched near him. I pointed a finger his way. "Pity to him," I said. "His reason? Anger. Betrayal. He is a man who fetched Gaius here, and received nothing for it. The shackles are his price for foolishness."

"Pity he gets, but no mercy," Antius said.

Eurydike shook her old head. "What of Laodamia's crimes? What of those? Surely, she too, had a reason to kill   Gaius?"

"Keep your calm, beggar," Laodamia said. "Let the centurion speak of your son."

I snorted at Laodamia. "Let us speak of both. Heartless. Eurydike is right. Pericles. Your family had lost its riches before you married Laodamia. Your family is ancient and has a name. Laodamia's is younger and has the coin. Together, you made a new, successful family. Alexander, he serves you well."

Alexander said nothing. He scowled at me.

I walked back and forth. "You made an ally of Meliton by agreeing to share your riches and blood, but in the end," I said slowly, "your wife cheated Meliton. Laodamia did. You, Pericles, likely promised Eurydike and Apollon back the favor you have apparently stripped from them for something foolish, and I suspect it has something to do with Lysirate, and your wife? Laodamia betrayed them, in your name."

She said nothing either. Lysirate smiled sadly. Pericles fought tears.

I went on. "They were your clients, Pericles. You let your wife harm them."

Pericles looked down. He put a hand on Eudoxia's shoulder, and the girl began weeping, her bravery spent.

"Laodamia," I went on, "did do you a favor. She saved your family from the two more powerful traders, by luring Gaius here. Apollon was the key. She likely sent others to make an impression. Many kings and queens did, so she was no different. The great man was the talk of the east, after all. Everyone wanted his favor. Then, she suddenly had Gaius. Here! Wounded, sad. Here! To imagine Apollon had managed it? She told them to wait and forgot them. Gaius did as well. That in itself, is enough for Apollon to have found a way in

259

there, into the study. He was Gaius's friend, once, and would have such trust from the great man."

Apollon shook his head, desperately. "I am still his friend. I was just upset…Kyrillos put Hiratius's body in my house. Not I."

I shrugged. "Perhaps. But look at Laodamia. She had Gaius. Riches began coming in, trade turning her way, favors given to chosen ones, and some very old families were suddenly suffering terribly. Everything depended on Gaius suddenly. How did you handle him? How did you indebt him to you? His money was gone soon, and he had to take yours? What else? You, as his consort? One of the girls? Others tried."

"You—" she hissed, but I slapped my hands together.

"Silence. How many people have you betrayed, Laodamia, for the wealth? How many for revenge? Apollon and Eurydike for some idiotic, ancient slight?"

Eurydike smiled sadly. "She hates us. You are right. She lied to us. Apollon set out to set our crimes right, and she promised us favor again. She forgot us. They won't let us have the theatre back. They even set that Kleitos over us, and told us to obey him in our own theatre? Bah. All this for their girls, for what they did. Lysirate, and Eudoxia both visited our theatre often. Lysirate wrote a play, and I allowed it. Her play was about a bitch of a harpy mother. Eudoxia, she told Laodamia, the poor little fool. After that, Laodamia set us all apart. She cannot forgive, no matter what services we do."

Laodamia didn't deny any of it. "And why would I kill Gaius? It sounds to me like I needed him."

I chuckled. "Why? I know not. Things change. He spent all his money, or perhaps it was stolen?" I gave Cassius a quick glance. He went pale as a sheet. I spoke on. "Perhaps it was stolen so you could make him yours. You paid for his expenses, his upkeep, and his way of life, and made him think he would be at home here. He attracted Roman business to you, and it paid off hugely, didn't it? Rich traders, new clients, people who offered much for access to your guest appeared, and gold flowed in your palm."

Pericles cleared his throat. "He didn't care about money. Laodamia does."

Laodamia shook her head. "Go on, centurion. Tell us more of your dreams."

I did. "And yet, what if he stayed? Would he slowly take over and bleed you dry? Would he control you? Would Augustus see an opportunity to use him? What if you relied on him and his patronage, and he changed his mind? What if he moved to Side? You would be left here, bereft of his person and support, and your once crushed enemies still at large. Would it not be better if he died here, and you were guiltless and could blame the soldiers who guarded him? Indeed, you might even worship him here, create a priesthood, a temple?"

"Fanciful," she said. "I shall have to remember all this. I will."

261

I didn't let her go. "Or, he insulted you, Laodamia. We have seen you don't forgive. Everyone thinks you seduced him. Perhaps he grew tired of you? Perhaps he grew to love coin after all? Augustus cut him off. Few of the high and mighty care for money before they have none. He demanded you share the coin he makes you?" I eyed the girls. "Or perhaps he rejected one of your girls? Perhaps for Corinne, Meliton's daughter? Eudoxia is, perhaps boring?"

Meliton shook his head. "I hoped he would take her, but he didn't. He was married and exhausted of women."

Corinne nodded. "I love Alexander. I still do."

Alexander looked down to hide the emotions on his face.

I spoke on to Laodamia. "Perhaps one of the girls you hoped to marry to Gaius didn't please him. He was divorcing Vipsania, after all, and might not have been exhausted of women. He might have had many. You have reasons to kill him, Laodamia. What was in the scroll that was stolen? What had he said? Did you find out something that displeases you? Gaius and his alliance to you, was a thing of fragility."

"It is all possible," Laodamia said. "But I didn't touch him." She held a hand over her belly, the hand shaking.

The silence was chilling.

"And Vipsania?" I said. "We all know why you would want him dead. Revenge, and perhaps to stop the divorce. Make it disappear!"

Vipsania looked enraged enough to kill someone with her eyes alone. Ariane looked down, terrified. Larissa, up to the roof, praying.

"I have no coin to buy anything or anyone," Vipsania said softly. "You know this."

I nodded. "Did the enemies of your hosts and husband find out about your misery and suggested a divorce could be stopped if you made sure he was dead. Did you work for Amyntas, Kyrillos, and Apollon, to save your marriage?"

She hissed. "I know your secrets too."

I laughed. "Share them! Your slave here, Ariane, she might have done it for you. Out of fear. The guard did like her, after all. She might have done if for Kyrillos, just to be at peace from you." I shook my head, walking back and forth. "Meliton, he was ruined. He could have been there, to avoid losing his fortune, and Corinne. Corinne, to avoid going to Rome. Bernike, for both reasons. Andromache, for revenge for Amyntas. Cassius, to silence the man, for Cassius might have known what Gaius had written down on his scrolls, the ones lost. Pericles, you too. You might have been jealous of his affairs with Laodamia. Eudoxia, for jealousy. Lysirate, for the spite you felt for him, and perhaps you sympathized with Amyntas, who is a rough man, isn't he? You must have known him."

They swayed there, shaking their heads.

I spat and shook my head. "Filth. Gaius touched every one of you, especially the women, in one way or the other. So many wanted to steal his heart and soul, and influence. And he said, 'no,' to most of you. Oh, aye, I doubt it not, that all you were offered to him for gain and power."

Corinne looked at me darkly. The tall Lysirate and the small Eudoxia wore neutral, calm faces. Eudoxia no longer wept.

Pericles cleared his throat. "You insult all of us. Anyone might a reason to kill another person. Few do. Few are deserving such a fate. It will be about money, no doubt, but not one of us—"

I looked at Cassius. "It might very well be about money. And there he is. There is one who knows all there is to know about the affairs of the house. A scribe, who is a man in love with slave Larissa. I see it in your face, Cassius. The huge bills Gaius was making. The gigantic one for the house? I am not sure it was Ennius who was stealing. Ennius sent all the information to Rome. Our people spoke to Augustus as well, sent him messages. A spy, if you will, spoke of Cassius, and Ennius, and riches that have disappeared. A relief from fraud, from getting caught, from stealing from Gaius, can motivate anyone to take advantage of the tragedies playing in the city. Where is Ennius? Did you kill Gaius, Cassius? You had access."

Cassius shook his head. "Nonsense. I am the diligent and honest one here. He left with everything he stole and tried to make me look like a thief."

"Indeed," I laughed. "Never seen an honest scribe.

And our valiant Alexander? The stone-face, the solider, the faithful warrior. What is your secret? Nay. Tell me not. You all had reason to hate him."

Alexander spat in anger. "You are a fool, Roman. You—"

I lifted a finger, and the handsome man went quiet. "Gaius might have betrayed you all without knowing it. Like a mighty storm, the Roman noble could topple you all with his ill will, or even with his ignorance, or even favor. He could have insulted anyone of you, without knowing or meaning it. Aye, one of you might have hated him enough to kill him or had other reasons to work with Kyrillos and Apollon, who poisoned him. One of you might have seen an opportunity to punish him, to make sure he died. That someone took his scrolls. He wrote something that night—some bit of business, his will, his confessions. Two bits of business, indeed. He told me both would change his life. One was a divorce from Vipsania."

"Show it to me," she hissed. "Otherwise, it doesn't exist."

"But there was also the will, his confession," I said. "That will, he wrote it because he feared going home, and of dying. It was an insurance. Someone took it all. Someone has his scrolls." I looked at Cassius and Pericles. "Someone knew of the will. Someone spoke of it. Someone killed him because they hated him or simply to punish him. Someone killed him, perhaps to hide something, or to benefit from him. You will all stay here, save for Alexander," I said. "You shall stay here, get rooms around this atrium, most of you, and you must endure it. Send words to your households and families, and tomorrow, after we return, we shall know which one of you were there. I will know which one of you opened his belly, as he lay dying, and which one of you have the scrolls."

They stared at me with rapt attention. Pericles stepped forward. "But I understand not. You just told us how anyone could have killed him, for any reason, and perhaps alone, perhaps not. How would you know the truth tomorrow?"

I smiled cruelly. "I know, you see. I have a hunch which one of you was involved, but I shall have Antius here question those two who guarded the door to Gaius's room. One of them admitted he knows who was in there but won't tell us because they want to honor Gaius. The other one is asking for coin. We shall remind them of their duty. Both have peeked inside that room and seen Gaius with his guest. They know who it is. Soon, I shall too."

I was about to leave.

Andromache laughed.

I turned to look at her. "What?"

"With Kyrillos, and Amyntas, or without them. For hate, for profit. All fine theories. But what, I ask you, will you do if it were Alecto, Megaera, and Tisiphone? What if it were the Furies, who punished him for your crimes against the innocent? They see all."

I cursed and kicked a pot down on its side. "There is no such thing as the Furies, you damned idiots! If there were, they couldn't solve this murder. I will. I shall. I piss on your fables, Andromache. Drag her and Apollon to their own rooms. Let them sit silently and think on their crimes."

I turned and left walked to stare at Gaius. I wondered at the wound, the crack on the floor, the blood. I heard Marius moving in the house, speaking to servants, who began preparing the house for so many guests. Alexander's voice was loud outside. People were coming. People were going. I watched them from the shadows of Gaius's study, all complaining loudly.

Hercules came to me, chuckled, and sat down, staring at Gaius as well. "We have seen it plenty before." His eyes were sad as a puppy's. "Young lives wasted. Poor boy. Augustus will die of a heartbreak. He will."

"He will," I agreed. "He shall be very sad. First Lucius, now Gaius. Young Postumus is not suitable. All sons of Julia are gone or unavailable. And Germanicus is too young and rash. He is of the blood, but...Augustus has a hard choice before him. In the meantime, we must find answers."

"Indeed, we must," he answered darkly. He gave me a curious glance. "You think this will work?"

"One way or the other, it will," I said. "One of them did it. The guards must know something, and now, they know I shall ask them. Marius ready?"

"He will be. By evening."

"Alexander must help us," I said. "But he will."

Hercules smiled. "He will, indeed. Marius will tell him what we shall need. He is happy you didn't blame him for anything particular. This is very risky."

I watched Segolia, who was walking in the atrium, shaking her head.

Perhaps she had seen my death. Perhaps her own.

"And if Alexander is the killer? What if he was sickened by the torture and wanted to revenge Lycia?" he asked.

"Then, we are fucked," I said crudely. "Tell Short and Tall what to do."

He nodded. "You have no idea who did it? You spewed a lot of fancy words out there."

"I only know," I said, "that we must find out who was in that room, and for how long." I also looked up the stairs. "I don't want to pry open all their secrets. If I fail to capture the murderer with what we are planning, then I will force all their evil out in the open. I will make Marcus and Avila speak, indeed, if we fail this night, but I will reveal all of their crimes if I must."

"Name one?" he said with a grin. "You are not this good."

I leaned forward. "Make sure Vipsania's meals are made by you still, and you guard her. Keep an eye on her. Someone tried to kill her last night."

I got up, and walked to Segolia, and left him gasping. She turned to me and rubbed her face. "Will you let

Antius do it?"

"If we are to find the scroll, we must," I said. "I am still a man worth knowing."

She didn't look sure. Then she looked terrified, for just one moment. "There is a killer in that room," she said. "I felt it. It wasn't done like you told them, for profit, for hate. It is something else. Sprits teased me. But there is something else. When you cursed the Furies, and said they would fail, you made a big mistake. A huge one. Something took great offence. It wasn't human."

She wrapped her hands around me and sobbed.

I pushed away the fear and replaced it with determination.

CHAPTER 9

That evening, I was staring at the surprisingly empty garden and atrium. Pericles had a large room with a desk near what had been Gaius's study, but the others, less fine ones. All were guarded, prisoners or not. Upstairs, Vipsania had retired into her own rooms. Outside the guarded rooms, dozens of legionnaires were preparing to sleep. All but ten had moved to the domus from the barracks.

Alexander was entering, looking around as if he were challenging a pit filled with wolves. He stopped next to me and joined me in my scrutiny of the guests and servants and the soldiers.

I turned to look at him. "Well?"

He nodded. "Marius made your request." He sounded reserved.

I smiled. "You are upset?"

"You insulted every single man and woman in the room. Even the prisoners. And you were wrong. It is Marcus, or some roman."

"I wasn't wrong," I told him. "I was entirely correct, about everything. Now, will you help me?"

He shook his head. "Yes. Reluctantly, but I will, if only to be rid of you lot. You want to take them outside the city?"

I rubbed my neck. "Look around you."

He did. The soldiers were observing me warily. "Oh."

"Yes," I told him. "Today, we fought together. If they see us take Marcus and Avila, they will want to challenge us. It is so with soldiers. So, if we must put the bastards to question, it must be done outside the city. There will only be a few of us. A risk, but I doubt anyone dare move in the night."

"Unless you are dealing with someone not in the house," he murmured. "Then, you might find yourself in trouble."

"A risk. I think I know who did it. But I want to confirm it. The bastards made a mistake. Trying to extort me? To deny us the knowledge? Fools."

He looked dubious and shivered. "Foolish, and unfortunate. Centurion Antius will question them? Did they truly peek into the room of Gaius?"

I nodded. "So, they claim. They know a secret, and I have a hunch. No. I know who was in there. Tomorrow, I will be sure."

He said nothing.

"And the city?" I asked. "It is simmering down?"

He looked troubled. "There is an uncommon silence in Limyra. The people are quiet, at least on the outside."

"Rome and Pericles will be grateful," I told him.

He looked troubled.

"You are not happy?" I asked him.

"I wonder what Gaius's death will bring us," he said. "It won't be forgotten."

I didn't deny it.

"You will be blamed as well," he said.

271

I said nothing to that.

"Just you and your few men?" he asked me.

I nodded. "Best not tell Marius that we will speak to his men in privacy."

"They will be ready in a moment," he said. "Your men managed to get them out of the garrison with some lie or another. They are going to be gagged, and hooded, and tied. Mine are coming. By the river's side, that's where we go." He shook his head. "It has been a long day."

"Why," I asked, "do you follow the family? For wealth? To captain your buffoons in Limyra is a great honor, is it not? The city is not large. The family gives and takes."

"Why?" he said, "I have pride. I'm a soldier, and a soldier's lot is to guard his city and family. Will Corinne be safe?"

I shrugged. "She will be. She did nothing."

His face was still. He was thinking hard.

"Myra is a mighty city," I said. "Corinne would have made a powerful wife to you."

His face didn't give anything away. He was a hard man to read.

I looked around. "Well. When?"

"Let us go," he said. "Come. Get your people."

I got Antius, and I saw Segolia coming after him. I frowned, but she walked past us for the servant's door.

We followed, not sure what she was doing. I looked around before we left the garden and saw people looking at us. Cassius, his fingers nervous, was staring at me. Eudoxia, her sister, and Corrina as well. Meliton was walking back and forth, and Larissa and Ariane, both in the kitchen area, stopped doing anything as I passed them. Hercules stood there, eyeing them, and he saluted us.

We moved out to the servant's side door and to the alley past the wall. I greeted the legionnaire on guard, and we passed the wall to see two Lycians who didn't look at me.

I stepped to the night and walked after Alexander.

We walked to the river's edge, and I found Tall there, huddling in a cape. He smiled as we appeared and whistled. Short gave him a handshake and rode back for the domus.

We waited for a moment.

Out of the darkness emerged horses and mules.

There were two of our men. There were two men of Alexander, and also, what I took to be Avila and Marcus. Both had sacks over their heads, both were gagged and tied up. We mounted up. Segolia trailed last, her face clouded with worry.

Alexander stared at the men as he rode south along the river. "This is distasteful. I find it dishonorable. Everyone thinks very little of Rome these days, and they are right."

"There would be a Lycian empire," I said, "if you were dogged in your duty and punished your criminals."

He said nothing.

"Take us to where we need to go," I muttered, and the man nodded.

Alexander went first, and the cats alone seemed to watch us from the river's bank. The horses walked the edge of the river for the walls below. They were snorting with fear and displeasure. The sun's light was long gone, and the torches flared unkindly in the shadowy walls, but the city was mostly dark. Segolia was coming along behind, muttering, and I wondered if she was calling for gods to help her. Alexander kept his focus forward, and we simply followed. His eyes were flashing, gazing around, and I knew he was worried.

"He's not stupid, this Alexander, is he?" I muttered. "He knows his business."

"He does, and that's worrying," she answered. "We are all in terrible danger."

I nodded. "We are. But I will protect you. Don't mention the spirits again."

She turned to me and opened her mouth. She closed it with a clack.

"Segolia, please," I said. "Fine. Tell me."

She looked at the high walls.

"Did you have a sight? That I shall die? Or you?" I asked.

She shook her head. "I told you all about that already. But no. I was thinking about you."

"Oh, shit," I muttered. "I am what I am."

274

She nodded. "All through the years when Father was in the Roman service," she said, "I admired the Guard. Tall, handsome, even if truly crude men, you all served a purpose. You kept the great men alive. You show the people Roman power and the loyalty of staunch warriors. In Gaul, such men guarded the chiefs. They were the best of men, the most powerful." She smiled. "Of course, some must have also been the worst of men."

I watched Antius, who turned to give me a small smile.

"Rome comes at a price," I said dully.

"It does," she said. "I have admired you. I have, like a fool, no matter if Father bred me to heal and fight, both, felt drawn to you. Then, suddenly, I grew up, and he grew old, and he will no longer go on missions with you." She shrugged. "I do not know I will, either. What we did…and what you do, I cannot do."

A dog ran past us and startled some cats, and for a moment, there was a terrible ruckus as the felines attacked the dog, and men shouted. Some guards looked down from the walls.

"Segolia, I—"

"He spoke of your women," she said mischievously. "Father did. He warned me of them. He loved you, but he loved me more, and so, he specifically told me about all your women, in all your missions. You are a young man, still under thirty, but you must have sired a village worth of people, Celcus."

I kept my mouth shut.

She nodded. "And still, I admired you. Nay, I desired you. I was a naïf fool." She shook her head. "It is, I suppose, best one grows up, and not only older. I imagined things when we sailed. Doing honor to justice, serving Rome, and having you were things I imagined."

"And I beg to gods, the ones I know don't give a damn, that you keep believing in the service to Rome, and keep loving me," I said tiredly. "The honor part, Segolia, is the part few can afford in this world of ours." I gave her a longing look. "I have had women. I have loved once. I was young, and I have a son I cannot meet. I don't know about village full of them, but the one that I know of wrenches my heart. I can see him, in many places in Rome. I have served the state, and Augustus, but the women are not—"

"I don't mind them," she said. "Father thought I am looking for a man who has had no others. I am not one either!"

"You are not—"

She smiled wickedly. "No. I am not. I serve Pretorian Guard, and I have seen some of them, on and off. Some have had me, and—"

"I don't want to—"

"But I never loved anyone of them. I loved the idea of you. Now, I know what we do. Torture. Amyntas. If I ever see you turning to Antius, I shall leave you. I can forgive you much, but not what you might become."

I shook my head. She meant to stay. I felt wings of

276

joy and smiled at her. She returned it.

We rode in silence, the wall twisting and dozens of tiny alleys opening along the wall.

"Beneath the walls of Rome, the golden glory of Rome," I told her, "there is a sewer where the miserable dead are hidden. I enjoy nothing of what Antius does, and I am not proud of some things I have done previously, but there are deeds that have saved thousands as well. When I go to sleep, I remember those." She said nothing. "And perhaps I need you to keep me from becoming a man like that scum. Thank you for staying."

Antius stiffened.

She said nothing. I decided to ride forward.

"Fine. Will," she began, and I turned, "torturing these men truly help?"

I shrugged. "I know not. But we must risk it."

She looked darkly at me. "And if it won't? Will you torture the others next?"

"If we must," I said. "We must find this person. You know it."

She nodded. "I do."

"This will be dangerous," I told her. "I trust you. I even trust you to do well in danger. I trust we won't die today. We talk about the rest later."

She nodded.

I smiled and rode on. Then, I looked at Antius and felt my heart harden into a lump of stone.

We reached the end of the road, came to the gates,

and the wall, with a large tower a short way away, was quiet. Alexander nodded us out of the gate. We followed, turned with the wall, and he was cursing.

The gates opened and then closed after us.

Alexander guided his horse towards the river.

"Where do we go to finish the filthy business?" I asked him.

He nodded forward. "To the woods. There is a small forest near the river, and it's secluded. That is what you wanted. Out of the city, and secluded. You had best do your business quietly." He looked at the two bound men. "At least they are Roman this time."

I nodded. "I have no stomach for it, either, Alexander. But we must know the truth."

He looked about to argue and then slumped in his saddle. "Whom do you suspect?"

"I suspect many things," I told him. "And only one person. We shall speak later."

He looked at me harshly. "I don't understand one thing. Wait, many things, actually."

"What do you not understand?"

"The coins," he said. "Why did Hiratius and the cook Dareios leave them behind when they left the house?"

Silence.

"Perhaps they were afraid they would be caught and searched and thought they would come back later, after the rebellion, to collect them?" I said.

He looked unconvinced. "Two bags, and two bad hideouts. They both visited the city and could have hidden everything deep in the soil. They should have ridden away."

"Why," he asked, "did you not turn Gaius around when you saw him dead?"

I laughed. "You question me? I respected him. I didn't want to see his miserable condition. And I didn't want to touch the shit, and the mucus."

"Oh, you are delicate," he murmured. "Where do you think Dareios is, by the way? He was paid, and he likely   was   killed."

"He might have been smarter than Hiratius, who trusted Kyrillos," I said.

"Did you ask Marius," he went on, "about the guards in the houses of the first victims?"

"I have had no time," I said. "Are we there soon?"

"Soon."

"We will be done soon," I said. "Marcus and Avila will know who were in that room. Then we can go home. We shall all be happy."

"I won't be, unless I get my own answers," he spat. "I doubt I shall get them, so I will remain unhappy. It seems to me that your legionnaires should be investigated much more than the rest of us," he added. "Make sure you won't fail. And fail or not, I think it would be the best if you left tomorrow and did your investigations later and elsewhere. Nefarious is still in the harbor, and you can leave."

I smiled. "Is that an order?"

"It is not. Yet."

"Will it be an order from you? Or from Pericles. Pardon me, from Laodamia?" I asked.

"It will be an order you should not ignore," he said. "It will come soon."

I nodded. "So, we shall see what we must do, when it does come."

He snorted and guided us out of the wall's shadows and rode forward to the river. A thick, shadowy wood emerged from the darkness. We were riding through a tiny necropolis, wind was moving branches, and it felt like the dead were watching. I saw Antius sitting on his horse, leading a mule, and there, his gear was clanking in bags. He seemed to have no qualms about hurting his own countrymen.

Alexander nodded at the two of his men. "They will know where to go. I will return and see that none will disturb you. The other man is my friend, a good friend. Ask him for a way back when you are done."

"I will ask them to stay out of it," I told him, as we rode past. "We shall know the truth this night, and then we likely need to kill another one of your countrymen. Or a woman."

"And perhaps," he said, "a Roman. Vipsania and her slaves, and your dubious legionaries are guilty, in my mind. That shifty thief, Cassius, perhaps in every case. I know he is a rogue." He shifted in his saddle. "Pericles and Laodamia will put me in charge of this investigation soon. She won't be trapped in a house filled with romans. Tomorrow, prepare to leave."

I smiled. "Shall we leave with our captives?"

He smiled and turned away.

***

The place was beautiful in the light of the moon. The trees shaded the small clearing, which was lit by torches. Mossy boulders, the silvery ripples of the river, stone-throw away, making its way down calmly, and the eternal wheat fields singing over the river in an endless dance with the wind could confuse one into thinking we were there to enjoy our time.

We were not.

On a flat boulder, not far from a pair of sturdy trees, sharp knives, daggers, and thongs were arranged. Some were tiny, as if surgeon's instruments, and yet others crude, meant for sawing at muscle and even bone.

Antius was walking back and forth. "Lycians. Tie Marcus onto that tree." He pointed a finger at one mounted man. "Avila, the next one," he added to my men.

Segolia was seated on her horse, and she rode around the area, looking down. She knew well what would happen.

The two Lycians were tying Marcus into a thick tree, his hands behind it. Avila, who was also being tied on another by my two men. Both were making muffled voices under the bag that hid their faces. The gags stopped them from speaking.

One Lycian grabbed the bag on Marcus's head.

"Leave it," I called out. "The fear is greater that way.

281

Let us deal with this."

He hesitated and then both stood up.

One, the man who had just been tied down by my men, was making most of the muffled, pleading noises, and then, he stopped as Antius toed him. "Shut it, Avila."

Marcus was panting. Avila was shuddering.

I nodded at the Lycians.

"Get out of here, boys," I told them. "This is part you need not see. Make sure you ride far enough up the trail not to be seen. We will come and fetch you when we are done."

The two took steps away, and a handsome, long-haired man nodded. "I shall step to the trail with my friend, and there, we shall wait. I trust you can manage this alone and with as little noise as possible. Make sure it is quiet."

"Trust me," I said. "Trust him. We will make them squeal, and when they want to talk, they will nod. Only then will the muffle come off."

They gave Antius a quick, frightened look and pulled their horses with them. The friend of Alexander nodded as they left. "Good luck, then. Make sure not to fail. Gods don't approve of this, I am sure of that, so make it count."

I said nothing as they took a path out of the woods, and then, I walked to the men and looked down at Marcus, whose covered head was bobbing up and down as he silently fought his restraints.

"Antius," I said. "They are yours."

"I need no instructions on this work," he said. The man was eyeing a pair of tongs and knives. "All very good. Something for delicate parts, others for larger parts, eh? No fire?"

I shook my head. "I thought you knew your part."

"Right."

I nodded. "We keep them chained to the tree. One by one, you make them talk."

Antius squeezed his eyes shut. "Avila looks like a weak link." He poked the man, whose covered head bobbed up and down.

I shrugged. "I don't care. We must find out what they know, weak or strong."

Avila made a miserable, squeaking sound and pissed his tunic.

"Oh, shit," Antius laughed. "He is a filthy boy, isn't he?" Antius mimicked a scared voice. "Oh, please," he whimpered. "I've done nothing. Just my duty!"

The man was shaking his head, mumbling.

Antius looked down on him like he would measure a chunk of mutton. "Ripe for death. Hades, Hel, or Bel, or even our own gods, will take him screaming to be made mockery of. Pissing his pants already. Damn it."

I turned away, and our two men walked back.

We left Antius to it.

Torturing a man, even one who has been tied up, is no easy feat. The poor bastards find the extent of your bindings, all the smallest of ways they might fight back, the end of your patience. They tend to fight, to kick, to bite, and scream, and they know that once they give up fighting, their misery is going to start, and they know the pain is the end for them. The other one, Marcus, was powerful. He almost broke free of his bindings, one arm swinging for Antius, but our two men surged forward, and he was dragged back to the tree. There, finally, his arms were again forced behind him, more rope tied around the wrists, and even his legs tied together again. He was finally sitting still, and then, Antius kneeled, and went to work.

I watched my hands and masked the slight quiver with a fist. I pushed myself to a place far from there and prepared for the worst.

The screams, even muffled ones, echoed over the river.

They attracted not a soul in the night, and even the birds' singing was subdued. Marcus lost his nails. He lost his toe, then a finger.

Finally, he howled and lost consciousness. Avila was weeping.

It had taken an hour, and more. The night was hot, and full of dread.

Antius grinned and turned to him. He seemed to have lost his mind and was speaking like a god to a condemned criminal. "It is just a game, boy. Begging is part of this, but usually only truth helps, see? Your pain is going to be great. I see it. Soon after? The pain will be terrible. It won't go away, like it did when I took a simple bit of toe from your friend. He must have been relieved I only worked on those, eh? Now, next it will be fingers. That will terrify you, boy. Toes we can lose and hop along. Fingers? Not so much."

The man was trying to speak but couldn't. He was begging, no doubt, but the gag stayed on.

Antius shook his head. "Fingers are different. Tell you what. I know what is worse. Cock. I'll suffer touching it, son. Perhaps first, though, your pretty face. If you get past the fingers, Avila, and stay conscious and survive until I start working on the flesh and skin on your face, you will forget all about the simple, previous pains. You will worry about your looks. Each cut, each lost bit of flesh, each broken facial bone will take you further from worrying about your ability to walk or to grasp a fork to eat." Antius grinned and kissed his forehead. The man was trembling, no longer a legionnaire. "And if you still insist on being a hero, you will still speak, but only later. If I take all that from you, all that you are on the outside, I can take it further still. Believe me, you will cling to me with hope."

The man was panting. Marcus was trying to break free, and then gave up.

Antius gave him a quick look. "You listen, Marcus, while I instruct Avila. I'll get back to you soon. Just listen. I don't have to repeat it. It would be tedious, and I shall be tired." He leaned close to his victim. "At one point, despite your courage, you shall be begging to survive this. You will be begging simply to live, even as a crippled, ugly shit. You will love me, if I tell you that I shall, perhaps, spare one of your balls, and you will kiss my cock, if I ask it. Don't worry—"

He tried to get away from Antius, but there was no going anywhere.

He tapped Avila's cheek. "Don't worry about it. It happens to the strongest of men. I shall escort you through hope, Avila. I'll take you to the darkness. I'll hold your hand. At final stage of this play, Avila, you will love me if I simply let you go. And I won't. Not until you tell us the truth. It is beyond truth, finally, when you shall be released from this world. You will walk to the river, your skin flayed, your misshapen body missing bits, and your family weeping for your suffering over the river. You will, in hope for a release, friend, tell us what happened in the house of Gaius. It will go like this. You cling to your flesh, then your beauty, then your hope for survival, and then begging for death, and you will go when I am happy. I've seen it often. It is no testament to your toughness, if you defy me to the end, but many do. Be not too brave, Avila! None shall remember it but I. Speak. Forget your honor. Don't worry about it. It will fall, and the truth will be born from its ashes. The centurion is right. We shall know everything."

The man was in a world of his own.

I took a step forward.

"That mad fuck," Segolia whispered. "He has forgotten why we are here."

Antius gave her a quick look and seemed to find his place for a moment. His lips were dry, his tongue flickering between them. His eyes gleamed, and the man was clearly possessed.

"Yes," Antius said sadly, the small blade flashing in the light of the moon. "Mother always told me that when she found me torturing cats." He turned back to the victim. "Here. Let us walk the way."

He leaned over Avila.

I lifted my hand. It had been hours. There was nobody coming. "Enough. It is not working."

"Truly?" Antius said. "He, too, must be broken. Might as well give it more time. Don't go soft on us."

And then, Segolia hissed. "Decimus!"

I turned fast. I pulled at my sword and stopped.

In the shadows of the woods, fog was playing. It slithered around us, over the water, and even past the fields, and it was thickest where the road to the city disappeared.

A figure was barely visible there.

It was human-like, swathed in dark clothes. Whites flashed in the depths of the hood, and it sat on a dark horse. A horned mask was swaying as it was looking at us.

There was a spear.

It was dripping blood.

I frowned. I had set up the trap and had expected one of those who feared for their lives to try to kill us. The one who had killed Gaius would have sent messages to their servants, and they would have come there in force. They would try to kill us, and Marcus and Avila as well, to silence them.

Except, under the hoods there was no Marcus, and no Avila, but two ruffians from the battle. Marcus and Avila were hidden in their barracks.

I had hoped to take few of those who come for us prisoner.

I had expected a captive, which would have told us told who sent them. That one would likely be the one who killed Gaius and took the scrolls.

That, perhaps, we could still get.

But the attack was odd. It was...terrifying.

The figure was alone, a disquieting, threatening presence. It was still as a statue, or an animal in the woods, stalking its pray.

It was no mob of Lycians. It was not a solider, or a savage drunk of the city. It was just one...person?

Segolia's voice slithered to my ear. "It is them. It."

It held out its hand. In it were swathes of skin and meat. On the horse's flanks were more pieces of skin and hair, and these were from the two Lycians who had guides us there.

It was looking at me as it let go of the mess. One might have been the face of Alexander's friend.

I took a breath and felt my two men and Segolia go around me, taking steps. Segolia's horse was silent as a grave. Antius was moving from his victims to pick up a sword.

"So," I called out. "Here we are. No Marcus, no Avila here. I know nothing. Not yet. I will. Who are you? Come, show yourself."

It shook the horned head. It was looking back to the woods.

I cursed. I could get to my horse fast enough and ride after it and perhaps capture it, but I didn't know the land. My eyes moved, and I looked at the darkness around us.

It would flee. It should.

But, apparently, it had no intention to do so.

It moved. It picked up a bag of something and lifted it up.

Then, it tossed it forward. Out of the bag rolled two heads. I looked at them with incredulity. One was Marcus. The other one was Avila. I could feel the pleasure in its very being.

Segolia had warned me. I had mocked what had never been human. The Furies.

The men had been locked in a room. They had been put out of sight. It was impossible they had died. And yet, they had.

I thrust away the dread that was coursing down my spine. Segolia was pulling at her dagger. and my Praetorians were drawing swords, stepping back, rather than towards the thing.

I snarled. "Stay your place. It is no ghost but the minion of whoever killed Gaius. We take it and make it pay."

From the sides of the figure moved two more of my men. They had followed us from afar, and over the walls. Both held swords.

Marius would be out there as well, with dozen men.

And yet, nothing moved out of the woods to surround the creature.

I walked forward slowly with Antius and my soldiers around me. "Get down from the horse, fiend. It is time to discuss Gaius, your master or mistress, and your thievery."

The thing moved. It lifted the spear and pointed it at us.

One of the men approaching the shadow from both sides fell on his knees and then his face.

Another creature came to sight, horned swaying, on a horse. The thing moved very fast. It lifted a bow, a dark, stubby, and powerful weapon, and it held a bundle of arrows in its hand.

It let go an arrow, and the shaft passed my face. It didn't miss.

Antius screamed and fell on his back. An arrow was jutting in his shoulder. The bow-wielding thing moved fast as a lightning and swiveled in its saddle. The arrow took the other man who had been flanking them in the face. The poor bastard fell on his side, howling like a beaten dog.

I charged, and so did my two men, spreading around.

Neither enemy ran. The spear beast kicked the

horse's sides.

It attacked.

"Mariuuuuus!" I screamed and attacked as well.

The thing's eyes glowed briefly. They glinted in the night, and a bloody flank of the horse twitched as the spear thing shifted in its saddle and kicked the horse's sides hard again. I roared, it charged, and my men were cursing as they converged on it. I saw short spear coming for me, saw the eyes widen in anticipation, and I dodged left, then right, but the horse smashed to one of my men, leaving him lying still, and the spear stabbed down at me as the horse trotted past.

It was coming for my chest.

I stabbed up, missed, and still survived, as the beast dodged, and the spear tore to my shoulder, tore my chainmail, but not my heart. The spear was tangled in my mail. I was rolling, the blade cutting at my flesh as the horse tore me out of my feet. The armor was rent, my flesh slashed, and I fell to the underbrush. I saw the rider on top of me, spear high, and then, it turned to deal with my last man.

I got up, spat, and cursed.

I watched my man stabbing at the horse with his gladius. It tore to the side of the horse, and the horse whinnied wildly and kicked up. The spear missed my man, and I ran at the figure. Sword high, I hacked down at the horse's back.

An arrow tore to my flesh, deep into my thigh, and spun off. I fell forward, the horse dancing over me.

291

I hazarded a glance behind and saw a figure walking out of the woods, aiming a bow. Slight, almost like a ghost, the creature was aiming at me. I rolled and struck the horse's hoof, then saw the arrow jutting just next to my throat in the mud.

"Centurion!" my man yelled. "Ware!"

I looked up and saw the spear coming, and the deadly anger dark eyes staring down at me. The spear stabbed down, and I hacked at it with my sword. Sparks flew, and the weapon was bashed to the side. The blade tore at the ground, and then, my soldier tried to stab at the rider.

He caught an arrow in his shoulder, then another tore to his face.

He staggered off, and I pulled myself up.

I turned and tried to focus and knew I'd get slaughtered by the skilled archer.

Then, there was a scream.

I saw Segolia, who, having ridden past the archer, was riding for me. Her horse was bleeding, and a third horned figure was coming from the woods after her, with spear.

I cursed and turned to see my soldier with a spear in his belly, and I jumped forward. I pushed the blade up, and it entered the rider's back.

Hissing, cursing, it rode off, barely holding on to the saddle.

I went after it, turned, and saw bow lifted, and then, Segolia's horse blocked the view. The horse screamed from pain, Segolia was yelling, but I couldn't hear her. I jumped and hung onto the wounded horse's neck, she kicked its sides, and together, we dashed off to the night, for the river.

I saw Antius, the horror in his eyes, and felt brief satisfaction at the fear I could almost taste.

The horse thundered through the woods for the close by water and then fell head first down a small bank. It rolled, we fell off, and crashed down a small hillside. Segolia was panting with fear as she pulled me up.

I felt an arrow thud into the tree next to me and another zip past my face. I hissed with pain, as my thigh was throbbing. Segolia was pulling at me, and we fell to the river. It was not steep. An arrow struck the water, one the muddy bank as we waded across. I looked back and saw a figure on a horse, half hidden by fog, crouched over the horse, like an evil spirit trying to see its meal. It was a disquieting sight, and Segolia sobbed with fear at the sight of it.

"Alecto," she whispered. "The dead eater."

I cursed, and tried to gain my feet, as Segolia pulled me to the wheat field and forced me forth, until finally, she pulled me down.

She eyed me carefully, panting.

"You'll live?" she whispered, looking towards the bank and the river.

I was nodding. "The thing...was so fast," I whispered. "Scratch here and wound here. I'll—"

She gasped. I followed her eyes and looked down at

my side. And arrow was jutting there in my flesh, having pieced my chain, and blood was flowing.

She touched it, and I hissed. I moved gently, and she grasped it.

"It was…there were two more," she said. "I saw the other one with a bow in the depths of the woods, and it… They know their weapons. Your soldiers?"

I heard a man screaming and got up to my knees. "Killers. Murderers. They killed them."

"They killed most of the squad," she whispered. "It was not a human. The others were, but not that one. They—"

"Come, we must get back," I said. I tried to get up.

"Hide," she whispered. "And fight on our own turf. Shh!"

I snarled. "This was supposed to be our turf. Marius didn't come. He failed. Those men of Alexander had better be dead too."

The screams ended.

Then, not soon after, a horn blared. It was deep, bitter, resentful, like a bull making its displeasure known. It rang many times. It rang nine times. Then, tenth.

Segolia shook her head. "The Lycians. Our men. Marcus and Avila. Did they kill the prisoners? No, we cannot go there. They are waiting."

I rubbed my face. "We wait. Hercules will come looking for us. As will Alexander, the bastard."

CHAPTER 10

Alexander was watching the scene with horror.

He stared at the torsos that were laid on the ground, one after the other. Ten obols would be needed.

But perhaps not.

Their heads were gone.

They had been removed and taken away, save for two.

I watched where the prisoners had been. They were nowhere to be seen. In their place, in the trees, were nailed two heads. They were Short and Tall, and the reason why Marius had not arrived. The boys had been following us and had meant to lead men to where we were, to come and help when the time was ripe, and I called, but instead, they had been caught.

Two bodies were those of the Lycian soldiers. Marcus and Avila, both were dead, and their heads had been recollected. Four were my men.

Antius had not had his horn blown. He was missing.

I rubbed my face, the pain acute.

I kneeled next to the corpses.

Antius. Was he alive?

All had been stabbed in a gut. Just like Gaius. After death.

"They mocked us," Segolia whispered. "They were already dead, but they wanted to tell us we failed by slashing them up like Gaius had been. They knew what you had said to those people in the domus. None else know, right? About the gut-wound. Only the few of us in that house."

I nodded. "They mock us, indeed. We failed utterly. Of course, we hoped one of the people inside would send word to their men to come and kill us, and that one might have told anyone about the wound, but I think you are right. They mock us."

Alexander was walking around his friend's body. "Pericles will want to speak with you right away," he whispered. "He won't be happy with this. This is…" He spat as flies were startled off a corpse by his shadow. "You are overmatched. It is as I said. You must leave."

"By what are we overmatched by?" I asked. "The enemy were alive. I probably killed one."

He shook his shoulders. "By what? You killed shit! Shit! This is a ghost. The Furies. The three Furies. You saw them, didn't you? Not human. You cannot kill one. You hurt one, but they won't die."

"We were surprised by a very skilled enemy," I said simply, looking at my dead men, and ignoring Segolia's fear. "They took our bait and chewed up our trap. No more, Alexander. I'll go back and make things very clear to people in this house. And we are not leaving."

He sneered. He waved his hand around. "I know your highness does not care for Lycian dead, but there are deaths a plenty in Limyra from the past. This one is not natural. This was not done by Kyrillos, or Amyntas, or anyone in that house. These are the killers who hunt Lycian criminals. They hunt murderers, traitors, and liars."

"They took Antius, and only left the boys their heads," I said. "They killed my men. I will take their heads."

"They want the boys to go to Hades," Alexander said. "They were a necessary kill, unlike the others. They had no guilt."

"The prisoners—"

"We look for them," Alexander said darkly. "I know the men. They did nothing, so they will be alive, and telling everyone about this shit. But you won't be here to make things worse. Pericles will see you out now."

I smiled and grimaced with pain. "Pericles can't see his cock out of his undergarments." I cursed and turned. I walked around the horse tracks in the mud and found an arrow. It was made of cane and had no feathers. I twisted it around and wondered at it.

I was thinking hard. "Our killer knew about the trap," I said.

He rubbed his face in frustration. "You only had your Marius and that Hercules there where you made it. And Antius. The girl. One of you betrayed the others. Come. Time to send you home."

Alexander turned and rode off.

We went to speak with the lord of the city.

On the way, people watched us with mixed emotions. They had heard the horns. Some looked pleased as they spotted blood on my armor. Others, worried. They feared Rome, but perhaps not as much as the killers who could murder its soldiers.

I looked at Segolia. She was shivering with fear. She touched my shoulder. "What will you do?"

"What?" I asked. "I'll expose the shits, and then, I'll have the lot killed, if they don't start telling me the truth. I'll pluck them out to the light one by one and see if one breaks." I gave her a quick look. "But I won't be Antius. I will not enjoy it."

She looked away. She was worried for me. And she was terrified of what she felt and had seen.

The Dead Eater.

BOOK 3: THE DEAD EATERS

CHAPTER 11

I was late afternoon when we watched the room where Marcus and Avila had been confined. The sun was going down. The room was at the end of the house, and it was well hidden in a shadowy corner. There were elaborate painted tiles on the floor, as there were in many of the houses in the area. Serpents in the trees, elks, and forests with a flowing river delicately made could be seen amid the trash and the old furniture.

"They were guarded?" I asked Marius.

He grunted. "Not very well, I admit. They were home, after all. Just kept out of sight. I don't understand it."

I looked at the floor. "I don't think we have been doing a very good job in Limyra, Marius. In fact, it has been a terrible job. You should know that I will have a word about this with the great man in Rome."

He bristled. "I simply follow orders, don't I? I'm a solider, not an augur. This is not the work of human beings."

"It is," I said, shuddering at his ominous words. "And we'll gut the lot."

"No poison in either," he said. "They were simply stabbed to death while they slept. And then…somehow…their heads…"

I walked the room, avoiding the great bloody pools around the missing heads, and looked at the streams that ran between the tiles.

I kneeled, inspecting the floors. "You have not been very observant, my friend Marius. I need to talk with the shits in Gaius's house. You will move all your men there. Most of the gear must go there, especially weapons. Leave what you don't need."

"Why?"

"Because," I said, "I will upset many people in a short while. We'll be in a hairy situation."

He nodded and rubbed his face. He reviewed my armor and saw the wounds on my side and thigh. He gave a critical eye on my scratches. "You going to stay alive?"

I nodded. "If I am lucky. Nothing vital was hit."

"How did it happen?"

"We were attacked, obviously," I snarled. "They brought the heads *there,* by the way. We saw them."

Marius spat in anger and shook his head. "The boys, they were butchered. The century wants to burn the entire city. They want to make a fitting pyre for our Gaius. I—"

"They are dead, cannot be brought back, and we are going to keep our heads cool for now," I said. "My men died as well, so I know how hard it is. We'll not burn the city, but we will roast the bastards who did this."

His eyes went large. "Your men died? No? The woman?"

I nodded at Segolia, who was walking in the atrium, her eyes on me. Marius looked relieved and turned back. "What happened? How many were there?"

"I am not sure," I told him. "Short and Tall are both dead. We were surprised. And you, sir, were not there. I don't blame you for it since the guides were surprised. They fought well, the enemy. There were three of them, one with a bow, and one was clearly a soldier. He knew the horse and the spear. He fought like they fight in the east, on horseback. In the west we dismount to have a scrap."

He shrugged. "While their militia is not worth shit, there are some good men here. Mercenaries as well. They all ride and shoot bows, especially the nobles. Hunting, ancient hobby. Their men carried bows with cane arrows to Salamis for Persia, they keep telling us." He shook his head. "I am sorry, sir. I should have found a way to find you. I was waiting for the two boys at the gate with ten men, and they didn't show up. I had no choice but to send for Alexander, and nobody found him."

I gave the mutilated corpses one final look. "It was a risky trap. I take the blame for that. But I wonder if I take the blame for much of the other things that have gone wrong. Rome has not been observant in here." I touched the floor and thought back on Drakon's words. "We'll find out soon."

He scratched his neck. "You had Antius torture the prisoners?" he asked me. "The plan was foolish."

"It had to look real," I said. "I could have had him torture these boys as well, but that is not something I do. Unless I must. For Rome."

He shook his head. "You are one cool shit, you are. But you know it would not be wise. That would not have sat well with the century," Marius said.

I sighed. "It seems Marcus and Avila didn't lie. *Nobody* used the door that night. And that makes this very complicated."

He blinked. "Nobody? I was sure they, or one, had failed in their duty and been off with a woman. They are both horny as shit. I was happy you didn't want their heads, but…"

"They didn't fail," I said. "They did their duty. Tell your men to start packing and move there. Now." I turned to go. "You will lock down the domus of Gaius. Tell the Lycians to go away, and man the doors, and have men drag furniture near the doors, so they can be blocked. Make sure the upper floors are guarded as well."

"Lock it down? What exactly will happen now?" he asked.

I waved my hands over my blood-stained mail. "I will go and have a chat with those shits. It's time to stop playing with them."

He scratched his neck and closed the door. "I think we must start considering the safety of lady Vipsania," he said, and eyed the doorway, which was half open.

"Lady Vipsania is one of the people we should indeed be worried about, and for," I said with a smile. "But there are others. All of them, in fact."

He walked with me. "They say Alexander is asking

us to leave. And that he thinks it was one of us who is to blame. You, Antius, me, or your man Hercules."

I nodded. "He does all that. But we all know it wasn't one of us, don't we?" I said, rubbing my face.

He smirked. "Aye, of course. And still, he is running about, telling everyone how unfair we are treating the people in that house. He is preparing a storm. They also say the prisoners you tortured are hidden in the city, speaking against us. He might not need to prepare a storm, see? It is coming."

I nodded. "Indeed. It is time you finally start being observant." I pressed the wound on my side and shivered at the memory of the speed and savagery of the attack. "They are very smart. Very brazen. I am not sure what they want."

"They say they are the Furies," the man said, "and Furies want to kill punish people. They punish those who commit crimes. There is—"

"One for murder, another for jealousy, one for everything else," I said. "Aye. But did they kill Gaius, or are they simply getting involved? No, they do not know who took Gaius's life, and the scrolls. They took Antius, after I told everyone I know. They would have taken me as well. I guess they are asking him questions. Alas, he doesn't know."

But he knew other things.

He blinked. "Well. That is no good."

"No good at all."

He spoke on. "They say they want to guard the land,

303

the city, the very ways of the people. I have been here months, and people speak of them. I studied them, didn't I?"

I pushed to the doorway. "I think you are putting too much weight on this dream, my friend. You were not supposed to start believing in local tales. And I bet, *if* they exist, they too, yearn for coin and power. Are not the gods themselves greedy? They are. I doubt they kill to protect anyone but themselves. They are fucking maniacs. They'll regret they took any part in our affairs."

"But—"

"People," I said. "They are people." I pushed Segolia's words away. "I do not know who killed Gaius in that room, not yet. As I just said, I think the Furies do not either. The Furies, I think, seek the scroll, same as I. Both the killer of Gaius, and perhaps one of the Furies are in that house. The Furies are arrogant shits. They kill our men, and slit the bellies, to mock us? They are playing, toying with us, and they want the scroll, I know it is so. It contains Gaius's crimes, and Roman shame."

He nodded. "That would be worth a lot."

"It is. Let us go. I have to speak to the lot again, but in a different note this time. We'll start stripping away their lies, and if the Furies have a problem with that, let them come out and complain. I'll get to the bottom of Gaius's death and I will save the scrolls, and then let the Furies take them from me, the scrolls."

He saluted me and turned to give orders, and I

walked out with Segolia, under guard to the domus of Gaius. I stopped before the sun-bathed house. "It is a peculiar place, is it not?"

"The city is a jumble of old grudges and new greed," she told me. "So far, we have been doing nothing to help Lycia."

"Aye," I said darkly. "Old and new. But, Segolia, we are here to help Rome."

She squeezed my hand. "Torture is not helping anyone. But I know."

"I never did any of that," I said. "But this is too important to fail in."

Segolia grabbed my arm. I turned to look at her. "What," she whispered, "will happen in there?"

"First," I said, "we shall see who might be missing, or wounded."

"But they were *all* under guard," she said. "And the house is as well."

"Less than we thought," I snarled. "Much less. It is my fault. I should have checked it out myself. We were not supposed to have to worry about anything but Gaius and Kyrillos's brood."

"Yes," she said. "You will not torture them?"

"I'll not torture anyone," I told her again. "But I'll not tiptoe around anymore. No fancy plans. I shall start prying open their fucking secrets like so many oysters. And if I must, I will simply hang them, one by one. No torture."

She nodded, her eyes horrified. "I see."

305

"This might cause deaths of nations, Segolia. That scroll must be regained, and Gaius was killed as well. Revenge must be had, or Rome is shamed. You go and tell Hercules this." I spoke to her, and she nodded. I went inside to the hall. Segolia walked past me to find Hercules. Behind us, the soldiers were coming in a stream, carrying their furca and many pila, and gear, and dodging back out again, to get more. The Lycian guards were looking on in confusion.

The guards inside turned to look at me.

Even the birds stopped singing.

Alexander had been speaking to Corinne and Bernike by the stairs. Larissa and Ariane took steps back as they saw me.

I turned to one of the guards. "Only Romans come in and go out. Save for Vipsania, and Cassius. They stay here too."

He began giving orders.

Alexander sneered. "Let *only* Romans in? You still think we must be blamed for this? No, we won't have it. This is why the city is such a quarrelsome pit of lies."

"Please, Alexander, do not—" Corinne began. "You must be patient."

"*You* are the one going to Rome," he said. "Your mother cannot bear the thought. No. I shall leave now. I have business I must attend to."

I didn't like the look in his eyes.

"Aye," I said. "That's all the attitude I take from you." I took the step that would change our stay in

Limyra. "Guards. Take his sword. If he resists, kill him."

Men stepped forward. Legionnaires pulled their blades and placed them on Alexander's chest. The man's face was one of incredulous shock. A legionnaire stepped forward and pulled out the sword.

"*Decimus!*" Vipsania said, leaning on the railing above. "Decimus! What are you doing?"

"This is preposterous!" Bernike said, her beautiful face twisted in shock. "Meliton!"

"Your husband hates trouble," I told her. "Don't mix him in it. Stay here, both. We are finding the underlying cause of many things here, this very night," I said. "That's what we will do. Vipsania! Get down here."

She looked enraged.

"Get-down-here," I snarled.

Ariane was weeping, and Larissa scowling, but I didn't care. I stared at Vipsania. My chainmail jingled, and I pointed my sword at the floor of the atrium. "Here. Get here or be dragged here. You are not above the doubt or being ordered about. You know who I am, don't you?"

"I know what you did, once," she said weakly, her eyes gleaming. "I will tell—"

"We can both tell him tales," I told her. "He will hear mine, as well."

She opened her mouth to say something and then walked down with jerky steps. Her eyes were gleaming with tears, but she held her head high as she stood next to Alexander, and Ariane and Larissa came to her sides.

I nodded and walked to the middle of the floor. "The rest of you! Come out. Come and stand before me. Get the prisoners here."

One by one, they did Appear. First, Apollon was dragged out of the room he had been locked in, blinking. His eyes were wet and afraid, and the chains on his wrists and legs jingled. He was dropped to the side. Andromache was next. Andromache was seated next to him. Eurydike appeared next to Apollon, holding a hand on his shoulder, her old eyes sad. She was muttering please. "Please, do not hurt him."

I shook my head at her. "I'm afraid I must withdraw my word, Eurydike."

Meliton came next, walking heavily. He stood next to Bernike, who looked enraged. Corinne did, as well, as she eyes Alexander. They were sweaty, dirty, and still proud.

I turned to see the sisters and daughters of Pericles enter. They were hastily dressed, their hair out of place. The smaller, Eudoxia, was looking around, lost, her eyes red-rimmed for crying.

She was searching for her mother.

Lysirate, the tall one, smiled and hopped to stand next to Corinne, avoiding Eudoxia.

Then, the bastard was brought in.

"I don't understand!" called out Cassius, who was pulled from his room by Hercules. Three of my men were standing before the door to Gaius's room, but Hercules came forth with Segolia. Cassius was pushed to stand before us. Hercules pulled his sword, his dark face beastly.

"*Where* is Pericles? And Laodamia?" I asked brusquely.

Lysirate took a step forward. "They are in father's new study. He is writing to Augustus. He said you are leaving today." She smiled pettily. "Go and see. Hopefully Mother will make a fight out of it. Irritate her, if you can." She smiled. "You can."

"Which room?" I asked.

She pointed towards the garden. There, I saw one door ajar.

I walked through the lot and straight to the door. I kicked it open and stepped in.

Laodamia lifted her head from whatever Pericles was writing. "Get out, Roman. I don't know what you are playing at."

I stepped forward and grasped her arm. "As your daughter asked, so it shall be." I pulled her after me and pushed her roughly out to Hercules's arms.

"Here, lady. Come along" he rumbled and pulled her along roughly.

"You dare—" she shrieked.

"They all say that," I wondered, "even after they know we *do* dare. Stand her still with Eudoxia, Hercules. At sword point, if one must."

I turned to Pericles.

He rubbed his eyes and smiled softly. "Come in," he said. "Do you like the room?"

I looked around it. The walls were painted with mermaids, swimming in a pond, delicate trees shading deer, and other wildlife. Snakes were plentiful in the trees. Birds were bright on the sky.

"I have seen worse," I told him. "I have seen plenty of the same, in fact. Get up and join the others, Pericles."

Pericles was sitting on a chair, leaning over a desk. He nodded, picked up the pen, writing furiously, and didn't look up at me. His face was ashen gray, terrified, perhaps, and his eyes took me in briefly. "I heard you. One moment."

"No time for this, Pericles. Get up," I said, with clear note of warning.

He nodded, like a child. "The writing is good here, as the mind rests. No sounds come from outside, other than what one must bear. Like the many horn blasts this night," he told me. "I half didn't expect you to come back."

"And I am," I told him. "I am sorry."

"Gaius's body has been prepared," he went on, without telling me how sorry he was for the way things turned out. He was in an odd mood. "It has been prepared for the journey. We will carry it to the temple of Zeus to rest. I don't suppose you can bury him here? I wouldn't mind."

"No."

"And as for whoever was in that room," he said dryly, "Alexander will take over investigating. You must go."

"Laodamia wants us gone, eh?" I said.

He shook his head at me. "*I* want you gone as well. He shall find the culprit. Your method is far too heavy-handed for the people. You will take Corinne as a hostage to keep Meliton in peace, and you will drag away Apollon for the death...of Gaius. Andromache as well." He shook his head and closed his eyes. "Yes. You will go back to Rome, to tell them your ruse failed, and that it wasn't our fault but yours. You challenge spirits, didn't you? You tried to trick them, you mocked them, and they tricked you, because no matter what Kyrillos, Apollon, and Amyntas did to destabilize our alliance, what followed has woken up the spirits in the land. Go and do not come back. Go, if you would live." He gave me a sneer. "You have no way of knowing what happened, anyway."

I shrugged. "There are things I can still do. And I will."

"What?" he asked, tiredly, incredulous. "We, the Limyran nobility, must leave this place soon. I must rule and show myself. So—"

"I cannot allow that," I said. "You'll rule later."

Pericles looked at me with worry. "What? Later? You came here to aid us. To keep us friends to Rome, to punish evil doers. It is done. Do not go too far, Roman. We have all paid a heavy price for our alliance, for our peace. A *heavy* price."

I waved my hand at my bloodied countenance. "I am in no mood to argue, Pericles. Come now."

He squinted at me for the doorway. "Where is Alexander? You must not push him too far. Laodamia does not understand him. He is not motivated by simple crumbs from our table."

"He is alive and well," I told him, wondering at his words. "He was never in any danger. But he, too, shall stay here."

He flinched. "He as well?" he asked. "This will not sit well with his soldiers, or Lycia. And not with him, especially."

I shrugged. "He is here now. And won't leave. *Come*."

He put down his pen and leaned back. "Some miss Gaius, others wonder if they get paid for his bills." He shook his head. "I must sign plenty of these payments now. He never had any head for coin."

"At least you can afford to," I told him, "for he gave you much of the Roman trade."

"It is true," the man said. "He did. But that can fade fast if we go to war. You were right in the things you said to my wife last evening. Gaius was a fragile tool for her. Some have already shown doubts about working with us. They know Gaius will be costly for Lycia."

"Get up," I said.

He didn't. "Fine. One day of butchery was enough. I will come." He gave me an unusually serious and brave look. "I warn you, centurion. Every man and woman out there, but I, deserve your doubt. They are all rotten deceivers. Gaius was a gentle, good soul in comparison to them. He was a very fine man. He worked hard to bring riches to those he liked, and even those he didn't. He believed in everyone and loved deep. And you came and scared him? To drag him back to Rome? Brute. I see why he was so happy here."

I pointed my sword at the door.

He closed his eyes and got up. He walked past me and joined the others in the atrium, and I followed him.

I walked back and forth before them.

Their eyes followed me. Laodamia looked proud as a lioness, and Meliton, stubborn. Alexander was very near ready to attack me barehanded. Hercules walked behind them, and legionnaires surrounded the lot, but the man was not happy at all.

"Let us get back to the things we spoke of yesterday," I said. "This time, let us get to the very bottom of them."

"You knew nothing yesterday," Laodamia said darkly. "You know nothing now. Just guesses."

I nodded and stopped. "What kind of fighters can take down Roman soldiers?" I asked them all.

"The beasts," said Eurydike. "Please, young man. I have been trying to tell you. They do not obey your laws. They see all and hear all. Flee now. Surely, they could have killed you as well. You mocked them."

She was right. They might have but didn't. Not that night. Not then. There was a reason for it.

"The Furies," said Pericles. "The dead-hearted beasts. She is right. You mocked them, and you paid."

"Ah, but I struck with my sword, and flesh was

313

parted," I said. "Aye, they are dead-hearted beasts, but living ones. Where," I asked, "is Antius? Where is the man who was taken by these three—"

"Three, like the Furies," said Eurydike. "It is so. They took him to find out who killed Gaius. Then, they will seek the killer out. They seek the same as you. The truth. Unfortunately, none of you knew the truth. Your Antius is dead. It was Kyrillos who did this, and be happy with it, and leave."

Eudoxia nodded. "She is right. My Gaius was poisoned. The scrolls matter little in comparison."

Vipsania sneered at her and shook her head. "Your Gaius."

Lysirate agreed with a serious face, for once. "What good does this do? Holding us here?"

"Where are the heads of my men?" I asked them.

They said nothing to that, either. They stood there, staring at me with fear. My mood was not unlike a rising storm.

I nodded and slapped my thigh with the flat of my blade. "Very well. Let us start. Show me your hands."

They blinked.

"Out with the hands," I snarled. "Palms up."

They pushed their hands out. "Dear centurion," said Lysirate. "You were outside, when you were attacked. We were inside."

I walked past her and eyed their hands. Every single one had calloused hands, save for Vipsania and Cassius. None had any marks on their forearms.

Pericles was frowning. "Archery marks? You are seeking, if one of us shot you with arrows? Dear centurion. We all ride and shoot arrows. We are, even if you might not believe it, warrior people. It is our pastime, hunting. We wear gloves and bracers. Even the girls—"

I nodded and waved him silent.

"Turn around," I told them.

Alexander didn't. The rest did, slowly. My eyes went to him. "Check his back. Right side, for a wound."

"You dare—" he roared.

"I still dare," I said. "I do."

Hercules rammed his fist into the man's back. He howled and fell on his knees. Two soldiers wrestled him down, and Hercules bent down to search for a back wound. He got up and shook his head.

"Bare your backs," I said brutally to the others. "Bare them."

"At least let the women—" Pericles started.

"No," I said. "*Here.*"

"You'll pay for this," Laodamia said. "You will."

Meliton lifted his tunic. Pericles was clear. The women, one by one, shifted their clothing, revealing leg, buttock, and back. They shivered with shame. None had wounds. I shook my head at Vipsania, who was hesitant. She lifted her chin and didn't move, but her servants did. They showed me their rears and backs. Eurydike was weeping softly with shame. She lifted her clothing, and her old back showed no wounds, and then, she fell forward on her face, shaking.

"Leave her alone," Apollon said as he scrambled for her, dragging his fetters. "She is old, and sick."

Andromache and Apollon bent over her and began helping her. Segolia did as well. There was blood as Eurydike had hurt her face.

"Turn and clothe yourself," I said.

Alexander got to his knees, holding his back with a pained grimace. He opened his mouth, but Meliton beat him to it. "Centurion. This is going too far. Far too far. You must end it. Myra, the city of my wife, will hear how you mistreat her. This will be far more serious than you think. I have agreed to pay for Kyrillos's crimes, and my girl is going to be a loss I cannot bear, but you cannot shame her like this."

"I care not for their legs and arses. I will end it when we have bared all your souls," I told him.

Laodamia smirked. "What next?"

"One of you heard us talking," I said. "One of you heard our plans in that study and acted to kill us. One of you is a very curious creature. More than one?"

Cassius laughed. "Centurion! We cannot hear you in Gaius's study!"

"Come, tell us, then," said Laodamia. "Shower us with your wisdom."

"I will deal with the Furies later," I said. "The revenge will be ours. But now I want to find the person who was in the study of Gaius and killed him." I turned to Aristomache, the pale, wounded widow of Kyrillos.

316

"I shall set you free."

She flinched, and Laodamia shook her head. "What?"

"What?" Aristomache also asked, her chains jingling as she got up from the recovering Eurydike.

"I shall set you free, wife of Kyrillos, to live your life, to bury your family, and to harbor whatever vengeance you wish to take on Rome, or on Pericles," I said. "For a price."

"And what would that be?" she asked me weakly.

I lifted a finger. "Wait. Meliton and you, Bernike. I shall free your daughter from the ties to Rome. She need not travel, and she can stay here. Also," I said, "you may keep your wealth."

"They many *not*!" Laodamia yelled. "This is preposterous! This is wrong! Pericles leads Limyra—"

"Silence, or he shall burn on a stake," I roared. "And you will burn with him."

She gnashed her teeth together.

I turned to the two families. "Aristomache, Meliton, and Bernike, you were desperate. Perhaps it was only Amyntas and then Kyrillos who killed our countrymen. Blaming you might have been just a mistake, a misunderstanding. A burning of passions and curious coincidences might have led us all to this dark place. The deaths that followed, ours and yours—a tragedy." They stared at me with interest. "You were desperate to fix what Gaius's arrival here had caused. You and yours suffered unfairly. You tried to speak to Pericles, to

Gaius, then, you were desperate to approach me and to approach Gaius through me. You hoped to mend things, for Rome to see reason, and you begged common sense would take over."

"What we had instead was a *travesty*," Meliton said. "A murder and a treason. I know not what Amyntas, Kyrillos, and that fool there," he said, and nodded at Apollon, "did—"

"I did nothing," Apollon howled, supporting his mother. "I was upset at Pericles. At Gaius, for our theatre. I didn't kill Hiratius. It was Kyrillos, and they framed me! I have no coin to pay Roman food tasters for murders!" His chains rattled as he tried to move.

Bernike nodded. "Please. Ask us. For Corinne, I will do anything."

I smiled. "I know. For your loved ones, you will do anything."

They were serious as statues.

I pointed my sword at Corinne. "Corinne is a tool to be handed around, isn't she?" I said. "First, to Alexander, and then, handed to Amyntas," I said. "She was offered to Gaius. But it was Amyntas, who was, by all accounts, a buffoon and a drunk, who would have had her. A drunken, violent man."

Aristomache looked down, trying to bear the words desperately without breaking down. Her fetters were jingling with the effort.

Meliton sighed. "It was an uneasy alliance, but one we had to have since Pericles had forgotten all the rules

318

of balance and was using Gaius to—"

"I don't do that," Pericles said tiredly. "I simply lead the city. Talk to my wife."

"Ah, Laodamia was doing all that," I said. "She was doing everything she could to grow the family wealth and power and hoping to create a permanent state of affairs which would ensure her house stand above all others. Alone, in fact. She knows Pericles here cannot lead a house. Gaius gave her all in exchange for peace and a sanctuary. And for his love for one of you."

Laodamia smirked. "We have all already spoken of this. Prove it."

I turned to Meliton and Andromache. "In fact, I shall only reward *one* of you."

They immediately lost their hope and then remembered that one might still gain it. The emotions lived on their faces as they gave each other angry glances.

I pointed my sword at them. "Hiratius and the cook Dareios, or perhaps only Hiratius, who was friends with the cook, were paid to poison Gaius. He was paid in the coin of Kyrillos. The other bag, filled with Meliton's coins with the crane. Did it come from one of you? Did someone else pay someone in the house for something?"

Aristomache stepped forward. "Meliton. Meliton said he has a spy in the house. I suppose Kyrillos paid this Hiratius, but Meliton paid someone as well. Was it the cook?"

Meliton rubbed his face, casting Aristomache an angry look. "She doesn't know who the spy was. Neither does Bernike. Spy, indeed."

"And who is the spy?" I asked.

"I want your assurances—"

"And you have them," I said and looked at Laodamia. "See, lady, how the veil begins to curl back."

She was glowering and looked ready to curse, but Pericles held her hand to still her.

Meliton looked at his hands. "I was sent word by lady Vipsania, two days ago."

We all looked at Vipsania, who shook her head with rage. "I? Roman lady asks for money?" she roared. "That is a lie!"

"It is not," said Meliton. "To my shame, it is true we were desperate. We were told she was in dire need of help. That she had debts to pay and couldn't bear to ask her husband for coin. Coin that belonged to Pericles and Laodamia. She didn't want to be in debt to them."

"And in return?" I asked.

"In return," he said, "she would let us know what was taking place in the house. She could let us know about the business Laodamia was constantly talking about with Gaius, and the traders and deals they discussed. She would try to help us. We had no idea Gaius was divorcing her. I grasped the chance and told Kyrillos we might have some help in that house of lies."

Vipsania was hissing, and I pointed a finger her way.

"And why do you suppose the coins were found in

the kitchen?" I asked.

He closed his eyes. "I am terrified to know. I gave them to be delivered to her."

Aristomache whispered, "They were paid for a murder. She paid for *murder*."

I nodded. "They ended up being exchanged for murder. Kyrillos paid Hiratius to kill Gaius. Someone else paid the cook Darius to kill Gaius, as well. They didn't know about each other's crimes, the two friends. They just died together to hide Hiratius's murder." I looked at Apollon.

He closed his eyes and shook his head. "I didn't—"

"Who did you give the money to?" I asked.

Their eyes went to Cassius.

"Now, wait a minute," Cassius said. "It was simply what I must do. I am serving people in the family. I have no part in any of this—"

"*Where* did you take the money?" I asked. "Before you lie, I will tell you this. I shall ask you questions about the disappearance of Ennius, the first scribe who faithfully sent Augustus the information about costs that kept accumulating in Limyra, and notes about his worry over the money that seemed to come from Pericles's house, and the people who were taking advantage of Gaius."

He flinched, and then, his eyes hardened. "Ennius stole and ran away with his papers. He stole and made it look like I am to—wait." He took a long breath and calmed himself. "He wrote to Augustus, pretending he was worried. He paid normal sums for things Gaius bought, reported triple the cost, and kept the coin."

"And where are all these things Gaius bought?" I asked. "The house is empty. The house itself I see, and there is nothing in it, but what it came with."

He flinched. "Ennius—"

"Enough!" I roared.

He spoke very softly. "I took the money from one place to another. The money went to Vipsania."

"And where is the money now, Vipsania?" I asked. "Was it not given to the cook Dareios? You trusted the man, no? You invited him up all the time."

She said nothing. Her eyes were gleaming with tears.

"You hired him to poison Gaius," I said.

She whispered, "No. You cannot prove that."

"No?" I asked. "When you told me, you needed something from me, Vipsania, you said you only had a day to get it. You knew he was going to divorce you. I'll not talk about your request, Vipsania, but you were going to poison Gaius. Then you tried it."

She hesitated. "No. It is *not* true."

I turned to look at Larissa. "Pay attention, Cassius and Larissa. I shall tell a tale. Ennius, the diligent, good man who fled on the night the traders were killed, is dead."

Larissa took a step back, holding a hand over her mouth. "No."

"Your lover, Larissa. Marcus mentioned it. He is dead, murdered," I told them. "Nobody counts

322

servants, when bodies start to show up. Four murders in one night. Not a soul care for the odd one. Alexander said none counted them. The witness, Lucius, saw no body on the alley behind the house, so the body came there later. The man's fingers had been cut, to hide the ink stains."

Every eye went to the fingers of Cassius.

They were blue as sky.

"His face had been crudely carved off," I said. "He had, no doubt, been told by someone to go there and to take stock of the killings. No horn was blown for him. He was betrayed, murdered, and his scrolls, no doubt, taken."

Cassius was cursing. "Do I look like a warrior?"

"Yes," I said. "Suns and stars are those Germani prefer in their shields. You were young when you were captured, but you are a Germani. A freedman with a violent streak, are you not?"

He said nothing.

"You are guilty of that, Cassius, of murder. Of theft as well. You were stealing from Gaius, all the time. Ennius wrote to Rome, remember? He wondered at the prices of some of the things bought. House, no matter how noble, cost terribly. This house, thrice as much as any in Rome. Jewelry and rare pieces of art. And yet, none of it was brought here. A renovation costs more than a house, Cassius, and it is unfinished. Ennius—"

He roared and interrupted me. "Tried to make me look like a thief. I cut no fingers. I gave the money to

323

Vipsania, and she no doubt spent it on—"

I snapped my fingers. A legionnaire brought forth a dinner.

It was what Vipsania had been served.

It was set before me. All eyes were on it. It was old, cold, and looked nasty, especially the broth.

"Vipsania hired the cook Darius to kill Gaius," I said. "She knew she was about to be divorced, so she wanted both to be spared the humiliation, and she hoped to be a widow, and more."

A mother.

She looked pale as a ghost. "No."

"Yes. The cook took the coin. It was possible to succeed. He knew what Hiratius would not taste. The fish. Everyone knew. Cassius told me this."

The eyes went to the fish on the plate, filled with flies.

I shook my head. "Vipsania sent one of her girls to find a woman knowledgeable in poison. The rest went to the cook. He hid the coin."

Ariane looked down, and Larissa at me, in fury, fear, and then tears.

"Larissa?" I asked.

She nodded.

I smiled. "And then, because Cassius was curious, and had a hold on Larissa, and did what Laodamia asked him to do—"

She hissed. "Lies! This is—"

Hercules slapped her with the sword's blade. She went quiet.

"That night, Cassius, who had replaced the inconvenient Ennius, and was Laodamia's spy in the house—"

"I was not!"

"He is not!" Laodamia added and got another slap from a sword's edge.

I rapped my fingers on the sword's hilt. "Cassius just said, and Vipsania said before, that he deals with *everything* in the house. You arrange *everything*. On the day we arrived, Vipsania asked you to get a wagon for her and guards. Gaius didn't care, but Cassius knew. The next thing we know, Laodamia knows about it. Then, the rest follow when they see her moving along with Pericles. I bet one of the girls do not know how to be quiet. The families might be in war, but the girls see each other daily." I looked at Eudoxia, who looked at Corinne. "Aye. We came in secret, and everyone were there, because Cassius tells Laodamia everything."

Pericles sighed. "Do go on. Laodamia and Cassius are well connected. We all know it."

The two culprits were pale and shivered.

I nodded. "Indeed. Kyrillos paid to kill Gaius," I said. "Hiratius poisoned the food for him. I saw how Gaius was served the meal. Hiratius was there, naturally. Hiratius, no doubt, poisoned the food while he tasted it. Ironically, Gaius might have been poisoned twice. One dose on the fish from Dareios, and the rest by Hiratius."

They looked at me with doubt.

I smiled. "But there was no poison on the fish of

Gaius. There was something harmless poured on it, for Laodamia and Cassius didn't want Gaius killed, and Larissa obeyed Cassius, for he promised her Ennius would come home if she did."

Larissa wiped tears off her face, and ignored the savage looks from Vipsania, Laodamia, and Cassius.

"The cook Darius was paid, but the poison was never delivered to him. Larissa, did you give him the poison?"

She shook her head. "Something else. Nothing dangerous."

"Nothing dangerous," I said. "The poison, however, went somewhere."

They all looked at the tray before them.

I pointed a sword at it. "Cassius intercepted Ariane when she was taking Vipsania her dinner. Hiratius had tasted it in the kitchen. Larissa took over. She put the poison in the food. Perhaps she had to taste it before she set it before Vipsania, but she knew where it is. Is this true, Larissa?"

Silence.

"Larissa?" I asked.

"Ennius?" she asked with a small voice. "They said —"

"Whatever Cassius told you about Ennius, he is *not* coming back," I said. "He is lying to you. They are. He is gone. Cassius there is a bastard thief, and a murdering shit."

Hercules went to stand behind the man.

"And as said, he was not alone. He stole, but did he

326

steal for himself? Where are the things the money Gaius brought here were used for? Statues, jewels? Laodamia? Did you and Cassius have a pact from the day he arrived? She had, after all, long conspired to get Gaius in Limyra. Did she enlist you to help her make Gaius dependent on her? You spent his coin, then spied on him for her? Did you kill Ennius for her, and then enlisted Larissa to help you?"

Laodamia stepped forward. "Are you saying he works for me? That I ordered Vipsania to be murdered? Do you claim I gave such an order to him? Is that what you are telling everyone?"

"You deny? Fine. For that, we must ask Cassius," I said. "He does, after all, have a lot to answer for. Personally, I bet our Laodamia learnt of the poison from Cassius and was afraid Vipsania would not stop with one failure. Vipsania had crossed the line and was threatening her business. Perhaps she was just tired with the tardiness with which Gaius was divorcing Vipsania. A death had to be arranged. It was a risk. Alas, Vipsania was not in a mood to eat. I found her weeping, with the scroll, where Gaius had told her the divorce would take place that night. She didn't eat. I took the tray. She is a killer, she is, but also almost a victim."

They were all quiet. Then, softly, Larissa spoke. "Is Ennius truly dead?"

"Who are you asking?" I said.

"Cassius," she said.

"Wait," Cassius began. "This is not—"

"You told me he is held hostage," she whispered. "And if I obeyed you, if I shared your bed, and told you everything about Vipsania and obeyed your orders, I'd be rid of her, and free with Ennius. And he is dead? Was I to die when you were done with me?"

Cassius looked back at Hercules and decided against running.

She held her face and fled, dodging past a guard. I nodded. They let her go.

Cassius opened his mouth, and Laodamia looked pale as a ghost.

I pointed a sword at the dinner. "You will have it, Cassius. You will eat it. You shall enjoy every last bit of it, won't you?"

He eyed the food.

"Laodamia will join you," I said darkly.

She shook her head, horrified.

Hercules looked at me. "Shall I feed it to them?"

"Yes, of course," I said. Cassius stepped away from him, and I lifted my hand. "Deny, and you *shall* eat it. You and Laodamia? At this point, Cassius, I can promise you a fast death. But you saw Amyntas. You know what it can be like."

He croaked something and tried to stand straight.

Hercules was behind him and placed a sword over his shoulder. He took a deep breath and closed his eyes. "She approached me when we arrived. She had done her very best to get Gaius to visit Limyra and was

328

parading her daughters before him. She had a suggestion for me."

"She offered you much," I said. "She knew Ennius was honest. He was famous for it. She knew much about all of you already. Had she not sent Apollon to Gaius's court."

"She offered me everything," he said. "We spent all his coin, everything he was sent from Rome as well, and Laodamia took everything we bought. Ennius, when an opportunity came, had to die. He had sent his missives to Rome with a courier, not a ship. We were supposed to stop his messages, but he was clever. So, we killed him, destroyed his scrolls and tablets, and claimed he had fled a thief. And as for the poison, and Larissa…yes. It is all true. Vipsania became a problem when she dared to approach Kyrillos and dared to plot to kill her husband." He sighed and went to his knees. "If I only had taken Gaius's money and fled…"

I looked at Vipsania, whose eyes were on Laodamia. "You whore," she whispered.

"You are a silly girl, dear," she answered, shivering with fear. "And I care little for your opinion. Really, centurion?" She turned to me and shook her head. "You have so far managed to prove that there have been two attempted murders in the house in addition to the one of Gaius. One was Vipsania, the desperate bitch, conspiring against her husband. The other one was an attempt on her own life. I say they all lie. Let me be judged by my countrymen, if I must be judged at all."

"No."

She spat and stepped towards me. "You have caught the killer of your Roman traders, and the actor, and you have killed Kyrillos, who killed Gaius with poison. You have Apollon, who at least helped Kyrillos get rid of the witnesses. Hiratius and Dareios both worked for them and were killed. You have Andromache, and you have Meliton's girl. You have your victims. And you still haven't told us who was in that room with Gaius. You have achieved nothing."

"I have found a reason," I snarled, "not to be gentle with any of you. And I shall not be."

She stepped forward again, like a lion. "None of us took his scrolls. It was, no doubt, one of your guards. They heard him crying and then left their post. They saw value in Gaius's scrolls, or his purse, and ended his life, out of pity. You shall never know. It might be really terrible for Rome to see it spreading around. Look to your men. Go and ask Marcus and Avila, and not I."

I frowned. Then, I smiled and walked back and forth.

"It is a curious thing, isn't it? That the guards might find coins from Gaius, who cared little for them," I said. "Indeed, who had none thanks to you. Perhaps they wanted to sell whatever Gaius had written down in his will? Perhaps?"

"Perhaps," Laodamia said. "I imagine there are a lot of secrets there. Ask them."

"Like, whom Gaius had in the room," I said. "I was wrong."

"Of course, you were," Pericles said. "There is none here who would profit in his death. Now, can we—"

"No," I said. "You misunderstand. Gaius was stabbed for a reason. It was not to make sure he died in Kyrillos's plans, or for benefit, or for hate. Segolia told me. It was for something else."

Segolia said. "It cut for love."

I nodded. "For love. Gaius was laughing. He was always laughing in that room. Whoever was in there *let* him go. For love. That someone eased his death, took the scrolls, one which was a divorce from Vipsania and his will, his confession that would embarrass Rome but himself as well. That someone is either going to use them to avenge his death, or to protect his secrets. For love."

They were quiet, and I watched their faces.

They held their calm but only barely. None made a move, which might be thought to be provocative.

"Which one of you girls, or women," I asked them, "was with him when he died? To which one did he read poetry, when he fell, poisoned, and died? Eudoxia? You are Laodamia's choice, since Lysirate seems not to please her."

"None of us," Lysirate whispered. "Not one of us. Not even simpering Eudoxia. The door was guarded."

"Which one was he going to marry?" I asked him. "Clearly, he was."

Eudoxia stepped forward. "Me, possibly. Corinne, he flirted with. He smiled to Lysirate, who found him repulsive, and he liked to speak with Bernike. But—"

"Silence," Laodamia said. "Be quiet, girls." She gave me a speculative look. "Aye. Of course, we spoke of it. I spoke with him of it many times. He agreed to marry one. Eudoxia, she was his choice. But Eudoxia was whom he was passionate for. Nobody could have entered that room past your soldiers, save the soldiers, centurion."

"Mother?" she breathed. "That is not…he was always kind, but never passionate. Never…"

Vipsania smiled thinly.

"In love," I said. "It matters little to your mother, dear. Now. To answer how you, or someone else who loved him, entered that room, and left, and how someone heard us planning, we must again ask a question. Gaius bought this house. Who did he buy it from?"

I looked at Cassius. "Remember Amyntas."

He sighed. "He bought it from Pericles. It was his house, originally. He has now another, newer one over to the north."

I nodded. "Now, I met a man on the way here. He said the house of Pericles is an ancient one. Older than the stones, and as stubborn. He told me how Pericles of old had once escaped his house though the very earth, slithering like a snake to a crack in a wall. That was amusing, and only lately interesting. I see snakes everywhere in this house. Mostly on the floors. Many on other houses around this one, which, no doubt, are those of Pericles? The soldiers wouldn't be allowed to have a camp there if Pericles hadn't arranged it. There are mosaics and wall paintings. All the rooms in this house are swept religiously. All the rooms have furniture, which is bulky. Many desks." I was nodding. "Is it not so, that this house is the Pericles family secret? The very center of their old power? And Gaius took it over, to meet in secret with his lover. Let us see the room again."

I walked past them and went to the garden. I heard them following and pushed to the doorway through my men. They spread behind me. Hercules was close, his sword out, and Segolia was there as well, eyeing the room.

I walked to the middle of the room, and we all stopped to look at Gaius.

He was laying under a sheet, to the side, on a bench carried there. He had been washed, but the floor had not, and there, dried excrement and blood ruined the floor ornaments.

I toed the crack in the floor. I tapped my foot, and a hollow sound echoed across the house.

I looked at Pericles. "How many know? How far do they reach?"

He took a ragged breath. "Many people in the city know the city is hollow. The exact location of these doorways in our house? I don't know who knows. We never speak of them."

I nodded at the floor. "The desk was moved off and

on and used to cover this spot. You are right. Someone knew. One of the women knew about them. Gaius's lover did know, and that one must step forward now."

Laodamia sneered at me. "And here we are again. You have no proof which one? It could be all of us. Or none."

I nodded at Hercules.

They turned to look at him. He held ropes.

They turned to look back at me, fetters jingling.

I lifted my chin. "It seems I cannot prove a thing. You are right, Laodamia. So, if the people in this room do not start talking, if the secret is not revealed, and I do not have those scrolls in my hands, we shall hang people from the youngest to the oldest. It is quite simple. You have all reasons to hang, as we have established, and we shall administer Roman justice right now."

They stared at me, their mouths open. A legionnaire grasped Eudoxia's hand, and Pericles stepped forward. "Centurion! No! I—"

Alexander moved forward.

He surged past Hercules, slapped his sword away, and pulled a dagger from under his armor.

I lifted my sword, but the man dodged under it like a lighting.

He crashed his fist on my wounded side, and I howled with the pain. The bastard placed the dagger under my chin and turned to look into my eyes. I watched him, not moving. "Out of all of them, you thought I was the only one," he whispered, "who had no secrets and desires? A man without any ambition, but to serve, and lick the crumbs off the table?" He snorted and pulled me with him. He kicked at the floor and pressed a tile. The floor tilted, and he pried the stone away, and eyed the hole below. "We all know about them, centurion. The holes. Why else would you block them with heavy furniture? We know about the hollow city. Pericles is a fool to think he is the only one. I already knew. These are no secrets, Roman."

"You did it?" I asked. "You were here?"

He shook his head. "No, of course not. I didn't. I had no wish to spend time with Gaius, Roman. No wish to do so at all. I followed Pericles and Laodamia, Roman, not because of loyalty and gratitude for my position, but because one day, they will overstep, and I will take over the family fortunes and power."

Pericles was staring at him in shock. "Alexander, what—"

"Your stupidity, and her greed and evil, uncle," he said darkly, "disgusted me. You damned bastards. The Furies you speak of? They defend the land? Nay, I shall do it. I care not, you decadent bastards, who was in here and killed the man. For love, or for hate, I do not care. I want you to know that. I didn't hate him. I just despised the weak bastard like I do you, Pericles."

"So, it was you," I said. "You sent the riders."

"No," he answered. "It wasn't I. I told you. I care nothing for the Furies. That was someone else. That was someone you have angered, Roman. Didn't you challenge them? However, it seems the time is past for you to go. It is too bad, really. This is too early for me. See, one day soon, I, Alexander, shall be a Tyrant of Lycia. I would have let my family grow richer, more prosperous, more influential. I would have known everything I need to know in order to destroy Roman sympathizers and to make plans. Now, I must take what remains and make the best of it. You will see, friends, how this end. In blood. But I do need a hostage."

He was looking at Vipsania.

She shook her head. "You cannot think I will let you..."

He sneered and cut my skin. "I shall have you, and hold you, like Paris held Helen, perhaps. Rome is right to fear rebellion in Lycia. The land is ripe for it. You lot came here to stomp it out, but you really just culled the weak ones. Now, I shall cull the rest. Centurion, say your prayers." He eyed the hole and tightened his hold on my throat. He would cut it and jump down to fetch his men.

At that, Segolia appeared.

She stepped from the side and stabbed her blade in Alexander's arm. It sliced to his shoulder, and he howled, pushing me back.

He cursed.

He took a step back.

He fell through the hole and took the tile with him with a terrible crash.

I whirled to look down and saw only darkness and

heard splashes as someone was running through caves.

I turned to look at the lot. "Hercules, tell Marius to prepare for an attack. If he is not here yet, then get Marius in here with the rest of the men right this moment. Send a man to tell him to hurry. Get pila, shields, and gather the men in here."

Hercules shook his head. "Alexander knows the caves below. They can come in from anywhere."

I nodded. "I know. That's why we must leave after Alexander now. We cannot leave Marius, though."

Meliton took a step forward. "But we cannot escape the city. Alexander is mad. He will stop us and kill us. There are walls, and he has far more men. Will you protect us?"

I nodded. "We came here to punish a murderer. I came to find a city so filled with greed and hate, and bitter, nasty family feuds, that I see no reason to guard you. You deserve to die, most of you. But you shall all come. We have the business of the scroll to settle."

"Yes," Meliton said. "It wasn't Corinne, so you don't have to—"

"Which one of you women did it?"

They all shook their heads, eyeing the ropes Hercules had tossed on the floor.

"How many ways are there inside, and where do they lead?" I roared.

Lysirate took a step toward me, trying to calm me. "You have lost too many men, centurion. It is clear Alexander did it and tries to blame us. Poor Marcus, who was always so happy. You must—"

Pericles took a small step forward. "Hush, Lysirate. Fine, Decimus. We will run into the darkness below with you. There are five to six ways to the house from below. We block them with heavy tables, but they can be forced open. From most all the bigger rooms surrounding the atrium, and the gardens, they can get in."

"Where do they lead outside?" I asked. "How did one of you come to this room?"

Pericles stared ahead, and the girls were shrugging. "Everywhere?" he wondered. "They lead everywhere."

I looked at Hercules, who was coming back. "Well?"

"Marius is late," he said. "I sent a man."

"I need a way to the southern part of the city," I said. "Tell me how? And save yourselves."

Apollon, carried forth by two guards, was speaking. "I can guide you. I have been running down there with the girls when I was young. I can probably take us to a necropolis that is near the southern gates. Beyond them, in fact. There is a stable near."

Eurydike shook her head and pointed a finger at me. "If Apollon saves you lot, if he spares you, will you let him go? I beg of you, let him be. The girls as well."

I nodded. "I will spare the one who gives me that scroll. You will all come with me. We go together, and later, we shall settle the scores with Alexander, the would-be tyrant. We must get to Nefarious. Guide us, and I will grant you—"

Horn rang outside. This was not a deep horn we had heard so many times, but a bright, brazen, military one, blessed with silvery notes. It didn't ring once, or twice. It rang constantly, wildly, demanding attention. It was a horn born of war, a horn of the Lycian troops, and Alexander had been ready.

"Sir!" called out a man on the doors. "There are men converging outside the walls!"

I whirled, looked below, and cursed.

I spoke to Hercules. "We are too late. Alexander has been preparing. Get the men in here! Everyone! Do not defend the doors, they can get inside! Here, make a line around this room! Defend the body of Gaius!"

Hercules turned to obey.

Somewhere outside, I heard Marius yelling orders to those men who were still in the barrack. I also heard the calls of Lycians and then the clash of steel on steel.

"Inside the room, you bastards," I hissed. "Alexander likes the lot of you just as much as he like us."

They shuffled inside the rooms. Vipsania tried to grasp my hand, and I pushed her away. I counted them and didn't see Larissa or Ariane. I looked at Segolia and nodded at Hercules. "Fast now."

The man roared orders. "A few men inside to guard the shit-hole on the floor!"

I pushed Segolia aside. I smiled at her. "So, is this where you saw us all die?"

"I said it is possible we die," she answered. "What

can we do? They outnumber us."

"We can fight? We will fight," I said. "And it is my fault."

She pushed my hair aside as Hercules tossed me my helmet. I watched her carefully and spoke to her gently. "Here. Take this." I gave her a scroll. "Take it to Nefarious. They will leave for Rome, and you go with them. It is for Augustus. Fish-Bait knows what else he must do."

She frowned and looked at me nervously. "And you?"

"We'll give them a proper fight," I said, and caressed her face briefly. "Apollon!"

The man was dragged forward and looked at me with frightened eyes. He was wringing his hands, and the chains were clinking. "Everything you hoped for your family, Apollon, if you get her to the Nefarious. Everything. All is forgiven, and riches follow."

His face brightened, but only until someone screamed from pain outside. He went pale as a ghost.

"What is below?" I asked him.

"There are caves, wet with rivulets of water, and streams..." he said. "Tunnels that run from here to the mountain. It is a maze. I know some ways."

"You must find one that you spoke of. Free his legs, not his arms." I gave Segolia her dagger. "Hercules! Send our men to go with them. Tell one to take them to Nefarious. You know what you tell the other two."

Hercules grasped our three remaining men and

340

spoke to them in hushed tones.

I found Apollon was speaking. "What?"

"I said, I am sorry," Apollon told me. "You know, I never did take part in Gaius's death. Kyrillos —"

"As I said, it will be forgiven," I told him. "Get going and good luck. Guide them. And Apollon, if you hurt her, if you do? I shall kill all the Furies in the world and rape them with my sword to find you. I have found men beyond the horizon before. One day, if you die, I will find you in Hades too. Trust me."

He grinned, nodded, and turned to Eurydike, who stepped forward and embraced him. She kissed his ear and held on, eyes closed, speaking to him gently, and then, he took steps back. Eurydike gave me a grateful smile. "To imagine," she said, "that we might actually fall on our feet if we work together with Rome. It shall be so. He will go. Alexander will have men below soon."

"Go, then," I said, and choked as Segolia followed him to the edge of the hole. He looked down, closed his eyes, and slipped below. Then, I saw his hand, and Segolia grasped it.

She jumped after him. One by one, my three remaining men jumped after her.

"Guard the hole," I said heavily. "The others, go and stand at the end of the room."

Two men pulled swords and stood over the hole, careful not to be seen, and the rest of us walked out. There were twenty men there, and two more were loping downstairs from the top. We spread to cover the doorway and stood in a double line.

I took the middle and Hercules was talking to an optio who was standing behind.

Their standard was in the other house.

They still had their pride.

The door was being banged on. There were calls, and some were coming from below the ground.

Let them hurry, I thought, and prayed for my men.

I grunted and stepped forward. I turned to look at the men. "Soldiers. You might wonder what the noise is all about?"

They grinned and nodded.

"There are a bunch of beggars," I said. "A group of misfits and thieves that wear armor, but who do not know how to fight. They fight like a child would, with their cocks erect from fear, and noses dripping. They'll come from the doors, from below, if they don't get lost, and they'll make a shoddy line before us. They'll try to look martial, they'll walk back and forth, and squeak their threat at us, but we don't care, do we?"

"No!" they called out. "Never!"

"Good," I said. "They'll get to preen all they want. Let them! Let them cry later. They are rebels. They are led by their captain, and that captain wants to molest the body of Gaius with his toy-sword, and he wants to take prisoner the thieving, greedy shits inside the very room, and then, they will take Vipsania. He wants her, you see. You know why."

Their eyes went hard, and they all seemed to growl like a pack of hungry dogs.

"We'll not let them do that, do we? No. Augustus would take a dim view on us if we did."

The soldiers turned their faces forward. They would not let Augustus think ill of them.

I walked back to the room and looked around. The two guards nodded, and the people stared at me, a row of bastards and opportunists, standing over dead Gaius.

Laodamia stepped forward, shaking. "There is no way to buy him off?"

"I don't know," I told her. "You may try after he gets past us. You seem to fear him more than you did me, just now."

She stepped closer still. "I do not, but he cannot be bargained with, and he will win. He has the men. Please, let us leave. Like we should. I can tell you, it wasn't me who slit Gaius's belly. But there is someone who did it, and who helped Gaius on his way. I can tell you who it was if it puts your mind at ease. That one can tell you more later. You will probably find the scroll as well. This person will have it."

I hesitated, cursed, and watched Eudoxia clutch Laodamia's arm in fear.

Cassius was walking back and forth, terrified. Vipsania was weeping.

Pericles knelt before the dead Gaius, and Lysirate, with Corinne and Eurydike, began to pray. Bernike was holding on to Meliton's arm, her uncanny beauty

343

shocked with fear. Aristomache stood alone, her eyes closed, as if hoping to die, the fetters jingling.

Ariane and Larissa were still missing.

I nodded at the men guarding the hole and turned to fight. "You take your chances, Laodamia, like the rest will. If we win, we shall speak more. If you think I can be bargained with, I suppose we can reach a deal, you evil bitch. Go away. Go to the others."

She walked back. "You will lose."

"Not if things go the way I planned," I answered.

There was a huge crash on the outer doorway. There were feet thumping and men cursing in Greek. There were doors opening in the atrium and then silent whispers.

I took my place before the doorway and cursed the mistakes that had been made.

We watched the movement and the men appearing. To our right, a door opened, and a Lycian stepped out, his shield high. Another followed, smeared and muddy, and few more.

Out of the atrium's doors, similar men appeared, swords out, and a great mass of men were marching through the main door. Their horsehair helmets and round shields filled the atrium, and the smell of sweat, and grease, and metal filled our nostrils. Calling out to each other, they looked up to the other floors, and to the room, but Alexander was amongst them, and he kept staring ahead.

He pointed his sword at us.

The thronging enemy marched towards us, emerging from the side rooms and from the atrium. Young men, men with no other prospects, not the brightest or the best, had been made into soldiers. They looked at us and our grim line with worry, but then, they looked at each other, saw they outnumbered us four to one, and walked forward.

I nodded. Hercules beside me lifted his sword, and wordlessly, the legionnaires lifted their pila. Hercules leaned over. "Well. If this is it, I'll be damned. Killed by shepherds. They think we are lambs."

"They'll remember us," I said. "We'll shear the lot, not the other way around. If not, I'll see you again, one day. Toss them."

"Throw!" Hercules howled.

And they tossed the pila.

They sailed across the garden with deadly, whooshing sound.

They sank to a line of the enemy soldiers, hitting shield here and there, and tearing into armor and the flesh beneath, dropping men screaming on their backs, knees, and faces.

"Again" I hissed.

"Throw!" yelled Hercules. The men obeyed. They had many pila and kept throwing them at the chaos before them. The enemy were trying to form a line, hoping to stand and hold, but the dead and the dying before and under them made it a futile effort. So, did the garden's trees, the furniture, and the shallow pond, the corridors. The pila crashed into more of them, and they howled and clawed at the bent spear shafts. Ten, twenty, many crawled away spattered in their own blood or that of their dead comrades, trying to get away.

Alexander, a bent javelin on his shield, was standing amid them.

He had a look on his face which spoke of an opportunity for glory being missed. Spittle flying on his falling men, he commanded them forward.

"Onwards! Onwards for your lives, for our glory! Take the usurpers to Hades, friend! Obol for them, and three steps to the gates of the dark god!" he yelled. "Kill them, charge them!"

And they did.

Climbing over their fallen, pushing away furniture, splashing through the pond, they howled and rushed forward.

We tightened our ranks, lobbing the last pila. One man caught the last such in his groin and screamed his life away at the edge of the pond, but dozens of them filled the garden before us, and we lifted our shields as they crashed into them. They came forward, short swords flashing, and as they struck us, we stepped forward, in a line of leather and steel, and bowled over many in the first line, forcing them to crash amid their next rankers. The chain mails jingled as our shield took the enemy shields and swords stabbed furiously. Ten of them fell. Ten others howled, screamed at their wounds, and the rest pushed at our shields, some past and through them, where the second line slammed shields on the jubilant, terrified bastards, and stabbed most down.

Two legionnaires died, stabbed from many sides, and one was hewn down by an ax.

I fought and put down men.

My next foe was a large man, as tall a bastard as I was. His curly hair was gleaming under his helmet, his face sweaty and bloodied, the huge eyes filled with anger. He rammed his shield into mine. I nearly slipped on blood. He hacked down with a half-moon bladed ax. It split my shield's rim, and he tried to pull me out of the ranks, but I stabbed at his throat, missed, and hit his eye, and the giant crashed down, dead and twitching like a fish on a hook.

Hercules was pulling me to the doorway, and there, we endured.

The enemy came, furiously, killing a man, pulling another among them, where Hercules jumped after the poor shit, stabbed one enemy in the neck, while the others pulled our man back to the ranks. Hercules, slashing with manic strength, killed another as he came back. There, we stood, and shields high, chanting encouragements, we killed. They came, they tried to find a way past our shields, and often found a blade in their thigh, crotch, belly, or throat. The throng came again, trying to ram into us, through us, hoping to break into the room beyond, but we bent and pushed back. The men in the second line stabbed at the men while we held them with the shields, and not even Alexander's cries could help out.

I heard warning in the room behind and hazarded a look. I saw a Lycian falling back to the hold, spitting blood.

I grinned, thanked gods for such a fine fight, cursed them for putting us there, and kept my rapidly disintegrating shield up.

"At them, at them!" Alexander howled. I saw him, not too far, barely unable to move, as his men tried. Panting, all tired, they pushed at us, and we, just as tired, kept pushing back and slaying.

"Come and kiss the blade of Mars!" I called out to Alexander. "Come, captain! Pit your pitiful sword against mine! I'll piss on yours after you die!"

He roared, his men pushed past him, the water in the pond splashing around, men jumping over wounded crawling from the battle and the dead.

A wave came at us again.

This time, three pushed past us. Hercules turned to kill one with a stab in the neck.

Another slipped past him, and two more.

Those men fought like mad things within our ranks. They stabbed at the sides and killed a legionnaire. They bowled over two men behind me. They slashed about with no discipline, no fear, full of rage, and I knew they had to die.

I turned and pushed my shield into them.

A hand was over my shield, another on my face.

Someone stabbed my back, but I ignored it. A blade was grating on my chainmail, and a knee caught my wound, but roaring, I stabbed my sword forward like a butcher. I took down one, cutting his shoulder and most of his arm off. I slashed and sawed at a man who crashed into me and tore his helmet off, then his throat. I hacked down and killed a man who was crawling away.

I turned to see Alexander and dozen men with axes coming to where the door was.

I held the door alone.

He hacked down at the captain, and I took his sword with the shield, and he still struck my helmet. I was dizzy as he pushed me inside the room, and his men spread to kill the men who had been cut from the door. Howling, killing, slaying like dogs, they attacked ferociously. I saw Hercules briefly hacking in a throng until a man stuck him with a hammer, and my friend fell, still howling challenges. I blocked the door just barely, fighting with Alexander, who rammed a shield into mine, and both our swords were locked together.

A spear, and then another was pushing over his shoulders, and one slashed to my helmet and under the cheek guard, cutting my face. I recoiled, Alexander stumbled forward and past me, and just as his men were coming in, the two guards in the room attacked them. Stabbing, pushing, roaring, they blocked the door, but Alexander was past them. He whirled, eyed me briefly, and attacked.

He had no skills for such a duel.

I dodged under his wild swing, kicked his knee, and stabbed my sword at his falling figure. I tore my blade's tip to his eye. It scraped along the side of his skull, cut away at his hair, part of his ear, and he crashed on the floor.

I stepped over him, turned to call for the enemy to stop fighting, and then felt a blade slipping to my back. I whirled, the blade came out, and I saw Corinne before me, her pale eyes wide, and I knew he had never let go of her. The dagger tore at my chain and flesh, and I pushed her back.

Bernike was coming, holding a hand over her face. "No! Do not—"

I knew then Alexander would never have let me take Corinne to Rome. He had made her promises and she loved him. He wanted her, for her connections and beauty. For his plans, Myra would be a great ally. Corinne had not killed Gaius. I was sure of that. Her eyes shone with love for Alexander. I felt sorry for Meliton, who would have to answer to Alexander for breaking their engagement.

Alexander whirled on the ground and kicked at me. Corinne, bravely, came on as well. I blocked the dagger, and then, I stabbed at Corinne, who fell on the blade, howled, and rolled to the side. Alexander kicked me again, trying to get up. He connected with my back. I fell forward, crashed to the hole, and fell below to the darkness.

There, trying to get up, holding my sword

ferociously, I felt hands grasping me and pulling me along.

The last thing I heard were men cheering their victory.

And I heard Alexander howling for Corinne's death.

CHAPTER 12

I woke up in darkness. I got up and felt dizzy. Then, there were hands groping for my face.

"Must be silent," said a small voice. "Please."

"Very quiet," said another. "And still. Silent and still."

I tried to see, but it was impossible. Then, I saw a light, coming and going, disappearing like a wraith, far ahead, and smelled the burning from an oil lamp that had been extinguished. The air was stuffy, earthy.

"Who are you?" I whispered and winced. I was pained all over, and my face was sore when I spoke. I felt myself bleeding down my chin. I put a hand on one shadow next to me and found a delicate arm. "Segolia?"

"No," said the voice. "Ariane. Larissa's here too."

I sat up and froze as my sword scraped the floor. It was beside me. The girls froze.

There was no sound. Nobody came, and the light far in the tunnels disappeared.

They dared to speak. "I followed Ariane down here," Larissa whispered. "She ran after me, and we found a room, and a trapdoor. Then, we heard the battle, saw men in the semi-dark. And you fell."

"You just found it, eh? Which one of you," I asked, touching the wound on my face, "was with Gaius when he died?"

Ariane shook her head. "I found it, the trapdoor, just now. Not before."

Larissa hissed. "Oh, shut up, both. Neither one! Remember, I was busy poisoning our damned mistress." I almost felt her smiling in the dark. "I supposed I should not have helped you. You don't seem grateful."

I rubbed my face and shook my head, but of course, she couldn't see it. "Do you know what happened up there? And do you know anything about this place?"

Ariane spoke. "I told you. We just found it. This place is a maze of tight tunnels, darkness, spiderwebs, snakes, and ghosts."

Larissa took a shuddering breath. Both were terrified.

She went on. "Some seem to be parts of an old city, and others are just caves. Wet all over, with streams trickling through the floor. Ice cold. In light, it looks like a sponge."

"You have fire to light the lamp?" I asked.

Larissa grunted. "Of course."

"Good," I breathed. "Very good. Now, did you hear what happened up there?"

Ariane sighed. "We don't. I know they sent men below to find you. We dragged you away and then hid behind a pillar of stone, and an old wall. We heard the Lycians celebrating, and the cries of Laodamia, may she rot, and her girls begging. There was a jingle of fetters. I heard that Alexander howling and cursing, and he called your name a few times. I don't think he wants to be a friend, though."

"I imagine not," I said.

Larissa took up the discussion. "I think they took some prisoners. They have men seeking the place, but I suppose this Alexander only knows some of the ways, and who they send here are suspicious and afraid. They just basically stay on the bigger paths."

"Vipsania?"

Ariane spat. Larissa spoke. "She was screaming. They took her away, I heard her voice receding. That Alexander, I hope he hangs her."

"I hope they feed her to the pigs," Ariane said. "She has beaten me for weeks. Ever since Gaius told me he will not take me a lover. Perhaps he knew Vipsania tried to spy on him. She didn't need to. He told her plainly he doesn't care for her."

I rubbed my face. "Alexander has been watching her with more than passing interest. She might find her virtues compromised."

Larissa took my arm and squeezed. "What do we do now? How do we get out of here?"

I was thinking. "If we are lucky, Apollon took Segolia away. With luck, they are safe and out of the harbor on Nefarious, blocking the place no doubt until morning, and then, the galley shall leave."

"We could try to get there fast," Larissa suggested. "Make our way there, take a boat, and escape."

I smiled. "Oh, we could. We could, indeed. And even you, Larissa?"

"Yes? Why not?" Larissa asked, exasperated. "Look.

I did what I did for Ennius. I helped you, so you let me go. I only want to be free. If he is dead, I have nothing left but the future I build for myself."

I sighed. "You tried to kill the wife of Gaius. No matter what she is, it is for Augustus to—"

"You were pardoning the others as well," Ariane said. "Meliton. Others. Aristomache."

"I was," I said. "But whether or not Augustus will, is a different matter."

"Roman lies," Larissa said bitterly. "We take our chances." She began moving.

"Wait," I told her, and grasped her hand. She tried to tug it out of my grip but settled when I didn't let her. "Fine. I will take you both back to Rome when we leave, and neither need to serve anyone again."

They were silent. Larissa spoke. "What for? That is surely an expensive gift. Wait. You don't mean to leave. You didn't mention the galley. You said, 'when we leave.'"

I laughed softly. "Girls. I'm a soldier. And when a soldier goes to battle, what does he do in order to win?"

Larissa hazarded a guess. "You pray?"

"We *prepare*," I said. "We are prepared."

"You nearly died," she said dully. "Many times. Your men died. Your preparations were terrible."

"We were surprised, and still, we are prepared," I said. "We just didn't have enough time up there. We are not lost yet. Had I died we still would have a chance of success."

They were quiet. I felt a hand on my helmet and then beneath it. "What are you doing?" I asked.

Larissa sounded calming. "You have hit your head, centurion. I am just checking —"

I pushed her back. "Oh, lay off. I am fine. I wonder if they took the lot to the Acropolis?"

Larissa nodded. I saw better in the dark now, though only shadows. "They would, maybe. That's where the original Pericles ruled from and where this Alexander hopes to rule from as well. I heard him. He would be a Tyrant. There, he has a wall to protect him, but also a fortress hewn into the mountain's side. I've seen it."

"And they'll search for me tomorrow," I said. "I'll find them first."

"You are hurt," she said. "Your mail saved you. You cannot possibly think you —"

"I have a sword, which suffices. Happily, I have something else as well."

"Ennius," she said. "He is truly dead?"

"Ennius?" I said. "Yes. Cassius killed him and blamed it on Amyntas."

"Amyntas," she said. "He always seemed strange…but a killer?"

"Amyntas, indeed," I said. "We must deal with Alexander."

"How?" she asked.

I shook my head, and rubbed my eyes, wincing at the pain in my side, and back. I was leaking blood all over.

Who had been in that room? Virtually anyone? Laodamia

would know. She almost told me.

Larissa was sitting patiently in the dark and staring at me. Ariane was weeping softly, and I put a hand on her shoulder, trying to soothe her. She leaned to lay on my lap, and I caressed her hair absentmindedly.

"He did that as well," she said happily. "Though nothing more."

I was nodding, thinking, and then looked down at her. "Who?"

"Gaius," she whispered. "I had once been close to him. He had even…you know. Touched me once, in Armenia. Never more than that. He said that he is not interested in such as I."

Snob bastard.

I rubbed my face and nodded. I had a duty. I had to get to the Acropolis, and I had to do it then.

For that, I needed friends.

"So, here is what we shall do," I said. "We must find a man."

Ariane, very close, was blinking. Larissa leaned forward and pulled Ariane back. "Oh, stop it. He wants a man, not you."

"Not any man," I said. "A historian. His name is Drakon, and he once offered to tell me about the Furies, the city, and its families. No matter what Alexander is doing, we must guard Rome. I must, and so you must as well, if you value your lives and freedom. Come, let us find a way out. Then, I shall tell you exactly what we are going to do. It is our turn to make our move."

Larissa leaned over and pulled me up. I winced for the pain, and they pulled me along and I kept my head low.

CHAPTER 13

The tunnels were wet, and sometimes, we waded in the water to our waist. The ancient remains of the walls showed marks of fire, and some parts of the buildings above had half-sunken to the ground. The oil lamp, held by Larissa, was sputtering as we jumped from rock to another, and then, after a while, she leaned up to look at a hole above us. I looked over her shoulder and Ariana over mine. There were bones far above, and a broken vase, and a coffin jutting just above us. "Necropolis," she whispered, as wind whipped across the room. "They have far too many of them."

I agreed with a nod. "Get up there."

She sighed. "I can't reach a handhold."

I bent down and cupped my hands, and she stepped on them. I pushed her up, pushed her buttock, and she made it. She turned to help Ariane up, and then, I grasped their hands, and we made it higher. We climbed a rough slop upwards for the tiny bit of shivering light past the bones, and soon, we were looking out of a hole next to an old, half crumbled tomb under some cedar trees.

"It's the stream, the smaller river that runs through the city from the springs below," Larissa noted.

"Aye," I said. There was a bridge, not far, and the small area of mausoleums was a forlorn reminder of death amid cluttered streets.

"See," Larissa whispered. "This underworld's no

secret. These holes are all around the city. It is just a matter of finding the right ones. It is terrifying, though, no?"

"You don't fear much," I whispered.

"I do not," she agreed. "I don't fear. When I was bought for Vipsania before she left for Asia with Gaius and Ariane as well, I had served a rich lanista for years. He taught me fear must be conquered."

"Lanista, eh?" I asked. "Fine. Shh, do not move." We stayed in the shadows, and I saw eight Lycian soldiers marching over the small bridge across the stream. A dog was following them, hoping for company or food. I looked at the two girls and their smudged appearance and looked across some of the mausoleums and tombs, many and well carved. "Death rules the city, indeed. Here is what must be done. Listen. The historian is called Drakon, and he lives near the temple of Apollon on the western edge. Wake the bastard up. Bring him to the inn. To the Flute."

"They'll be looking for you there," Larissa said. "They will be waiting."

"They will come, if they are not there already," Ariane said desperately. "Please, you must not! They will come and arrest you—"

"I need a drink," I said. "Get Drakon in there. No matter if he sleeps. I think he won't mind helping such pretty, young girls in distress. Bat an eye and show him some thigh if he is not willing to come."

They gave me an evil eye.

I rubbed my temple. "Fine. Just get him there. Tell him   Rome   needs   him."

"Temple of Apollo?" Larissa asked. "The city is a dangerous place for two girls at night."

I smiled. "I pity the city, if it challenges you two. Take this. First, one of you must do something. It might be dangerous." I gave Larissa a dagger and then leaned closer to the redhead beauty and pulled Ariane near as well and whispered something to their ears. I let them go, to see if they understood.

Both looked shocked and shook their heads.

"Do it."

Larissa nodded. "I will do it. Then, Drakon."

I nodded.

Ariane grinned nervously and pulled Larissa along. Both wore dirty tunica, ripped in places, and I decided they would indeed succeed to convince Drakon to come along. They disappeared to the stream, and I walked for the agora which I could see near. I moved forward, the sword ready, and passed the agora in shadows. I passed a few drunken bandits and beggars, and none looked at me twice.

Most were celebrating, even the poor ones, and no doubt felt proud Rome, which had butchered men of Kyrillos, had been humiliated.

"I'll show you bastard shits some humiliation," I whispered to no-one.

I thought of Hercules, my friend, begged Segolia was in safety, and cursed Fortuna, who had left me in deep shit.

I had to get to Laodamia. She knew. She at least knew the person who had been in that room if she was not the one.

It had not been Corinne, likely. Vipsania, of course it had not been her. Eurydike was too old, and honest. Neither one of the slaves fit the picture, and they had saved me.

Lysirate, Bernike, Eudoxia, Laodamia.

It had been a woman. The smudges in the sofa suggested the company Gaius enjoyed there was more than intellectual. One of them had been there.

It had been so close.

If not for Alexander, if not for the one I had thought to be too dull and foolish to matter, I would know all by now.

He had mattered. And now, I had to fix it.

I needed help to learn all I could of Alexander, the acropolis, and the Furies, if they showed up. I needed Laodamia, and I had to get her fast.

We were in deep shit.

I found the street back towards the River Limyrus, looked up at the acropolis, the Pericles's Tomb, the lit walls, and the temples and necropolis below, the theatre as well, and cursed the city again.

Happily, as I had told the girls, I never went to war unprepared.

I kicked away a rat which scuttled my way and walked for the inn, which was empty.

On the doorstep sat the boy who had tried to steal from me. I walked to him, and he got up, wiping his fingers on his tunic. "Sir."

"Boy," I said, and fished him a coin. "I need to know something."

He nodded. "They came."

"Truly?" I asked. "They are there?"

"Indeed," he said. "They are."

I leaned down on him. "And did not any of my men come here this very night, not long before?"

He shook his head. "None of your men came."

"Oh, really," I said, knowing it was unwelcome news. "Go and tell the boys this." I leaned close to him and gave him another coin. This one was a silvery one. "Use it for my journey to Hades, if I die in there." Then, I told him what to do.

He grinned, saluted, and ran off.

I entered the inn.

The room was quiet and empty. A cat was seated on a man's lap, and that man was drunk as a sailor. It was the inn keep. He eyed me as I leaned on the doorway and dropped the cup he had been holding and the cat as well. It shattered to thousand pieces, and the cat peered at the carnage with interest. "Oh, please," he whispered. "Do not, do not kill me, oh, ghost! Leave me alive, and I shall pray on you and on your success in the afterlife."

The cat jumped down to lap up the wine, and I walked in, in terrible pain. My leg was bleeding, my side as well, and my face was caked in blood from a cut under my helmet.

"I could use a drink," I said. "And I could use it now."

He shifted in his seat, stood up, and then sat down, full of wonder. "They came here, seeking you. They said you are a fugitive, or a corpse."

"They were not looking for my corpse here," I told him as I limped to the bar. "They know I am alive. So, serve me. I am parched and pissed off." I looked at him carefully. "I asked the boy already, but you didn't see any of my men here today?"

"No," he breathed. "None came. I am sorry."

"Wine," I said darkly.

He hesitated, turned, and poured me wine. He walked to me, placed the cup before me, and stood by with the jar full of it. "Best get drunk, sir. As drunk as you can get, even. They'll find you, and they'll make an end of you. It might hurt less if you are half senseless. Alas."

"Alas?" I said and drank the wine. He poured me more. "Alas for what? By all means, join me." I placed another coin on the desk. It would more than cover his expenses. I was frivolous with my wealth, for he was right. I should not be alive. Alexander should be jubilant, and I should be a corpse amid my men. Instead, I was having wine, and Alexander would be up in the Acropolis, full of hopeless anger, seething in rage. He was wounded, not quite as pretty now, and Corinne, likely dead in his arms.

His men were on the walls, and no doubt in the harbor, spread around to seek me.

There would not be many up in the Acropolis. There would be fewer still, soon.

I drank and nodded at him. "Ask."

He squinted. "I guess I will not get paid for the rent of the inn? And my services?"

I shrugged. "If I keep my head, you will be paid. But I must be frank with you, friend. If I die, it is likely one or two legions who will visit Limyra in a year or two. They are not bringing you any coin, though. They'll be pissed as shit, like I am."

He squinted. "You don't look too good. I think you need a doctor."

I nodded and drank some more. "I need a historian first."

"Eh?"

"A historian, friend," I said. "Then, a medicus. More wine. The better one." He got up to get it, and I saluted him with the cup. "You are in it deep, friend. For the better, or for the worse, you are with Rome now. It won't be long. Rome will start ruling here. No more alliance, freedom, or Lycian League. We shall bring our soldiers here. We'll pull the Acropolis down and make a fort on the plain. We'll build a better, new theatre, and finer temples, and we'll make your roads decent. It will be a different world. The people who help us won't be forgotten. Your sons and daughters will do well in

Limyra. But today?" I shrugged. "Today, you must be brave. Here."

I handed him two golden aurei, and he wondered at them.

"Down payment," I said. "For your services. For your friendship. Were you discreet, friend?"

He nodded. "They came here, soldiers, a few times. They were seeking you this night, and I said you haven't been here. I showed them your gear, what little there was. I mentioned nothing else, of anything else. I admit, I did it for greed, but also because they were unpleasant and arrogant."

I smiled. I drank more.

"Make a bill, and I shall take it to Rome with me," I said. "And I am sorry, but you might have to come along, for a time."

He looked at me with his eyes agog, and he wiped his face. "Why?"

"Because," I said, as I put my wine down, "there might be a bit of a mess in your fine tavern and possibly a small battle. I have invited some friends to a feast of blood. Ah, they come."

I heard steps outside and so did the inn keep. He blanched as the jingle of armor and weapons echoed from the windows and doorway. I grinned, picked up my sword, and, wincing, walked up to the stairway. There, I stood and turned.

Lycians came in.

They were the very bunch I had seen crossing the

bridge. They entered the tavern with spears in their hands, their shields getting in the way. They were a bloodied lot, a tired bunch, and an irate looking, large bastard led them. His sword was out, and the horsehair on his helmet looked better than that of most of his men. He was an officer with a silver belt. The large fellow was not so irate any longer when he spotted me on the stairs. He smelled success, coin, and praise.

There were eight of them.

They even had the hound with them, a lanky, fleet creature, and the dog growled at me, its teeth gleaming.

They spread around and walked up to me, keeping a careful look at the innkeeper who looked terrified. He was mumbling and grinned at the Lycian officer. "Thank you, Zeus, for sending you to aid me. You came to save me!"

The leader kept his eyes at me. "Zeus had shit to do with it. A beggar girl saw this one trying to sneak in here."

I smiled and waved my hands around. "You caught me!"

The officer went on. "He was drinking wine. Your wine?"

"The thief had a sword on me," the innkeeper complained. "A bloody sword on me! He threatened to kill me. He took wine and cursed Lycia."

The leader glanced at the bar. The two gold coins were there. "Oh? He decided to pay you after the threat and the curses? What did you do to merit such riches?"

I slapped my sword's edge on my thigh. "Ah, lay off the poor sot. He is terrified as he is."

"Put the sword away," the officer said.

I shook my head, whistled, and slapped my leg. The dog's ears pricked up, and it ambled towards me, waging its tail. I crouched to look at it, and then I rubbed its neck vigorously.

The men were staring at me with incredulity.

"So," I said, and looked at the officer, "did you kill my men, and the others?"

"Centurion Marius," said the officer, "is alive, as are eight of his men. The big, dark one is tied up. All are up there. We'll kill them with the other captives, perhaps, but we shall see. Now—"

I nodded and patted the dog and let it lick my bloody hand. "The people. Meliton. Bernike, Andromache, and the girls? Laodamia and fucking Pericles?"

He stepped forward, and his men were close, spears out. "Why, in the Acropolis. There is a comfortable citadel in there, and all the snakes fit in. Only Eurydike, and that Bernike, and of course your Vipsania get some comfort on the second level, but the rest rot on top. Do not worry for them, Roman. Worry for yourself. Alexander will not put you in there. He doesn't have men like your friend Antius, who knows how to make a man squeal skinless, but he'll let someone practice on you."

"I see," I said. "I do see. He'll make me squeal. How is his Corinne? She—"

"His Corinne is dead," the man said darkly, looking at my sword. "Dead and will be buried tomorrow. You'll not attend the party. Put down the sword."

"You'll not like me when I get mad," I told him. "Don't interrupt your betters, you sheep-fucking peasant." I saw the dog lifts its head and growl at the shadows.

"Sheep—" he breathed.

I got up and towered over the men. "Listen, this is what I need you to do. I need you to strip your armor, and not to piss your tunics. We'll need it all intact and clean."

The leader stared at me as if I had sprouted wings. He opened his mouth, and a subdued laugh escaped his lips. He turned to his men. "The dog-lover wants us to strip. He thinks we are going to take it up the arse, perhaps? Take him down. Alive."

They lifted their shields, glared at me from behind the rim, their spears aimed to my direction.

The dog bolted upstairs. The cat followed it, with wobbly steps.

The officer opened his mouth as he flanked his men.

Then, he took a pilum in the mouth.

The man fell on his back, as if by hit by a lighting, and his heels thrummed the floor. They enemy turned to see dark shadows coming from the corners of the inn, from the front door, and there were many of them.

The men rushed forward.

They lobbed pila, and the enemy took them with

their shields, save for two, one of whom caught a javelin in his side, the other on his arm. The shadowy men rushed at their enemy, swords out, and tore to the men. They dodged past the shields and began stabbing the enemy to death. Two had a bow, which killed a particularly angry Lycian, one dancing from the rushing men, and the rest pulled the enemy out of their feet.

The cries ended into gurgling, bloody pain.

"Save one!" I called out, as I walked down. "Just one. The one with a clipped wing!"

The men turned to look at me and grinned, and one young man was spared, his mouth open in pain, for he was the one who had caught the pila in the arm.

The men held a sword on top of that one, while the others sneaked around the room, looking out of the door.

There were twenty of them.

"Nothing there, sir," said one.

I nodded, and the inn keeper walked forward to look at the carnage. The officer was dead, and the soldier who was alive looked at me.

"You alive?" I asked him. He was a young man and in terrible pain. "Get him wine."

The inn keeper rushed to obey.

"You had more than one contubernium," he said in pain. "You had three." He was looking at the soldiers around him.

I looked at the men, wolves the lot, who were

prowling in the room. "Yes. I had more men. And a place where they could hide. That's how you stay alive. It was an inconvenience we were spotted coming in, but I never play fair, boy. They had been stashed in Nefarious as rowers." I gave them a grin. "Did the lazy bastards good, I say," I said loudly. "They were growing fat in Rome."

They grinned and then went grim.

"And still," I said, "my own men failed to escape the house, and fetch these lads to the battle. If Segolia failed to reach safety, boy, I'll take it out on you."

"Please, I don't—"

I clapped his face and got up to speak to the men around me. "The others are dead," I told them. "Centurion Antius, may he rot, and the men died, though Hercules might be salvaged. And we shall do just that. Optio Longinus."

"Yes, sir," said the optio, leading the men.

"Strip the enemy of their gear," I told him.

They got to it.

"The best fighters dress up," I said.

They began arguing about who was the best fighter.

"Let this one keep his," I said, and nodded at the young man, who was drinking wine. "Be smart, boy, and you get to see your sheep again. Be a hero, and you will die. Do you understand?"

He nodded fearfully.

"Good," I said, and sat on the stairs.

Suddenly, everyone froze.

We heard steps outside. The soldiers tensed, some in the middle of undressing, and turned to look at the doorway, where one of our men was looking outside. He turned to me. "An old man, and two women?"

"Let them inside," I said.

The door opened, and Larissa entered. She had the pugio, and she looked at the sight before her. Her eyes went over the naked soldiers, the corpse, and then found me. She hesitated and then pulled her red hair over her shoulder as she stepped aside.

Drakon entered, smiling nervously, and yelped when he saw inside. He held a hand over his mouth, eyes wide.

I waved my hand at him. "More wine, inn keeper." I winked at Drakon. "Mind your step, good historian. You do not want to slip, do you? Some blood right over there."

He didn't move until one of the soldiers pulled him inside. Ariana followed him, and the man closed the door. Larissa walked forward with him and stopped to stare at me. "Well, we did it. I see you found the patrol I told about you."

I nodded. "So, Drakon. You look parched. Take a seat."

"I am, thank you," the man said, and walked to the side, eyeing the corpses and the wounded with a horrified expression on his old face. "I am not sure your help on the Nefarious covers whatever you are going to ask for. It was just a hat. They are dead!"

I laughed as I got up. "They asked for it."

The girls stepped forward, eyed the teaming hoard of men with worry, and then sat down together on the stairs. I walked to the inn keeper and took the wine and mugs. "Serve the men as well."

He turned to obey, puffing and cursing, and I walked to Drakon. I sat down before him and pushed the mug and the pitcher for him. "There is a lack of servants currently, I am sorry to say. Here, serve yourself."

He nodded and helped himself. "I have known how to do this for ages, I have. I have no servants." He smiled, and rubbed his face, shaking his head. "I must ask; how did it go?"

I gazed at him and laughed. He grinned and rubbed his eyes, still smiling.

"It didn't go too well," I said. "We caught the killer of the traders and Kleitos, the killer's father caught Gaius, and when I tried to find out who actually slit his belly in a room that is seemingly inaccessible, I found everyone is a liar and a thief, and also that the city is hollow. I remember you said so, in a very mysterious way."

"I did say so," he answered tartly. "I told you so, kind of." He took a breath. "And have you run into any odder trouble than elusive killer of Gaius?"

I nodded.

"They took interest, then?" he said. "Oh, dear."

"You claimed the Furies are real," I said. "So far, I have seen a group of three people who wore dog-masks, horns and all. They took a man of mine prisoner, alive. I had claimed, you see, that we know who killed Gaius. It seems to me they seek the same as I do. It seems the killer and these Furies are not the same person. Or they are simply trying to silence us and make a mess of everyone's lives. Why would they do that?"

"They would have silenced you as well," he said darkly. "But they spared you. They do have an agenda, no doubt."

"Coin, and power, I think," I said.

He grinned. "I have no idea of the details, but I suppose it is possible. They might be the defenders of Lycia, but who doesn't want riches. The gods themselves do, why not their demons." He leaned forward. "Look, you brought me here to help you? You want to know more about the Furies, yes? Of a myth you showed no interest in?" His eyes twinkled. "I cannot tell you who slit the belly of Gaius, but I can tell you these things are real."

"Aye," I said acidly. "I want to know about them. I now want to know *all* about the Furies. Just do not claim they are really spirits or demi-gods."

He sobered. "The Furies are real. I told you. Spirits."

"Tell me about them," I sighed.

He nodded. "Fine. But first, tell me a few things so I understand why I must help a Roman against my own people."

"Ask."

He waved his mug around. "So, how do you like the

house of Pericles, as it stands?"

I looked at my hands. "Pericles seems a good sort, and I suppose the girls are not too bad. Lysirate…asked me to take her to Rome. Eudoxia, mother's girl. It's the mother that is the problem. It is too bad the family they married into were greedy as well as clever."

"Laodamia is known to run the house," he informed me. "Though, perhaps she should. The family was impoverished thanks to the lack of business acumen of this Pericles of ours. She was of low origins, and he of high, but she had the coin. Who has the coin should rule, no?" He squinted at me. "If the rumors are true, it is a different spawn of the original Pericles that is trying to lead Limyra into a new, glorious, golden future. Alexander rebelled?"

"It is," I said. "It truly is. Alexander is thinking about becoming a Tyrant of Lycia if you can imagine. First, he simply takes over the Limyra. He was upset Corinne was given to Amyntas. I think he always meant to kill the lot. He hopes to use Meliton's daughter and Bernike's connections to Myra to grow in power in the Lycian League before making his move. Corinne died, though."

He chuckled and leaned forward. "Bernike is a fetching woman, is she not? She can still bear children, even. He might divorce Meliton from her with his sword and have her."

I blinked.

He could, indeed.

375

It was possible.

And Vipsania was in danger as well.

"Where, one must wonder," I told him, "would one be without clever minds like yours? We must deal with Alexander, no matter whom he marries. That is the only way to save Limyra from fire and legionnaires. Just look at the magnificent bastards. Do you want them coming here as your enemy?"

He glanced at the men drawing on Limyran gear, and others washing blood off them. Many stood in silent ranks around the room, and before the doors.

"No, I wouldn't want that," he said. "That is not good."

"We shall deal with Alexander, indeed," I told him. "But there remains a problem. The Furies. And the killer. And something the killer took. I tell you now, if the killer is not found, the scroll recovered, and these Furies try to stop me, or benefit from this, and I fail to kill them as well, things will go bad for Limyra."

"The killers of Limyra," he breathed. "the tale you were bored with. I suppose I should help you, then, for Limyra."

"For Limyra, aye. And I am not bored now," I said. "You claimed they have been around for hundreds of years."

"Yes," he answered. "The Persians butchered the people and burned much of the city, but at that time, what was worst for Lycia was the fact so many were turning from our old ways into those of the enemy.

There were old families in the city. That of Pericles, and others. Persian ways, immorality..." He shrugged. "Some say Alecto, the Eternal, the most powerful of the demonic Furies, chose one family to do justice for the slain, the molested, the raped, the hurt. One of the oldest families was chosen, and still, one that had been wronged, left in shame."

"Chose them?" I asked. "The family of Pericles. You are saying they are—"

"No," he said. "The family of the Ptolemy. The Ptolemy's bastard—"

"Ptolemy's bastard?" I asked. "What?"

He smiled. "We worship the line of great Alexander and that of his generals. The Ptolemaion, a temple not far from here, was set up for one of the original general's sons, Ptolemy II Philadelphos, a great general who fought here for our people against the Galatians, who are Celts like your woman. Where is she? She isn't—"

"She is still no...she should be in the ship."

"She is too just for you, I think, but she is also in love with you. She'll make her move one day," he laughed, "though you will have to explain to her why the two girls are attached to you."

I glanced over my shoulder at the two girls. Both stared at us.

"They...no," I snarled. "They are here to help themselves. I—"

He rolled his eyes. "You have put your cock in a noose and now claim it is not tight."

"My cock has not touched either noose," I said icily. "You were saying?"

"The Furies chose a family, the Ptolemy family."

"But the Ptolemy's ruled a great deal of Alexander's lands," I said dubiously. "Why would they be in Limyra? A rural town of little meaning?"

He snapped his fingers at me. "Pay attention. I spoke of a bastard. This woman of little importance, a minor noble, once made an impression on the great king who waged war here, and an offspring was born. She called him Ptolemy, the child, risking much. It was a secret, of course, and she should not have done that, but she was allowed to live. The boy grew into man and had three daughters, and war swept across the land again. The Seleucids raided the city, and many people died. Some say the old Ptolemy had especially ordered the death of his bastard offspring. The woman died. A small girl of this bastard Ptolemy died and another. He died holding them." He leaned closer. "The last one, she hid herself, and buried her people. She wept, cursed, and asked the gods to send her an avenger."

I smiled. "I know this story. After this, the Furies chose the remaining child to defend the land against evil doers."

He nodded. "They did. Alecto made the girl her own. She possessed her. She has ruled the shadows ever since. They have, they say, killed hundreds of evil doers across the land through all these years. Hundreds."

I rolled my eyes. "Possessed her, eh? And then the

offspring of this girl?"

"Aye."

"Aye," I said. "And the other furies? Are they, too, immortal? Why do they not simply, being demi-gods, know who does what and strike us all down?"

He sighed. "I know not if there are all three Furies. I don't know if one, Tisiphone punishes people for murders, or another for crimes of love, this Megaera. Dog-headed and horned masks are not beyond the skills of humans to create, nor are skills of murder impossible to train. I have no idea if this Alecto knows who is to be blamed for what with but a blink of her eyes. I know not if they can see our crimes, or if the human forms they possess are as vulnerable to wounds as we are. I don't even know if they are beyond unjust murders and greed themselves. But I know people die steadily every year. Headless people are found, and often, they are rich and evil. There have been no horns blowing before this Amyntas and Kyrillos began undermining Pericles with the killings. There were only missing heads. I think the Furies, they were upset someone tried to take their mantle, and I think they, too, want to know who slit the belly of Gaius. Their motives? To punish? To benefit? I know not."

"Are they women, like Furies?"

He laughed. "I said they possess a body. Spirits do this, and while the Furies are women, my friend, they take what they must."

I looked at him. "Have you ever seen anything like

this?"

"Demons, spirits?" he asked. "I don't think it matters what I say. You have a sword, and you think that solves your trouble. Try, centurion! Spirits may lose a body, but they will come back."

"How would I find them?" I asked softly.

He shrugged. "I have never tried to find any. They might be women, they might be men, but I bet Alecto still possesses the with Ptolemy blood. Ptolemy's symbol was the Eagle of Zeus."

I held my face.

"It is in the Ptolemaion, hacked in the stone. It was in the tomb of the first bastard, and his family," he said.

"Where is that tomb?" I asked him.

"On the side of the mountain, near the theatre," he said. "Some hundred ancient tombs are placed there. You must be very careful, centurion. Spirits or not, the tales of these things…they say they take the heads, so their enemies may never go to the afterlife. They are malicious. No obols for the ones they hate. They are patient and seek the truth, and they stay hidden in the middle of the hairiest of situation. They welcome danger, and they welcome war, and they welcome pain. They bear it with supreme skill. They know medicine, poisons, and potions, better than most, and can act like few others. They will play the game to the end. They hide in plain sight and make few mistakes." He shook his head. "The heads they take? They eat the flesh off the skull."

I rubbed my face. "They heard us making plans. They knew exactly how I planned to roast out the killer of Gaius. They heard about the belly wound. At least one of them must have been in the house. The killer of Gaius might have sent them after us, they might be the same, and still, they took Antius alive."

"They didn't kill Gaius, but they do want to know who did," he said. "One of them, or all of them, were in the house when you set this trap."

"I wounded one," I said. "And none of them had a wound."

He frowned. "Then, one of them was in that house. You checked them all?"

"They all lifted their—"

"Not all," said Ariane. "Not all."

I frowned. And then, I got up. "But he was in chains!"

"Apollon," Drakon said, "is an actor, a soldier, and an acrobat. He can do many tricks."

Larissa spoke softly. "And he was locked in a room with a hole on the floor."

I held my face. "He can slip from fetters? He seemed so simple. Easy to understand."

I remembered the acrobat from the day we arrived. He had slipped from ropes.

I was thinking about Segolia and fought the terrible urge to rush out to find her.

Drakon spoke softly. "You think spirits are simple? They appear to be anything but clever. They seek to confuse you, to hide in plain sight. One is kind and caring. Other one is foolish and harmlessly stupid, and one might appear to be brazen and too obvious. This Apollon is the son of Eurydike, the one who owns the theatre? The Eagle's Joy?" He groaned. "Oh. They don't hide it much, do they?"

I nodded. My head was spinning. "I sent Apollon with Segolia, to Nefarious. I sent a message to Augustus."

"Centurion?" said a man from the doorway. "You should see this."

I shifted and walked to the doorway, and the man was pointing a finger to the south. He was looking at the harbor, and beyond.

There, something was ablaze.

"I bet it is the Nefarious," said the soldier softly. "Somehow, they burned it."

I watched the ship in flames.

Segolia.

It was burning from stern to the bow, and I saw how fire would kill the ship of Fish-Bait, and the good, kind girl I had loved. I turned and looked at the two former slaves. I walked to Larissa. "Tell me, when Vipsania sent you to buy poison, who did you buy it from? Who was the woman versed in poison?"

She blinked and looked at Drakon. "Speak, girl. I know who it was."

She spoke softly. "Eurydike. She knows all the potions, poisons, and pain relievers. Everyone goes to

382

her."

I thought of Apollon, and the day I had seen them performing in the Agora, fantastic feats, and I closed my eyes. Eurydike had been singing there, looking at us exploring the murder site. She had been curious then. Later much more than curious.

Apollon.

The bastard knew how to slip out of fetters. The bastard was one of them.

Eurydike, the other one. Perhaps the main one. Alecto.

I watched Drakon. I cursed and walked to him. "So, I know who carries the blood of Ptolemy," I said. "Tell me, old lord, has Apollon the actor ever been to war? You called him a soldier just now."

He shrugged. "Yes. I did. He is far older than he looks. Your age, perhaps? He spent years a mercenary in Egypt, and only later, he went after Gaius to perform his art. He is a wonderful actor and an acrobat. He can slip out of anything. He can twist his thumbs in every direction imaginable and bend over to lick his own arse if he wants to."

I laughed bitterly.

"And who is the third one?" I asked him. "Does Eurydike have another child? Can she be one?"

"She can," he said. "But she has no other children."

Silence. I was thinking hard. Then, I held my head and laughed again. "Oh, she said it."

"What?"

"Never mind. The play," I said softly, and looked up

to the ceiling. "The reason Laodamia hates Eurydike, who seems to get along with everyone else. Do you know about it?"

The man smiled. "A local scandal that. Eurydike owns the theatre, and though she sings very well, it is Apollon who acts, and they hire some boys to play the female parts. There was a play few years past. It was all about a harpy as a mother, a terrible, bloodsucking beast. The whole city loved it, and everyone speculated it was about Laodamia."

"It was," I said.

He nodded. "Laodamia blamed Eurydike, and she admitted it. Later, Eudoxia, in a rage of jealousy, admitted that they had been with Eurydike, and Lysirate had written the tale with her. The girls, both of them back then, went to Eurydike to complain about life, see. Laodamia never forgave Lysirate, or Eurydike."

"Why would the girls go to them?" I asked. "What is she to them? Eurydike is no noble, or rich."

He winked. "She is liked by all the children. After all, she tells them adventures, and they have been listening for a long while. She is a client of Pericles, if not that of Laodamia. She used to wet nurse the girls." He looked at me with curiosity. "There was some other reason for you to think it were Lysirate?"

I leaned forward. "Laodamia told me to investigate Marcus and Avila just before Alexander's escape and attack. She didn't know they were dead. Lysirate told me to my face how sorry she was for Marcus."

"Brazen and evil," Drakon said. "She was baiting you."

I balled my fists. "Segolia might be dead now as well. It seems to me that the Furies want a fight. Apollon wants us to stay, since he torched the ship, Lysirate mocks me, and Eurydike works hard to find out who killed Gaius and who stole the scroll."

"Does he know about the soldiers?" Drakon asked. "These men?"

I shook my head. "Eurydike, Laodamia, and Lysirate are all up in the Acropolis. The killer of Gaius is there as well."

Drakon leaned back. "This is very fascinating. Very much so. But can you guess who killed Gaius?"

I rubbed my face. "He was laughing with someone. Laodamia knows which one of the girls it was. Well, it wasn't Lysirate. Or Laodamia, after all. Eudoxia, Bernike. Andromache possibly, but she is so…blunt and unloving. The list is short. I must find out which. Someone might have seen me there, in that room. Someone took something Rome must hide. We have killed the poisoner of Gaius, but we must find the lover of Gaius."

He nodded. "Who knows him best? Ask his best friend? He was happy with someone."

"Nobody," I said. "Ennius is dead. Vipsania, he hates her. He lets few people close to him. Even Apollon might have known him better than Vipsania."

385

Silence.

"Apollon," said Ariane, "is a handsome man."

"I don't know about that," I said. "I have no interest in him, other than to plunge my sword in his belly. If he hurt Segolia—"

"When Vipsania told me to seduce him," Ariane said, "he said he is not interested in my kind."

"He is after nobler blood, obviously," I said.

Larissa cursed and tossed a cup my way. It struck my helmet. I turned to her, angry.

"You damned idiot. You think like a man. Women swoon at the sight of you, Celcus, so you think with your cock. But Gaius, he was never a man like you. Think! How had Apollon convinced Gaius to visit Limyra? Why not Myra, Side?"

Apollon had convinced Gaius to visit Limyra.

How, indeed.

And then, I knew how. I groaned.

"It is no big deal in Greece, or here," said Drakon. "Only in Rome."

I nodded.

It had been Apollon, once, who had made Gaius visit Limyra. It had been so, because he had seduced Gaius. Gaius had had streams of women offered to him all through his life. He had staunchly rejected all but Vipsania. It had been his duty, his purity, and everyone admired his strength...

"Laodamia," I began, "said Eudoxia would marry Gaius. She said it like she knew what she was talking about."

"A cover," Drakon said. "A cover only."

I nodded. Gaius had found Apollon beautiful if foolish. Not like the soldiers around him, but…delicate. So, when he had been wounded, and on his final tour in Lycian cities, he had willingly followed Apollon, wounded, terrified of his duties in Rome, in love with Apollon and had agreed to stay with Pericles, the head of the city.

There, Gaius had stayed, and he had been used.

I shook my head. "If he is one of the Furies, then why did he agree to help Laodamia? Laodamia promised to let them play again and promised support for the theatre, but surely a Fury would not—"

"He is a man, as well as a Fury," Larissa said wisely. "He wanted an adventure or just to see Gaius. Or perhaps they wanted to see how far Laodamia is going to go. It did go pretty far. The demons like to play games with their prey."

Fool Gaius.

He had been offered happiness, a holiday, a paradise, under the roof of Laodamia and Pericles. There, he had been offered women, by everyone, and he had turned them down.

Apollon was soon forgotten.

I wonder if that hurt Apollon? It had. He was vain.

There, in that house, Gaius had found a man, who was not pretty like Apollon, but who loved poetry, who cared as little as he did of duties, and of power, and the terrible demands of those who would take an advantage of him, and he had turned increasingly to this man.

It had been Pericles.

Pericles had visited him in his study, where they could read, smile, and compete in poetry, in tale-spinning, in philosophy, and in their hatred for their wives. Had Laodamia learnt of it? Had Cassius seen the will of Gaius and told her? Had she realized none of her girls would marry the great man? Or had she told them she didn't mind, if Eudoxia was their cover?

As long as the coin kept coming in, I doubted Laodamia cared.

It had been Pericles who had taken the scrolls. Perhaps Laodamia after, if they contained filth on her family.

He, a wise, gentle man, had lost his love.

He had seen Gaius writhing on the floor, dying, and he had suffered as Gaius suffered, and he had, with his sword, for no man traveled the city without one, over or under ground, helped him die.

He had wanted Kyrillos dead, savagely so. He had acted. He had acted to save his family, his city, for he knew, that this secret would destroy nations.

Had he been there, hiding in the shadows, as I was there?

He had. He had been there.

He had seen and heard us, as I had been the only one who had threatened Gaius with violence. He had sneered at that, in the study.

He had seen and heard us.

I got up and looked around. The girls rose.

"Right. We will go up to the Acropolis. We shall go up there, we'll fuck Alexander with our swords, and we'll take the heads of each and every one of them. All the heads. We will want Gaius's body, and we'll clean up. Apollon is sure to go up there, isn't he?"

Drakon looked uncertain. "When you say you will clean up, do you mean me?"

I smiled. "No. Of course not. And if Limyra still rebels, we shall call on Side to subdue the city, and Myra. They have lots to lose as well. Roman century, a Roman galley? Gaius? We'll settle Limyra. But dear Drakon, while we will get inside, is there something more you can tell us? Tell us where these fuckers hide, if they get away from the Acropolis."

He got up. "They have a stable and their ramshackle house, where you visited, and the theatre," he said, shivering by the look in my eyes. "They have those. They have horses, and probably that's something the girls have arranged." He leaned closer. "The Eagle Stone," he said. "That's what the tomb is called. It is, everyone says, haunted. People stay far from it. The cursed blood of the Ptolemy and their dead, murdered kin lie there. Right next to the theatre. They say there are ways to the mountain inside for the dead to walk, and a gate to Hades. Intriguing."

I smiled. I wished I had asked him more in the galley,

the day I met him. "We are going to the Acropolis. Before this, you will show this place to me. You shall do this, and if we die, you will write to Augustus and tell everything that has transpired. You do it to save Limyra, and the girls. Also," I said, and grinned at the innkeeper, "tell Augustus this man stayed faithful."

"We are coming along—" Larissa said.

I shook my head at them. "I have something else for you two. Drakon? The Eagle Stone?"

Drakon nodded. "I will do this. Of course. It is a pleasure."

I smiled down at him and pulled him along. "Dear historian, as Segolia knew, to her sorrow, Rome and its servants are both murderers and liars, and occasionally, we also betray the trust of those who welcome us with open arms. Pleasure has nothing to do with serving Rome."

I looked at the seven men dressed in Lycian gear, and our prisoner. I turned to look at the rest of the men. "Three men come with me. The rest, listen to me. First, get Gaius's body from the Temple of Zeus. Hide it in our hideout. Then, when they come and try to put out the fires, make sure to kill all the soldiers you can find. All of them. Hit and run and start some new fires as well. Many of their fighters will come down soon from the Acropolis. The optio knows what to do. Chaos is the word."

He nodded and turned to growl orders to his men, who looked ordinary ruffians all, but wore chain under the tunics, and their swords were sharp.

Drakon sputtered. "What do you mean by this? What fires?"

I pulled him along as with my Lycian infiltrators. I grinned and looked at the innkeeper. "Please do not be angry, dear friend, but you and your boy," I said, and looked at the boy in the shadows, "will go with Drakon. Later, you come with us. Take the cat and the dog. We need to, unfortunately, burn this place up. Ariane, come here. Listen."

CHAPTER 14

The people were rushing around like ants, their nest kicked over. The city was in fire, and flames were reaching to the heights of the trees, which were blazing as well. The houses next to the inn were catching fire, and though the water was plentiful in the city, with stream, wells, fountains, and the river, no one was giving orders, for Pericles and his family were held prisoners.

The shouts and chaos below were terrible, and I grinned like a fiend, for I saw isolated Lycian soldiers being stabbed to death while the speculatores disappeared.

"Why must you kill them?" Drakon asked me.

"Because they killed Roman soldiers," I said. "They'll never forget this night."

Then, I watched the tomb.

The Eagle Stone.

We were standing in the shadows of the theatre, and everyone eyed the odd, ancient tomb with apprehension.

It was large and had once been carved full of glorious sights of victory of the great Ptolemy. It had likely been an awkward decoration, a shame exposed, and I saw someone had chiseled away at the names and faces.

It was overgrown with weeds, glistening with mold, and seemed slightly dilatated.

There were pillars, and between the pillars, there was

a cracked doorway.

I jumped down and walked for it. My men, reluctantly, followed.

I looked inside and saw a broken stone urn, and perhaps bits of bone. There was rubble, and there were further chambers.

The spiderwebs were broken.

I turned to Drakon, the innkeeper, and bowed. "No matter how bad it looks, remember; it will all be far better than the city in flames. We shall perhaps see you soon."

One man escorted them away for our hideout.

I led the men away and took a road up the mountain side—a winding road, broken by craggy rock formations, sparse vegetation, some cedar trees blocking the view—but we made steady headway.

Then, horn brayed on top. There, up the hill, we saw an elaborate building, the Heroon of Pericles, the original Pericles's bones under the small temple's roof, and then some walls and a gate.

The gate was open.

"Make it look good," I said. "And you?" I turned to the prisoner. "If you want to live, tell the men up there you did well to capture me."

The man with a wound in his arm was nodding. He looked like a coward, and still, like Apollon had, could be faking the entire fearful countenance. I didn't care.

"Shit terrible to take," said one of the men, pushing at the horse hair hanging before his eyes. "Looks like a killer. Eight-foot-high walls, parapets, and towers. All point our way, south. See, the road before the gate swings left, and two towers can punish you were no shield—"

"We are friends," I said. "And we shall walk in."

They held me, hands behind my back, bloodied, mail filthy. I winced with each step but made the effort to climb. "The gates are open."

"They are," said the man. "See? Men are leaving."

Indeed, dozens of men had already left the fortress. Dozen more, all armored but carrying no shield, were rushing to help with the fires. I looked behind. They were ranging across the Agora now.

As were our men.

We stopped on a bend of the road, sweating profusely, and the soldiers rushed by, giving me furious glances. One stopped to hit me. Then, he moved on.

I grinned, spat blood, and was pushed forward. Up and up we went, and I felt unease as we went up. I felt death waiting above, an old, ancient deceiver looking down upon me, and also, Alexander.

Spirits? Or people?

Just people.

I spoke to the man as we walked below the towers. "You make it good. You tell them cheerfully, that you caught the killer of Corinne, the man your lord wants skinned and dead, and you be good."

He nodded.

"How many men up there?" I asked.

He shrugged. "Usually, we have nearly two hundred men. Of course, in truth, many are on a leave, and we had hundred and twenty yesterday. Now, sixty or more are down below"

"We killed some," I told him.

He frowned and looked at me with dark anger. A sword poked into his flesh, reminding him of wisdom of calm. He was nodding and breathing hard, holding his arm. "You killed and wounded thirty men. We took ten prisoners."

"They will be held where?"

"The keep, right after the gate, on the slope. It has a third floor. They will be there. There's the roof, but the supplies and prisoners are chained on the third floor."

"And Alexander?"

"He has his rooms on the middle, while soldiers and the horses stay on the bottom. There are stables, and armories on the second level, and such, but—"

"Shh," I said. "They are looking."

"The gates are still open. There will be nearly thirty men there," I said. "And we have no idea what is waiting for us in the keep. Be ready."

They were. We marched forward, and five men, gate guards, were squinting at us. One, a helmetless man without armor, was stepping forward. He had a wound across his scalp. It was bleeding still, though it had been sewn. "What do you have there? What news from the city? The fire?"

I growled at the captive. He showed the man his arm.

"A fight! The Roman shit torched the Agora, and he had help. Some more of his men. We fought and captured him."

"Oh, thank Zeus!" he yelled, and laughed sharply. "Who burned their ship?"

"I know not," the man said. We walked forward and were almost upon them.

"Never mind," he said. "The captain will know. That actor just came in, rode like a mad thing, and wanted to speak with him. Said he comes from the harbor and begged for his mother's life."

"Aye, well," the captive said. "We shall take him to the captain then. He may join the others."

He had killed my men.

Perhaps Segolia.

I will kill him slowly.

"In death, soon," the guard said, as we stepped inside the gates. "The people are going to be put to death. Save for the simple actor and his mother, of course. And save for Bernike, Meliton's wife. She shall survive it. I think. She is, after all, daughter of Myra." He slapped his thigh. "To imagine, we have Vipsania a prisoner. The captain is thinking about that, isn't he? He might make her a Helen, while he dons Paris's armor!"

Apparently, Alexander loved to make that comparison.

And yet, Paris died miserable and pleading for his life.

The guard stepped forward and spat at my face.

I saw the five men were laughing, but then, I ignored them, for beyond the gate, there was a fort—thick, wide, evil, and lit by torches. Some men were pulling horses along before it, and none else moved.

Then, the horn rang.

It was not the military one, the clear, strong one.

It was the same kind as we had found on Amyntas, and on Hiratius, in Apollon's place. It was harsh, blunt, and brutal. It rang over the land and silenced the guards. All of them turned to look at the citadel. "The Furies?" whispered the man who had spat at me. "Again? Here? Why?"

"Look!" called out a man.

And indeed, high on the roof of the place, I saw a dark, horned figure. It was dancing and held a curved thing in his hand, likely the horn. It bent back to blow it again. Beneath, someone was screaming in pain, and then, the scream was cut off.

The horn rang. It rang again.

"Three," I whispered.

"What is happening?" the guard wondered. Then, we heard Alexander screaming. He was roaring orders inside. The men with horses abandoned the beasts and rushed through the gates for the citadel.

The horn was lifted to the lips yet again. It rang and then rang again. It rang so many times the hills and mountains seemed to echo with a thousand horn blasts. Finally, the figure turned and disappeared.

"Kill them," I snarled.

My men flipped their spears and attacked, the round shields flashing in the light of the torches. They went forward fast, savage, and deadly, and pushed the spears in to the men's back. The enemy fell on their faces, screamed briefly as my men stabbed repeatedly, while kicking at them. I turned to our captive and pushed him to the side.

"Sword," I said.

"Wait, you promised—"

I was handed a sword, and I bend low to cut at his leg. "You'll live, perhaps," I said harshly. "The promise has been fulfilled." I pulled the blade.

He fell amid shrubs, howling, and I walked for the citadel.

The men came after, pulling away their helmets to make sure we knew who we would send to Hades. A man rushed from the top of the walls from one of the towers and stared down at us aghast, and when I looked up at him, he fled.

We came to the citadel, and I pushed inside. I looked around. To the right, there was a hall filled with tables and doors to kitchens and stables. A dog got up, wagging a tail, and then rushed off towards a stairway. I walked that way, past racks of armor and weapons and shields, a smithy, and a pile of spears.

I loped up the stairs and came face to back with a chaotic mass of men, all trying to push up stairway and through a doorway, which had apparently been locked from the inside. There were rooms to the left and right, but little else, save for stairs to the top.

The would-be-tyrant was standing in the middle of the stairs, just below the gate.

"Push through!" Alexander roared. "Get inside! We *must* get inside!"

With him, was Bernike, the wife of Meliton, mother to dead Corinne, who had apparently taken her place, no matter her age. She was holding onto Vipsania for Alexander. Around them were men, waiting for the door to break, as were the men on the stairs. Vipsania had been weeping, her eyes red. She hugged herself in terror, and the murderous girl was clearly praying.

The doors shuddered as the men pushed at them. Chain jingled inside.

Whoever was inside would have done a bit of killing.

Apollon will have begged to see his mother, like a fool. He will have been let in. In fetters, without them, he will have surprised a guard and locked the doors.

He would have freed Eurydike and Lysirate.

The rest?

They will all be dead. Our men, included. If Pericles or Laodamia had the scroll, then we should hurry.

Segolia, and Hercules.

I needed to get inside the doors. The enemy stood between us.

"Get us there," Alexander roared again. I caught a glimpse of his face, hideously wounded. One eye was missing, most of his ear as well, and skin and flesh had been torn off. I kissed my sword blade, counted nearly twenty men, all without shields and spears, few with axes, around the doorway, few of them hammering at it. They had been at it for quite a while already, judging by the damage.

I turned to my men, who nodded, grinning.

They lined up with me, and we attacked.

It takes mad bravery to attack an armed enemy.

It takes a desperate bastard to go and get recruited to the legions, but when you have survived many battles, and realize what a terrible thing war, and a battle, is, you become cautious and try to avoid taking part in either. If you must, you fight, but you do not risk your neck.

Such men do not become speculatores, especially for Augustus.

The men with me had never understood the word 'caution' and were enjoying themselves immensely. They rushed forward, chain jingling and I saw spears striking the first men. One fell on his face and dragged others with him, his eyes huge and fingers grasping. Another tore to the mass of men, and then, as we ran, the rest of the men tossed the heavy battle spears and left many of the enemy gutted.

Four, five of them fell, and I jumped forward, forgetting the pain, the losses, as I went forward. I stabbed at a young soldier, and he fell away, howling. I jumped to the midst of the enemy. My men came after me, stomping to the stairs over falling enemy, then up them, like a pack of bulls.

The enemy turned to fight.

Some fell off the stairs, and others stabbed down, and two of our men fell, one wounded, the other one spitting blood, his chest open. The rest of us pushed up, and up, and the enemy was flattening against the wall as we killed them like lambs.

I winked at Alexander. I hacked down a man and pushed him off the stairs.

The would-be-tyrant of Limyra was above me and held a blade on Vipsania's throat. "Stay back!" he howled. Bernike looked shocked to the bone, clutching Vipsania hard.

I ignored his threat. I walked over one of his wounded men and stomped the man's face to the stairs.

We attacked the remaining eight men.

I saw him hesitate, then he took the weapon off Vipsania's throat and hacked the sword at me with a roar.

I blocked.

I reached out from under our blades and pulled Vipsania away. I threw her behind me, noticed Bernike was still attached to her, and let them both fall. I looked at Alexander's eyes as his sword was again swinging. I dodged and cut his thigh. He howled and tried to push me down with his free hand. I dodged left and surged forward, crashed into his midsection, and lifted him. Then, I pushed him up and over my shoulder. He fell, and I tripped, and he pulled me along by hair. We crashed heavily to the bottom of the stairs, in a tangle of legs and arms. He tried to climb over me, and I rammed my sword's hilt to his face. He was stunned, spitting blood, and I pushed my blade into his thigh. He shivered and let out a hissing breath. I twisted the blade, and he dropped his sword and threw up with pain.

I climbed up, looking where four of my men were stabbing down the last of the foe. I placed the sword on his chest and slid it to his throat. I smiled. "Alexander the Tyrant."

"Bastard," he hissed, and laughed. "You shit."

I nodded at the door upstairs. "Apollon in there?"

"He?" the man asked. "Yes. How did you know? It matters little…" he began and looked up to the doors. "Apollon is one of them."

"He is Apollon of Ptolemy, and a murderer of the murderers," I said. "And I do believe he came here to take heads and free some of his friends."

He nodded and looked up to the ceiling. "I was going to let him see his mother. He begged me to. Said they were just actors. And they are."

"Oh, yes," I said. "Though not better than Limyran nobles. He had a sword?"

"He slipped his fetters and took a guard's sword, then blocked the door with the chains," he said. "He is very skillful. He killed my men. And I cannot even avenge us now."

"He, or his friends used the blade on the prisoners," I said. "Including my friends and men. I'll do the avenging. Trust me. See what I did to you, eh? Can they get out of there?"

He shook his head. "Of course, he can. You can climb down. Ladders and ropes. Who are they?"

I nodded at my men, who grasped the axes, and got to work. I watched the dead and wounded, and then, at the door thrumming with ax blows.

"Lysirate, Eurydike, and him. He has a horn, and he has a blade," I said. "No doubt, he has a damned rope. You are right. Just not a Tyrant."

Alexander twisted to look at the door. "Lysirate? And the old lady?" he asked, wondering. "You reach high, Roman, when you are low. And I had Corinne." Tears fell from his eye, and blood from the other. Bernike stepped closer, but I shook my head.

"And sometimes, you burn to cinders, Alexander, when you reach the sun," I told him, and pressed the sword to his throat, leaning down until he was still.

"No!" Bernike vailed, though Vipsania was smiling softly.

I turned to look at Vipsania, and then at the door. She came forth, walking slowly, and I lifted a finger her way. "Augustus might spare you, Vipsania, not I. Save your prayers to him. Bernike?"

She sobbed.

"You will come with us when we leave," I said. "Stay out of sight for now."

I watched the door splinter, and with a metallic crash and wooden jingle, it was broken.

It yawned open, and I whistled to the men. "Two of

you. Guard the women. The rest, come with me."

I walked forward, and two men joined me.

The top of the fort was a warehouse and a prison. If housed everything one might need to run a citadel. There was anything from building materials and buckets to horse harnesses.

Half was a clear area with chains attached to the walls.

On some of the chains were slain Roman soldiers. Some were still alive but would die soon. They had been stabbed to death with brutal efficiency.

Hercules wasn't there.

As for the others, they were there.

There was Cassius. He had died with a slit throat, and he had shat himself.

There, too, was Andromache. She was dead as a stone, her face bloody.

Meliton, he had struggled mightily, for his chain had nearly been pulled off the wall. Still, he, too, was dead.

I saw that in the corner was the corpse of the woman, who was cause of much of the grief. There, Laodamia was dead, hacked to pieces so crudely, her arm and leg were severed, and throat cut to the bone. On her lap was dead Eudoxia, with a blessedly simple deadly wound on her back.

"Nothing here," said one of the men.

"Pericles, behind the gear?" I asked.

"No, sir," he said.

I nodded and looked up to the ceiling. There was a

trapdoor, and up to the roof, led a ladder.

I watched it and went for it. I climbed it carefully, listening and looking around.

On top, I looked around and froze.

I saw Marius. The Centurion was on his side, laying in his pool of blood. He had been killed, his throat slit. A look of dread was on his face.

Then, I saw Hercules.

He was on the far side of the roof, but I couldn't mistake his large body. I might have imagined, it, but he moved.

Last, I turned to watch Pericles, who was seated in the middle of the roof. He wasn't alone.

"So, which ones are they?" I asked. "Alecto, Tisiphone, and the last?"

"Megaera," said Eurydike, tiredly. "Indeed, the murderous one is Apollon, of course. He is the solider in the family, the true artist. He is—"

"He was the lover of Gaius, his friend, and then, ultimately, rejected for this one," I said and smiled at Pericles. "Oh, poor Gaius to reject such as he, a handsome hero."

She nodded, smiling coldly. "Truly, Decimus, I had no wish to tangle in the petty crimes of Laodamia. I cared little for Kyrillos and Meliton and their small tragedies. We Lycians have ever fought amongst ourselves, and only sometimes, do the Furies take note."

"When?"

"When the crime is great, the killer or the criminal a famous one, and when it pleases and intrigues us," she said. "This has been all that, you see?"

I looked at the woman.

Alecto. The Eternal.

She looked like an old, beautiful woman, but there was something to her eyes that left me uneasy. They compelled you to look at her. Like she had been from the start, she was charming and kind, save for the fact she now held a dagger to the neck of Pericles. She smiled, and I fought not to answer the smile.

I forced myself to look away from her, and looked around me, at Hercules, and she waited.

"Gaius?" I heard below. I looked back, and saw Vipsania, the guards hissing orders at her. "Take me away from her. I—" She climbed up and saw us. Bernike followed us, as did our men.

"Let them stay, centurion," Eurydike laughed. "I don't mind."

I spoke. "Moral guardians, punishers of the wicked, eh? But are you not wicked yourselves? You let others kill, and yet, others get away with it. You—"

"We do that," she agreed. "Indeed, we do. We are not your kind. We make the rules. We don't listen to your meowing complains, human. We are the hunters, not you. We eat you, not the other way around."

The voice was harsh, crude, and not quite human.

I kept a grip of my sword. She was an actor. That's what she was. Trying to scare me.

"I admit," she said, again Eurydike, "we took offence at the murders of the traders and the actor. We didn't understand the game. Apollon, Lysirate, and I, we watched and wondered. The stupid Kyrillos, the proud Meliton, the mouse-like Pericles? And Gaius, whom the bitch-queen wanted to live in her house. Ah, how she was surprised to see Eudoxia had no effect on Gaius, but Pericles did!"

I nodded. "It was a shock, no doubt."

"She still endured," Eurydike said. "She thought she could make it work. Gaius wanted to stay and didn't mind being used. Eudoxia would find a lover while married. She thought she might even benefit from the death of Gaius, for you are right. That temple to Augustus will be a shrine to Gaius. People will shower it with money. Alas, she has no use for it."

I smiled. "You left her with the head."

"Unfortunate," she said. "We have no time to hack off heads now."

"So, Alecto," I said. "The demon in the second last Ptolemy."

"Oh, I hardly think I am the second last one," she said, smiling. "There are others elsewhere. The man was a goat. In Myra, Side, we live on. I know some of them. We won't die, Decimus. We shall go on. And Alecto favors the old blood. They made a pact, see."

"I doubt it not," I told her. I walked around and looked at her carefully. Then at Pericles.

He smiled tiredly, and I noticed Eurydike had a

dagger on his neck. "You wish to speak to Pericles?" she asked. "I know what you will ask."

"I do. But first, where is Antius," I asked her. "And did he tell you anything?"

"He didn't," she said sadly. "He was too hurt and died. He did assure us you and he had no idea who killed Gaius, and who took the scrolls. We had little time to play with him. So, we decided to let you play your crude game to the end. Alas, for Alexander. But he has paid, no?"

"He has," I said.

She laughed. "He didn't make it too hard for us, though. You are a fool. You forgot to check the prisoners for a wound. Then, Apollon took your opportunity, centurion, to get us an insurance and to sink your galleon. He would have slipped his bonds here anyway. We were safe enough. He killed your men, by the way."

Her eyes glinted. I didn't ask about Segolia.

It upset her.

She went on, pressing the dagger under the skin of Pericles. "And since your crude methods worked, and Laodamia told everyone she had the answers, we didn't mind going with Alexander. We had Laodamia here, and Apollon was coming. Then, we only had to wait for you." She looked at Vipsania and then me. "I spoke with Laodamia."

"I saw her," I said.

"She told me about Pericles," she went on.

"Obviously."

"And Pericles, he gave me a scroll," she said. "I don't have it on me. It is safe."

I nodded. I looked at Marius.

"Well," she said with a wicked grin. "Antius did mention something else."

"Did he?" I asked.

"He said, that you came here to make sure Pericles would rule," she said. "That the weakest, and most roman-minded ruler in Lycia would stay in power. It was a worry in Rome since you have plans for the land. Antius told me Marius was ordered to perform four murders. He was to get a witness, and then, the rest of it, would be an act."

Everyone were quiet.

"I asked Marius that, as well," she said. "You came here to kill innocent people for Rome, to guard your interests. You came to cripple Kyrillos and Meliton. And you came to fetch Gaius home. By force, if you had to."

I spread my hands to my sides.

"And?"

"And I couldn't understand," she said, "why you spared Kyrillos after killing his son. Why did you put him in that house of his? I asked Apollon to free him, for I had a hunch something else was going on. I had him raise the rabble to rebellion, to mix up the pot."

"You are right," I said. "We should have killed Kyrillos, and Meliton both with the boy. Kyrillos bought the murder of Gaius, after all. It is our fault."

"Whose idea was it not to kill them, but to spare them with humiliating terms?" she asked.

Pericles was shaking his head, sorrow and fear etched on his face.

"They were my orders," I said.

"Truly? From Augustus, the Kind?"

I nodded.

"It is true, I couldn't understand other things," she said. "The petty secrets and Vipsania's treason towards her husband and Rome aside, there were a few things I didn't understand. The roman guards in the murder scenes? None asked them anything. Nothing was asked. The insulting horns, were odd. The coins, that Hiratius left behind?" She smiled. "Very odd. The cook, Dareios, where did he go? He left the house with Hiratius. Did you kill him, because you know you must kill everyone who knows about Vipsania? He left the house with Hiratius, but you made sure he was found, and thrown to the river? That big one did it?"

I shrugged and looked at Vipsania.

"I must protect her," I said.

"She has secrets over you, and you over her," she agreed. "My, but now I am intrigued. Here is what I know. Hiratius and Kyrillos didn't poison anyone. Just like Amyntas had nothing to do with murders, Hiratius and Kyrillos had nothing to do with the death of Gaius. Dareios tried to kill him, but he failed thanks to Laodamia. The two left together that evening as they always did, to drink. You knew where they were. Your men killed both, for different reason. Hiratius was to be made a scapegoat, and Dareios was simply silenced for her."

I walked back and forth, listening to her.

"And why were Kyrillos spared?" she asked. "For Rome needed yet another scapegoat."

"Did we?" I asked.

"Pericles," she said. "Tell him what you saw that night."

I saw his fingers were broken.

"You were his lover," I said.

He nodded. "I was. He was mine, I was his. Apollon was before me, but he found in me the peace he needed."

"The scroll," I said. "It can shake up Rome?"

He laughed and then cried softly. "It can. It has poison, and honey. His love for me and hatred for Rome are both penned down in it," he said. "He listed all the lies he had heard in Palatine, all the betrayals by Augustus, all the murders in the name of the state. He spoke of all of it. It can upset half of your Roman world, it can." He cried and wiped them clear. "It wasn't all dark, as I said. He spoke of love he had found here. For me. We would have lived happily, pretending marriage to poor, silly Eudoxia, but he would have been with me. And I with him." He sighed. "He was too pure for the world, and I, too afraid to make that scroll public after I had helped him die. I only told Laodamia, for she knew about it, and us. She wanted to hide it, of course, for to

411

benefit from Gaius's death, he couldn't be seen a traitor."

I walked back and forth, and Eurydike's eyes gleamed with amusement.

She whispered to his ear, "He wants the full pie, Pericles. Let him eat it."

He took a ragged breath. "How heavy is the truth. For Lycia, for my family, I was willing to let it go, to let him die without the truth, to let my wife hide it. I was willing to let it all be to save my land. I decided; let it be Kyrillos, and Amyntas who were the murderers of Romans, and of Gaius...I let it be so. Kyrillos, Amyntas. The killers."

"Aye, they were," I said.

"But it was a lie too," he said miserably. "Why?" It was a question, asked through flowing tears.

"Why, Decimus? Aye, why?" Eurydike said, leaning her face on the shoulder of Pericles, the dagger at his throat. Her eyes gleamed with unholy joy. "Why? You had taken the anti-roman families apart. You had won. Why did you spare Kyrillos for one day? Many things went wrong in your plans, but why did you do it?"

I walked back and forth. "Why, what?"

"Answer him," Eurydike said.

Pericles spoke miserably. "I saw it. I was there, hiding in the shadows below, just under your feet. That crack, I saw you."

The bastard had been watching me. He had been there.

She whispered to us, like a snake. "You spared Kyrillos, at least for a night," she said. "Because Gaius was still the problem. You have a special mission, and perhaps only you. Antius, Marius were both there to kill the families of Limyra, those who hated Rome, but you? You went further."

I said nothing.

She spoke on. "Gaius was not going home. You threatened him, told him he would be *carried* home, and watched him. He refused. He was given a choice, and he refused. So, you gave him olives of Augustus. Tell me, Decimus, why did Augustus want to kill Gaius? The bottom olives? Pericles was lucky not to eat those ones. They were sure to share. You gave him his death."

I stared at Pericles, who was trying to understand. "Why? Because he said 'no.' Because he did more. He dared to betray Augustus, Rome, to risk war and misery to be allowed to retire. He let others use Rome and his influence, to unbalance the land and trade. Then, he threatened Augustus. If you threaten Augustus, and threaten the peace of Rome, you cannot expect to be trusted in the future. We came here, expecting him to go home, but anticipating he might not, and when he threatened to speak of Roman affairs?" I shook my head. "Augustus is full of sorrow. But he is...Augustus. He rules millions. Gaius was one man, who failed."

Pericles wept.

Eurydike smiled. "I understand him. Someone else must rule, for Gaius would kill the line of Augustus, and perhaps even Rome. Someone else must do it, and Gaius will be buried, and his crimes disposed of. Oh, how you must have suffered when you saw the wound and no sword. How you suffered when you saw his scrolls gone."

Pericles wept. "They were all guiltless. Kyrillos, Meliton. I didn't know Rome killed those traders and Kleitos. I was so afraid to tell of them to Augustus, but he had...we were tricked. We invited the killers in."

"Aye."

He tore at his hair. "And Laodamia, the greedy Laodamia, was so eager to see them all dead. They simply wanted to keep their houses and trade, and all the people who died...poor Gaius. What a dismal fate. You poisoned him, Decimus. I curse you for it."

Eurydike pushed the blade into the back of Pericles and then got up, as he fell on his face.

She walked brazenly to me, old, still proud, and beautiful, and cocked her head. "I taught Lysirate to ride and Apollon how to fight. Don't chase them. They are gone with the scroll."

"Augustus wants it," I said. "I thought that much was clear."

She smiled and patted my cheek, and her eyes gleamed dangerous. I felt fear coursing through me. "Such a handsome boy. Seen so much. I suppose you won't insult the gods again, or their servants, eh?"

"I suppose I won't."

She laughed softly, as she eyed Vipsania, whose face

was white with fear.

She knew she was now in danger. Bernike was shaking with fear. Our men, they were looking down, faces hard.

Eurydike sighed. "I suppose I cannot kill you with that sword in your hand. Listen. Leave. Take your men and captives and just go. Clean up. Kill those who would speak of this. Throw them to the sea. We shall not even punish Vipsania for her crimes. If you do not," she said, and tiptoed before me and gave me a kiss on the lips, her eyes mad with anger and odd desire, "I shall send that scroll around the world. It will embarrass you. It will hurt your Augustus. It will do more. Remember those millions of people Gaius had to die for. You leave, Decimus. Lysirate left your man alive, to show you our good will. Apollon wanted to skin him."

I turned to look to the side where Hercules was tied up and looking at us feverishly.

"He is a gift," she said. "Just a gift. We shall go now, and perhaps you will hear a horn braying when we are done. To celebrate our success. One more death. The city will rise again, purer, and better. In a way, Decimus, you are much like me. You punish those who would degrade your land."

"A gift," I answered. "I thank you for the gift. And the kind words. And still, I fought for Rome. I fought and worked to keep Rome pure, and safe, and I shall forever be cursed for the blood in my hands. However,

415

lady, I cannot go without that scroll."

She smiled. "You will never find it. Not ever. But consider it leverage that will never be used."

I smiled. "Why, exactly, do you leave me alive and free to go? Why are we even talking? Why do you feel so safe? Look around you."

She gave me a smile, and my men. "The Furies are not alive, love. You cannot kill the unliving. They shall rise again. This is my city. It shall always be so, and I guard the gate to Hades. I decide on the right and the wrong. However, even such as I deserve some happiness every now and then. When you go, I want you to give us something."

"Happiness?" I asked. "What are you after?"

She smiled. "The city has no rulers."

"You would…" I began and laughed bitterly. "You would *rule* the city? What of your high and fine duties? You call yourself Alecto, the Guard of Morals? The leader of the dog-headed pack of mongrels? You would—"

She lifted her chin, and her eyes gleamed with pride, her face taut with indigitation. "The Ptolemy blood runs deep in the family's veins, and is it not better than the Pericles line? It should have always been us, and not them, who live their lives in wealth. Nay, Roman, do not look at me like this. Never like this. You have no right. I am both a Ptolemy, and inside me, the great Alecto. That is who and what we are. Even the unliving love riches, and power. We have lived in the shadows for a long time. Now? Perhaps we should find ourselves elevated. What say you? I tell you again. You will *never* find the scroll."

I nodded. "You say you cannot be killed?" I asked. "Let us see, because I think I know where you sent the scroll, and I cannot go home without it."

I stabbed my sword into her belly, and she fell over it, holding to my arm painfully. She was wheezing and shuddering, and I pushed her off the blade. Her eyes were full of incredulous pain and such rage as I had never seen. They burned hot as coals.

"Let me start cleaning this up, with you," I said softly.

She shuddered and closed her eyes.

I leaned down to search her and came up with nothing. Then walked to Hercules. He was gagged, beaten, and wounded in back and thigh, but nodded at me, nonetheless. I cut his bonds, and he sat up.

He spoke, trying to keep his balance. "Laodamia had the scroll. They tortured her, Marius, and killed our men."

"I know," I said, as I pulled him to his wobbly feet.

He spoke while groaning. "I was sure I would follow. I didn't, happily. They gave the scroll to Lysirate. She is a different sort of girl when she is with Apollon and that one. Not frivolous at all, is she? Grave, I would say. She killed her sister and mother." He smiled. "Imagine, she thought we would make her true ruler of the city."

"Imagine that she thought I could be bargained with.

Come, we must finish this."

We were about to leave when Eurydike turned to look at us, wheezing. We stopped to stare at her. Her finger was pointed at me. "Alecto will find you, one day. It is only fair. Did you know for whom that final horn blast would have been? Apollon came back with your girl."

We stared at her until Hercules stepped up and on her neck. It cracked agreeably, but I kept staring at the thing.

Then, I turned.

We rushed down, took our men, and ran out of the citadel. We hurried down the mountain side, watched the flames in the city, the surging people, and the remains of our ship, far away, and ran on. We reached the tomb, and there, we found one of our men, getting up from behind a boulder.

"Well?" I asked.

"They came here," said the man. "Segolia, sir. She was with them, tied up. It was that Apollon and the lady Lysirate. They took her inside."

I nodded and entered. I looked behind me, and Hercules was following me.

"Come after me, in a bit," I said.

And alone I did go down, holding a torch.

CHAPTER 15

The tunnels ran for a long time. They were tombs, to be truthful, deep, and dangerous. River Limyrus and the springs made the tomb wet again, and sad, broken sarcophagi littered the many alcoves.

On the end of it, a doorway had been left ajar.

There, deep inside, I heard the sound of the river. Rivulets of it ran across the walls, and some of it would be pushed back up to the surface by springs, but much of the water would be going down to Hades. I was sure we were under the mountain now. There, the dead, if they had been paid the obol, would travel for Hades. Far below me, I saw darkness deeper than any and took steps to my right, three of them, and then seven to the left, and I saw the room.

I walked the dark, slippery corridor for the noise of the river and for the pale light. It was an eerie sound, like a gurgling, strangling man fighting for breath on his last steps in life. I went forward, ever towards it, against all my instincts. I held my gladius, and my chainmail was heavy and cold around me, but neither offered me any comfort. The past days had given me no reason to believe in steel when dealing with the killers of so many of my men. I walked forward, holding my hand against the wall to my left, and tried to hear something besides the gurgling noise. Only echoes met my ears, mostly my steps. I passed under roots hanging from a ceiling and imagined moist, dead fingers touching my face as I pushed past them. I arrived in an old cave.

It was lit by many small fires and by dozens of oil-lamps.

The way in had begun in a tomb, and the road ended in another. There was an ancient, old as time, block of stone, carved with figure that had lost its features long before. A river, part of Limyrus, was gushing to the side, its waters unnervingly silent, dark, dangerous as a beast, as they rushed far down to the roots of the mountain, and the world below. The sound of warbling death came from far below where the chilly water surged beneath the stone.

The sight was eerie, but not as eerie as the room itself.

There were holes on the walls, moist and dark, deep black, and large as doorways.

Skulls lined the walls.

There were hundreds.

They were the victims of a generation of murderers, a generation of killers who had come there with their trophies, denying their victims the afterlife, mocking them with the very gates of Hades. They were the seeds of Ptolemy's bastard, the price for slain children.

"Obol for the ferryman," I whispered. None of these had had a mouth where the coin could be placed.

No obol for their mouths.

They were all dead, most long dead. I felt, I swore it, the ancient dead—lining the room, staring at me, staring down to where the river should have carried their souls for Hades—wept.

There, too, were people I had known.

On one wall, there were heads of many of my men. One was Antius. They stared ahead in frozen horror, and I saw rats, and something else had gnawed on their ears, on their noses, and some had lost eyeballs, leaving behind a garish, pale-red hole filled with meat.

All had lost flesh to something else. They had been carved with a blade, the cheeks gone, and I knew the mad bastards had eaten the flesh.

And then, I felt immense relief.

There was also Segolia, gagged, by the river's edge, tied on a stake.

Before her, there was a bottle.

"Come out, and play," I called out.

I stepped closer and felt malignant eyes on me. They might have stared at me from the depths of the hole where the river plummeted below. They might have stared at me from a dozen cracks in the walls. They were filled with anger, full of hate, righteous rage. They hated me.

I heard a voice.

"Tell me, centurion," the voice of Apollon demanded, "will Eurydike come here? We were not expecting you. How did you find us?"

"No, she won't. She lost her head."

The malignant silence lasted for long moments.

"Will you pay for your crimes?" he asked hoarsely. "Will you pay for the many lies, for the evil plans you have been part of? Tell me, centurion, will you pay the price those who commit crimes in Limyra *must* pay?"

I stepped forward, trying to locate the noise. "My head stays attached," I said. "Tell me, Apollon, how much did Gaius's betrayal hurt you? He chose an old man over you."

Apollon chuckled. "And you, the murderer of your Gaius? Poison, centurion? Using poison to be rid of your foes? Filth!"

"Great states are built from filth, Apollon. You have seen them. War, service, and duty. All filth. You have seen it. Lysirate? What do you think? Should we accept duty can be painful?"

Her laughter echoed softly in the room. "Oh, do not worry about me. Duty to family is done. Eudoxia had everything, and still, I have what I love best. Adventure and my life."

"Your Alecto is gone," I said. "I murdered her. Get on with it, Tisiphone, and see why I stand here, and not her."

Apollon hissed. "You came to the house of death, centurion, to rescue and to recover. But in truth, did you not come for another reason?"

"I came," I said, "because I serve Rome. I always did."

"Aye," it answered. "You serve Rome. You always did, I doubt it not."

I looked around and couldn't see where it was. I stepped forward and held my sword by my thigh, ready

A figure emerged and tossed a horn across. It rattled

across the floor and stopped before my feet. "A nice addition, this. Perhaps we will use it in the future. Marius came up with that himself?"

"Aye," I said. "They were not supposed to do anything different from what was being done here, anyway."

I watched Apollon, a dark thing with horns protruding from under the black hood.

I felt the dread in my chest, but instead, took another step forward.

Another figure walked forward. The masks were snouted like dogs. The horns were red, and their gear made of dark, precious silks, and wool. Apollon held the spear, and Lysirate, a bow.

I watched Segolia, who was breathing but unconscious. "You spared her, then?"

"Apollon here," said Lysirate, "simply put her to sleep. I tell you what. We were going to give her poison, and send her down to the mountain's heart, but she may live yet. I doubt she ever did anything wrong, even for Rome."

"The poison is in the bottle?" I asked.

"Hemlock," Apollon said as he came closer, stalking towards me. "Hemlock and you have a choice. You drink it," he said, "or she will." He nodded at Segolia.

"And if I do?"

"She said it," he murmured, nodding at Lysirate. "She is guiltless and goes free. We will let her run along. You choose."

"And the scroll?" I asked.

He smiled and patted a large bag on his hip. "We shall think about it. Our mistress may decide. I imagine she might use it to her best advantage, or she might expose you lot for what you are. Scum."

I eyed the bow aimed my way. "Truly? I killed her."

"She *cannot* be killed," Apollon said. "She is eternal, endless. Alecto. A demon can never die. The rest of us? Yes, but not her. Let us not ruminate on the mortality any longer. The bottle. Drink it. Then she goes. Or do not, and we toss you both down to Hades."

I walked next to Segolia.

The arrow was turned my way, and Apollon was close, holding the spear low and ready. The man knew how to use it.

I picked up the bottle and eyed it carefully. Then, I tipped it and poured it to the river.

Apollon jerked. He took half a step ahead. "You coward. You—"

"I dislike this place," I told him. "Stinks of old grudges and piss. Though, I am somewhat less disgusted than I was when we came here earlier."

Apollon frowned. "Kill him."

The bow shivered, Lysirate pulled the weapon taut and prepared to kill me.

Four people appeared from the darkness behind them, four people I had told to wait there, hidden, until the enemy came, or I fetched them.

Ariane ran out first and stabbed Lysirate in the back

with a dagger before she could so much as blink. She released the arrow before a soldier appeared and stabbed her as well, and Larissa pushed her dagger to Lysirate's belly. I stepped to the side, the arrow clattered to the darkness, and she fell on her face, the mask shattering. Ariane was on her knee before her and looked at Apollon. "You well, centurion?"

Apollon was staring at them with his mouth open. "Who is she? She is no slave."

I pointed a sword at her. "Remember when I said we had been told about Gaius and the situation in Lycia? Pericles wrote to Augustus, Ennius, Vipsania. But we always have one of our own with such a party as that of Gaius. Or course we have someone close to his. She has been telling us plenty of stories of your issues here. She told Marius what to do. Alas, that she couldn't help much before this. Surely you appreciate her acting abilities, woman or not. Now, as for you. The scrolls. Then; your life."

Apollon hissed, cursed, and bolted. He ran back the way I had come from, and there, at the doorway, froze. He thrust quickly forward, a man screamed, and then, he tried to hop back.

Hercules's fist crashed into his face. The giant jumped forward and grasped the man's black tunic and came away with half of it. Apollon danced away, to me and Ariane, and tried to spear me. I dodged. He feinted and then stabbed deceptively from under my sword. The spear passed my face, then my chest, and I dodged back. He slapped Ariane back, saw Hercules, and two Praetorians and Larissa coming for him and dodged away, panting. He tried to cross the black stream and hoped to disappear to some unknown tunnels beyond in the dark.

Segolia, groggy, lifted a foot, and the man toppled on it.

He crashed to the stone and rolled to the river.

I jumped after, stopped his tumbling decent towards the depths, and held him under the water. I put my sword on the chest, and the man seemed to give up.

I pressed the blade deep, twisted, and pulled it out. I grasped the belt, and the bag.

Then, I let him tumble away and fall to the heart of the mountain.

I watched Segolia as the others spread to search the rooms. I took the scroll out and kneeled next to Segolia and began cutting her free. "It was very brave. We caught them good."

She nodded. "Deceitful. Filthy. Unkind. Like the entire mission."

I showed her the scroll. "In this, Gaius is talking about rebellion. Not with so many words, but all the things he talks about are fuel to those who hate Rome. Such a man, love, cannot be allowed to remain alive. A thousand lives pales in comparison to hundred thousand. Lycia will fall to Rome one day, allies or under agreement, or not. If there is no Rome, Segolia, there is strife. Your father joined us to find peace for

Gaul. It is best achieved under the eagle. Gaius was dangerous. Germanicus will do better. Augustus did this with a heavy heart."

She nodded and put a hand on mine. "I will try to learn."

"They were mad, murderers and thieves, no matter what else they claimed to," I said. "Segolia, I—"

"We shall talk about it on the trip back home," she said with a smile. "Larissa and Ariane and your men and me. You lost many. What is Ariane?"

I smiled. "Not a soldier, and still, she *is*. She serves Augustus well. Marius was a good man," I said. "He would have been a praetorian, as Augustus promised. No matter what mistakes were made, not knowing about the land beneath the city, the addition of the horn, and missing Alexander's ambitions and madness, Ariane gave him his instructions, and he did well. I am sorry this was a shit-terrible mission. There will be others."

"I am not a medicus now," she said. "I promised the gods I would save lives."

I kissed her hand. "You are a soldier like Ariane now. Mine as well. Come. We shall go to Myra and take a ship from there."

EPILOGUE

Days later, with the corpse of Gaius on board, and citizens of Myra and Limyra trailing the coast, wailing for the death of Gaius, our merchant ship was moving to the southwest, for Rhodes and Crete. Myra had had two visiting roman ships, one a galley, and it had been no coincidence. The tale we left behind was already changing. The legends of a prince of Rome, and of the terrible Furies, and of the deaths of so many in Limyra were told wide and far, but the story that was in the scroll, the one I held in my hands, the tale of bitter, mad Gaius, a product of Palatinus and Augustus, would not change, and it would not even be spoken aloud.

It would be forgotten, and Gaius buried with honors in the mausoleum of Augustus. There, he would join the sister of Augustus, Lucius, Drusus, Marcellus, and his father, Agrippa. There, those who died or failed Augustus would wait until Rome died.

Lucius the witness, Bernike, Drakon, and the poor innkeeper, and his boy would also be forgotten. They would disappear, and never say a word to anyone about Gaius, and his scroll. They were aboard now, but blissfully unaware of what was coming.

It was their fate.

Gaius had sealed their fates as well.

As for the four men who had heard Pericles and Eurydike? They too, would find accidents, and assignments that would not be good for their health.

Augustus trusted in me. And in Hercules.

None other.

I watched the coast, the multitudes of people trailing us, Segolia, Larissa, and Ariane were in a cabin, and Hercules was leaning on the mast next to me.

"And what of her?" he asked me.

I sighed.

I heard Vipsania's voice below. She was singing, happy.

"Augustus was clear," he rumbled.

"He was," I said. "He told me if Gaius betrays Rome, she too must die. He doesn't want to risk anything. She might know this and that. Even Ariane couldn't keep her fully in dark."

"And yet she is here," he said. "Augustus was clear. He thinks she is to be blamed for what happened to Gaius. What he became. He thinks she sapped his soul. He told you to make sure she doesn't come home." He leaned close. "And even worse, she heard it *all*. She knows about you."

"Augustus doesn't see clearly," I said. "He needs to blame someone. And I knew her father. He *made* me."

"She is wickedly selfish," he said. "She will come to a bad end. She will take you with her."

I rubbed my forehead. "I knew her father. I loved him. I know things about her as well. The murder attempt, for one."

He laughed. "If she will come to a bad end, it doesn't matter how many people she has murdered. Fine. She

429

will go to Rome. What makes you think she will survive Augustus?"

I knew I would have plenty of trouble with her. I was fully aware of it. Still, I had made up my mind.

I had served her father, I could not hurt her. I had gotten rid of the cook, and Larissa served me now. I had cleaned all traces of her treachery, out of the table.

If she betrayed me, I would have to think again.

"He needs new blood to rely on," I said. "Augustus. New people in the family."

"Too bad she is not pregnant," he rumbled.

I smiled. "I have no idea is she is, or not. But it would indeed change the way Augustus thinks about her."

He gave me a suspicious glance, and then held his head. "You didn't. Does Segolia know?"

"She knows I am trying to save Vipsania's life," I said vaguely. "She suspects. I have no idea what Segolia and I might become, but we are not there yet. I cannot just leave Vipsania. Tiberius asked me to make sure she survives. Drusus always loved her well."

"Bastard. You were between her thighs?"

I nodded.

"And does she demand more of your seed?" he asked.

"I have no idea," I said. "She seems very happy, and grateful Gaius is dead. And I am still free. Segolia has not made up her mind."

He groaned.

I put the infamous scroll on a bag and closed it. Filled

with stones, I tossed it down to the sea, along with the scroll that divorced Vipsania from Gaius.

I turned to go. I froze.

I saw Segolia on the deck, staring at the coast. She was shivering and hugging herself tight.

My eyes followed hers, and I saw something that made hair rise on the back of my head.

I saw a woman, clad in gray, standing in the surf. She didn't move, and to this day, I swear the lean, tanned face was that of Eurydike, looking at us emotionlessly. Her neck was twisted, and the head rested on her shoulder, her hair was b

She lifted a finger towards me, and then at Segolia.

I knew we had made an immortal enemy, and one that would follow us to the edges of world, and beyond.

THE END

AUTHOR'S NOTES

If you have read any of my other work, you will notice that mystery is part of each story. There will always be that surprising twist, and unexpected turn, and something you might have missed.

Writing a <u>full </u>mystery, is a challenge one does not expect, before diving into it.

Especially, when you are making the lead character the murderer, and hope to mask the fact with many lies, and still leave a hint here, and there, and have a delightful story. I tried to serve you a hero, a trio of villains, and to show the fragility of human nature.

Hopefully the book managed to surprise, and please you.

I do apologize for typos and editing issues. I still cannot fully afford a full-blown editing service.

**

As for the setting of the story, ancient Rome has always fascinated me.

Let's go over some of the things that might displease the more educated readers.

Speculatores, the spies and infiltrators of the Roman army, also fascinate me. Of course, there is no way to really know, what sort of organizations the praetorians, for example, had in place. I am sure Augustus had plenty of men and women, who would go on unpleasant, unsavory missions for him, and for Rome. So, I invented something I think must have existed. We have a group of praetorians who knew their service would be far in the field, and not in the halls of Palatine.

Lycia. The land is a mystery. Settled between east, and west, it has a long and bloody history. A mix of ancient gods, worship of the Ptolemy and Alexander, and of course; of Augustus, it was indeed land of the gods. It was in Limyra, where Gaius died. His memorial can still be seen there. The land is fertile, and wet, the mountains are beautiful, and if you visit the place, and see the many a necropolis littering the land, and the remains of the acropolis, the tombs and ruins of the walls, the roman theatre that came later than the one in the story, it will impress you all. Forgive me for adding an underground land in Limyra. When I walked the city ruins, I spotted several holes in the ground, and always shuddered at the thought of going deep to see what might be found. At this time, much of the old Lycian ways and language had fallen into disuse, but I apologize for making most *everyone* Greek, and for not knowing enough about Lycian Federation and the ruling mechanism, and the armor and particular ways of these people. Also, there is nothing like the Necromantion in Limyra. There is no recorded road to Hades, or river that carries the spirits inside the mountain. Pure fiction. I did my best with what I knew and had available.

Gaius and his influence in the lands he passed has also fascinated me. Such a man like him, cannot help but cause turmoil in the old towns and cities he visited.

However, I have no idea what sex Gaius preferred in the matters of love. In this book, he prefers men. If this offends someone, I actually don't really care.

I could go on.

I won't.

In short; there is probably a lot to be desired with the accuracy of many of the things I have served you. I shall hide behind the shield of fiction, and will point out, as writers always do, that in order to entertain, one must deviate from the accepted facts, at least a bit and pay more attention to the plot, than whether there Lycian soldiers wore horsehair on their helmets, or not.

Thank you for getting the book. Check out the next page for more information.

REVIEWS

Thank you for getting this story. If you enjoyed it, I would be grateful if you could leave a review. You need not write an elaborate one, just one line and a rating is enough. Readers who do not enjoy the story, will write such reviews, and a bad rating will make it hard for any author to sell the story, and to write new ones. Your help is truly needed, and well appreciated. This author reads them all and is very grateful for your help.

NEWSLETTER

Do sign up for our newsletter at: www.alariclongward.com. You will find our blog, latest news, competitions, and lists of our stories in these pages.

FREE BOOKS

We are often offering free e-books for our readers. These are not short stories, but full, often gigantic tales. In many cases, you might get Book 2 free, by signing up to our newsletter. Please check out our author pages in the various retailers, or in our homepage to find out what is available.

OUR OTHER STORIES

If you enjoyed this story, be sure to check our other historical and fantasy tales. We have many related series that often tie together and are related. We have Medieval stories, several Roman Era tales, story set in the Napoleonic Era, historical mysteries, and many Norse Mythology related fantasy series. None of them are suitable for children, and will serve people who enjoy a surprising plot, fierce battles, and practical heroes and heroines. You can find list of these in our various retail author pages, and our home- or Facebook pages.